The King's Coat

The Alan Lewrie Naval Adventures

The King's Coat
The French Admiral
The King's Commission
The King's Privateer
The Gun Ketch
H.M.S. Cockerel
A King's Commander
Jester's Fortune
King's Captain
Sea of Grey
Havoc's Sword
The Captain's Vengeance
A King's Trade
Troubled Waters
The Baltic Gambit
King, Ship, and Sword
The Invasion Year
Reefs and Shoals
Hostile Shores
The King's Marauder
Kings and Emperors
A Hard, Cruel Shore
A Fine Retribution

The King's Coat

Dewey Lambdin

The Alan Lewrie Naval Adventures #1

McBooks Press, Inc.
www.mcbooks.com
Ithaca, New York

Published by McBooks Press, Inc. 2018
Copyright © 1989 Dewey Lambdin
First published in the U.S.A. By Donald I. Fine, Inc., New York

Cover painting by Dennis Lyall

ISBN: 978-1-59013-756-7

Library of Control Number: 2018942138

Visit the McBooks Press website at www.mcbooks.com.

Printed in Canada

9 8 7 6 5 4 3 2 1

To my mother, who always thought I could do
it, but most especially to my father;

Lt. Cmdr. Dewey Lambdin (USN)
  • 'Boot' Seaman in 1930
  • 'Mustanged' in 1941
  • Died in line of duty, 1954

"So hush, for the wind's his Lorelei
And he wants to hear her calling,
where the wave-tops flash
with the light of God,
in sparkling, salt-teared Mercy
for those who commit themselves
to The Deeps."

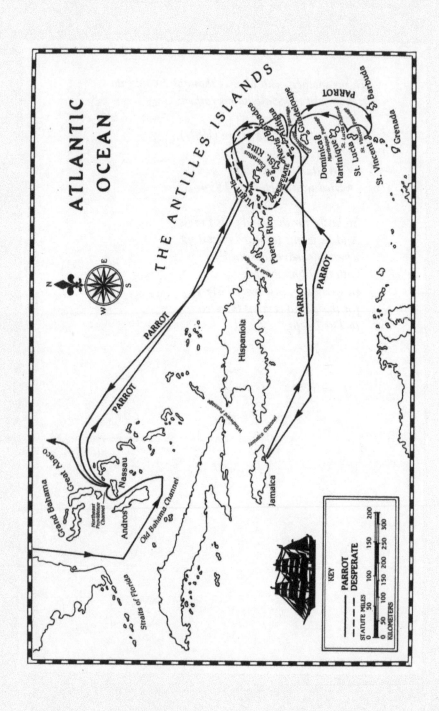

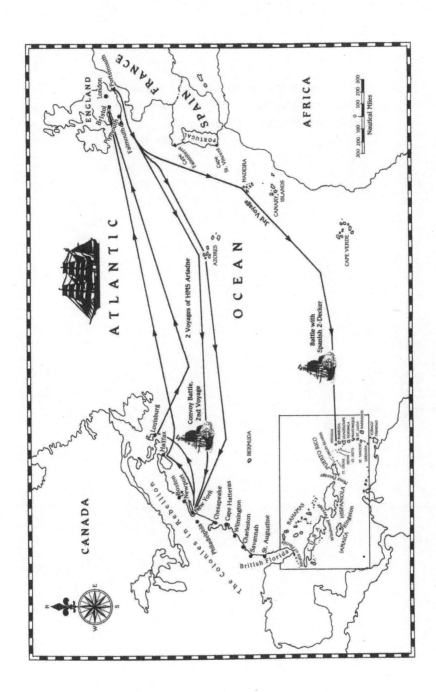

CANADA

ENGLAND
London
Bristol
Plymouth
Portsmouth
Falmouth

FRANCE
SPAIN
PORTUGAL
Cape Finisterre
Cape St. Vincent
MADEIRA
CANARY ISLANDS
AFRICA
CAPE VERDE

ATLANTIC

OCEAN

2 Voyages of HMS Ariadne
AZORES

Convoy Battle, 2nd Voyage

3rd Voyage

Battle with Spanish 2-Decker

Louisburg
Halifax
Boston
Newport
New York
Philadelphia
Chesapeake
Cape Hatteras
Wilmington
Charleston
Savannah
St. Augustine

The Colonies in Rebellion

BERMUDA

British Florida

BAHAMAS
Windward Passage
Mona Passage
PUERTO RICO
VIRGIN ISLANDS
ST. CROIX
ANGUILLA
ST. MARTIN
ST. KITTS
ANTIGUA
GUADELOUPE
DOMINICA
MARTINIQUE
ST. LUCIA
ST. VINCENT
BARBADOS
GRENADA
TOBAGO
TRINIDAD

Florida Strait
HISPANIOLA
JAMAICA Kingston

Nautical Miles
300 200 100 0 100 200 300

N
W   E
S

"We are precarious, uncertain, wild, enduring mortals, and may we so endowed continue, the wonder and balance of the universe."

—JOHN BYNG

Prologue

I N retrospect, perhaps, getting into his half sister's mutton was not the brightest idea that Alan Lewrie had ever had. Not, he told himself later, that it had been his idea at all; Belinda had been the initiator and he merely the recipient of her favors, which were ample. That she had been the object of desire for half the blades in London, both old and young, made it imperative that he try her at least once, just for the sake of comparison, much like a book critic would sample some Gothick fright and flummery so he could say he had read it. That half those blades had already preceded him really didn't bother Alan.

After all, Belinda never dallied with anyone less than aristocratic (unless one counted the odd stable boy, ostler, shopclerk, tinker or tradesman who happened to be in the immediate vicinity when her blood was up), and since Lewrie knew half of them anyway, he could be fairly sure she wasn't poxed.

Admittedly, he had suffered some pangs of concern that they were related, but since he was a Willoughby by blood if not by name, they had submerged wherever guilt pangs go when faced directly against Willoughby nature. Run shrieking for the nearest window, he surmised to himself, if they have any sense at all.

Belinda was a fetching girl right enough, an auburn beauty with creamy skin, breasts that threatened to spill over her bodice, and bold eyes for any man of comely proportions. And, being a Willoughby, hot as a pagan Hindoo with the morals of a monkey.

Alan was seventeen, two years younger than she, but already sure of his abilities to please at what he thought was the Prime Sport of Kings, a well-knit young man of middling height that could turn heads at a ball or on the Strand even without his 'Macaroni' clothing. With the Christmas season over, and the City Season pace dying down, he had little to look forward to until spring, and invitations to country houses, and had wearied of maids and mopsqueezers. 1780 was looking to be a damned dull year until the last explosion of parties in spring, so what could be more delightful than a dalliance at home, where one did not have to brave the elements, the Mob, mud, dead cats and streets full of garbage, or a shower of night soil from some window? This will cut down on my gambling debts, and my clothing bills, so everyone should be grateful.

He had been surprised that Belinda would show interest in him at all, since he was the younger adopted but natural son born out of wedlock, usually referred to as "that filthy little bastard" by everyone, including his father, and Belinda herself. But suddenly, instead of irritable toleration, there had been a week or two of sultry looks, some covert fondling, seductive conversation and deep breathing that led up to this night when all the servants were out of the way. Gerald was off chasing fellow sodomites so he could scratch his particular form of the Willoughby itch; Sir Hugo and his manservant Morton were both away, most likely drinking and wenching themselves into the gout again, and no one to interfere. Alan had pinched a silk condom from Sir Hugo's travelling kit (half sister or not, he was only *fairly* sure of her latest amours) and had finally succumbed eagerly.

They were gloriously engaged, and Belinda was trying to emulate the sound of a pack of hounds after the fox had gone to earth, when he thought he heard a scuffling noise in the hall, which he thought damned odd, odd enough to put him off stride, which didn't seem to affect Belinda's squirmings and View Halloo much. He knew servants never came upstairs after dinner, not if they knew what was good for them, and everyone else would be away til dawn at the earliest.

Then he heard the door latch snap open.

"Suffering Christ," he breathed, his passion cooling precipitously. "Belinda, leave off, quick!"

She grappled him even tighter to her, yelping aloud now, her transports of joy turning into full fledged yells which he took for dumb lust. "Not now, you silly mort, someone's here."

"Merciful Father in Heaven," a voice quavered as the bed curtains parted with a jerk, spilling candlelight on the scene.

Alan gulped at the sight of their parish vicar. Now what's the amen curler doing here? God, is he up next with her?

Belinda pitched into a screaming frenzy as Alan disengaged and crawled away from the scene of the crime. Then, he saw the others; his brother Gerald, grinning wickedly; his father's catch-fart Morton, who had a pistol in his fist; his father, even redder in the face than his usual brandy-induced hue, exercising his thick fingers on a walking stick; God help him, even their family solicitor Pilchard was there, bringing up the rear and trying to peek over their shoulders for a better view of Belinda's charms as she screeched her way up a full octave.

"Your own sister!" The vicar appropriately shuddered. "You godless ... animal!"

"Half sister," Alan corrected as coolly as he could clad only in a silk sheath condom and kneeling about as close to *flagrante delicto* as one could.

"He raped me! Help!" Belinda screamed.

"I'll see you hang for this," Sir Hugo said, advancing with the walking stick swishing the air.

"Rape, hell," Alan shouted in defense, thinking it a poor one even as he said it. "The jade was the one invited me!"

"Lying hound!" Sir Hugo took a swing at Alan's head that barely missed the vicar, and, if Alan had not gone flat on his back, would have half beheaded him. "I'll kill you for this, you little bastard."

Alan did the sensible thing at that point; he ran. He leaped from the bed and made for his clothes. Morton came for him, but he was a well-fed slowcoach, and Alan had retrieved his breeches and was well on his way to freedom past Morton's outstretched arms when Sir Hugo's cane came down like a thunderbolt from on high and struck him on the shoulder, which caused him to draw his length on the parquet.

"There, there, girl." The vicar pawed Belinda's bare arms and back and reluctantly allowed her to draw a sheet up over her magnificent young breasts. "You're safe from him now!"

Sir Hugo got the toe of his shoe in, spinning Alan about on the bare boards like a top before he fetched up against a table which came down with a crash, but allowed him space to rise. Belinda went into another paroxysm of wailing as the vicar slobbered over her.

"Vicar, I swear before God this was not totally my doing," Alan shouted, dodging about the room from Morton and his father. Gerald and Pilchard huddled in the doorway, unwilling to get too involved but ready to form a blocking force. "I don't know you well, and I doubt if you know this family well, either, but if you did . . ."

"Take him, Morton," his father said. "Take him now!"

The one safe road was not another lap of the room. Alan vaulted a table and dove back into the bed, rolling to his feet by the vicar.

"If you would only listen to me, sir . . ." he begged.

Belinda's feet flew into action, pummeling him around the groin and up against the quavering old churchman. "You . . . you . . . Absalom," the vicar finally managed to say, just before hitting him inexpertly in the chin with a lean and bird-like fist. It was enough, however, to put stars in his vision and brought with it the odd urge to sneeze. As the others rounded the bed to lay hands on him, he sank to the floor once more, feeling the thump of the vicar's foot slamming his ribs.

"Here, that's not quite...cricket," he protested.

As he was jerked to his feet and hustled out of the room, he got a chance to lay eyes on Belinda once more, and she was staring at him with a curious smile on her lips and a crinkle to her eyes, the sort of smile he had seen her deliver to a particularly tasty stuffed goose at remove, after she had had her fill and was quite satisfied.

Damme, what's this all about, Alan wondered groggily, still smarting from the kick in the ribs from the otherwise saintly seeming reverend. With his arms full of clothing, he was hustled upstairs in Morton's steely grasp.

"I must beg your forgiveness for striking him, Sir Hugo," the vicar said, gratefully accepting a brandy in the first floor study. "I've not raised a fist in anger since I was twelve, but the utter audacity and cock-a-whoop gall of him quite overcame me."

"I understand totally," Sir Hugo said without humor. "Perhaps if I had allowed my temper to break on him more often when he was young, we would not be engaged as we are tonight."

"You did not strap him as a child?" the vicar asked.

"Very rarely. He's a thoroughly spoiled young man," Sir Hugo said, pouring himself a glass. "You are new to the parish, so I must explain. In my youth, before I settled down from serving the King as a soldier, I was more forward than most with the young ladies. His mother was beautiful, my first love, a proper girl from a good family."

The vicar made agreeable cooing noises, which Sir Hugo ignored.

"Before I went overseas, she and I consummated our love for each other, and then I lost touch with her, my letters returned or never answered. I was heartbroken," Sir Hugo muttered, looking only stern, but not in the least heartbroken. "By the time I had returned, and married someone else, I discovered that she had borne me a son. She had been turned out by her own family, and had died, little better than a prostitute, and that boy a pitiful parish waif. I could not refuse to own up to my sin, could I, father?"

"Well..."

"To atone for all, I took him in, you see."

"A heavy burden brought about by the lust of the flesh, sir," the vicar said, now on familiar ground. "But a common one, I am sad to say. In these evil times in which we suffer before our admission to the higher reward..."

"Yes," Sir Hugo said. "As I was saying, I took him in, fed him, clothed him, sent him to the best schools, and never could find the sternness in my heart necessary for his proper upbringing, because of my guilt and shame of abandoning her, even though she was too proud to tell me. My second wife died, leaving me the sole parent of three poor babes. Even then, I could not raise a hand to him, not after ruining his poor mother, for being the one that caused her untimely death."

"Er, which mother are we talking of?" the vicar asked.

"*His* mother...father!" Sir Hugo snapped. "Alan was the very image of her when he was a boy. How could I strike him? How could I deny him anything his heart desired?" He sank his face into his hands.

"You poor fellow," the vicar said, patting him on the back.

"God most assuredly is aware that you tried, Sir Hugo," the vicar went on. "For we have all sinned not only by commission but by omission as well, and come short of the glory of God. Any small act of contrition and amends is—"

"He is a rakehell," Sir Hugo said, shooting to his feet and going for the brandy decanter, away from the vicar's petting.

"Indeed."

"A gambler, a Corinthian, a brothel dandy and the bane of any pretty maid in London," Sir Hugo went on with some heat. "He's fought a duel, so please you, for his alleged *honor*, brought comment on this family by his shocking conduct, wasted my money to clothe him in that ridiculous Macaroni fashion ... he was *expelled* from Harrow, sir."

"Merciful God," the vicar gasped at this last revelation.

"Something about emulating the Gunpowder Plot and the Governor's privy. I do not see him mending his way in future, either."

"God forgives all, Sir Hugo. Even the most practiced sinner," the vicar reminded him with a beatific smile, and a brandy glass that was dry as dust on the bottom.

"Even the attempted rape of his own sister? The rest I could live down, but this! Belinda will be ruined! What good man would have her, even with her dowry and prospects? How shall I face the world as the father of a boy doomed to be hanged like one of the filthy Mob?" Sir Hugo filled the vicar's glass and then threw himself into a facedown sulk behind his desk. He waited for an answer but heard only the sound of sloshing and a moan of contentment from the vicar. "I mean to say, how may I retain the good name of Willoughby?"

"Ah, yes, the poor young lady," the vicar finally said, not without a gleam coming to his watery eyes.

"Yes?" Sir Hugo prompted, trying not to seem impatient.

"Transport him. Or send him to the country," the vicar decided.

"But the courts involved ..."

"Ah, yes, well ..." The vicar shrugged and made free with the decanter on his own.

"I shall of course, disinherit him," Sir Hugo announced. "I'll not have him spend another moment under this roof as one of mine. Then it shall be up to him to succeed or fail under his own name."

"He is not known by Willoughby?"

"Lewrie, his mother's maiden name, father."

"Let me see ... some form of punishment, or banishment, that will not reflect on your own kith and kin, remove him from the scene and make a man of him," the vicar said. "I have it!"

"Yes?"

"I know a captain in the Royal Navy, Sir Hugo. With this dreadful little rebellion going on in the American colonies, one more young volunteer for service would not be looked on amiss." The vicar fairly beamed.

"And ship him out as a seaman?" Sir Hugo grinned in return.

"Heavens, Sir Hugo, be merciful at the last, I beg you. To be a midshipman is punishment enough, but to be pent with the common rabble, an educated young man raised as a gentleman...besides, there would be unfavorable comment if he stood out from his surroundings too well."

"I suppose so," Sir Hugo said unhappily. "So I shall have to buy him his kit. And his commission as well, I suppose."

"Not at all, Sir Hugo," the vicar assured him. "Well, he must have his kit, but a commission in even a poor regiment is four times the cost of a willing captain. I am sure my friend Captain Bevan can find your son a commander desperately in need of hands and midshipmen. Like much else in our times, the zeal of the populace for naval service is akin to the lack of zeal for the true sense of Christ's teachings."

"Desperate enough to take young Alan?"

"Fifty pounds in the right pocket in Portsmouth could put him in any ship of the line."

"Preferably one going to foreign climes, the farther the better. And your friend can do this?"

"Most assuredly, Sir Hugo. Why, I recall in my last parish there was a young widow with a son who was—" the vicar reddened at the memory that Sir Hugo thought touched a bit too close to home—"at any rate, the Fleet is full of young lads who are not exactly welcome at home."

"Shameful," Sir Hugo said. "Well, please be so good as to have your nautical friend...Bevan, did you say?...attend me as soon as he can. And, just to clear this up as a legal matter, I wonder if I could prevail upon you to attest to what you witnessed this evening with my solicitor, Mister Pilchard? He is gathering statements in case we have to call the watch and have Alan imprisoned, should he prove to be intractable."

"Mosht happy to oblige you, Shir Hugo," the vicar said, barely able to bring glass to lip any longer. "I shall not keep you longer, Shir Hugo. I believe we have all shuf... suffered enough tonight."

"Indeed we have, sir." Sir Hugo nodded somberly.

Sir Hugo rose and bowed a courteous goodnight to the stumbling sermonizer as Morton held the door for him and took him in charge to the parlor, where Pilchard waited. Sir Hugo sat down and mused happily over his brandy. It seemed an age before the wizened solicitor stuck his head around the door, waving a sheet of vellum to dry the ink, much like a flag of surrender to his master's temper.

"Is that sodden hedge-priest gone?"

"Just this minute, Sir Hugo. I saw him to the door myself." Pilchard grinned, entering the room fully as Sir Hugo waved him forward. He laid the document before his employer like a great trophy. "Here it is, Sir Hugo. And considering his vulnerable state and the witnesses against him, I anticipate no problem there..."

"Excellent, Pilchard, excellent! Everything is in order, then."

"All but young Alan's signature, Sir Hugo."

"I wish you to make an addition to that, Pilchard."

"Sir?"

"Have a brandy and sit down, for God's sake," Sir Hugo ordered, irritated at the *outré* deference his solicitor always showed him but secretly still pleased that he could engender that sort of deference. Pilchard obeyed the instructions and took a seat on a settee, perched on the edge of the cushion with knees close together.

"The vicar came up with a most interesting suggestion, Pilchard. And a perfect excuse for Alan not to be present when this matter comes to its fruition."

"And that is, Sir Hugo, if I may inquire?"

"Naval service, Pilchard, naval service!" Sir Hugo boomed it with a hearty chuckle. "The boy is not come to his majority, and is overseas, preferably far overseas, on the King's business, when we enter the court. Write it up so that I am his guardian or whatever, so that his signature, which you assure me of, gives me total control over everything he is due, in the first instance, and hang the rest of what you had planned."

"But if he survives to return to England, Sir Hugo, he is then heir, and can take you to court for all of it. I believe he should sign away all claims, as we initially laid out."

"Now what are the odds of a midshipman returning?" Sir Hugo stood to refill his glass. "Off to the Americas, the Fever Islands, or the East Indies among all those pagan Hindoos?"

"Not good, sir, but not certain, I'm afraid."

"But no problem until the war is over, at any rate. He knows nothing now, and can learn nothing thousands of miles away. It strengthens our appearance, does it not, safeguarding the interests of my . . . son, as he fights for England, his King? Oh, shout Harroo for England and St. George! And should he survive and return, it will be much too late to do anything."

"He is a clever little devil, Sir Hugo. God help me, but I think he may tumble to it . . . eventually, that is."

"Then the second part, the part you first suggested to me, shall be a secret agreement between him and me, obtainable for reasons you make clear, and only the first part of the document, concerning guardianship, shall be presented in court. Surely that shall suffice."

"I believe that would work, Sir Hugo. Though I still worry that asking him to put his name to so many documents will bring his suspicions up—"

"To the devil with his suspicions! The means of removal has to come up from Portsmouth, so we shall let that little damme-boy stew in his own skin for a few days. By that time I am sure he shall be most agreeable."

There was a soft knock on the door, and Belinda entered

the room, now dressed in high fashion and bearing a cloak, hat and muff for an evening out. She crossed to her father and planted a gentle kiss on his cheek. He put an arm around her.

"Off, are you?"

"Lady Margaret is giving a drum," Belinda said calmly. "Now I shall be fashionably late for it. Did I do well, father?"

"Excellently well, my girl. And you shall share in my gratitude and munificence once this is behind us."

"I never doubted it father." She beamed, then bade them both goodnight, leaving Sir Hugo humming to himself, and Pilchard fidgeting as he thought upon his new document's form and content.

"WHERE'S the chamber-pot, then?" Alan demanded as he was shoved into a dark and cheerless garret servant's room at the back of the house.

"Criminals don't deserve none." Morton smirked.

"I'm sure you know about criminals, Morton, you were born one! Candles, too, and a bed."

"An' why not a bottle an' some bird, an' a servant girl while you're askin', young sir," Morton jibed back. "Scandalous goin's on, I swear to heaven. Rapin' your own sister!"

"And you the innocent babe just down from the country. Goddamn you, fetch me light and some sort of bedding—"

"I'll fetch ya a ticket to your own hangin', and that's all, you little bastard," Morton said, shoving him back into the dark room with a horny fist and slamming the door. "Ye'r not the high 'an mighty little buck a' the first head now, are you, young sir?" he crowed through the wood, then laughed his way down to the landing and out of hearing.

There was a thin slit of light under the door, which did little to banish the gloom of that tiny garret cell, and Alan sat down next to it, arranging his coat over his knees and chest as a makeshift blanket.

Now what the hell is this all about? he pondered again,

now a bit more levelheaded than when the posse had broken in on him. Why should they all show up at the same time, as if it were arranged...?

There had, though, never been much sense in the household, from the way Sir Hugo ran his own affairs to the way he allowed Belinda and Gerald to run riot with their own pleasures and interests. Sir Hugo had never shown much discipline toward them, or much affection, either, too far gone in his own cares even to notice his children. Alan had come into the house a three-year-old waif in rags to a paradise of food and good clothing and the life of a moneyed scion of a great man, or so it seemed. Quite a change from the parish poorhouse he had known since birth and the death of his mother (at least they'd told him she'd been poor and was dead). He had been prepared to be grateful and loving, but there had been a vast gulf that he could never bridge, made of his father's icy indifference. By the time he was breeched and off to the first in a long succession of schools he had stopped trying to bridge the gulf and only took advantage of the man's largesse. He had wanted for nothing, had been allowed to run riot like the son of a titled lord with few warnings to correct his behavior. And now, suddenly, this...?

"What in hell did I do?" he asked the darkness. "Hopped onto my half sister. Well, that's almost fashionable these days, isn't it? All the good families do it, and without witnesses, too. Now I'm on my way out because of it. Why?"

He tried to think that he had crossed Sir Hugo's interests in some way but could not think of any woman he had had that Sir Hugo wanted. He wasn't exactly champion wasteful with money; in fact, he had a fair amount of his allowance hidden away, since he had gotten his fingers burned gambling the year before and had lost his taste for the tables. He had not purchased anything extravagant, or at least nothing so extravagant that would make his father bite furniture over it.

God's Balls, he thought suddenly. The old fart's gone smash over some investment and I'm now expendable. He can't afford to keep all of us and I'm only half a son, not like Gerald. If I'm not careful I'll end up some drudging clerk. Maybe someplace brutal and nasty, like Liverpool. But why not just call me in and tell me I'm chucked...?

He shivered with the cold, and with his misery, clamping his knees together to control his aching bladder, and waited for the dawn, soon too foxed by wine to keep his eyes open, dreaming of revenge and triumph.

It was four days before Alan was freed from his cold and gloomy garret prison to be brought down to the study. He did not make a very pretty picture by then. His light brown hair was lank about his face and his queue was loose. He wore no neckstock, and his fashionable white silk waistcoat all sprigged with red and blue flowers was crumpled from service as a pillow. His silk stockings had ladders in them, and his tightly cut grey blue satin suit looked more like a stained and bedraggled bad bargain from a ragpicker's barrow.

On the way down he had seen Gerald entertaining a strange man in the parlor by the fire, the man swathed in a voluminous dark blue cape held open for warmth from the grate.

Court official? Alan wondered. Or one of Gerald's lovers getting his equipment to room temperature? But there's no sign of the Charlies about. No one seeming to be a member of the watch, usually spavined oldsters with cudgels, was in evidence, and he considered that a reason for cheer. God knew he needed some badly at that point. He had fretted and pondered feverishly all the time of his confinement as to what last straw he had broken, if any, and what was to be his fate.

He was led to face his father, who glowered at him from the study fireplace. Pilchard stood behind the writing desk with his most serious legal face on.

"You know Mister Pilchard." Sir Hugo began. "He has paid you out of trouble often enough in the past for you two to be good friends by now, hasn't he? Well, hasn't he?"

"I suppose so, sir."

"What could have possessed you?" Sir Hugo demanded. "You realize this isn't some country girl to be fobbed off with twenty pounds. This is your own *sister* you tried to rape. You are finished, boy."

"What rape?" Alan shot back, but shuddering cold inside. "Not until that Bible Thumper stuck his beak in, it wasn't rape."

"You're facing a hanging offense." Sir Hugo intoned.

"But it wasn't rape. She was the one that wanted to do it and I went along with it. You know her nature, surely—"

"What's worse, I know yours." Sir Hugo shot back.

"Then you know I wouldn't have to depend on rape. The town's full of quim to be had, without a bit of struggle."

"That nature of yours could get you hanged, Alan." Sir Hugo said. "You were caught in the act, and we have witnesses."

"And I can provide a platoon of witnesses for myself, and for my dear sister's character as well, if it comes to that."

"Only if it comes to trial, boy."

"What is this? Just what do you want from me? Since when have you gotten so holy?"

"Sir Hugo and I . . . that is, we . . . have come to what we believe to be a most salutary solution to the contretemps which you brought about by your unnatural act of forcible rape upon your sister," Pilchard said from behind the desk. "For the sake of your family we—"

"Oh, don't prose like a front bencher in Parliament, Pilchard," Sir Hugo said crossly, going to the sideboard for an early morning brandy. "Get to the meat of it."

"You are to be banished," Pilchard summed up. "You may never more lay claim to the Willoughby name—"

"I never did, you miserable ass."

"Pray allow me to continue, young sir," Pilchard said, wagging a finger at him. "You must go away, for the family's best interests. You can no longer reside under this roof, in

London or in England. And it would be most inadvisable for you to return, for obvious reasons."

"You're raving—"

"If you do not, then we shall summon the watch and have you taken before the magistrate. We have no choice," Sir Hugo warned, making happy sounds from the brandy decanter with his back to the show.

"Your sister is the one who wishes to prefer charges," Pilchard informed him. "While we wish to spare her reputation, and the family reputation, she has decided otherwise. If this does go to court you would throw undying shame on your own family, and it would most likely cost you your life. At best, commitment to Bedlam as an uncontrollable lunatic. Do you understand the seriousness of what you have done?"

Alan was stunned into silence, beginning to doubt his memories of the incident. *Belinda wants to prosecute me? She's a brainless whore. No, there's something here that isn't right.*

The whole thing was astonishing, too astonishing to be credited. Part of the shock to his system, admittedly, was the realization that he would have to give up his whole life, even if he, by acquiesence, saved his mere existence. There went the girls, the money, the parties, his circle of friends and fellow roisterers, all the pleasures of the world's greatest city. Not to mention the perquisites of the moderate wealth of even a second son.

"We have here an agreement which Sir Hugo hopes you have the wit to sign, which will spare your family any further loss of reputation."

"What reputation did you have in mind? The good name of Sir Hell-Fire Club over there, my sister the open beard, or my brother the butt-fucking Molly?"

Morton must have been in the room behind him all that time, for Alan's arms were seized at the elbows and forced high behind his back, bringing a yelp of pain and surprise from him as he was forced into a half-crouch to the floor.

"I hope you're enjoying this, you butcher's dog," Alan managed to get out between clenched teeth.

"I am, sir," Morton whispered into his ear. "An' about time, too, let me tell ya!"

"Now listen to me, you little bastard," Sir Hugo said, leaning over the edge of the desk so he could stare into Alan's face. "What we want from you is for you to be gone. And we don't want any public trial, so there won't be one. You'll have to leave the city and the country, but you'll be alive. And with some money in hand to spend on your beastly habits."

"My beastly habits? What about yours...? Oww!" Alan went to his knees as Morton applied more pressure. "I suppose you want me to admit to a rape I didn't commit, too."

"Not at all," Pilchard said. "You merely have to sign this and go."

I'm as good as knackered right now, he told himself sadly. I haven't a hope in hell of fighting this, whatever it is.

"Father," Alan asked as sweetly as he could under the circumstances, "just why is this necessary? Was I any bigger a sinner than the rest of us? Have I cost you more money than Belinda does? She spends more on the Strand in a day than I do in a month. And half of London knows all about Gerald. Last time he went to Bath he was lucky to escape alive. I'm not going to inherit anyway, so why are you doing this?"

Let's put our contrite face on now, laddy, he told himself. Maybe I can save this situation yet.

"I beg you, father," he said with emotion. "Don't disown me like this. Don't turn me out. From the moment you pulled me out of that parish orphanage and claimed me as yours, I have been full of gratitude and love for you."

"Don't abuse my wit, boy," Sir Hugo said. "You love your purse and your gut and your prick, but I doubt this sudden affection for me. We cannot keep you around after this, and you know it."

Well, it was worth a try. Alan sighed heavily. Old bastard knows me too well. I've had it.

"Um, you mentioned money?" Alan asked. At this, Sir Hugo smiled and waved a signal to Morton to relent his hold so Alan could rise to his feet. "Just how much did you have in mind?"

"Fifty pounds per annum," Pilchard said.

That's four pounds...three shillings a month. Alan quickly figured in his head. This is ludicrous. I spend more than that in a month, and that's with food and lodging all found! Even in some hog's-wallow of a village in the North, I'd starve to death. Not to mention being bored absolutely shitless.

"I want a hundred." Alan stated, testing the waters.

"You're mad, raving."

"For whatever reasons you have, you want me gone." Alan told him, resigned to his fate but anxious to get some of his own back. "If you're broke and have to sell up, say so, but why go to this ridiculous charade? You don't want this to go to a trial, so there must be some blunt in it for you somewhere. I want some of it, if there's any to be had. I don't know anywhere a gentleman can live for less than three hundred pounds a year, so consider this a bargain price."

"Gone smash, have I?" Sir Hugo laughed. "Is that what you think?"

"The thought had crossed my mind."

"You're going because you are despicable, and I'll not have the Willoughby name tied to anything scandalous."

"As if it isn't already?"

"Gentlemen's vices, discreetly handled as befits a gentleman. Not like the get of a two-penny tart who shows the dirt of the gutter every time he opens his lips. And you want to go as a gentleman. Damn what you want."

"Damned right I do."

"Alright, Alan." His father relented suddenly, turning so mild Alan was immediately put on his guard for some high-handed move. "One hundred pounds a year. On certain conditions."

"In that case, make it guineas."

His father tried to stare him down. Alan didn't back down. Sir Hugo finally nodded his assent.

Pilchard began to scribble on the document on the desk, muttering to himself as he found room to add the amount, which gave Alan satisfaction. Pilchard presented his amended work to Sir Hugo, who nodded his approval.

"Now sign the damned thing and get your guineas."

Alan was released from Morton's grasp to free his arms, and took the excuse of massaging feeling back into his arms to take the time to read the document, looking for traps and pitfalls.

No more claim to being a Willoughby...that's no loss, is it? Out on my bare arse with one hundred guineas a year remittance. I still think he's gone smash! I was down for five hundred per annum, last time I snuck a look at the will. Leave the City, leave England. I wasn't expecting much more if the old bastard had dropped to hell, anyway. Second sons can't expect much, and God knows Gerald wouldn't give me a dilberry off his fundament, much less a *rouleau* of guineas once the old boy croaked. What?

"Here, what's this bit about mother's estate?" he asked. "She didn't have one, did she? She died penniless, right?"

"That is a legal form only." Pilchard said primly.

"Now I see...you never told me anything about her except she was pretty and dead. Her people have money, do they?"

"And just what estate do you think a bawd could leave her bastard when she was doing it upright in doorways just before she died?" Sir Hugo sneered, which was something he was right good at. "Explain it to him, Pilchard."

"Yes, explain it to me, Mister Pilchard."

"Miss Elizabeth's parents are still alive," Pilchard began. If Alan had had eyes for his father at that point, he would have been amazed to see eyebrows climb for heaven. "They are desperately poor wretches but still with us. They have, for many years, tried to find someone to take them to court to sue Sir Hugo for support, knowing that he had taken you in. We sent them fifty pounds per annum to keep them satisfied. We do not wish to have them known as part of the family. Or you." He did not add that Alan could be considered an heir through his mother's side. "To spare Gerald and Belinda any legal difficulties upon their inheritance, we included this clause. You shall receive your hundred guineas, as they get their money, as long as you live, for much the same reasons."

"Better I had left you in your squalor than claim you as mine in the parish register." Sir Hugo busied himself pouring another morning brandy. "It's all a formality to spare us your *presence* in future. That's it. Now sign the damned thing and be quick about it before I lose my patience and summon the watch and to hell with the Willoughby name..."

Alan quickly read to the bottom of the long page, noting that his father was still to be his guardian, though he was banished. Much like what some of Alan's wilder friends had faced: exile and frigid relations. Much like living under the old fart's roof.

"And what do I do after I sign? Have you arranged that, too?"

"Overseas would be best."

"Who pays my way? And what do I do once I get there?"

"Pilchard?" Sir Hugo snapped, turning his back on things.

"To make your disappearance from society credible, and without throwing any light on this despicable incident, we could not have you transported, or 'prenticed, without comment being made."

"Thank bloody Christ for that, anyway. And I'm to go as a gentleman?"

"Yes, but as a Lewrie, *not* a Willoughby," the solicitor told him.

Right, it's the army for me. This is going to cost him dear. An ensign's commission must go for at least four hundred pounds nowadays, even in a poor regiment. To buy my colors and my kit will have to cost near a thousand pounds...

That meant most likely that he would soon be in the American Colonies, facing constant danger from Red Indians and lawless Rebels. But there was a chance he could prosper; he could ride well, he could fence (he'd already dueled once and won handily) and he was a crack shot at game. With one hundred guineas in addition to his army pay he could get by, barely. Certainly, they would not choose a fashionable regiment for him, so he would not have to worry about high mess bills. Besides, there were damned few fashionable regiments fighting the war; they were still parading and wenching at home. As a soldier, a gentleman ensign, he could still carouse with a pack of young bucks as much as he pleased.

"Very well," he said carefully. "If you foot the bill for my kit and my commission." He was delighted to see the involuntary responses from both his father and Pilchard. What a discovering little slyboots I am to see to the heart of it, he told himself.

"Oh, we shall indeed," his father agreed.

Alan leaned over the desk and took the proferred quill from Pilchard's outstretched hand. He signed his name to the document and stood back up, waiting while Pilchard sanded the wet ink and glared at him in a prissy, satisfied way. When Sir Hugo smiled broadly, Alan was filled with a sudden foreboding.

"Well, I wish to express my gratitude for all you've done for me, father. Up until now, mind."

"Piss on your thanks, boy."

"Need me anymore? No? Well, I shall go pack then."

"That has been done for you." Sir Hugo told him. "You'll not spend another hour under my roof."

"You will surely give me time to gather a few keepsakes—"

"That has been done as well. Including your hidden money. I am sure there won't be a dry eye in Drury Lane when word gets out you've gone. Your wastrel friends will think you all brave and noble. Quite unlike you, but we have to maintain appearances. You were born a low bastard in a knocking shop, but thankfully you're no longer my bastard to worry about. Once you leave here, you're welcome to go to hell in your own way."

"As are you, father. And what regiment am I due for?"

"Regiment? Oh, yes. Morton, have that Captain Bevan come up, would you?"

The mysterious guest that Alan had seen by the parlor fireplace entered the room a moment later, no longer tented by his dark blue cape.

The stranger wore white breeches and waistcoat, a dark blue coat with white turnbacks at cuff and collar, trimmed heavily in gold with gold buttons that bore fouled anchors.

"The *Navy*." Alan was suddenly aware of what waited for him. "Sweet Jesus, no! Not the bloody Navy. I'd...I'd sooner go to Ireland. Even Bedlam—"

"I am so pleased by your reaction. Captain Bevan shall take you to Portsmouth, where you shall enter the King's service as a midshipman, a *gentleman* volunteer. He shall supervise the purchase of your kit and see you into a suitable vessel."

"You are now under King's Regulations and the Articles of War, boy," Captain Bevan told him. "Desertion from my custody is a hanging offense. To prevent that I have brought my coxswain with me."

That petty officer stood in the doorway, a solid block of low-browed elephantine muscle with a devilish black expression on his face. He wore a brace of imposing pistols in the waistband of his loose striped sailor's trousers, and a heavy cutlass hung on a baldric over his shoulder. His hands dangled loose, near enough to draw his personal choice at a moment's notice, and while he might appear slow to make up his mind just which instrument he preferred under a particular circumstance, once committed he appeared altogether competent.

"And you call *me* a bastard?" Alan shook his head. Damn 'em all to hell, they'll sit on me all the way to Portsmouth. Probably some chink in it for them, too. I am so well and truly fucked now. Ah, well, nothing for it but to go game...

"Father, it's farewell, then." Alan said manfully. "And you

have my most sincere wish that you rot in hell as soon as possible."

Morton took him by the arms again, and began to hustle him into the tender custody of the Navy.

"Give my regards to Belinda, too," Alan called out. "Have you not tried her already, you'll find her a right short-heeled wench, and a *most* obliging sort of girl."

Alan saw a look cross his father's face and had to laugh in spite of the circumstances. "By God, I believe you already have."

"Shameless. Come on, you," Captain Bevan ordered.

"I'll pay you all back, you know," Alan threatened as the coxswain took charge of him at the door with huge hard hands. "You, and Belinda, and Gerald, and that pettifogger Pilchard, and your brainless helpmeet Morton."

Gerald was waiting at the base of the stairs, pleased with the world. "Do us all proud at sea, won't you, Alan dear? Don't bother to write, though."

"My brother, Captain Bevan," Alan said by way of a hasty introduction. "Sews his own dresses and, what's the naval term...he goes in for the windward passage? God rot you too, Gerald. I hope to see you in the stocks for buggery one day, you poxy sodomite."

There was no servants present in the front hall, just a valise and his cloak and hat awaiting him, a much too small tricorne trimmed in white lace and adorned with a long feather. It was jammed onto his head, but without his usual tall, oversized wig it came off once they were in the street.

"Have you no shame?" Bevan demanded. "Comport yourself quietly into the coach, for your own sake, if not your poor family's."

"Then have your trained bear let go of me."

He shrugged himself into his coat and cloak, picked up his fallen hat and entered the coach. The coxswain got in and sat across from him.

"My name's Bell," the man announced in a deep rumble.

"Do you really believe I give a fuck what your name is?"

"Give me an excuse ta cut yer nutmegs awrf, boy. Ya sing

small wi' me an' sit quiet er ya won't live ta sign aboard a ship."

"Take your choice, young 'un," Captain Bevan said, seating himself next to his coxswain and sweeping back his cloak to reveal a pair of small pistols in his waistcoat. "Go a gentleman, or suffer the consequences."

"I shall keep that in mind, thank you, Captain Bevan," Alan replied archly, wrapping his cloak about him closer. Even a windy and wet January morning could not explain the sudden coldness he felt as their coach rattled off to rendezvous with the 'Dilly' for Portsmouth.

CHAPTER

1

ASULLEN, icy wind blew across the King's Stairs in the city of Portsmouth as Midshipman Alan Lewrie waited for the boat to fetch him out to his ship, the sixty-four gun 3rd rate *Ariadne*. Many naval vessels tossed and gyrated on the heaving grey green harbor waters, and Alan swallowed hard, and became a touch ill just watching them. He was also still in a mild form of shock over his fall from grace, and his sudden banishment. From one moment of being a buck of the first head and caterwauling with his friends all over London, chasing women, eating and drinking his fill, gambling and playing, and with little thought for the morrow, to this seaborne exile was just too hellish a wrench.

The trip down had been rough; bad roads and bad company, with both Bell and Bevan eyeing him like hawks. Even a bath and a shave at the inn had not revived his spirits. There had been no chance to escape. To listen to Bevan, it wasn't that bad a fate to go to sea, and over the past few days, the terror of it had slipped away. He would be a midshipman, not a common sailor, a junior warrant officer with authority, carried on the ship's books as a gentleman, berthed with others of his kind, with servants and stewards to care for his clothing and his table.

Bevan had told him about prize money, and how some ships' crews had become rich beyond measure, and how midshipmen took a larger share, of how fellows much like himself had gone on to fame and fortune and had set themselves up as gentlemen once they came home.

And during the process of buying his kit, Alan had reveled in a form of revenge on Sir Hugo. Bevan had a letter of credit from his father—he did not strike Alan as the sort one would trust with a full purse—and since it wasn't Bevan's money, they ended as confederates in spending it properly. Six full uniforms, three of them the best the town could boast, more silk and linen shirts than anyone could need, silk and cotton stockings, breeches and working rig slop trousers, personal stores of extra fine biscuit, jam, tea, paper, and the proper set of books, such as the latest edition of Falconer's Marine Dictionary.

Alan was sure that even a *royal* bastard could not make a finer showing, and secretly, he thought he looked especially handsome in the uniform, even if it was on the plain side. There had been a saucy darkhaired chambermaid at the inn that had thought so, too, his last evening ashore. After a dinner that had filled him to bursting, two bottles of claret and several brandies, he had gone to his room to discover her ready to turn his bed down for the evening and fetch a warming pan. When he suggested she warm it instead, she was out of her sack and stays in a heartbeat. Thankfully, Bell relented and stood guard on the door, and not in the room with him, showing some mercy to him on his last free night. He had no civilian clothing anymore, so he could not have run away. Like a condemned man, he had eaten a hearty meal, and had bulled her all over the room until the sky was grey.

Both Bell and Bevan had been tactfully silent after he had washed up and joined them for breakfast, much like executioners who had the good grace not to crack jokes at the wrong time. The girl's send-off, all the drink, and little sleep had damned near killed him, and a cold breakfast had almost finished the job, and still gave notice of trying.

"I am in no shape to do this," he said to Bell, who took no notice. And there was the boat from his ship, approaching fast.

"Here, you." Bell said behind him to a waiting bargee. "Help the gemmun with his chest."

The sense of shock was gone, also the hope of escape, and Alan's passing interest in prize money and uniforms and little revenge faded as reality approached. Here was the end of one life and the beginning of another that felt much like penal servitude. Had he not heard or read somewhere that the Navy was like a prison, in which one had the chance to drown?

"Bell, I have money," he said, turning to the coxswain.

"A tuppence'll do for the bargee, sir."

"No, I mean..."

"Best do it like a man," Bell said. "Sir."

Alan shrugged and tramped down to the boat at the foot of the stairs. One man held it to shore with a boat hook while eight more sat with their oars held aloft like lances. There was a boy by the tiller, a midshipman of perhaps fifteen.

"Hurry it up, will you?" he called. "Our first lieutenant's watching. Well, get in the goddamned boat. We won't bite you...yet."

Alan stumbled across the gunwale and sat in the boat at the stern by the boy who had addressed him, while two of the oarsmen took hold of his chest and placed it in the bottom of the boat with a loud thump. Alan flipped a coin to the waiting bargee.

"Shove off, bowman," the boy at the tiller said. "Out oars. Backwater, larboard...give us some way, starboard."

Alan looked up at Bell, who spat in the water as he waved him a sardonic farewell. Alan sighed and turned to look at the men in the boat with him. The nearest oarsmen were both tanned a dark brown, with skin as wrinkled as a discarded pair of gloves. They also sported impressive scars which stood out like chalk marks on their arms and faces.

"Give way all," the boy called. "Stroke, damn yer eyes, or I'll see someone's back laid open for shirking."

That could cheer me up, Alan told himself. Not like a hanging but possibly entertaining.

He turned to look at the tillerman of his version of Charon's ferry and marked him down for a brutal little get of a type he was familiar with from Harrow (and sundry other schools from which he had been expelled), a right bastard made even worse with power over fags and new boys. At least once he was aboard ship, he would have the same power, as if he had been made prefect over a whole shipload of fags. But the men in the boat didn't look like the pink-cheeked little victims he had bullied in the past. Neither did they look like the popular illustrations of Jolly Jacks and True Blue Hearts of Oak. In fact, they resembled more last session's dock at the Assizes, surly, uncouth and dangerous brutes, the gutter sweepings from the worst parts of the city, cutthroats and cutpurses he normally wouldn't give way for, unless they were the pimps he knew. These men looked like the sort who would do him in for a little light entertainment. And that brought him full circle to the dicey situation in his belly.

"God, it can't be sick already," the tiller boy crowed.

"Oh, hold your tongue," Alan snapped, making sure to keep his own mouth as tightly sealed as possible.

"So that's the way you'll be, milord," the boy said with a cruel laugh. "Well, you'll sing a different tune when we're at sea, that I promise you. I said row, you damned sluggards."

Within minutes they were close to *Ariadne* and steering for its starboard side. It seemed immense to Alan's eyes, much like a country house on a large estate. Unfortunately, a country house that seemed to bob and roll with a life of its own. The bowman grappled them to the side with his boat hook by the mainmast chains.

"Up you go, my booby," the boy said.

"Up there? How?"

"Jump onto the battens, grab hold of the manropes and climb to the entry port."

Alan perceived a ladder of sorts made of wooden strips set into the hull much like a set of shelves, with red baize covered rope strung through the outer ends to make a most shallow sort of banister rail. This led upwards from the waterline, following the broad curve of the hull along the tumble-home to an ornate open gate cut into the ship's side, very far overhead.

"Can't they drop a chair or something?" Alan asked. God, I'll be killed if I try to climb that. I'll bet this is some kind of nautical humbug they pull on the newlies.

"You in the boat. Get a move on," a voice shouted down through a brass speaking trumpet which appeared over the rail, then withdrew.

Alan realized there was nothing for it but to go. He got to his feet shakily as the boat rocked and rolled and bumped against the heaving ship hellish lively, which made him swoon. He was also not a swimmer and feared the grey water. A seaman offered a hand and shoulder to steady him as he put a foot on the gunwale of the boat. He waited for the two craft to get in harmony, then leaped for the ladder. But his foot pushed the gunwale down and the ship rolled to starboard as he fought madly for a grip on the sodden manropes and slick battens. Clinging in terror, he was dunked chest-deep in the freezing water and screeched an obscenity, also catching a solid whack in his back from the side of the rowing boat. As the ship rolled back upright, Alan scrambled for his very life and arrived through the entry port with his teeth chattering. There was a hearty general round of laughter at his arrival which didn't do his composure much good, either.

"Well?" a person who appeared to be some sort of officer demanded, hands on his hips and his chin out almost in Alan's face.

"Sorry about that. Must have misjudged my timing," Alan said. "Is there a place I could change? It's devilish cold."

"You'll doff your hat to me." The officer was within an inch of his nose, "you'll say *sir* to me, and report yourself aboard this ship properly, or I'll shove your ignorant arse back for the fish to gawk at, you simple fucking farmer!"

Alan stared at him for a second, shocked to his core that anyone could yell at him in such a manner, and with such filthy language. Not that he was above using it himself, and prided himself on being a true Englishman when occasion demanded harsh words. But to be the recipient was much like his recent cold bath. His lips trembled as he desperately tried to remember what Captain Bevan had instructed him to say.

"M... mid... midshipman Alan Lewrie," he finally said. "Come aboard to join, sir." He raised and doffed the cocked hat he wore.

"You *are* a young one, ain't you, now," the officer said. "What a cod's-head. You'll never shit a seaman's turd."

"Is that required?" Alan asked, instantly regretting it.

The officer stared at him with eyes as blared as a first-saddled colt, unable to believe what he had heard. "Bosun. A round dozen of yer best for this idiot."

"I believe, Mister Harm, that if the midshipman has just come aboard to join, then he is not on the ship's books, and is not yet subject to punishment," another officer said after stifling his laughter.

Thank bloody Christ, Alan thought wildly. That dozen of the best didn't sound like a round of drinks.

"Goddamn you, you'll get your ass flayed raw before the day's out, if I've any say in it," the officer so appropriately named Harm said. "I've my eye on you from here on out, little man."

"Yes, sir," Alan replied, galled to give this screeching parrot any sort of courtesy, but thinking it might mollify him.

"That's *aye aye, sir,*" Harm said, but sauntered off.

"Sufferin' Jesus," Alan whispered sadly, still standing at a loose sort of attention and doffing his hat.

"You are a bit old to be joining, aren't you," the second officer asked. "Why, you must be all of eighteen."

"S . . . seventeen, sir," Alan said between chattering teeth.

"What *were* your parents thinking of to wait so late?"

"My father . . . he did not agree with my choice, sir," Alan said, thinking his reception could get worse if they knew his real reason for being there, or the fact that if he could get a good knockdown price, he would sell the ship for his freedom, and care less if the crew was carried off in a Turk's galley.

"Newlies usually go to the gun room, but you're too old for that. Might be the orlop for you with the senior midshipmen."

"The . . . orlop," Alan replied, trying the new word on for size. He peeked about the deck to see if he could spot one.

"God's teeth, what a prize booby you are. I cannot wait until Captain Bales sees his latest acquisition. You'll need dry clothing. Mister Rolston?"

"Aye aye, sir," said the grinning imp who had ferried him out to the ship.

"Show Mister Lewrie below to the gun room and see he gets into dry things. And the proper hat. Soon as you're presentable, Lewrie, get back up to the quarterdeck and we'll take you to the first lieutenant, Mister Swift, so you can be properly entered in the ship's books. By the way, I am Lieutenant Kenyon, the second officer."

"How do you do, sir," Lewrie asked, offering a civilian hand.

"Oh, God," Kenyon said as Alan dropped his hand and doffed his cap once more. "Yes, I expect you shall be most entertaining for us. Now get below."

He allowed himself to be led below from the gangway to the waist of the ship while a pigtailed seaman named Fowles staggered along behind with his chest, suffering in silence. He staggered down a steep double set of stairs to the lower gun deck, a dank and dimly lit and groaning place full of guns, mess tables, stools, thick supporting beams and the columnlike masts. Glims in paper holders shed light on hundreds of men and doxies and quite a few children scampering about. It was more like a debtor's prison than a ship. Rolston led him aft to an area which was screened off from the rest of the gun deck by half-partitions, and filled with chests and tables.

"This is the gun room," Rolston told him. "The master gunner Mister Tencher and his mates berth here, along with the junior midshipmen. You can stow your chest along one of the screens and it'll be your seat. And you'll sleep in a hammock, instead of your soft little feather bed. I trust it will be up to milord's usual standards."

The smell of cooking grease, some foul egestion wafting aloft from the bilges, the fug of damp wool and unwashed bodies was fit to make him gag, but he forbore manfully. "It is not St. James's," Alan said acidly, turning to look Rolston up and down, "but good enough for some, I shouldn't wonder."

"You'll not last long in this ship with your snotty damned City ways, Lewrie. Just you wait until—"

His tirade was interrupted by the arrival of Fowles with the heavy sea chest. But as the ship groaned and creaked into another roll, Fowles staggered and performed a shaky dance to waddle past them, bump Rolston and crash to the deck atop the chest almost on Rolston's shoes.

"You clumsy fool!" Rolston slapped the man on the arms and chest in anger. "You did that on purpose. I'll see you on charge for it. Laying hands on an officer, for starters."

"Beg pardon, sir," Fowles said. "Sorry, sir."

Alan saw real fear in the man, and was amazed that a grown man of nearly fourteen stone could be so bullied by a mere boy in a blue coat.

"It wasn't his fault," Lewrie said, wishing they would all go away and let him be as ill as he wished. "The ship rolled heavily."

"Thankee, sir," Fowles said, knuckling his forehead gratefully, "I were clumsy, sir, but meant no harm, sir."

"That's all, fellow. You may go," Alan told him.

Fowles ducked out like a shot, leaving Rolston blazing. "Goddamn you, Lewrie. Don't interfere like that again, or I'll make it hard on you."

"You," Alan said. "Buss my blind cheeks, turkey cock. Pigeons could sit on your shoulder and eat seeds out of your arse, hop-o'-my-thumb. Now go push on a rope, or whatever, before I decide to hurt you."

They faced each other for a moment, one frailer boy whose voice had not broken completely, arms akimbo and chin out like Lt. Harm; the other broad shouldered and man-sized, coolly amused and at the same time threatening. Rolston was the one to finally give way. With a petulant noise he whirled about and fled the compartment, utterly frustrated. Once he was gone, Lewrie sank down onto the nearest sea chest and began to strip off his wet clothing. He unlocked his own and dug down for dry breeches, stockings, not forgetting to pack away his cocked hat in its japanned box and fetch out the boyish round hat he had hoped not to wear. Once dry and in fresh togs, he collapsed in misery, letting go a moan of despair and sickness. He clapped a hand to his mouth.

"What the hell are you, then?" a drink-graveled voice asked. "A new midshipman? Should have known...look at yer chest, all on top an' nothin' handy. What's yer name, boy?"

"Lewrie," Alan said, ready to spew. "What are you?"

"Mister Tencher, Master Gunner. You'll say *sir* to me, or I'll have you kissin' the gunner's daughter before you're a day older."

"You want me to kiss your daughter?" Alan wondered aloud. She must be a real dirty puzzle if he meant it as a threat.

"Are you that ignorant? I've a feelin' you and the gunner's daughter will be great friends right soon."

"Not right now, if you please. I'm feeling a bit ill at the moment, sir."

"You've a sense of humor, anyway. Sick, eh? Had your breakfast, then?"

"Oh, for God's sake," Alan said, feeling the bile rise.

"Biscuit n' burgoo'll fix you right up." Tencher grinned.

"Where could one...uh?"

"Need to shit through your teeth? Try it in this bucket."

Once empty, Tencher had prescribed his own version of
nostrum, a hot rum toddy and a turn about the decks in the
frigid January air. Lewrie choked down the rum and staggered topside. He had to admit it worked; after an hour, no
one gaped at his pallor any longer. He was ice cold down to
his bones, but the cold had a reviving effect, as did the occasional splash of salt spray that plumed off the wave tops
and smacked him in the face. Once free of immediate distress, he began to take note of his surroundings, and it was
awe-inspiring to see all the miles of rope that made up the
maze of rigging coiled on the decks, on rails, all leading
upward to the masts that swayed back and forth over his
head, all the blocks and all the ordered clutter of the guns
and their own ropes and blocks and tackles.

It was all so overwhelming, so confusing, that he didn't
think he could ever even begin to discover what each did,
much less become competent in the use of such a spider
web. His physical unease became lost in his anxiety over
how he had been received so far, and his nagging fear that
not only was he stuck in the Navy for the duration of the
war, but possibly for life. What career could he undertake
after this? And if it was to be his career, he had a sneaking
suspicion that most likely he would be a total, miserable failure at it!

What a terrible, shitten life this is going to be, he
brooded. And I've made such a terrible start on my first
day.

Suddenly he jerked to a halt in his perambulations about
the deck. Had not Kenyon told him to come back right after
he was dressed to see the ship's first lieutenant? And was
that perhaps a whole hour or better ago? Oh, damn me,
they'll beat me crippled.

He turned to dash aft toward the quarterdeck, where he
had seen officers, but before he could, shrill whistles began
to blow some sort of complicated warbling call, and the ship
became alive with running men.

That's it, they're going to hang me as soon as they catch

me. He felt a tugging on his sleeve and looked down to behold a very young midshipman, a mere babe of about twelve.

"You must be our newly," the tiny apparition said. "I'm Beckett. Better get in line with us. Captain's coming off shore."

"So then what happens?" Alan asked, wondering for his safety.

"Get in line here with the rest of us, I told you."

"Down here, you. By height. Between me and Ashburn," a very old-looking midshipman told him. He had to be twenty if he was a day. Alan shouldered between him and a very elegantly turned out midshipman, if such a thing was possible in their plain uniform. The other boy was about eighteen, handsome, with grey eyes and a noble face.

"I'm Keith Ashburn," the youth whispered. "That's Chapman, our senior."

"Alan Lewrie," he said.

Then there was no time for more talk as all the officers turned up in their blue and gold and white, their swords glistening. There were Marines in red coats and white crossbelts, slapping their muskets about, their sergeants holding half-pikes, and two officers; one very young lieutenant with a baby face, and one very lean and dashing looking captain of Marines who resembled a sheathed razor. Such members of the crew also appeared, that were not below out of discipline.

"Boat ahoy," someone called down to the gig, and the answering shout came back '*Ariadne*', meaning that the captain was in the boat. After a few moments, the Marines presented their muskets and the officers presented swords while the bosun's pipes shrilled some complicated *lieder* that Lewrie found most annoying.

A bulky man in the uniform of a post captain came slowly through the entry port and briefly doffed his hat to ship's company.

God, what a face, Alan thought. Looks like a pit bull dog I once lost money on.

The captain of *Ariadne* was in his late forties, a gotch-bellied man with very thin and short legs. He wore his own hair, clubbed back into a massive grey queue, and his eyebrows seemed to have a life of their own and danced like bat's wings in the breeze.

"Dismiss the hands, Mister Swift," the captain said.

"Aye aye, sir. Ship's company...on hats. Dismiss."

"You, there, the new midshipman. Come here," Bales thundered.

"Yes, sir?"

"You are Lewrie?"

"I am, sir. Come aboard to join, sir."

"Then why have you not reported to me and you've already been inboard half the morning?" the first lieutenant, Swift, said. He was a reedy, thoroughly sour looking man with a permanent scowl on his dark face.

"I shall see you in my cabin directly, Mister Lewrie, after I have conferred with Mister Swift. Following that, you will not tarry about signing on board in a proper fashion."

"Yes, sir," Alan replied crisply as he could, but secretly terrified that he was about to catch absolute hell.

"And for God's sake, Lewrie, the proper form is 'aye aye, sir'," Captain Bales said petulantly. "Try it, will you? Even the Marines do so!"

"Aye aye, sir," Alan said, turning red.

The captain turned to go aft, but the first lieutenant took Alan by the arm and shook him like a first term student. "Salute and show the captain respect, goddamn you."

Alan doffed his hat and threw in another one of those meaningless "aye aye, sirs", ready to weep. After they had gone, and the other midshipmen who had witnessed his ignorance had finished laughing and had gone below, Alan turned and staggered to the rail to look out at the shore, which was rising and falling in a regular pace. Alongside the petulant anger of a spoiled young man who had been humiliated before his new peers like the merest toddler, he felt such a rush of self-pity that he could not control his face screwing up in a flushed grimace, or hold back for long the acid-hot tears that threatened to explode his eyes. How could he stand this, he wondered? How could he survive all the hateful abuse, the wicked laughter at his ignorance about a career he would never have chosen in a million years? How tempting that shore looked, where people safely ate and drank and slept snug at night with never a care for this sort of misery. He contemplated finding a way to run away from all this, no matter what the consequences. He thought of killing himself, his death flinging shame on his family forever. Besides, suicide was damned fashionable these days—everybody did it.

But then, who would care if he died? A few of his friends, and a girl or two might sigh over his coffin, but most of London would most likely feel a sense of relief. That was no way to go.

He shoved his hands in his breeches pockets to warm them, and leaned on the solid oak bulwark, growing angry and snuffling away his tears. There was no escape—this was his life now, and he would have to make the best of it he could, until he found a way to get even.

"I'll make you pay for this, you filthy old bastard," he told the harbor waters. "I'll find a way to break you, and Pilchard, and Belinda, and Gerald, and Morton, and even that damned vicar. I'll make all you shits pay. You want me to die, let the Navy kill me for you, but I won't do it. I'll be back."

"Lewrie," Lt. Kenyon said behind him, making him leap away from the railing and spin to face him.

"Aye aye, sir," Alan sniffled, stained with tears but his face hot with anger.

"Young gentlemen do not ever lean on the railings. Nor do they ever put their hands in their pockets."

"Aye aye, sir."

"You had better go aft to the captain's cabins and be ready for your interview," Kenyon said.

"What can I do to avoid making even more of an ass of myself, sir?" Alan asked him. "Though I can't imagine doing worse than now."

"Follow me," Kenyon said. As they walked aft, he told him to be sure to salute, to remove his hat once in the cabin, to speak direct and not prose on, and to remember to salute before he left.

Alan mopped his face with a handkerchief after they had passed the wheel and entered the passage under the poop deck that led to the captain's quarters. Kenyon pointed out the first lieutenant's cabin on one side, and the sailing master's to the other. They stood by the ramrod straight Marine sentry by the captain's door until the first lieutenant emerged.

"Who be ye, sir?" the Marine asked.

"Midshipman Lewrie, to report to the captain," Kenyon said.

"Midshipman Lewrie...SAH," the sentry said at the top of his voice, crashing the butt of his musket on the deck.

"Enter."

Alan stepped through the door into a large set of cabins that spanned the entire width of the ship. There was a dining room with some rather fine chairs, table and sideboard to his right, and a study to his left filled with charts and books and a large desk. Far aft, there was a day cabin and another large desk before the stern windows. Lewrie strode up to the desk, and his bulky captain seated behind it. He tried to keep his balance as the ship groaned and rolled and pitched with a life of its own. He came to a halt three paces from the desk, hat under his arm and gulped down his alarm at the sight of the town swinging like a pendulum beyond the stern windows.

"Midshipman Lewrie reporting, sir."

"Lewrie, my name is Bales." The captain frowned, as though disappointed with his own name. "A Captain Bevan offered me your services as a midshipman. *Ariadne* is at present fitting out and so is short-handed in prime seamen, warrants, idlers and waisters. And midshipmen."

Alan didn't think a reply was in order, but he did nod.

"To be expected in wartime," Bales continued. "So, I

looked on Captain Bevan's offer quite favorably, to get such a well-recommended young man."

And I'll bet someone slipped you some chink, as well, Lewrie thought. What's place for, if you can't make money out of it.

"Then Captain Bevan hands me this letter from your family solicitor, a Mister Pilchard of London."

God rot the jackanapes. What sort of lying packet did he send? Oh God, did he mention Belinda?

"He states that you have been sent to sea to make a man of you," Bales said sourly, "that you have been a wastrel, a scamp and a rogue. So you will understand if I feel that I have been handed a pig in a poke?"

"Yes . . . aye aye, sir," Alan said.

"Well, I do not intend to allow you to be a bad bargain, for me or for this ship, or for the King, Lewrie," Bales said. "Beggars can't be choosers, especially in what's becoming an unpopular war. We have to take what we can get, by the press gang if necessary, so consider yourself press ganged if you like, but you're mine now. This letter goes on to state that you were banished."

"Aye, sir," Alan said, hoping the reason was unknown.

"And that you had to leave . . . Society," Bales said, making Society sound like an epithet. "Was it a duel?"

"A young lady, sir," Alan said, pretending contrite apology with perhaps the hint of an ill-starred affair.

Damme, that sounded right good, he told himself. I said that devilish well. Pray God he eats it up like plum duff.

"You may have noticed that we already have the dregs of the hulks and the debtor's prisons. Perhaps next Assize will flesh us out, Lewrie. Now, we have you. You know nothing of the sea, do you?"

"No, sir."

"You'd much rather be rantipoling about and playing balum rancum with some whores, wouldn't you?" Bales asked.

"Well, frankly . . . yes, sir."

46

"Believe you me, you shall know something of the sea before I'm done with you, even if it kills you. England needs her Navy now more than ever. I wouldn't count on our Army to pull a drunk off its sister, much less save the nation. And the sea is a fine calling for a man. I shall not allow you to abuse that calling."

"May I be honest with you, sir?" Alan asked.

"You had better not ever be anything else, boy," Bales replied, picking up a shiny pewter mug of something dark and aromatic.

"I am indeed banished, sir," he began, hoping he could win the man over. He could charm when it was necessary. There were even some addled old fools back in London that considered him a manly, upright young gentleman. "I realize that I know nothing, sir, and I shall endeavor to learn, with all my heart. If this is to be my life, then how can I succeed without knowledge?"

"Hmm," and Bales nodded, studying him over the rim of the mug. "I tell you this, Lewrie. If you apply even a tenth of yourself, we can beat you into some sort of sailor. We can do that with anyone."

"Aye, sir." Saying it only once sounded a little more English to his ear; saying it twice was like higgledy-piggledy.

"Your Mister Pilchard goes on to state that you show some promise as a student...some Latin...Greek...a little French...mathematics...had good tutors. If you throw yourself wholeheartedly into your work and your studies, you may make someone much better than your background suggests. And your bottom won't get half as sore."

"I shall try, sir," Alan responded heartily, all but piping his eyes and breaking into a chorus of "Rule Brittania."

"Yes," Bales said, setting his mug down. "You are seventeen."

"Aye, sir."

"You are much too old for the gun room. And I doubt if we want our younger midshipmen corrupted by any habits you might have picked up in London," Bales said, almost mellowing toward him. "Pity we did not get you sooner. Most midshipmen come aboard at ten or twelve and spend six years before being examined for a commission. At least that is what Master Pepys laid down, though it is not followed much in these times. But since I doubt you have much influence with our Lords Commissioners of The Admiralty, we'll assume you have six years. We will put you in the cockpit with the older midshipmen, where you may pick up their knowledge the quicker with people closer to your own age. When you see Mister Swift, give him my compliments and that you shall shift your dunnage to the cockpit on the orlop."

Damn, there's that word again, he thought. "Aye, sir."

"Bevan has given me your per annum allowance."

"Aye, sir?"

"An hundred guineas is quite a sum—too much, really. I shall hold it for you, and should you have any need for it, you shall request of it through my clerk, Mister Brail. I have deducted five pounds for schooling with the sailing master, and another five pounds for your initial mess charge. As a midshipman you do not receive pay, so I shall ration you to one pound ten shillings per month of your allowance. That should be more than enough at sea."

"Aye, sir." Not paid? Nobody told me that!

"Then be so good as to sign to that effect."

Alan bent over the desk and placed his signature to a sheet of paper that banked his money and allowed the deductions.

"That shall be all for now, Mister Lewrie."

"Aye aye, sir."

"Dismissed."

Alan saluted and got out quickly. He stopped by the first officer's door and knocked. Swift bade him enter.

"Ah, Lewrie. Ready to sign aboard now?" Swift asked.

"Aye, sir. Um, the captain presents his compliments and asks that I be assigned to the cockpit on the orlop, sir."

"Thought he would," Swift said, presenting him a large

bound book. There were many names entered, many with X's for mens' marks.

"Here. Copy of The Articles of War. Make sure you learn them. I am assigning you to the lower gun deck should we go to quarters. Sail making stations shall be the mizzen mast for now. Brace tending will be on the poop with the after-guard."

I know it must be English, he thought. I can make out a word now and then.

"See Lieutenants Roth or Harm and get a copy of your quarter bills so you may memorize all the names of the hands in your larboard division, and for the afterguard and lower gun deck, especially your quartergunners and gun captains. Got all that?"

"If not now, then I shall by morning, sir."

"Don't be flip with me, Lewrie. You'll live to regret it."

"Aye aye, sir," Alan said, on his guard again.

"That's all, then. Dismissed. Get below."

"About my luggage, sir?"

"Yes?" Swift smiled, almost pleasant for once.

"Could you give me some men to help carry it, sir?"

"Think it might be worth a penny for me, Lewrie?" Swift asked.

"Oh . . . I wouldn't presume . . ."

"Take care of it yerself fer God's sake! Dismissed!"

Alan staggered out onto the quarterdeck, glad to have escaped without a physical attack or something direr. Damme, it's hellish bad enough just being on this filthy ship. Do they have to be so hateful?

He looked about the quarterdeck but did not see anyone exactly menial. It was inhabited by a few people in blue coats, red waistcoats, cocked hats and breeches. It was only below the quarterdeck rail that he saw men in checked shirts and red and white striped ticken trousers, or short blue jackets, some wearing flat tarred hats. He descended to the ship's waist, into that stirring crowd of men, determined to give as good as he had gotten lately.

Dewey Lambdin

Let's see if this junior warrant power works, he thought, bracing the first man he saw. "You there. What's your name?"

"Bostwick, sor," the man replied, startled and suddenly on his guard. "Oim a larboard waister, sor."

"Grab another hand and go down to the gun room. I shall want my... dunnage shifted to the orlop," Lewrie ordered, hunting for the right words.

"Roight away, sor!" The man nodded, relieved that the new midshipman only wanted something trifling done. "Here, George, bear a hand, laddy."

Had Alan not followed them below closely, he would have been lost. They hoisted his heavy chest and he followed them back to the companionways, down another ladder to the orlop deck, and slightly aft to the cockpit. If the gun room had been gloomy, then the cockpit was the netherpit of the deepest, darkest hell. There were two deadlights of Muscovy glass that let in weak beams of light from God knew where. Glims burned in paper holders here and there to relieve the darkness. There was a long mess table with chests down both sides as furniture. Four miniscule cabins not much bigger than dogboxes were set two abeam. The headroom between the thick beams that supported the lower gun deck over his head could not have been much over five-and-a-half feet. There were several midshipmen lounging about, obviously bored, dressed any old how. The air was thick with the smell of pipe tobacco, bilge odor, sour clothing, mildew, salt, tar, and a generation of pea soup farts. All in all, it was a damned sight worse than Harrow even on the worst days Alan could remember.

The hands set his chest down with a crash at an open space near the far end of the table. "Er... beggin' yer pardon, sir," the fellow known as 'George' asked, knuckling his brow. "Does yer want me ter be yer 'ammockman, sir?"

Am I being put on, or does that mean what I think it does? He wondered. I heard the Navy was a bunch of bum wallopers, but I thought it was illegal.

"Keep yer togs all spiffylike, sir," George said.

50

"You already do for the ward-room, Jones," the young midshipman named Ashburn said. "Lieutenants do not get dirty, but midshipmen do. You'd have Mister Lewrie looking like a rag tag and bobtail in a week. Off with you, now."

"Aye aye, sir."

"Thank you, Mister Ashburn," Lewrie said as soon as they were gone. "Should I have tipped them something?"

This drew a chorus of hoots and laughs from everyone.

"Christ, no. They're more used to a rope's end on their fundaments," one young man said, looking up from a book he was trying to read in the light of a small candle.

Lewrie peeled off his coat and hat and found a spare peg on which to hang them. He also unfrogged his new dirk, an especially showy one with an ivory grip and what the shopkeeper had assured him was a heavily gold plated lion pommel.

"Pretty little sticker," Ashburn said.

"Anyone ever use one of these things for real, or just prying open jam pots?" Lewrie asked.

"I'd sooner have spent the money on a letter opener," Ashburn replied. "Take off your neckcloth and make yourself to home. Pass that toddy down here before this newly gets his death."

"Thank you," Alan said, getting comfortable on top of his chest, arms resting on the scarred mess table.

"Let me do the honors," Ashburn said, pouring a battered pewter mug full of steaming toddy. "The bookworm over there is Harvey Bascombe. This is Alan Lewrie, I believe. Bascombe is a total waste of time, and doesn't even have a sister, so he's not worth knowing."

"Hello."

"That's Chapman, our senior midshipman," Ashburn said, indicating the older man that Alan had rubbed shoulders with on deck. "We all toe the line when Chapman speaks, don't we, lads?"

Chapman was a carrot-haired lout with not a sign of intelligence behind his eyes, but seemed kindly. Lewrie got the idea that Ashburn was japing the fellow with his comment, a comment that went right over the man's head.

"The mathematical genius over there with the slate is Jemmy Shirke. Do *not* trust his sums, ever. And never let him navigate any boat you're in. Young Jemmy, on the other hand, has three sisters in Suffolk, all willing tits, or so he tells us."

"What a reception you got," Shirke said, putting aside his slate and coming to the table to sit down next to Lewrie. "Were you really wandering about adrift without reporting to the first officer?"

"Yes, I got soaked coming aboard," Alan said, feeling at his ease for the first time of the day. "Had to go change."

"What was your last ship?" Chapman asked as he helped himself to the battered rum pot, pouring a larger tankard than the others.

"There wasn't one." Alan had to admit.

"You don't mean you're a true Johnny Newcome," Bascombe said.

"Right in here with us practiced sinners," Shirke added. "Not a whip jack, much less a scaly fish. Now what got you here at your age?"

From hard experience with the cruelty of youth (and he had dished out his share of it, so he ought to know), he realized that he was in for a rough time if he did not establish some sort of standing in their order at once. He was totally ignorant of their chosen trade, while they could sport years of experience at sea. If knowledge could not help, perhaps bravado could win the day, letting them know that he was wise to their games and not to trifle with him, much, anyways.

"It was a bit of a scandal, really," he said with a knowing leer. "There was a young lady I knew who turned up with a jack-in-the-box and all sorts of hell to pay for it. When I refused her, her brother came for me and I had to duel him. Everyone was happy I left."

"And did you kill your man?" Shirke asked.

"Honor was satisfied. She and her family weren't," Alan

told them cryptically. "Next thing I knew I was buying my kit."

"But you've never actually been to sea?" Ashburn asked.

"Well, no. Not until necessary," Alan said with a bluff smile.

"I think this is going to be fun, don't you?" Bascombe grinned cunningly at the others, and Lewrie realized the game was blocked at both ends. I don't think I'm going to enjoy the next few weeks...

CHAPTER

2

FOR nearly a month more, *Ariadne* heaved and tugged at her anchor while the business of commissioning continued. Warrants were put aboard by the various Navy Boards, powder and shot came aboard to be stowed below, sewn up into cartridge bags. The holds were filled with new casks for fresh water, barrels of salt pork and salt beef, barrels of rum, tobacco, purser's supplies, slop clothing, large bags of ship's biscuit, galley implements, muskets, cutlasses, boarding pikes, miles more of cordage for spare anchor and towing lines, standing rigging and running rigging—all the needs of a ship of war that would allow her to be free of the land for months at a time. More hands were recruited, most willingly, but some gathered in by the press gangs and allotted to the vessels in harbor in need of men, a few at a time.

For Alan, it was a time of learning. He was not going to be allowed ashore, and the ship had no amusements other than reading, so he read, mostly his Falconer's. And if the descriptions seemed vague or made no sense, then he found practical examples in the ship.

He learned the names of the sails and masts, how they and their yards were raised and lowered. He found out what most of the running rigging did, tracing lines from pin rails to blocks to where they were terminated aloft. He prowled the length of the ship, plumbing secrets of cable tiers, carpenter's walks, bread rooms, spirit rooms, where the surgeon plied his trade, where the firewood was kept. He learned a bit about how *Ariadne* was constructed from the carpenter. He learned how to actually sleep in a hammock at night, and how to wrap it up in the required seven turns so it would be snug enough to pass through the ring measure each morning and be stowed along the nettings on the bulwarks. He also learned how to tell if one of his mess mates had taken liberties with how it was slung; one fall had been enough, as well as one good blow on the ears that had left Shirke sneezing.

Ellison, the sailing master, loaned him a book on trigonometry so he could get a head start on solving navigational problems, at the least learning how to handle the numbers obtained from the daily sights.

It was indeed fortunate that he had not joined a ship ready to go to sea. Safe in harbor, or fairly so, and with none of the daily activity of working the ship to be done in his first few weeks, he had a chance to pick up enough knowledge without killing himself in the process. And he was spared most of the officers' disgust with an ignorant newly—officers did not stand harbor watches except to supervise loading and storing, and what drills or exercises were ordered.

Alan was fortunate, too, that Keith Ashburn was deputized to be his unofficial mentor, since they were both London boys and had come from a station above the usual squirearchy.

When they were not working for the purser, the bosun, the sailmaker, carpenter, cooper (and to be honest, the work was either clerical or merely standing around appearing like they knew what they were doing), Ashburn delighted in his duties as guide, for it kept them out of trouble from senior warrants who detested the sight of a midshipman with idle hands.

Not that Ashburn didn't have a cruel streak, himself.

"YOU'RE going aloft, Lewrie," Ashburn told him, leaping for the mainmast chains.

"Could we not wait until tomorrow?" Alan asked, looking up at the incredible height of the mast. It was one thing to stand on deck and follow lines to understand their use. He was hoping that midshipmen would stay on deck and supervise, or something.

"Up you go." Ashburn wore a shark's expression.

The first part wasn't so bad, going up the ratlines of the larboard mainmast shrouds, for they were angled in toward the maintop; not much worse than the ladders down to the holds. It was at the mast that it got frightening, where the shrouds crossed to either side of the top. Marines might get to go inside the crisscrossing and proceed through the lubber's hole to the top platform—real sailors had to grab hold of the shrouds that were now over their heads and angled out to the edge of the top, actually hang on with fingers and toes, and scramble up the outside angle before gaining the top platform.

"Well, that was exciting," Alan said after getting his breath back. "Nice view. We can go down now, right?"

"Up." Ashburn laughed.

The next set of shrouds were much narrower and set closer together, and they did not lead to another platform where there was much room to stand, but the small cap and trestle trees that supported the topmast. Ashburn thrust an arm between the topmast and the halyards and stood on the cap, while Alan gripped the mast with both arms and held on for dear life. It seemed a terrifying distance down to that very substantial deck, far below. And the ship was still moving, and the masts swayed a considerable distance with each slow roll, heave and pitch, plus the snubbing jerk as she tugged at her anchor. And the mast seemed to hum and vibrate on its own in the steady wind.

Alan's heart was thudding away in his chest and his limbs felt cold. There was a tingling emptiness in the pit of his stomach, but not in his bladder, and he knew that if he did not get down from that precarious position, he was going to fall and kill himself, or piss his breeches.

"Now we'll lay out on the t'gallant yard!" Ashburn shouted to be heard over the wind. "Do what I do!"

Ashburn reached up and scrambled like a monkey onto the small crosswise yard that rested on the cap and rapidly went out to the end of it.

"Oh God, you have to be kidding me," Alan said, feeling sick at the very idea.

"Be a man, for God's sake, Lewrie! Come on!"

The yard seemed like a toothpick. "To hell with your nautical humbug, I can't—"

"Can't? No such word in the Navy, Lewrie. I promise you you'll spend half your life in the rigging. Might as well learn now."

"I would very much like to go down."

"And what do you think Mister Swift would do with any-one who had no guts, who refused to go aloft because he was frightened?" Ashburn asked, swarming back to the mast, and Lewrie's shaky perch on the crosstrees. "Disrat-ing, three dozen lashes, put forward with the common rab-ble! There'll be some dark night when it's blowing a full gale and you don't want to go. They'll *drive* you aloft and the best thing you can do then is jump and die, because if you don't have bottom, every hand'll be turned against you! Or they could just hang you for refusing to obey a direct order—"

"Jesus Christ!"

"He was a carpenter's mate, not a sailor," Ashburn said. "Now listen to me . . . grab hold of that yard, use the harbor gaskets to hold onto. Put your feet on the footrope. Now lean into the yard and hook your elbows over it. Whatever you do, don't lean back. Now come out here."

Alan was panting now. There was not enough air in the whole wide world to fill his lungs. But he did as he was told, and slowly, painfully, trembling like a whipped puppy, he crabbed his way out to the end of the yard, until it was no longer the ship he would strike if he fell, but the harbor. He was one hundred and twenty feet up, with nothing but ocean below his feet.

There he stayed for long minutes. The footrope was not all that bad, if he hooked the heels of his shoes along it, and if he kept leaning forward.

"How do you work up here?" he asked with only one eye open, and that directed at Ashburn, not down. Anywhere but down.

"One hand for yourself and one for the ship," Ashburn sing-songed. "The trick is to reach over the yard, keep your arms locked down or an elbow. Even with a full crew, work aloft is like church work, it goes slow. No one but a fool would rush things if it's blowing hard."

"Can we go down now?"

"Take a look around."

"Jesus!"

"Have to climb higher for that. Look around. You can see down-Channel fairly well today. And there's a lovely frigate beating down past us."

There was the Isle of Wight, the grey waters of the Solent, the harbor mole and the old forts, and the Channel beyond. There was a frigate, taking advantage of a favorable slant of wind to make her way west down-Channel, her sails laid as close to the wind as she could bear and well heeled over.

"Are you well?"

"Just thumping wonderful, thank you very much for asking..."

"That's my bully buck. We'll make a sailor of you yet."

"My ass on a bandbox!"

"Got to set your mind to it or you won't get on in the Navy. Not just reading about it, but doing it, like this. Turning into a real tarpaulin man."

"Like Chapman?" Lewrie asked sarcastically.

"Well, Chapman," Ashburn said. "There's a blank page for you. He's failed the exam twice now. A good sailor but sharp as an anvil. I expect he'll always be a midshipman."

"Can one do that? I mean, that would be awful—"

"You're an educated type, Lewrie. You're miles ahead of most of us, you know. Social skills, good tutors. Can't expect eight year olds to come aboard as a captain's servant and learn much more than the sea. Think how you and I shall stand out when we become officers."

"What about Rolston?" Lewrie asked. He had been plagued by the little bastard, showing off his skills and knowledge, finding subtle ways when they were working together to belittle Alan's small contributions, or toady to the officers and warrants and shine at Lewrie's expense.

"Now that's a real Welsh mile, he is! I feel sorry for whatever crew gets him as a post captain. Well, let's go down."

"Thank God..."

"Make your way back to the mast without killing yourself, and we'll go down one of the backstays."

"Why can't we just climb back down the way we came up?"

"Not seamanly. You'll have to cross your legs over the stay and let yourself down hand over hand."

"You keep finding new ways to scare hell out of me."

"If I beat you down to the deck I'll make you climb back up here and do it all over again."

Lewrie was closest to the mast, so he reached a backstay first, but took a moment to decide how to proceed. With a death grip, he had seized the stay, levered himself out into the open air, flipped a leg around the rope and cocked it behind his knee. It was then that he discovered that standing rigging is coated with tar, which can be slippery. He could not hang on, and he could not remain in one place. Even with both legs about the stay, he was sliding slowly down, gaining speed as he went! There was nothing to do but try and go down hand over hand, but in a moment he was moving too fast to brake his descent with his hands, which were burning on the hemp rope. With some heartfelt (and very English) words of pain and terror, he screeched his way down to crash feet first onto the quarterdeck and tumble in a heap, his hands on fire.

"On your feet there, young sir," Captain Bales said angrily. "I shall teach you that I shall have no blaspheming in my ship. Bosun's mate? Half dozen of your best for Mister Lewrie. At once, sir!"

Alan Lewrie finally met the gunner's daughter, bent over a quarterdeck nine pounder and slashed on the buttocks by a bosun's mate with a stiffened rope "starter". Once chastised, Bales ordered him aloft again, to climb each mast in succession and lay out on each topsail yard in turn until Bales was satisfied with his progress. And Bales had a great deal of patience in watching him.

"MISTER Lewrie." Turner, one of the master's mates, called to him as he paced along the starboard gangway above the waist one damp and dreary afternoon.

"Aye, Mister Turner."

"Captain Osmonde 'ere wants a boat ter go ashore an' fetch out cabin stores fer the wardroom. Yer it," Turner told him, standing rat-scruffy next to the elegantly uniformed Marine officer.

"Me, sir?" They hadn't allowed him outboard since he had joined, and he knew nothing about boats.

"O' course, yew, sir, now git wif it."

"Here is the list, Mister Lewrie," Osmonde said, handing him a sheet of paper. "The particular chandler's name is on this bill, and his place of business. Be sure and get a receipt."

"Aye aye, sir."

Now, how do I do this, he wondered, turning away. The duty bosun's mate has charge of the boats. I'll try him...

Lewrie hustled up Ream, a husky young man, explained what was needed, and a boat's crew was there in a twinkling, scrambling down the side to an eight-oared cutter tied below the main chains. Alan went through the gate and lowered himself down the ladder to stumble into the boat and make his way aft to the tiller. The crew sat waiting for him to say something, but for the life of him, he could not think of what the proper order was.

Well, we can't go on staring at each other like this.

"Let's...shove off, then," he said, and the bowman undid the painter and fended them off from the ship's side with his boat hook.

So far, so good, he told himself shakily. Now we need these oars in the water. "Out oars," he said with a confidence he did not feel.

Eight men lowered their blades into the water and shipped them to the rowlocks, then sat looking slightly over their shoulders for the next command.

"Give way...er...starboard."

Sounds as good as any, he thought.

The oarsmen paused for a short moment, took the opportunity to look at each other, and then the four starboard oarsmen dug in for a stroke. Naturally, under their thrust, the boat swung back alongside *Ariadne* and nuzzled her timbers with a series of bumps much like a piglet would prod her sow for a teat.

"God strike me blind, but you're *hopeless*," came a strangled wail from the quarterdeck.

"Oh, stop that," Alan said, waving at the starboard oarsmen. "Shove off again. Give way...over here!"

Someone in the boat began to snigger, choking on a laugh that could cost him a dozen lashes if he was not careful. The boat made it away from *Ariadne*'s side this time. She also continued to circle to the right until she was pointing back at the ship.

"Today, you clown," came a shout from above.

"Just what does he expect, Jason and the bloody Argonauts?" Lewrie muttered under his breath. Two more oarsmen began to laugh. I couldn't look any more stupid if I sank the damned thing. "I'm open to suggestions," he said with a grin.

"Easy all, sor," the closest oarsman whispered.

"Easy all," Lewrie parroted aloud.

"Tiller, sor," the other closest man muttered. "Center it up." He took hold of the heavy tiller bar and laid his arm along it, lining it up in the direction of the bows.

"Ah, yes. Now . . . give way all," Lewrie said, remembering those instructions that Rolston had used weeks before.

The two closest hands winked at him and began to set the pace for the stroke. The boat began to pick up speed, lifting and rising through a slight chop, with a pleasing sort of surge forward each time they dug in with the oars.

He was headed in the general direction of the shore, but there was one slight problem; from water level, he hadn't a clue where he was going, and nothing looked remotely familiar. He was lost.

"Anyone from Portsmouth here?" he asked.

"I am . . . sor," one of the forward men said between strokes.

"I am looking for a certain chandler's named Kenner & Sons. Do we have to land at the fleet landing and walk, or is there an easier way?"

"Pale . . . brick place . . . sor. There's a . . . red n' white gig by it right now . . . sor," the man said. Lewrie found the distinctive gig and gingerly turned the tiller, first the wrong way, then back to the other side a few degrees, which brought them in a gently curving path toward the particular landing where they needed to go.

Here, that's not so tricky, after all, he marveled. Now when we get there, we don't want to go this fast, so I should tell them to . . . ease the stroke, I guess. Easy all stops 'em. Now what do you say to get 'em sticking up? God, I can't remember and I don't think my Falconer's mentioned it. You're just supposed to know . . .

As they approached, he told them to ease the stroke, and the speed fell off. The bowman stood up with his boat hook ready. They had to come alongside the stone wharf sideways, Lewrie knew, but how he was going to do it was beyond him. He steered directly for the dock until the bowman began to cough alarmingly, and he took it as a cue to throw the tiller over.

"Toss yer oars," the bowman called, and all eight oars were unshipped and raised aloft as one, Lewrie realized he was sitting on the stern mooring line, and he raised up and dug it out from under his bottom, but neglected the tiller and the boat swung away from the dock, and the bowman almost went overboard trying in vain to hook onto something solid. On the second try, he caught a ringbolt and pulled the cutter's bow in close enough so that Lewrie could grab hold of another ringbolt and pass the line through it. He made a hash of his knot, but he had arrived.

"Boat yer oars." The bowman ordered softly, and down went the blades, to be stored alongside the gunwales.

"Thalt never make a sailor-man," a toothless oldster on the dock said with a grin.

"Go to the devil, why don't you? Is this Kenner & Sons?"

"Aye, so it be, young 'un."

"You come with me," Lewrie said, indicating his starboard stroke oar. "Who is senior man? Keep an eye on 'em, bowman." He scrambled to the dock and entered the chandler's shop.

He found a clerk, presented the list, and began the task of having his men carry the cabin stores to the waiting cutter, noticing he was ferrying mostly wine for the officers to drink. It gave him a thirst for something himself. The only things available in *Ariadne* were rum, Miss Taylor, a thin and acrid white wine, Black Strap, a thin and acrid red, and small beer, which at least stayed fresh longer than the water. What he wanted was a good ale, a stout English ale foaming in a pint mug. There was a keg behind the counter of the chandler's, and a row of wooden mugs. Why not?

"Here, let me have a pint of ale. How much?"

"Penny a pint, sir," the counterman said and Lewrie flipped a coin out to jingle on the counter. He got his mug and started to lift it to his lips when he saw stroke oar staring at him with a short look of disgust.

Hell, they did get me here, he thought. And they've been at hard work loading those cases.

"Here, man. A pint for every hand," Lewrie said, slapping down a shilling.

"Thankee, sor, thankee right kindly," the bowman said for all of them as they began to guzzle and sigh with pleasure. "Nothin' like a good wet afore rowin' back to the ship, sor."

They were halfway into the boat after finishing their drinks before Alan realized that they were a man short.

"Who's missing?"

"Uh...Harrison, sor," the bowman said sheepishly. "'E must be takin' a piss, sor. Not run."

"Hell he is," Alan decided in a panic, "you stay here and keep your eye on the rest of the hands. You, come with me, and we'll search for him."

Lewrie and his stroke oar began to dart about the dock and the storage areas. There were a million places to hide among all the barrels and crates, a thousand ways out of the dock area into the town. How could he have let him slip away? And how much hell would he catch if he went back a man short? They had warned him; the men were signed on for at least three years of commission with only rare spells of freedom, and it was common for men to pay off one ship and go right into another with no chance to see wives and families. When in port, it was safer to let wives and children come out to the ship and live on the man's rations and pay until the ship was placed back in full discipline. Let them go ashore and it was good odds they'd run inland as fast as their legs would carry them. Once into "long clothing" beyond the immediate reach of the watch and Impress Service, and they were lost to the Fleet. Most desertions came from new crews in home ports; they had told him to be vigilant.

"There, sor," stroke oar said, pointing to an area behind the chandlery. Lewrie saw his quarry, a youngish man in a brass buttoned short jacket, hugging a thin and poorly clad young woman. One dirty child clung to her skirts, and she held another still in swaddling clothes.

"Harrison," Lewrie snapped.

"Comin' zurr," the man replied sadly, letting go his woman.

"Coming? So is Christmas!"

"'E weren't run, zurr," the woman said, fearful for her man. "Juss wanted ta see 'is babbies, zurr."

"Why didn't you come out to the ship, then?"

"Ah didn' have no money, zurr," Harrison told him. "Ah had no way ta have 'em come out ta the ship."

"It been a year they been wi'out their daddy, zurr. Just a few minute more?"

"We have to go. Harrison, go back to the boat with this man."

"Aye aye, sir," Harrison said, giving his wife one last quick kiss and patting the dirty little boy on the head. The oldest child was wailing, and Lewrie wanted to get away from the damned noise. He turned to follow his men but the girl took him by the arm.

"'Tis a hard service what never pays a man but in scrip, zurr, an' that two years behind, if 'e's lucky. Bum boat men an' jobbers give 'alf what the scrip's worth. Don't 'ave 'im flogged, please zurr."

"Well..." Lewrie managed, embarrassed by her tears.

"Anythin' ta keep 'im from bein' flogged, zurr."

By God, she's a pretty thing under all that dirt.

"If ya don't tell on 'im, I'd...I'd..." She shuddered, pointed to a building across the alley that was obviously cheap lodgings.

God, even I'm not that low, he told himself. Well, maybe I am, I'm a Willoughby. No, I have to go back to the ship, now.

"I'll not make a habit of this," Lewrie said, digging into his breeches and fetching out coins. He gave her two half-crown pieces and watched her eyes go wide in astonishment. "You get some food for these children and pretty yourself up, and come out to the *Ariadne*. And I won't say anything to anyone, if you won't. Can't have the hands thinking I'm a soft touch, can I?"

"God bless you forever, zurr, ye're a true Christian!"

"Er... right," he said, and trotted away from her.

Once in the boat he glared at Harrison. "Just 'cause I sported you a pint is no reason to think you can take a piss on my time behind a crate, Harrison, or I'll have you up on a charge."

"Aye sir," Harrison said, nodding his relief.

"Out and toss your oars. Shove off, bowman. Ship your oars. Give way starboard... backwater, larboard. Easy all. Now give way all. Row, damn your eyes!"

He arrived back at *Ariadne* in much better fashion than when he had left, coming alongside gently and issuing the correct commands at the right time, so that they hooked on and tied up properly. He arrived on deck very proud of himself, but no one took the slightest note of his improved performance. He organized a party to hoist the stores up from the boat on his own initiative, and saw them delivered below to the wardroom, just in time to meet Mister Swift.

"Lewrie, where the hell have you been?"

"Mister Turner had me take a boat ashore and fetch wardroom stores, sir," he said.

"And what took you so damned long?"

"Well, after the boat was loaded we had a pint of ale, sir."

"You stopped and had a pint of ale? You let the hands purchase drink, sir?"

"I... uh... treated, sir."

"And what if *Ariadne* were ordered to sea and we had to wait for you and nine hands to finish your little drink? Have you no sense?"

"I am sorry, sir."... Damned if you do and damned if you don't. I'm out money and not a speck of credit for getting there and back without drowning anybody. If he's mad about me being late, I should have gone ahead and bulled that skinny wench while I had the chance...

"My word, you're a brainless booby," Swift said. "Your

only concern is what the Navy wants, not what you want. You'll have to do better than this in future if you wish to be a sea officer."

"Aye aye, sir."

"Now go below. No, stay a moment. From now on you're on rowing duties. Good practice for you. And I'll time you from the moment you shove off until the second you return, and God help you if I see you skylarking ashore, got that?"

MORE hands came aboard, calf-headed innocents who had been gotten at recruiting rendezvous at various taverns, where an officer and several reliable hands had bragged about *Ariadne* and all the prize money she would take. More came aboard from the Impress Service, willing and eager volunteers for the security of the Navy, even merchant sailors seeking better food and less work in the over-manned fighting ships; though the pay was less, they would not be cheated by a bad master.

Many more came from the tenders as volunteers, or from debtors' prison, fleeing small debts and giving tops'l payment with the joining bounty, men snagged by the courts for various crimes, but which were crimes against property, not crimes of violence. Lewrie soon lost all sympathy for them, since no one had any to spare for him. *If I'm here then it's their tough luck to be here, too. Should have run faster.*

They came aboard in ragpicker's finery cast off from the great houses, perhaps even stolen from their masters. They came from shops and stores and weavers' lofts still trying to play the upright apprentice or freeman. They came in country togs from the estates where the owners no longer needed field hands, or from the villages that had been wiped out by enclosure of public lands. They came with the prison stink and the farm stink on them, or dredged up from the cities' gutters. Up to the first lieutenant to sign or make their marks, then out of their clothes to shiver under the wash deck pumps, and the decks ran with the accumulated grit they carried aboard on their skins. Deloused, perhaps for the first time in months, and then, chicken-white and pimply, down to the gun deck with their slop clothing, where they got sorted out into "hands". They would, the bulk of them, serve guns in battle, haul on braces to angle the sails, tail on the jeers to raise the yards, tail on the halyards to make sail, and be the human engines to shift cargo, so that *Ariadne* would live. The younger ones would be cabin servants and stewards, or be trained as topmen who went aloft to fight canvas.

As *Ariadne* approached something like her full complement, Bales decided the time had come for sail drill and gunnery exercises. Alan knew a little, which was reams more than most of the new hands knew, so he found himself leading men about the deck like tame bears, so they would know where to stand when ordered, what rope or sheet to seize when needed, what part of the deck they would scrub.

Lewrie saw what captain Bales had meant when he had told him they could make sailors out of any material they laid their hands on; slowly the crew began to fathom what was required of them. Slowly, he began to do the same, going aloft when top and t'gallant masts were struck and re-hoisted, sails were shaken out and drawn down, then reefed over and over again until the exercise was no longer a complete shambles.

With the ship back in full discipline, and with her company hard at work, the officers were out in force once more, and though *Ariadne* had fourteen of her required sixteen midshipmen, he felt that he was the only name anyone knew when it came to extra duties, or something especially filthy to do.

Now he sat at the mess table in the cockpit. He had a navigation problem due to Mister Ellison in the next forenoon, but his mind refused to function. He had been up since four in the morning, and it was now six in the evening. Supper was on its way from the galley, and he slumped over a hot mug of flip, wondering if he would be able to stay awake long enough to eat.

"Let's play a game after supper," Bascombe suggested. "Let's build a galley."

"Let's not, unless you're the figurehead, Bascombe," Alan said wearily.

"Heard of that one, have you?" Alan had fallen for some of the usual pranks. He had been sent up on deck to listen to the dogfish bark; that cost Bascombe a sore shoulder. He had been sent to fetch a Marine private named Cheeks, and had dashed about the ship "passing the word for Private Cheeks" until Ream had told him it was a butt-fucker's insult, and even got the Marines mad. He had *not* gone to fetch gooseberries from the foretop, or most of the other dumb games midshipmen played on each other. He had heard of "building a galley" and had asked Lt. Kenyon about it; it involved one boy being the contractor and the rest being the boat, linking arms in an oval to make the sides, their feet together to be a keel. The one named the figurehead leaned forward until the contractor demanded that he wanted a gilt figurehead, at which point the mark was given a dash of shit in the face with a brush, and everyone ran for their lives.

"Gun drill tomorrow," Shirke said, sipping his drink. "Surely we should be doing more of that."

"Don't we work enough already?" Alan asked.

"'Cause we've got people listed for the guns that don't know a cap square from a cascabel, and what do we do if we run into a French line of battle ship going down-Channel?" Bascombe asked.

"A cap square," Alan laughed. "Is that something you wear?"

"I'd like to see you wear one," Bascombe snapped. "Speaking of Country Harrys who can't even steer a damned cutter."

"Hark that from our best bargee," Alan shot back. "The great sailor, Tom Turdman. Learned his trade at Dung Wharf!"

"I'll thrash you for that," Bascombe shouted, leaping across the mess table. Lewrie sprang to meet him and the brawl was on. With the others cheering (and the senior warrants of their mess absent), it was a wrestling match just to work off tension and excess energy, only half-serious.

"Here, you spilled my brandy, you lout!"

"Ow, fight fair, you bastard!"

"Kick 'im in the nutmegs, Lewrie!" Shirke cheered. "I'll take a shilling on Harvey."

"Done!" Ashburn said, putting aside his book.

Until Lewrie noticed that he had hold of a silk shirt as he grappled with Bascombe. Bascombe was from a poor family; his kit was of middling quality, and it most definitely did not run to silk shirts.

"Wait a minute! Where the hell did you get silk, Bascombe?"

"Chapman gave it to me," Bascombe lied, knowing the fight was about to become serious. In their mess, things were borrowed back and forth to make a presentable showing on deck in front of the officers, but they were mostly asked for, not taken.

"Chapman doesn't have one, and he doesn't look *that* stupid!" Lewrie said. "Have you been in my things?"

"Me? Why should I dig in your rag box?"

"Because you're a ragpicker, Bascombe. Now take it off and put it back where you got it."

"I'll not, it's mine—"

"Hell, it's yours, you parish waif, now have it off!"

Bascombe took a serious swing at Lewrie and caught him on the side of the head. Alan shot a fist straight into his face and bloodied Bascombe's lips and nose, dropping the other boy to the deck.

"Damn you!" Bascombe wiped blood from his face on the shirt sleeve, got to his feet and ripped his waistcoat off, then the shirt, balled it up and threw it at Lewrie. "Here's your damned shirt, I hope you *choke* on it."

"You'll hand it back to me clean, or I'll make it a gift. If

the blood won't come out, then you'll have exactly one silk
shirt—"

"'Ere now, 'ere now," Finnegan, one of the master's mates,
said as he came into the compartment. "Christ, wot a pack
of yowlin' ram cats; Mister Bascombe, I see summun tapped
yer claret. N' nice Mister Lewrie alookin' like Goodyer's Pig
—never well but when in mischief. Wot is it, then, summat
seryuss enough fer the captain, er does it stop 'ere?"

"Just a little wrestling match for a glass of flip, Mister
Finnegan," Ashburn said. "Got out of hand."

"Flip, ya say? I'll take a measure. Now let's git this cockpit
stright fer eatin'," Finnegan ordered, knowing exactly what
had happened, but relieved that he did not have to report
it, which would reflect on his ability to supervise the midshipmen.

Alan tossed Bascombe the shirt with a sly smile and
watched as Bascombe dashed out of the compartment to
fetch some seawater to staunch his nose and lips.

"You really know how to make friends, Lewrie," Ashburn
said in a low voice after they had sat down away from the
others.

"He took that shirt from my chest, didn't he? He'll not
have my blessings to take what he wants, when he wants."

"But you don't have to rub his nose in it," Ashburn replied. "There's no harm in him, he just had to look good to
attend the Captain's gig this afternoon. I'd have loaned him
one but all mine were dirty."

"He could have asked."

"He doesn't know you well enough to ask. Besides, your
usual answer to sharing is 'no'," Ashburn said. "My family
could buy up yours a dozen times over, most like, but that
don't make me as purse-proud as you! You haven't gone
shares on anything in the mess yet."

"It's still stealing," Alan insisted, blushing red.

"Not stealing . . . borrowing."

"Aye, if the hands 'borrow', they get flogged for it, but if
we do, it's Christian charity." Alan said sarcastically.

"For your information, Harvey's the son of a country parson. I doubt he's got two shillings to rub together and no hope of more. His father probably makes less than thirty pounds per annum."

"Shit," Alan said. "I didn't know. But what's mine is mine. I have to protect it. I don't have enough to keep a gentleman in the first place and my family won't part with another pence for me, not if it was for a coffin. Let's say the splendor of my kit was a very firm goodbye."

"Just be civilized, Lewrie. You'll get by with us a lot better. Now Bascombe's going to get his own back on you and I don't know what he'll do, but it won't be hurtful...much. Don't take it to heart. We don't need a Scottish feud down here."

"Damn you, Ashburn," Alan muttered. "You always find a way to make me feel like such a low bastard..."

"That's because you are. Mind now, I like you, Lewrie, I really do. You're a ruthless, uncivilized young swine, and I doubt you'll ever be buried a bishop, but you're an interesting person anyway. You'll go far in the Navy. Like me."

Supper was decent, since they were still close to shore and had the opportunity to send for fresh meat and vegetables. And when Ashburn raised the suggestion that they go shares on some cabin stores, Alan did offer to help out, so they would have some drinkable wine and some livestock of their own in the forecastle manger to delay the day when they would have to live totally on issue salt meats.

Before lights out at 9:00 P.M. Lewrie took some bum fodder in his hand and made a postprandial journey to the heads up by the beakhead under the bowsprit. At sea the heads would be scoured continually by the sea, but in harbor no waves reached high enough to relieve the odors, or remove their source. At least at sea, there would be no Marine sentry standing over him to prevent desertions over the bow, as one now patrolled in port.

He returned to the cold orlop deck that was buried in darkness, for after lights out, no glims could burn except where permitted by the ship's corporals. He found his hammock by touch, slipped out of his clothes and rolled in, drawing the blanket over him gratefully.

"Oh my God," he muttered, feeling the cold and sticky semifluid substance against his legs and buttocks. "They've shat in my hammock!" He raised a hand to his nose, expecting the worst, and detected a sweet odor tinged with sulfur. "My hammock is full of molasses."

"Bascombe, I swear to God I'll murder you," he shouted into the dark, bringing snorts of laughter from the others, and shouts from the senior warrants to shut up and let them sleep.

CHAPTER

3

THEIR last morning had dawned grey and miserable with a fine, misty rain that swelled the running rigging until it would have difficulty passing through the blocks and sheaves. But the wind had come around to the northwest, and *Ariadne* was in all respects ready for the sea. The ship was still about twenty-five men short of full complement but that could not be helped in wartime. Captain Bales evidently did not have private funds for recruiting at taverns, or for paying the crimps to deliver warm bodies with all their working parts in order who would wake and discover they were in the Fleet. He must have heaved a great sigh of relief that he was in shape to sail at all, for if a captain could not gather enough men to crew the ship out of harbor, he could lose his commission (and his full pay) and some other captain would be given a chance, while the failure went on the beach at half-pay, there to remain for the rest of his natural life. Those men he had gathered had been pummeled into some semblance of a crew, through fire drills, sail drills, gunnery exercises and the like.

Alan had been disappointed that he had not been given a

chance for a final run ashore. If the awful day had indeed arrived when he cut his last ties to the land, he at least wanted to remember it with a stupendous farewell, but it was not to be. The boats had been hoisted inboard and stored upside down on the boat tier beams that spanned the center waist of the upper gun deck, so there was no excuse to be used for a last quart of ale, a last dinner or a last rattle.

"Anchor's hove short, sir," Lt. Church, their feisty little third lieutenant called from the bows.

"Get the ship underway, Mister Swift," Captain Bales said, looking like a hung over mastiff in the dawn light.

"Hands aloft and loose tops'ls. Stand by to hoist fores'ls."

Lewrie joined a mob of topmen as they sprang for the shrouds and swarmed up the ratlines for the mizzen top. He was no longer dead with fear about going aloft; merely scared stiff.

Off came the harbor gaskets. Hands tailed on the jeers, hoisting the yards to their full erect positions on the masts. Others tailed on the sheets to draw down the sails as they were freed, while more men stood by the braces to angle the sails to the wind as they began to draw air and fill with pressure.

There was a difference aloft. The masts were vibrating even more, the freed canvas was flapping and booming as the wind found it like a continual peal of thunder, rattling the yards and jerking them into an unpredictable motion that was like to shake hands out of the masts like autumn leaves. Then, as the topsails began to draw, the yards tilted as the ship paid off heavily to the wind, swinging through great arcs that brought cries of alarm from the newest hands, and made Lewrie moan in sheer terror as he tried to find his balance as footropes and secure holds began to slide from beneath him. The footrope he was on on the mizzen topsailyard was down at a forty-five degree angle, and new men were skittering it until it almost tucked under the yard in their panic. Senior topmen cursed them into stillness before they all tumbled to the deck.

But the topsail was set, and no one was calling for t'gal-

lants yet, so Lewrie could look forward and upward to the
other masts to see hands working calmly, could look down
to the huge capstan head on the upper gun deck, where a
hundred men at the least trundled about in a small circle on
the bars, and the clank of pawls filled the air, while on the
forecastle, the strongest hands in the crew were walking
away with the halyards for the stays'ls and jibs, while others
of their kind drew on the sheets to bring control of the jibs,
laid out almost level to the deck as they strained their great
muscles to gain every inch of rope aft to the belaying pins.

Ariadne was no longer sailing sideways from the wind
after paying off from her head to wind anchorage, but beginning to make steerage way for the harbor mouth; she
had changed from a helpless pile of oak and pine and iron
to a ship. Admittedly, her crew's efforts must have raised
some cruel amusement from more fortunate captains and
officers, but she was under control, and unless taken suddenly aback from a capricious shift of wind, would make
her way out of Portsmouth and past the Isle of Wight into
the Channel without mishap. For a new crew made up of
mostly landsmen, it was the best to be expected.

"Aloft there on the mizzen, set the spanker."

Back to the mast at the crosstrees, then straight down the
mast to the spanker gaff. Experienced topmen walked out
the footropes to free the big driver, which was furled on the
gaff and would hang loose-footed to the boom that swept
over the taffrail. Lewrie had to join them and lay on his
belly over the gaff. By this time, his immaculate white waistcoat, working rig trousers and jacket cuffs were turning a
pale tan from the linseed oil of the spars and streaked with
the tar of the standing rigging, even beginning to smell like
rancid cooking fat and pick up grey stains from the galley
slush skimmed off boiling meat that was used to coat the
running rigging. It was almost impossible for a midshipman
to stay clean and presentable on a ship, and he knew he'd
have the hide off his hammockman if the stains would not
come out.

Finally, they were called down to the deck, with *Ariadne*

fully underway and clumping along like a wooden clog down the Channel coast. Lewrie mopped his face with a handkerchief and made his way to the starboard gangway to watch England drift by. It did not look as if any more would be demanded of him for awhile, and he now had time to take note of his hunger pangs, and the soreness of his muscles from being so tense aloft. His hands were aching from the climb down a backstay, and were red from unused exertion, but beginning to toughen up. He could rub them together and feel the difference in them from a month before. He looked about him and took note that the ship was now organized—the monumental clutter and confusion of braces, halyards, sheets, clew lines and jeers were coiled or flaked into order.

The anchors were catted down up forward, the stinking anchor lines were stored away below in the cable tiers to drip their harbor filth into the bilges, wafting a dead fish tidal smell down the deck. Except for the watch, the hands had been dismissed below. Those with touchy stomachs were being dragged to the leeward rails to cast their accounts into the Channel, and those that could not wait were being ordered to clean up their spew. He thought about going below out of the brisk wind and misty, cold rain, but the idea of hundreds of men who at that moment resembled death's head on a mopstick down on the lower gun deck, and were being ill in platoons, dissuaded him. He was dizzy from the motion of the ship, a lift and twist to larboard, a plunge that brought spray sluicing up over the forward bulkhead, and a jerky roll upright that did not bring the deck level.

"Mister Swift, I'll have a first reef in the courses," Captain Bales said. Seconds later all hands were called, but the mizzenmast had no lower course, merely a cro'jack yard to lend power to the braces and hold the clews of the mizzen tops'l down, so he could sit this one out. He went aft to the quarterdeck and stood by the larboard rail with the afterguard should he be needed to trim the braces. He could see Ashburn standing with the first lieutenant, pleased as punch to be underway, who turned and gave him a wink when Swift was too busy to notice. Lewrie became fascinated watching the water cream bone white down the leeward side, just feet away from him with the ship at a good angle of heel. The hull groaned and creaked as before, but now *Ariadne* also made a continual hiss as she turned the ocean to foam, and made an irregular surf roar as she met an oncoming wave.

There were ships coming up-Channel in a steady stream with the wind on their quarters and Alan had to admit they made a brave sight to see, heeled over and rocking slowly, and he wondered if *Ariadne* was much the same picture to them.

"Lewrie, quit skylarking and keep your eyes inboard," Lt. Harm snapped at him as he headed for the ladder down to the waist. Harm was making good on his promise to keep a chary eye on him, and being such a surly Anglo-Irish bog trotter, was eager to find any fault in him.

"Aye aye, sir," Lewrie answered brightly. Cheerfulness seemed to upset Lt. Harm very much, so Lewrie made it a point to be as happy and eager as possible around him.

"Mister Lewrie?" Lt. Swift called, "Come here."

"Aye aye, sir?" Lewrie doffed his hat.

"I watched you on the mizzen. You did that right manfully enough, and you're too old to be wasted on the mizzenmast. See me in my quarters and I'll move you on the watch lists and quarter bills. I think we'll move one of the new lads to your place and you may serve on the mainmast."

"Aye aye, sir." He secretly dreaded that, for the mainmast was much taller, had longer and heavier yards, carried the main course and the largest tops'l, was the place where studding booms had to be rigged in light airs, and meant a quantum leap in work. The mizzen was manned by the oldest topmen, or the very newest and clumsiest, the nearly ruptured and the ones with foreheads as big as a hen. Some eleven- or twelve-year-old sneak was going to get a soft touch, and he was going to work his young ass off. Still, it did have advantages. He would no longer be in Lieutenant

Harm's division or watch, but would get to serve under Lieutenant Kenyon, the second officer, who was considered much fairer and so much more polite.

Lewrie went forward to the base of the mainmast, where Kenyon and a bosun's mate were chatting and pointing at something aloft. And when Alan told him of the transfer he welcomed him to the starboard watch most pleasantly.

"Very glad to have you with us, Mister Lewrie," Kenyon said. "Though I am sure you realize that much more work is involved. Still, I can use such a well-set-up young fellow like yourself."

"Aye, Mister Kenyon. And I may learn the faster," Alan answered, thinking that it never hurt to piss down a superior's back. Actually, he would be working much the same duties in any watch or subdivision on deck or aloft, for the watches rotated equally each four hours, using the much shorter dog watches in late afternoon to make sure that the same men did not have to work two nights running, and everyone turned up at 4:00 A.M. to begin the ship's working day, washing and scraping decks and standing dawn quarters, so there wasn't much to choose, really.

"Well said, Mister Lewrie. We shall make a tarpaulin sailor of you yet, though the bosun despairs of your ropework. You are not seasick yet?"

"Well...no, sir," Alan replied, realizing with a shock that he wasn't. He was clumsy as a new-foaled colt on the tilting deck, and he staggered from one handhold to another, but the ship's motion did not affect him overly. All he had in his stomach was a raging hunger.

How disgusting, he thought. I am getting used to this.

"When do I make the changeover, sir, from one watch to the other?"

"Ship's day begins at noon, at the taking of the sights for our positions," Kenyon said. "I'd suggest you go see Lt. Swift as soon as he's had his breakfast. Then show up for the second dog watch."

"Aye aye, sir."

"Oh, by the way, Mister Lewrie," Kenyon said, calling him

back with a drawling voice. "We have a man missing from my division. He has run. Went out a gunport last night, probably. There's a rumor he was smuggled money and some street clothing. Heard anything about it?"

"Who was it, sir?" Lewrie said, having a sneaking suspicion of exactly who it was and where the money had come from.

"Harrison, one of my main topmen. Had a wife and family in the port, so I'm told."

"He was in one of my boat crews, sir. Had to hunt him down about two weeks ago, but he swore he was only taking a piss behind some crates and barrels."

"Hmm, that was after you had stood the boat crew to a pint?"

"Uh, yes, sir, I did see a woman with two children but I didn't connect them with him."

"Well, you weren't to know. What I regret is that he was no green hand, but a prime topman. He's probably halfway inland by now. There are some hands in this ship you can trust with your life and your sister's honor, and you'll find out who they are quick enough. There are also some men I wouldn't approach with a loaded pistol. Since you'll be closer to them than I, it is up to you to discover the shirkers and the ones who work chearly."

"Aye, sir."

"You can't treat them all like scum, Mister Lewrie, though they are halfway scum when we first get them. Neither can you be soft on 'em. Someday, you may have to order a great many men not only to do something dangerous, but maybe tell a whole crew to go die for you," Kenyon went on at some length. "I do not expect my midshipmen to be popular with the men, nor do I wish them to be little tyrants, either. The men respect a taut hand, a man who's firm but fair, and a man who's consistent in his punishments and his praise, and in the standards he calls for. Don't court favor; don't drive them all snarling for your blood. If you are so eager to learn the faster, as you put it, there are good les-

sons to be had from the older hands. I suggest you find
them."

"Aye aye, sir," Lewrie said with a hearty affirmative shake
of his head, though he regarded it much like a lecture from
a travelling Italian surgeon who might see salubrious bene-
fits for mankind in the cholera.

"Now be off with you. I can hear the wolf in your stomach in full cry, Mister Lewrie."

"Aye aye, sir."

ARIADNE butted her way through the Channel chop until
she was out past Land's End, and began to work hard in the
great rollers of the unfettered Atlantic, and up into the
Irish Sea to meet her duty.

It was not blockade work for her, that was for the largest
3rd rates that mounted more guns. Since *Ariadne* was much
older and armed lighter, her lot was convoy duties. She met
her first convoy off the Bristol Channel; forty or so merchant vessels under guard by *Ariadne* and a 4th rate fifty-
gun cruiser named *Dauntless*, and if she was anything to go
by, it was going to be devilish miserable work; *Dauntless* was
sanded down to the bare wood on her bows, and her sides
as high as the upper gun deck ports were stained with salt,
and her heavy weather suit of sails was a chessboard of
patches of older tan and new white.

After getting the convoy into a semblance of order, *Ariadne* took the stern position and let *Dauntless* lead out past
Ireland for New York in the Americas. The weather was
blowing half a gale when they began, and the bottom fell
out of the glass within forty-eight hours. *Ariadne* rode like
an overloaded cutter, pitching bow high, then plunging
with her stern cocked up in the air, rolling her guts out and
shipping cold water over the gangways by the ton. The
hatches were battened down and belowdecks became a
frowsty, reeking hell where it was impossible to get away
from several nauseous stinks, impossible to cook a hot meal,

impossible to sit down in safety, impossible to get warm or, once having been soaked right through on deck, to find a speck of dry clothing for days on end. Even in a hammock, one was slung about so roughly it was impossible to relax enough to really sleep. Gunnery exercises were cancelled, and sail drill became sail-saving, as lines parted, sails were torn or simply burst in the middle and flogged themselves to ribbons of flax or heavy cotton. With new rigging, it was a constant war to keep the tension necessary to support the masts as new rope stretched.

A watch could not pass without all hands being summoned to reef in or totally brail up the sails, cut away those that had blown out and manhandle new ones aloft and lash them to the yards and their controlling ropes.

'I want to die,' Alan kept repeating to himself as the afternoon wore on on their tenth day of passage. He was soaked to the skin, half-frozen and his tarred canvas tarpaulin was turning into a stiff suit of waterlogged armor that he swore weighed twenty pounds more than when he had put it on. He had not eaten in three days and had lived on rum heated over a candle. He honestly could not have choked anything down that could possibly scratch on the way back up.

"I hate this ship," he screamed into the wind, sure he could not be heard over the howling roar. "I hate this Navy, I hate the ocean. And I hate you, too. Rolston..."

Rolston stood nearby at the quarterdeck nettings, looking down at the upper gun deck, a slight smile on his cocky face.

"You love this shitten life, don't you, you little bastard?" Only the wind heard him. The ship gave a more pronounced heave as a following wave smashed into the transom, rolled heavily to port, and Alan dropped to the deck, his feet ripped from beneath him. He slid like a hog on ice along the deck that ran with water until he fetched up against coiled gun tackle and thumped his shoulder into a gun-truck wheel.

"Goddamn it," he howled, looking straight at Captain

Bales by the wheel binnacle. Bales nodded at him with a vague expression, not knowing what the hell he had said.

"Resting?" Lt. Swift boomed near to him.

"No, sir," he shouted back, hoping Swift hadn't been close enough to hear what he had said, though a full flogging could not hurt much worse than being bounced around like this.

"Then get on yer feet," Swift barked in a voice that could have carried forward in a full hurricane. Alan scrambled to obey and clung to the nearest pin rail, trying to rub his shoulder where he had smacked it.

"Go forward and check on the lashings on the boat tier," Swift ordered.

"Aye aye, sir," he screamed back, inches from the officer's nose. "Bosun's mate!"

The duty bosun's mate, Ream, could not hear a word he said, so he took advantage of the ship's roll upright to dash over to him and cling to the man as the ship rolled to port once more and threatened to take him back where he had started.

"Come with me," he yelled into the man's cupped ear. "Boat tiers!"

Alan muttered curses at everything in general all the way along the starboard gangway, clinging to anything that looked substantial. Ream fetched a couple of hands along the way, and Alan took notice that Ream and both hands were also moving their lips in a canticle of woe and anger, probably directed at Alan, but he could have cared less at that point.

They reached the thick timbers that spanned the waist of the upper gun deck between the gangways and stood studying the lashings on the stored boats that were nestled fore and aft on the massive beams.

"Chafing," Ream shouted into each ear, pointing at the ropes that were wearing away slowly before their eyes each time the ship did a particularly violent roll and pitch. "Tell the first lieutenant."

Alan made his way back aft, getting freshly drenched in waves of spume and spray until he could stagger to the mizzen weather chains, where Swift stood, one arm hooked through the shrouds.

"Chafing, sir," he shouted.

"Rolston!" Swift bellowed. "All hands on deck!"

Rolston's mouth moved but no sounds were to be heard as he relayed the message, and in moments men began to boil up from below and muster on the upper gun deck below them.

"Rolston, take windward with Mister Kenyon," Swift ordered. "And, Mister Lewrie, go to looard with Mister Church. Oakum pads and baggy wrinkle on old lines, and new lashings doubled up."

"Aye, sir," Alan replied, knuckling his forehead. Shit, new words again. Baggy wrinkle? Sounds like my scrotum about now.

He went forward with their little third officer and tried to explain what was desired to each man, but Church simply roared out one command, and everyone fell to with a sense of purpose that left Alan standing about.

"Go keep an eye on 'em," Church barked, shoving Alan toward the boat tiers. He realized that he would have to scramble out onto the timbers to the upturned boats, and that timber could not be more than two feet wide and deep, with absolutely no safety line of any kind.

He took a deep breath, waited until the ship rolled about as much upright as she was going to, and ran out onto one of the timbers. The ship slammed her bows into a wave as the stern lifted once more, the beakhead buried in foam, and she lurched as if she had been punched right in the mouth. The beam seemed to dance out from beneath him, but Alan was close enough to fling himself forward and grab onto one of the lashings that stood out from the nearest craft, the jolly boat. One leg dangled into the waist, but he had made it by the merest whisker.

He scrambled up on top of the jolly boat with the help of one of the older hands and clung to her keel with a death grip. The man smiled back at him, teeth gleaming white as foam in his face.

Don't tell me this cretin enjoys this, Alan thought...

"New lashin's first, er baggy wrinkle, sir?" The man asked, coming close enough to carry the smell of his body.

Alan clung tight as *Ariadne* rolled once more to port. He felt more than heard the grating as more than two tons of wooden boat shifted against the tiers to the leeward side—the boat he was sitting on.

"New lashings!" he decided quickly, bobbing his head nervously.

"Aye aye," the man yelled, then scrambled over to the next boat, with a grace that Alan could only envy, and shout something to the rest of his party, then hopped back over to Alan.

"How do we do it?" Alan asked when the wind gusted a little softer than normal. "I'm not too proud to ask."

"Stap me if I know, sir, thought you did."

And that's the last time I am not too proud to ask, Alan promised himself as the man beamed his stupidity at him.

Alan bent over as far as he dared and studied the existing lashings, the way they threaded under the beams, crossed under like a laced up corset and crossed over the boats.

"Give me a...bight on the forward timber," Alan shouted. "Then make sure it's wrapped snug in oakum or old canvas. Take it up and over the boat, under this beam we're on, and on aft...then back forward, like...well, like a woman's bodice is tied up, see? Double lashings this time."

"Aye aye, sir."

Ship work on a heaving deck or shaky spar was, as Ashburn had prophesied, much like church work; it went damned slow. Alan inspected each point where the new ropes could rub on wood and had them padded and wrapped. He thumped on each bight until satisfied that they were as taut as belaying pins so there would be no play after they were finished. Lt. Church made his way out to him and gave him an encouraging grin, squatting on one of the boat tiers.

Once his men had gotten the idea Alan swung his way over to the centermost boats, the massive cutter and barge, to watch from another vantage point. He was feeling very pleased with himself, in spite of being wet as a drowned rat and aching in places he hadn't thought one could ache from.

"Being useful?" Rolston shouted into his face, taunting him.

"Yes, damn yer eyes," Alan shot back, and was disappointed that he had to repeat himself to be understood. His throat was almost raw with the effort of making himself heard.

"Church tell you to do that?" Rolston shouted back.

"Do what?"

"Rig new lashings before padding the old...that's wrong."

"What if the old ones part before you have new ones on?"

"They won't part," Rolston shrieked into his nose. But he didn't look as confident as he had earlier, which prompted Alan to look at what his hands were doing. Rolston's team was applying a single lashing without any padding or baggy wrinkling, and were loosening the frayed lashings to pad them.

"Then what the hell are we doing out here?" Alan demanded. "Did Kenyon tell you to do it that way?"

Rolston looked away.

Alan made his way further to starboard over the barge to the captain's brightly painted and gilt-trimmed gig, which was being lashed down in much the fashion that Alan had thought correct, providing him with a tingle of satisfaction. He waved to Lt. Kenyon, who clambered out to join him. But once out there Kenyon took one look at the way the two heaviest boats were being treated and frowned.

"Rolston, you young fool," he shouted. "Leave those lashings be!"

"Sir?" Rolston cringed, not able to believe he had done wrong.

At that moment Shirke came from aft to request some topmen to go aloft and secure a corner of the mizzen tops'l that had blown out her leeward leach line.

Alan looked at Rolston, gave him a large smile, then went back to his own hands, who were busily doing things all seamanlike.

He climbed over the keel of the biggest and heaviest boat, the barge, and was about to traverse the short distance to the jolly boat when he felt the barge shift underneath him. A frayed lashing gave way and came snaking over past his head with the force of a coach whip. It struck the jolly boat and cracked like a gunshot, leaving a mark in the paint.

"Jump for it," he yelled, wondering if he could do the same.

There followed a series of groans and gunshots as other lashings parted under the tremendous weight they had restrained, and he was on a slide along the timbers toward the jolly boat as the barge came free.

One of his men had been sitting on the boat tier between the two boats. He turned to look at the weight that was about to smear him like a cockroach between a boot and a floor and screamed wordlessly. Alan leaped over him, one foot touching the man's posterior, and flung himself across the keel of the jolly boat. The man grabbed at him and hauled away, which pulled Alan down off the keel and down the rain-slick bottom of the upturned boat. Using Alan as a ladder, he got out of the way and disappeared over the far side.

The ship now rolled back upright for a moment, snubbed as her bow dug deep into a wave, and came up like a seal blowing foam. The barge shifted back to the starboard side, making a funereal drumming boom against the cutter.

Rolston came over the top of the barge to check for damage as Alan hoisted himself out of harm's way, just in time to meet Lt. Church and the panicked working party. The ship tucked her stern into the air once more, rolled to port, and Rolston fell between the barge and the jolly boat. He was face down on the boat tier as the barge began to slide down on him, a leg dangling on either side of the thick beam.

Wonderful, Alan thought inanely, I'm about to see a

human meat patty and it couldn't happen to a nicer person...

Then, without really thinking or calculating the risk, he planted his feet on the boat tier, leaped forward and grabbed Rolston as he flung himself off the tier to drop to the upper gun deck, which was about eight-feet below them. He had the satisfaction to land on Rolston, who landed on a thick coil of cordage at the foot of the mainmast. Overhead, the barge slammed into the jolly boat to the sound of splintering timber.

Now why in hell did I do that? he wondered, trying to get his lungs to work again after taking an elbow in the pit of his stomach. For a moment he thought he was dying, until with a spasm his lungs began to function again and he could suck in fresh air. As for Rolston, he was stretched out like a dead man, but Alan could see his chest heaving.

"Merciful God, are you all right, young sir?" Lt. Roth asked him, kneeling down by both of them.

"I believe so, sir," Alan said, trying to sit up, which was about all he thought he could manage at the moment. Roth hoisted Rolston up in his arms and slapped him a couple of times, which cheered Alan a bit. In fact he wished that he could do that to Rolston himself.

Rolston rolled his eyes and groaned loudly, trying to shrink away from that hard palm.

"Stupid get," Lt. Kenyon shouted down from above. "Get your miserable ass up here. Now."

"Aye, sir," Alan shouted back, thinking it was a summons for him.

"*Both* of you," Kenyon added.

Lt. Swift and the captain were there on the gangway by the time they had ascended to that level by the forecastle ladders and gone aft to join the officers.

"Silly cack-handed cunny-thumbed whip jack of a sailor you are, sir," Swift howled, spitting saliva into the wind in his fury. "A canting-crew imitation tar would know better than that. There's a jolly boat stove in and the barge damaged as well because of you."

"Sorry, sir," Alan said along with Rolston.

"Oh, not you, Lewrie, at least not this once, it's *Rolston* I'm talking to." Swift's face was turning red as a turkey cock's wattles. "Get back to work, Mister Lewrie."

"Oh, aye aye, sir," said a surprised Alan, not on the carpet for the first time since he had joined *Ariadne*.

"If it wasn't for Lewrie you'd be pressed flat as a flounder, and good riddance to bad rubbish..." Swift was going on as Alan scrambled back across the boat tiers to leeward out of earshot.

I should have let him get mashed, damme if I shouldn't have, Alan thought. But now I've done something right for a change and somebody else is getting grief.

AN hour later, they finished lashing down the boats and by then the watch had changed. Alan went down to the lower gun deck and sniffed at the odors of sickness and bodies. Even as bad as the weather was topside, he almost contemplated going back on deck rather than stand the atmosphere down here, but he peeled off the sodden tarpaulin and began to work his way through the swinging hammocks toward the after-ladders to the orlop. He passed the junior midshipmens' mess, where there was a single glim burning. The master gunner Mr. Tencher had a stone bottle by his elbow on the table, secured by fiddles, and was humming to himself.

"Lewrie," he whispered, not wanting to wake up his sleeping berth mates. "Want a wet?"

"God, yes, Mister Tencher, sir," Alan croaked in gratitude. He seated himself on a chest and locked his elbows into place on the table so he wouldn't slide about. The gummy wetness of his clothing that had been soaked in saltwater for hours almost glued him to the dry wood.

"Cider-And, boy," Tencher promised, pouring him a battered tin mug full of something alcoholic smelling.

"And what, Mister Tencher?" Alan asked, sniffing at it as it was handed over to him.

"Good Blue Ruin, Holland gin." Tencher laughed softly, his leathery face crinkling. In the fitful light of the glim he looked as if he had tar and gunpowder permanently ground into his wrinkles.

"God in Heaven," Alan choked after a sip. He had ordered Cider-And in country inns and had usually gotten rum or mulled wine as the additive. Plus, he was never partial to gin, but he took another sip, grateful for the hot flush in his innards.

"Hear ya done somethin' right tonight, Mister Lewrie."

"It was nice not to be caned or shouted at for a change, Mister Tencher," Alan said, tears coming to his eyes from the fumes of the gin.

"No gunner's daughter fer you, eh?"

"Until tomorrow." Alan gave Tencher the ghost of a smile. The man had run him ragged, trying to pound the art of handling artillery into him, and had had him caned more than once when he didn't have the right answer. He could not feel exactly comfortable with Tencher but he meant to be civil if the man was going to trot out free drink.

"Rolston should owe you a tot fer saving his life, ya know," Tencher said, filling his own mug again and taking a deep quaff.

"Well, we shall see," Alan said, forcing himself to choke down the rest of the mug. He knew that if he made it to his hammock without passing out he was going to be a lot luckier than he had any right to be. "Thankee kindly, Mister Tencher, that was potent stuff. I shall sleep like a stone if they don't call all hands again."

"Don't mention it."

Alan made his way out of the mess, clinging to the top of the half partitions toward the double ladders. Someone took him by the arm in the dark and spun him to a stop.

"*Lewrie.*"

"Rolston?" he asked, thinking he recognized the voice.

"Think you're a clever cock, do you?" It was Rolston, all right.

"I'll not let you make me look ridiculous like that again—"

"You don't need any help from me to be ridiculous." Alan tried to judge just where Rolston's head might be so that when he hit him, as he felt he soon must, he could get in a good shot.

"I'll *settle* you." Rolston's voice was shaking.

Alan could barely make out a face but he knew the fellow must be almost weeping with rage by then. "I'll square your yards for you for good and all—"

"No, you won't," Alan said, prying the hand from his arm and pressing it back away from him against Rolston's best effort with an ease he would not have had weeks before. "And if you lay hands on me once more I'll kick your skinny arse up between your ears, right where it belongs."

"Watch and see if I don't get you Lewrie."

"Watch out for yourself." Alan chuckled. "I might not save your miserable life next time...*farmer.*"

Alan took a few cautious steps toward the coaming of the hatch, wary of a sudden shove from Rolston that would send him crashing to the hard deck below, ready to dive flat and let Rolston go arse-over-tit instead. But Mister Tencher came out of the mess area with his glim and a handful of scrap paper for a trip to the warrant officer's heads in the roundhouse before the focs'l, and Rolston had to turn on his heel and go forward to his own berth space. Alan, relieved, went below to his own, where he slid out of his wet dripping clothes and sat on a chest to towel himself down in the dark.

His skin was burning with saltwater rash and he could feel the chafe in crotch and limbs, where boils were erupting from the constant immersion and the sandpaper effect of wet wool. He rolled into his hammock nude, wearing a blanket wrapped about him like a cocoon. He tried to inventory what he had dry to wear but was so sleepy, exhausted, battered and drunk that he soon fell into a swoonlike sleep, dreaming once more of getting everyone

who had been in any way responsible for his current predic-
ament in the Navy all together in one place, and roasting
them over slow fires.

Two days later, once the weather had moderated, they only
found twenty ships of their convoy at first light. Perhaps
fifteen more came straggling back into sight over the next
few days. It was likely that the five missing merchantmen
would never be seen by anyone again. At first Alan was a bit
irked that no one said anything about his saving Rolston,
then realized that it was just one of those things that was,
after all, expected from a midshipman or a sailor, with no
thanks needed or expected.

What a shitten outlook they have in this Navy, he sighed.

CHAPTER

4

DAWN was a rosy hint rising over the humps of the sea astern, lost in the grey gloom of another spring morning in the wind-swept North Atlantic. The taffrail lanterns, and the candles in the wheel binnacle lost their strength, and one could begin to recognize people on watch by their faces instead of their voices. Like wraiths the ships in convoy began to loom as dark shadows ahead of them to leeward on either side of their bows now that another long voyage was almost over.

Alan clung to the starboard shrouds halfway up to the main top, shivering with chill and trying to steady a heavy telescope to count ships. Lt. Kenyon was below him at the quarterdeck ladder, his eyes flying from one vantage to the next, judging the strength of the wind, the set of the sails, *Ariadne*'s position to the rest of the convoy, a first reassuring sight of *Dauntless* out to leeward and far ahead of the convoy, eyeing his watch to see they were awake and alert. Lewrie wondered if he was making nautical plans for certain eventualities, or merely sniffing the aromas that occasionally swirled back from the smoking galley funnel. Today was a meat issue day following a Wednesday 'Banyan Day' on which the crew was served beer, cheese, gruel, soup and biscuit.

Lewrie clambered down to the rail and jumped the last few feet to the deck. "Twenty-five sail to starboard, sir. Some very far out of position, but all taffrail lanterns burning."

"Very good, Mister Lewrie," Kenyon replied, referring to his pocketwatch. "Almost five bells. Prepare to rotate the watch."

"Aye aye, sir."

Five bells did indeed chime from up forward—two pairs of quick chimes, and a last single one that echoed on and on. Or was it merely the sound of so many ships around them raising a chorus of bells later than *Ariadne?* Lewrie kicked awake one of the ratty little ship's boys so he could turn the half-hour glass at the binnacle. Wash deck pumps were stowed away—hands stood erect from buffing the deck with bibles and holystones to remove the filth of the day before—others boiled up from below with their rolled up hammocks for stowing. The pipes shrilled for the lower deck to be swept clean. Pump chains clanked as the bilges were emptied of their accumulated seepage.

"Twenty-two ships to larboard and ahead, sir," Midshipman Rolston reported to Kenyon, "and *Dauntless* is shaking out her night reef, sir."

That was the main wrench of being in Kenyon's watch; having to share it with Rolston. Even after two round voyages Rolston still gave off a hatred so deep and abiding that he positively glowed, and Lewrie found himself walking stiff-legged about him, waiting for the knife in the back, or the studiedly awkward push at the wrong moment.

"Very good, Mister Rolston," Kenyon replied. "My respects to the captain and inform him that all ships in convoy are in sight, spread out from the night, and that *Dauntless* is making sail."

"Aye aye, sir," Rolston answered, giving Lewrie a haughty look as if to say that *he* could never be entrusted with carrying a message aft to their lord and master as Rolston could.

Alan's belly rumbled.

"Hungry, Mister Lewrie?" Kenyon grinned.

"Always, sir." He never got enough to eat, not like back home in London, and ship's fare was plain commons. He could spend half the watch dreaming of all the spicy substance of the buffets he had seen at drums, the hour upon hour dinner parties of course after course, even the hearty filling nature of a twopenny ordinary, or the choices available at a cold midnight supper after the theatre. The midshipmens' mess always exhausted their livestock quickly, and had to settle for biscuit hard as lumber and alive with weevils; joints of salt pork or salt beef that had been in cask so long one could carve them into combs; thick pea soup, cheeses gone rancid, and that only twice a week, an ounce of butter now and then, and a fruit duff only on Sundays. He no longer looked askance at the hands who offered him rats that had been caught and killed in the bread room. They were three-a-penny, fat as tabbies, and surprisingly tasty; "sea squirrel," he called them.

Now that his once fine palate had been jaded, he had to admit that the food wasn't all that bad. He had seen coaching inns and low dives in the East End of London that served worse. It was the unremitting sameness of boiled everything. And once the gristle and bone had been subtracted, there was never enough on his plate to leave him comfortably stuffed.

"Captain, sir," Lewrie whispered, catching sight of Captain Bales coming on deck from his great cabins aft. He and the mate of the watch, Byers, went down to leeward, leaving the starboard side of the quarterdeck for Bales to pace in solitary splendor. And after making his report, Kenyon joined them.

What would he have done if he had not gotten into Kenyon's watch? he wondered. The captain was so remote and aloof, and rarely seen. The first lieutenant, Mr. Swift, was a testy butler who always found a power of fault—no one could please him. The third officer, Lt. Church, was cold as charity and silent, while Roth, their fourth, and Lt. Harm, the fifth, were both full of harsh invective and bile. Kenyon was the only one he could remember who actually smiled now and then, who didn't deal out floggings and canings and viper-tongued screeches against one and all. Kenyon went out of his way to teach, to admonish his failures as faults to be corrected and not catastrophes that called for humiliating tirades. He would go to the heads aft off the wardroom in the middle of the watch, leaving Lewrie and Byers alone on the quarterdeck, totally in charge of twelve-hundred tons of ship plunging along in the dark of night. While Kenyon did not court favorites, and disliked being toadied to, Lewrie had a sneaking feeling that Kenyon liked him. When his part of the watch stood on the quarterdeck, he got quizzed by the second lieutenant. And there was time to talk softly in the black hours of the morning; Alan found himself confiding in Kenyon, as he never could with the others, even Ashburn. Had it not been for the difference in rank, Kenyon could have become much like an older brother to him. He did not think Kenyon and Rolston shared the same regard.

"As soon as the hands have eaten, we shall endeavor to round up this flock of silly sheep once more, Lt. Kenyon," he heard the captain say. It was the same each morning of every convoy; the masters of the merchant ships would never trust the station-keeping of their own kind and would scatter like chickens going for seed corn every night, which required *Ariadne* to spend half the day chasing after them, herding them back toward the pack and chivvying them back into order. And merchant captains did not take kindly to sharp commands from the Navy. More than once they had fired a blank charge to draw a moody merchantman's attention to their signals.

Under the captain's sharp eye, Lewrie tried to appear busy. He went up into the larboard shrouds of the mizzen to use his telescope on the convoy, now that the gloom was being chased to the west by the watery rising sun behind them. He also noticed, with some amusement, that Lt. Kenyon was trying to appear intent on his duties as well.

He turned his glass on *Dauntless.* There were flags soaring up a halyard of her mizzen, and he dug into his pocket to consult a sheet of paper that contained the meager signals for day or night. "Strange sail...south!"

"At last!" he crowed, leaping down and dashing to report to Lt. Kenyon. This close to New York, strange sail could be those Frenchies from their base in Newport, or rebel privateers. We're going to see some action.

"Strange sail, is it?" Captain Bates said, hearing the report. "Aloft with you to the maintop, Mister Lewrie and spy them out!"

"Aye aye, sir!"

"Mister Kenyon, my respects to the master gunner and I'll have a signal gun fired to starboard. Day signal for the convoy to close up, followed by strange sail to the south."

"Shall we beat to quarters, sir?" Kenyon asked.

"No, let the hands be fed first. Time enough for that."

Lewrie made it to the mainmast crosstrees to join the lookout already there, his heart beating from the exertion, and the excitement.

"Seen anything to the south?"

"No, sir," the lookout replied. "Not yet, sir."

Lewrie scrambled up onto the topmast cap and hugged the quivering t'gallant mast, unslinging his glass which had hung over his shoulder, as heavy as a sporting gun. He steadied his hands and peered to the south.

"Aloft there!" came a leather-lunged shout from the deck. "What do you see?"

"Not a bloody thing, damn yer eyes," Lewrie muttered. "Tell him nothing yet."

Lewrie went up higher, onto the t'gallant yard to sit astride the narrow spar. "Now, that's more like it."

In his glass, he could see a tiny sliver of a tops'l, with just the hint of a triangular sail right behind it. That might be a schooner or a brigantine. He scanned further west behind that ship and found a pair of tops'ls, and then, bringing up the rear, three tops'ls close together; possibly a brig, and a full-rigged ship, their sails painted rose red as spring flowers by the dawn.

"Deck there!" he bawled. "Three strange sail to the south!"

"What?" Lt. Swift shouted back through a speaking trumpet.

Lewrie left the glass with the lookout and descended rapidly to the quarterdeck by way of a backstay.

"Three ships to the south and southwest, sir," Lewrie said. "Due south a topsail and what looks to be a gaffsail together."

"A brigantine or schooner." Swift nodded impatiently. "Aye."

"Aft of her two topsails... a brig most like, sir. And three topsails to the southwest, perhaps a full-rigged ship."

"Mister Swift, signal again to those damned merchantmen to close up." Captain Bales said. "Then have *Dauntless* move to the southern corner."

"Aye aye, sir. Mister Rolston, bring your signals, sir."

Six bells of the watch chimed from the forecastle belfry — seven in the morning. The sound of the signal gun had brought everyone up from below out of curiosity. The other officers now congregated on the quarterdeck.

"Mister Lewrie," said Kenyon, "where is your glass, sir?"

"I left it with the lookout at the crosstrees, sir, for him to see the better."

"Good. You'd better take your portion of the watch below now. I doubt if you'd have much chance for breakfast if you waited til the end of the watch."

"Aye, sir. Thank you." But Alan only got as far as the wide companionway to the lower gun deck before the first lieutenant called for all hands to hoist more sail and shake out their night reefs to make more speed. With a sigh, he dashed back to the ratlines.

Ariadne turned due south away from the easternmost end of the convoy, which by now had seen the possibly hostile sails for themselves and were fleeing northwest away from them. Alan presumed that they would pose a threat, well up to windward and ready to dash down on the raiders as they tried to close. He was much too busy for many minutes to pay attention, as *Ariadne* also set her t'gallants for more speed.

But by the end of the watch, they were faced with a new alignment. The schooner furthest east was now behind the convoy, and had crossed *Ariadne*'s stern, while a fast privateer brig was dashing dead north for the convoy with the wind on her quarter, while the frigate-sized ship was challenging *Dauntless* for passage to the west of the convoy. Alan turned from the bulwarks and the hammock nettings, now full of tightly rolled and numbered hammocks which would act as a barrier for the Marines when action was joined within musket shot. He saw some ship's boys gathering with their drums and fifes and trumpets. The *Ariadne* was beating to quarters, really stripping herself for a battle! He could see the captain on the quarterdeck, pacing back and forth by the foremost netting rail overlooking the waist of the ship, looking like a fat duck on his thin legs.

Alan took himself down to the waist, then down to the lower gun deck, which was his station at quarters. The deck was rapidly being transformed, as mess tables were slung from the overheads, the hammocks already removed, as were the screens and partitions from the Marine and midshipmens' berths. Chests and furniture were being carried below to the holds for safekeeping, and to lessen the danger of being shattered and turned into deadly clouds of wooden splinters.

The *Ariadne* was a 3rd rate ship of the line, mounting a total of sixty-four guns, twenty-eight of them on her lower gun deck, massive thirty-two-pounder pieces that weighed over 5,300 pounds, fourteen to each beam. The ideal crew would be thirteen men to each gun, but since there was little likelihood of fighting on both sides at once, there were only three men on the disengaged side to starboard, while the bulk of the men slaved to prepare the larboard guns for action.

The deck was gloomy, for the gun ports were not yet opened, though the guns had been rolled back to the extent of their breeching ropes for tompions to be removed and to be loaded with cartridges and balls. Gun captains stood ready with powder horns, portfires with a burning length of a slow match on one end and a pricker on the other to clear the vent of their gun and pierce the cartridge bag. Bundles of firing quills were ready to hand, goose quills filled with a fastburning and fine-grained powder that had been soaked in wine (and supposedly a bit of gunner's urine) that would be stuck down into the cartridge bags and lit off to transfer the spark that would fire the gun. Loaders rolled cannon balls from the thick rope shot garlands or the shot racks around the hatches to find the roundest, most perfect iron balls, which would fly straight for long range work. Rammer men plied their tools to tamp the cartridges down snug against the vents, then a hairy disc-shaped wad, a ball, and another wad. Other men stood by with crows and handspikes to shift the guns from left to right with brute force once they were drawn up to the sills and run out. Most of the gunnery crew stood by at the side tackles and overhauled the train tackles to haul those guns up to firing position. Lieutenants Roth and Harm had charge of the lower gun deck, though should they close to pistol or boarding range, Harm, as the fifth lieutenant, or lieutenant-at-arms, would go on deck to oversee the boarding parties which he had trained at musketry and the use of the pike and cutlass.

"Bout *time*, you." Harm fairly spat at Lewrie.

"I was at the masthead, sir."

"Take station to starboard and stay out of the way. You might be good enough to run messages, if you've wit to remember them."

Ariadne was allotted a complement of sixteen midshipmen, and it was galling to see the youngest and smallest boys getting assigned to the engaged side while Lewrie was rated more useless than even Striplin, an eleven-year-old who was not half the height of an average sailor. Harm and

Roth, and their quartergunners in charge of four guns, had to put tools in the hands of some men, shove others out of the way of possible recoil, while Alan, who had found that gunnery exercise was one of his least hated duties, had to stand silent.

Once the lower gun deck was arranged to Roth's satisfaction, the deck became fairly silent, and long minutes passed as *Ariadne* drew up to their foe.

Alan amused himself reciting the fourteen steps of gun drill he had memorized. He daydreamed about delivering brave messages to the quarterdeck, or having both officers shot dead before him...Please God, most especially Lt. Harm...and him taking charge and performing some feat that would go down in glory. When that grew dull, and he realized that an immediate commission to lieutenant might not be in the cards, he worked on other remembrances and fantasies.

There was what he would have liked to have done with Harrison's slim little West Country wife, her with her burring accent from Zedland. There was that last glorious night with the little chambermaid to be relished, or the lady at Vauxhall Gardens who had found him so pretty she had taken him home to her lodgings and half-killed him with kindness. Then there was a ball in the country, where he and his hostess had struck an arrangement after the host had drunk himself into a stupor. The crotch of his slop trousers became uncomfortably tight just remembering what a rogering buck he had used to be. If I don't get ashore for some mutton in New York this trip, I don't know what I'll do...

After what seemed an age, little Beckett dashed down and spoke with Roth, who ordered the gun ports opened. As they hinged up out of the way, the deck became a painfully loud cavern as the heavy guns were run out to stick their black muzzles from the ports. Alan made his way to midships and knelt down to spy their target. It was the rebel privateer brig, tacking heavily to make a dash past *Ariadne*'s bows to get at her prey in the convoy!

"Stand by," Roth called. There was a loud bang from the upper deck. "As you bear...*fire!*"

One by one, each piece discharged with a monumental blast that had Alan's ears ringing most painfully, but it was glorious! So much noise, so much power, so much smoke and recoil and the great guns all rolling back to snub at the end of their groaning breeching ropes! He had not taken part in a live firing yet, merely drills and he knew at once that if he could play with cannon, he could make a career in the Navy and not half mind all the rest of the stupidity.

It did not appear, however, that *Ariadne*'s bite was quite as impressive as her bark. In point of fact, Alan could see quite a few tall splashes as heavy balls impacted with the sea. Some were far beyond the brig, having passed over her harmlessly, perhaps twitching a sail with the wind of their passage; some struck short, incredibly short, so close to *Ariadne* that he at first thought it was the enemy that had fired at them and missed; there were a few (frankly, more than merely a few) splashes far in front and far astern of the privateer brig where they may have killed an injudicious fish or two, but had no effect on their foe.

"Goddamn my eyes!" Roth called as loud as the broadside after the last thunder had died away. "What a pack of duck-fuckers. Try to keep your eyes open and *aim* at something this time. Swab out yer guns!"

Ariadne began a ponderous turn to starboard to keep the enemy on her beam and within the arc of her guns. Alan could see a gay flag on the privateer, a red and white striped banner with a blue canton to the upper mast. They were almost close enough to discern a circle of tiny white stars on the flag as the guns were run out again.

"Point yer guns! Handspikes and crows, there!" Harm ordered, "Aim the goddamn things, now!"

They let loose a second broadside. It was about as effective as the first. Jesus, how can we miss at this range? Alan thought miserably. He spans two gun ports so he must be no farther than three or four cables away from us. It's impossible to miss!

And then the privateer brig sailed out of their gun ports to the north, outreaching the much heavier and slower *Ariadne*.

The hands labored at swabbing out their hot barrels, slipping in fresh cartridge bags, ramming home wads and fresh shot, then straining to roll the guns squealing on their ungreased wooden trucks back up to the sills.

Beckett appeared once more at Lt. Roth's side. "The captain's respects, Mister Roth, and you are to prepare to engage to starboard."

"Lewrie, supervise the larboard guns and see they're secure," Roth told him, leading all but three of the numbers from each hot gun over to starboard. Alan made sure that no cartridge bags had been pricked, that all vents were covered from sparks, and that the ports were securely closed, and the heavy guns were snubbed in place by the train and side tackles with no chance to roll about and crush someone.

By the time he and the excess numbers had finished that chore, the starboard guns were speaking, rattling the fabric of the ship. He bent down to see out, and could not detect any improvement in their aim as they fired at a much smaller target, the privateer schooner, which was in the process of cutting out a slow merchantman. And by the time the most experienced gun captains and quartergunners had found their enemy's range and had begun to slap balls close about her, she had danced out of reach and gun arcs to rush down on another prize. *Ariadne* now turned about and chased after their earlier target, the brig. The men stood behind the guns in long swaying lines for what seemed like an hour. There were sounds of gunfire far off, light six- and nine-pounders, occasionally the deeper boom of a twelve-pounder. And then it was over; they were to secure from quarters. Charges and balls were drawn, and the guns were securely bowsed down.

By the time the mess tables were being lowered between the guns, and all the other officers had left, Lewrie shrugged and went up on the upperdeck gangways. Down south to windward, or off to the southeast astern, stood the three raiders, safe as houses with *Ariadne* and *Dauntless* now far down to leeward to the north in pursuit of a panicky flock of merchantmen. The privateer ship had a fore-top-mast missing and showed a few scars, but was still afloat. More to the point, five tubby merchant vessels that had lately been part of the convoy were also down to windward, prizes of the privateers.

Seven bells chimed from the belfry, and bosun's pipes began to shrill. "D'ye hear there? Clear decks an' up spirits!" The bosun shouted as loud as a gunshot. Eleven-thirty in the morning; as if to confirm it, Lewrie drew out his gold-damascened silver pocketwatch and opened it.

So that was a battle, he thought. I can't see anything we accomplished. If this is the glory of naval life, you can have this nautical humbug. How do you make all that prize money or make a name for yourself when you're down below getting bored to death?

Lewrie took himself off to the cockpit for their issue of rum, then came back up to perform noon sights, which he got wrong, as usual, resulting in an hour of racing up and down the mainmast.

Later at dinner, he noticed the many long faces around their mess table. Finnegan and Turner, Mister Brail, the captain's clerk, a couple of surgeon's mates, Shirke, Chapman, Ashburn and himself. Bascombe was in the day watch. Except for the sound of cutlery, it was dead quiet.

Well, perhaps not *too* quiet; there was the sound of the master's mates, Finnegan and Turner, as they chomped and chewed and gargled and hawked—both of them were what were termed "rough feeders".

"Um...this morning," Alan said, clearing his throat, which raised an involuntary groan from everyone as they thought of their poor performance. "What exactly happened?"

"Nothin' worth talkin' about," Finnegan mumbled.

"Bloody shambles," Chapman said with a blank stare. For him to make a comment of any kind was rare.

"We weren't handled at all badly," Ashburn said between bites. "Placed right clever, if you ask me."

"But the gunnery..." Alan prompted.

"Aye, that was awful," Shirke said. "It's like Harvey was telling us, we haven't spent much time at gun drill."

"We've drilled," Turner said. "Jus' never fired the damn things, 'cept fer salutin' and pissin' off merchant masters. Good gunners gone stale, new uns couldn't hit a spit kid if it were tied to their mouths."

"They were pretty fast, too. I expect that didn't help," Alan said.

"*Dauntless* did alright," Keith Ashburn said. "Got hits on her foe, chased her off, and chased off that brig once it got past us. No one could have caught that schooner once she got past us, though. Lost five ships. Not a bad morning's work for 'em, damn their eyes."

"And there's no way we could get them back?" Alan asked.

"Beat up to windward against more weatherly ships, and leave the rest o' the convoy ta get took?" Finnegan shook his head. "Ye're a *young* booby, ain't ya? Wot it's all about is, we got beat, see, younker? Them damned rebel Jonathans done beat us!"

ALAN saw New York again, but only from the anchorage at Sandy Hook. He got to go ashore, but only as far as the fleet landing with a cutter full of demoralized and sullen hands, who had to be watched constantly to keep them from drink or the many brothels. Fresh supplies had to be ferried out, more coal and firewood, fresh water, livestock and wine, and crates of fruit and vegetables. The bumboats were out, offering women, rum and gewgaws, but the ship was not allowed out of discipline. Only Bales and the purser actually got to step ashore for pleasure.

The officers sulked in their gun room aft, lolling over long pipes and full mugs when there was no drill, exercise, or working party. The midshipmen and mates stood anchor

watch in their stead for the humdrum task of waiting, envying the men in the guard boats who rowed about to prevent
desertion, or watch against a hostile move. It was an unhappy existence. The ship lay at anchor for days, stewing in
the blustery early spring rains and fickle winds, too wet to
stay topside, and too warm and airless to stay below. *Ariadne*
shifted her beakhead to point at the colony, then at England, groaning her way all about the compass. The seeming
lack of purpose, and their recent poor showing, began to
grate on everyone. People began to put in requests for a
change of mess, a sure sign of trouble below decks. There
were more floggings for fighting, more back-talking and in-
subordination, more slow work at tasks assigned. God knew
where they got it, but lots of men were turning up drunk
and getting their dozen lashes on the gratings every forenoon watch.

If he didn't have to set some sort of example, he wouldn't
have minded getting cup-shot himself, Alan decided. Here
I stand, dripping wet, can't see a cable, the food stinks, the
people stink, and I still can't get ashore for sport. Why can't
I help out on the press gang or the patrol?

"What a nautical picture you make," Keith told him as he
climbed to the quarterdeck to join him. "Perhaps a water-
color is appropriate."

"Water is the word," Alan agreed, feeling the wet seeping
down his spine under the heavy tarpaulin he wore.

"Mister Brail and the Jack In The Bread Room said we
could buy fresh food from shore on the next trip for cabin
stores. Any ideas?"

"A warm, dry whore for starters."

"Seriously," Keith said.

"Potatoes," Lewrie said with some heat. "I'd love some
boiled potatoes. And carrots with parsnip. Turkey or goose
...coffee, wine."

"That's one meal. How about some onions?"

"Drag it back aboard and I'll go shares. God, what a shitten life this is."

"It will get better once we're at sea. This idling is bad for us," Keith said.

"What's the bloody difference?" Lewrie eyed a passing barge with the spy glass. "Ahoy there!"

"Passing," came the faint reply.

"Boredom and deprivation in port is pretty much like boredom and deprivation at sea, only not as noisy," Lewrie said.

"At least at sea, we're too busy to care."

"Of all the ships I had to be put on, why this one? Why not one that can shoot and do something exciting?"

"We'll do better," Ashburn promised firmly. "Now we see how bad we did, we've been working the gun crews properly."

"Do you really believe that?"

"Of course, I do, I have to."

"Is the rest of the Navy like this? Because if it is I'll be glad to make my fortune as a pimp soon as we're paid off."

"That's disloyal talk, Alan," Ashburn told him.

"Oh, for God's sake, Keith. You're educated. You've been in a couple of ships now. Let's just say I have a fresher outlook. Tell me if you've seen better ships. And don't go all noble about it."

"Alan, you must know that I love the Navy," Keith said.

"Believe me, after listening to you for three months, I *know.*"

"It... *Ariadne* is not the best I've served in," Keith muttered. "What's your concern? You're the one was dragooned here. It's all I've ever wanted."

"All your talk about prize money and fame," Alan said. "What do I have if this war ends? A small *rouleau* of guineas and that's it. In peacetime, I'd end up selling my clothes in a year. I can't go home, and without a full purse I can't set myself up in any trade. I think I could make a go of this, miserable as it can be at times, if I were on another ship, one that could fight and shoot, and go where the prize money is."

"Hark the true sailorman!" Keith was amused at Lewrie's sudden ambitions, which made him sound like any officer or warrant that Ashburn had ever listened to. "Bravo! We'll make a post captain of you yet."

"Or kill me first," Alan said. But the fantasy was tempting. If I were a post captain, wouldn't that make all those bastards back home bite on the furniture? Now that would be a pretty crow pie...

ARIADNE finally weighed and sailed, and it was back across the Atlantic to England with another convoy. Once home, she swung about her anchor in Plymouth, in Falmouth, in Bristol before shepherding more ships across the Atlantic to Halifax, Louisburg or New York, facing the same winds, the same seas, the same food and hours of gun drill and sail handling with the same job of replenishment and loading at each end until *Ariadne* could have done it in her sleep. Some men died, fallen from aloft and vanished astern. Some sickened from the weather and came down with the flux. Some could not stomach the food, though it was more plentiful and regular than what they would have gotten in their country crofts, and more healthful than the dubious offerings of a slum ordinary.

Some were injured by cargo or gun carriages, and suffered amputation. Men were ruptured by heaving on lines or cables. Men went on a steady parade to the gratings. So many miles were rolled off astern across the ocean in all her moods and weathers. So many pounds of salt beef, pork, biscuit, peas, and raisins and flour were issued. So many gallons of small beer, red wine and tan water were swallowed. It all blended into seven months of such a limitless, unremarked and pointless existence that hardly anything seemed to relieve it of its sameness.

There were some small delights, even so. He crossed swords at small arms drill with Lt. Harm and thoroughly humiliated him, to the clandestine joy of the other midshipmen (and most of the crew).

And there were moments of freedom, when the ship was moored so far out that rowing supplies out would have half-killed the hands, and Alan discovered the pleasure of sailing a small boat under a lugsail, racing other cutters to the docks on a day of brisk wind, then a quick quart for all hands before racing back.

With his new determination to succeed burning in him, he pored over all the books on the ship, and the only books were nautical in nature. It was impossible not to learn something. One can only practice a task so long without gaining the knowledge of how to do it, and more importantly, when, unless one were like Chapman. Do a bad knot, get a caning or a tongue-lashing, so one learns a world of useful knots. Do a bad splice and be called a booby by people who have your career in their hands, and one learns to do a good splice.

Execute the steps of gun drill so often, get quizzed on the amount of powder to be used in various circumstances until you're letter perfect, and you no longer get abused. Go aloft until you know every reef cringle and clewgarnet, block and splinter of spars, and one finally is allowed a grudging competence to be able to fulfill one's duty, from both the officers, and the senior hands.

Measure the sun at noon and work out the spherical trigonometry often enough and you soon learn what is right and what is wrong, whether you really like doing it or not, and navigation can become a tedious but useful skill, and not a horror of stupid errors and their price.

And with each slowly gained bit of knowledge, with each more seamanly performed chore, with each more day full of danger and challenge that was experienced, Lewrie noticed a change in the way he was treated. From the Captain, from Kenyon certainly, old Ellison the sailing master, the mates, the bosun, the Marine captain, even from Mister Swift, he found less harsh shouting or exasperated invective, fewer occasions to be bent over a gun "for his own good". There was a gruff acceptance of him and his abilities, as though he and the blue coat were one, and he could do anything that any other blue coat on a blustery night-deck could do in their seagoing pony show, and his new anonymity was blissful.

And when he performed something so particularly well that even he knew it, there was now and then a firm nod, or a bleak smile, or even a grunt of approval that was as much a treat to his spirits as an hour with a wench with the keys to her master's wine cabinet.

There were, too, the reactions of his fellow midshipmen to go by.

There was Ashburn's bemused acceptance, Shirke and Bascombe's sullen scowls of disdain at his progress. There were Chapman's heavy sighs as he realized that he was being surpassed by yet one more contender for commission, and that his own chances were flying farther from his poor grasp every day. And there was the unspoken deference of the younger boys like Beckett and Striplin, who were already cowed by his size and seeming maturity, and now by his knowledge which had accrued faster than theirs.

Most especially, there was the hot glow of dislike that Lewrie felt whenever he was around Rolston that was so warming that he thought he could easily toast cheese on it. Ashburn had been the top dog in a blue coat, then Rolston, in the officers' estimations. It was only natural that an older boy such as Lewrie, once he had attained Rolston's level in skill and sea-lore, would be thought of as more competent by those worthies, which would automatically force their opinion of young Rolston down to third place, perhaps lower.

Much as it galled him, Lewrie realized that life had become more tolerable since he had, in the parlance, taken a round turn and two half hitches. But that is not to say that he did not secretly detest and loathe every bloody minute of it.

CHAPTER

5

BY the Grace of God, and the pleasure of the Admiralty, *Ariadne* was saved from her ennui by new orders. Lewrie could have kissed them in delight. He still shivered with cold as the ship was driven hard to the west-sou'west by a stiff trade wind. It was a grey, miserable afternoon with an overcast as dull as a cheap pewter bowl, and the sea a pale green and white humping high as hills on either beam. The ship held her starboard gangway near the water as she forged her way across the Atlantic to their new duty station in the West Indies. Somewhere over the larboard beam was Portugal, and she was beginning to pick up the trades that sweep clockwise about the huge basin that is the Atlantic and blow due west for the islands. Soon she would turn the corner and run with a landsman's breeze right up her stern for an entire, and exotic, new world, and Alan wondered what it would be like to be warm all the time, to get soaking wet and not consider it a disaster, to see new sights and smells and delight in the fabled pleasures of those far harbors. Like having a woman again—any woman.

Four bells chimed from the forecastle belfry—6:00-P.M.

and the end of the first dogwatch. Soon, unless sail had to be reduced for the night, they would stand to evening quarters at the great guns. Then he could go below out of the harsh winds for more of the smell and the damp and the evil motion of the ship.

Lewrie sighed in frustration...about the women, or the lack of them, about the irritating *sameness* of shipboard life and the need to see an unfamiliar face, hear a new voice telling new jokes; about the bland and boiled mediocrity of the food; and most especially about the *eternity* of life in the Navy. It had been eight months now. With an educated eye he could see that *Ariadne* was broad reaching on the larboard tack, with the wind large on her quarter, utilizing jibs, fore and main stays'ls, two reefs in the tops'ls, and three reefs in the courses. The glass was rising and the seas were calming after a day of bashing through half a gale.

Captain Bales strode the quarterdeck deep in thought, and the sailing master Mister Ellison leaned on the waist-high bulwarks about the wheel and binnacle, squinting at the sails. Lt. Swift loafed by the mizzen shrouds on the lee side with the watch officer, Lt. Church. Bales would peer aloft, at the seas astern, and sniff the air heavily. Alan grimaced as he knew what was coming; they would have to take in the courses and take a third reef in the tops'ls for the night. He was halfway to the weather shrouds before Captain Bales shared a silent eye conference with the sailing master and made his decision.

"All hands!" Swift bellowed as the bosun's pipes shrilled.

"Hands aloft to shorten sail."

To ease the wind aloft, *Ariadne* came more southerly to take the wind abeam. Waisters hauled in the braces to larboard. With the third reef came the need for preventer braces and backstays, parrels aloft to keep the yards from swinging and flogging sails, not so much with an eye to sail or yard damage, but to keep the topmen from being flung out and down by a heavy smack by the flying canvas.

Lewrie left his hat on deck, not wanting it to disappear in the harsh wind. Going aloft had not gotten any easier for him. It still brought his scrotum up to his navel each time.

"Go, lads, go," Captain Bales shouted from below as they passed onto the futtock shrouds. "Crack on, Mister Lewrie, speed 'em on."

Fine day to get singled out by the old fart, he thought miserably. Now I'll have to be all keen with him watching.

The wind was a brutal live force aloft, buffeting him and setting his clothing rattling, and the higher he went, the harder it was to breathe as the wind made his cheeks flutter. They assembled in the main crosstrees. Once the yards were braced to satisfaction, and the preventers and parrels rigged, it was time to lay out on the yard. The top captain went out to the weather side first, Lewrie following. Rolston went to the lee side after the number two man. The yard had been lowered slightly and was drumming like a pigeon's wing as the top captain prepared to pass the weather earring to the third reef line.

"Haul to weather!"

Facing inboard on the yard and footrope, they hauled with all their might to shift the weight of the sail as it was clewed up.

Once hauled up, it was Lewrie's "honor" to duck below the yard and pass the earring through the reef cringle to the third man seated astride the yardarm. Once secured, and hugging the spar for dear life, it was the lee arm's turn to perform that dangerous duty. Then it was nail-breaking, herniating exertion to reach forward and haul in the flogging sail, tucking the folds under one's chest, until the third reef was gathered snug.

Then came another dangerous chore, no less so now that the sail was under control and the reef tackles had tautened. One had to *squat* down on the footrope, one arm from the elbow down the only secure hold from a nasty death, and reach under the yard once again, one's shoulder *below* the yard to grab the dancing reef points and bring them back up so they could be tied off. Lewrie could hear Rolston giving someone absolute hell on the lee yardarm for not getting his on the first try.

The first and second top captains surveyed their handiwork and found it good. Below them, other men were still tidying up, taking in the main course. The forecourse would be left at three reefs, since it was a lifting effect on the bows.

"Lay in from the yard!"

Thank Christ, Lewrie thought, glad to have survived once more.

They gathered in the top and began making their way down to the deck. Lewrie took hold of the preventer backstay that was already twanging with the weight of the men who had preceded him and began to descend, after glancing over to sting Rolston with a smug look. He lowered himself away quickly and neatly, hand over hand, smearing his clothing with tar and tallow. Then there was a shrill scream...

He took a deathgrip on the preventer backstay and locked his legs about it tighter than a virgin without a further bit of thought. It definitely saved his life. He glanced up and the whole world was filled by a dirty blue and white checked shirt and a man's mouth open in a toothy rictus of terror. Horny fingers raked like talons on the sleeve of his jacket, ripping one hand from his grip, and unconsciously he clenched his hand, as though to grab back, though it would have been his own death to have tried. The desperate hand caught on the white turnback cuff of his left sleeve and ripped it loose. Then the man fell past him, and Lewrie watched him with dumb amazement as he performed a lazy spin face upwards and limbs flailing, to smack spine first onto the inner edge of the starboard gangway. Lewrie could hear the man's spine snap over the harsh, final thump of the impact. And then Gibbs, late maintopman in the starboard watch, dribbled off the edge of the gangway and fell to the upper gun deck like a limp sack of grain.

His bowels turned to water and his own limbs began to so tremble he was himself lucky to reach the deck without accident. But he had to satisfy his morbid curiosity, so he made his way forward until he had a good view, after the bosun's mates had shooed away the hands. Captain Bales was standing over the man sadly while the surgeon tried to discover some sign of life. The surgeon stood up to signify that it was hopeless. Gibbs would be commented upon in the log and the ship's books with a very final "DD", "Discharged, Dead", washed by the surgeon's mates and sewn up for burial in the morning by the sailmaker and his crew.

"A brave attempt, sir," Bales said to Lewrie, showing the scrap of white cuff he held in his hand.

"Sir?" Lewrie asked in shock. Does he actually think I tried to save the poor bastard?

"Hawkes," Bales said to the second top captain who had been on the lee yardarm, and who was now weeping openly for his dead friend. "You must keep a better control of your people aloft. I'll not have them skylarking in the rigging."

"Aye, sir," Hawkes said, cutting a black glance at Rolston, who, Lewrie observed, was standing near and eyeing the corpse with a bright fascination, and licking his lips as if in satisfaction.

"What happened, Mister Rolston?" Bales demanded.

"Gibbs overbalanced on the footrope, sir, reaching for a stay before he was on the crosstrees," Rolston answered quickly, unable to tear his gaze from the bloody body bent at so unnatural an angle, or unable to face Bales' hard stare. "It was too far to reach."

Did he indeed? Lewrie wondered. You had it in for him for back-talking, everybody knows that, had him gagged with a marlinspike half the day watch yesterday. Nobody's so stupid as to leap that far for a stay! There's something going on here, and I don't think you're the innocent Bartholomew Baby you appear to be. I could square your yards right proper with this, if I handle it right.

"Was that what happened, Hawkes?" Bales asked.

"I . . . I suppose it was, sir." He wanted to say something else but not knowing how to in front of his betters, he sounded more resigned than anything else.

* * *

ONCE they were below after evening quarters, Lewrie searched for a way to begin. Supper was over, the dingy mess cloth removed and hot rum punch circulating in lieu of decent port. The surgeon's mates were absent, still preparing the body. Finnegan and Turner were munching on hard cheese and biscuit at the head of the table. The captain's clerk, Brail, was writing a letter.

"Lord, what trash," Keith said softly, wincing at the bite of the rum. "I'd give anything for a run ashore, and a real port for an afterdinner treat."

"At least we'll be able to buy fresh stores at Antigua," Shirke said. "The ship's even running low on well-fed rats to cook."

"Two-a-penny now, not three," Bascombe said, rubbing his eyes in weariness. "It's amazing what an English sailor can eat."

"If he can catch it," Finnegan said boozily. "Now me, I'd admire me a quart of strong ale. Ya can have yer Black Strap n' yer claret n' yer port. Ale's a good...Christian drink." The pause had been to release a spectacular belch. Turner nodded agreeably, making a gobbling noise through a cheekful of cheese.

"And for you, Chapman?" Shirke asked, nudging Bascombe so he could appreciate his wit. Chapman, ponderous and dim, was always good for a laugh.

"Oh," Chapman pondered long, knowing he was being made fun of once more and determined to respond in kind but not sure quite how. "Country beer was always nice back home. Cool stoup on a hot day."

"After bringing in the sheaves," Shirke said with a straight and innocent face.

"I like wine, too," Chapman said, his face flushing with the effort of erudition and repartee. "A nice white now and again."

"Miss Taylor, I'll wager," Bascombe said, naming the thin acrid white issued by the purser.

"I'm partial to ale." Chapman's fists clenched. It was dangerous to goad him further, for he was a big and powerful lout who could explode if pushed too far. Lewrie had made that mistake once and had been bashed silly for it, before he learned to recognize the warning signs.

"Did you really murder that topman today, Lewrie?" Shirke asked, turning to safer game.

"No, but I nicked him with my dirk as he went by," Lewrie said with a grin. A hand's spectacular death plunge *had* to be a topic of conversation in so closed a world sooner or later, and Alan was more than ready for it. It would have been remarkable if no one had thought or said a word about it.

"Did he sass you, too?" Bascombe laughed. "Wasn't gagging with a marlinspike good enough?"

"I looked up and there he was, and I distinctly heard him say, 'Bugger all you officer shits,' quickly followed by 'aarrgh splat'," Lewrie went on, giving a shrill sound by way of punctuation, which had them all smiling and nodding.

"'Ere now, 'ave some respeck fer the dead, young sir." Turner said. "I'll not 'ave it."

"Sorry, Mister Turner," Lewrie said, trying to sound contrite.

"Men die in a King's ship," Finnegan said into the awkward silence. "No need to make fun of 'em a-doin' it. Gibbs was a good hand."

"Indeed he was, Mister Finnegan," Lewrie said. "I never found him a back-talker or a sea lawyer. Very reliable, very steady."

"Not steady today," Shirke said softly, bringing grins back.

"There was danger enough to reef tops'ls before the wind," Keith said, shaking his head sadly. "But he fell when all that was over with, on the way down. What happened to him?"

"Rolston says he jumped from the footrope to the preventer backstay and overbalanced," Lewrie told them. "I heard him say it."

"How cunny-thumbed can you be?" Bascombe said. "How dumb."

"And what do you think?" Brail asked, looking up from

his letter and speaking to Lewrie. Brail was close to the captian and the affairs aft, but did not trade on his confidences or what he could learn, so he was most reticent in the mess, never initiating conversation.

"Well...," Alan began, thinking, I have to be careful here. I cannot accuse, but will have to plant seeds instead to take Rolston down a peg. He's such a bullying little shit, it'll do everyone a favor to have the captain sit on him with some stiff warning.

"Hawkes didn't look too happy about it. I mean, Rolston was riding Gibbs. That might have upset his judgement," Alan said as calmly as he could, extending his left arm and sleeve, which still sported the torn cuff as eloquent a sign of his supposed bravery as a ribbon and a star of knighthood.

"What do you mean about Hawkes?" Brail asked, putting on his legal face. Brail held himself aloof from the common herd because he had been a lawyer's clerk at one time, and fancied himself as a man who could see his way to the kernel of an argument with the discerning logic of the law, though any clerk who had to give tops'l payment and take sea service automatically was suspect of being a bit less acute than he thought himself to be.

"Hawkes did agree with Rolston, but I don't think his heart was in it," Lewrie said, pouring himself another measure of grog.

"But you are not suggesting that Rolston actually did anything aloft to make Gibbs fall to his death," Brail pressed. Lewrie knew any scuttlebutt from below decks would reach the captain through Brail. "God, that would be unthinkable, I totally disavow any notion, Mister Brail."

"Rolston was... riding him, you say."

"Well, shouting at him to get a move on, that sort of thing..."

"And where were you?"

"On the weather yardarm. Rolston and Gibbs were on the lee. I was next to last down from my side, except for Blunt. And then here came Gibbs, screaming down right at me."

"So you did not actually see anything," Brail concluded.

"No, I did not, and Mister Brail, the way you're asking these questions, you seem to think there was something... wrong done. Now I told you, I refuse to place blame on anyone."

"But it does seem queer that a steady topman like Gibbs would take such a risk," Ashburn put in. "Who was left from the lee side?"

"Oh, Keith, not you too," Alan said. "Well, Gibbs, Rolston, and Hawkes, who would have been at the lee earing and cringle. At least, I think so. I wasn't paying much attention to anything but just getting down to the deck myself once I got to the crosstrees. Now look here, you're pressing me to make some kind of charge against Rolston, and I'm not going to do it. Granted, he's a little swine and I dislike him more than cold boiled mutton, but it *has* to be an accident, doesn't it? Accidents happen all the time, no matter how careful one is."

"Maybe Gibbs was stung by something Rolston said that took his mind off safety at the wrong moment," Shirke said. "Maybe just being on the same yard together was enough, after the way he had been hazing him. We'll never know."

"I know I'd hate to be on the same yard with Rolston," Bascombe said, expressing everyone's general opinion.

Brail left it at that, agreeing to take a bumper from Ashburn, but Lewrie knew that he was still puzzling about it inside, and that his suspicions would get back to the captain. Rolston would be called aft and given a roasting, maybe even caned over a gun for not keeping proper concerns for safety uppermost. It would be a tidy comedown for him in every officer's mind. That would make the little bastard seethe, Lewrie thought, and make him a little less eager to bully and bluster. And his own reputation would shine in comparison, which was the primary goal. Lewrie rolled into his hammock and blankets quite pleased with himself that night, and happily fuzzled by too much hot grog, slept peacefully as *Ariadne* rocked along in the night.

Gibbs' funeral was held the next morning after dawn quarters and deckcleaning. Bales read from the prayer book as the men swayed in even lines, since *Ariadne* did not carry a clergyman. As the sun rose in strength on what promised to be a bright day of sparkling waves and blue skies, the body was slipped over the side, sewn up in scrap canvas, with a final stitch through the nose to make sure that Gibbs was really a corpse to satisfy the superstition of the hands, rusty round shot at his feet to speed his passage to the unknown depths below.

Immediately after the hands were dismissed, ship's routine reasserted itself. Hammocks were piped up from below, and the hands were released for breakfast. Hundreds of bare feet thundered on oak decks as the man took themselves off for a hearty meal. And Captain Bales crooked a finger at Rolston, summoning him aft to his cabins, which sight delighted Lewrie.

Breakfast was also delightful, porridge and scraps of salt pork and crumbled biscuit in a salmon-gundy, with "Scotch coffee" and small beer for drink. Lewrie was taking a second helping when Rolston appeared in their mess.

His face was as white as his coat facings, except for two dots of red on his cheeks. Before anyone could say anything to him, the angry young midshipman leaped for Alan. "I'll see you in hell, you vicious bastard—"

He cleared the table, scattering bowls and plates and mugs in a shower of food, then dove at Lewrie as he attempted to rise from his seat on his chest. Lewrie fell to the deck with both of Rolston's hands on his throat and his weight on top of him.

Damme, I didn't expect him to try and kill me, Lewrie thought in shock as he struggled and flailed to free his throat. There were other hands there in a moment, however, prying Rolston loose and hauling them both to their feet.

"You miserable, lying bastard! You said I killed Gibbs! I'll kill you for it!" Rolston cried, wriggling to break free.

"The hell I did!" Alan shot back. I didn't say it, actually. Just hinted round it, he qualified to himself. "In the privacy of this mess I said it was a shame you were riding him, and that's all! Nobody is going to make me make a false report, not even against you."

"It was an *accident*," Rolston said. "But it's all over the ship I pushed him or something, and it's your fault. I want you *dead*."

As he said it, he shoved hard to his left, breaking Bascombe loose from him and dragging free of Keith's grip. Before anyone could restrain him, he drew his dirk and dove at Lewrie with the point held forward. Alan ducked across the compartment as Finnegan and Turner and the surgeon's mates seized Rolston again, this time disarming him and forcing him to kneel on the deck.

"Stand to attention, the lot of you!" Lt. Swift ordered from the doorway. He had the master-at-arms and two ship's corporals with him. He stepped inside, taking in the dirk in Finnegan's fist, Rolston held down and raging, Lewrie looking as pale as a spirit, and the mess littered with overturned utensils and bowls. "Now what's all this about? Did I hear you threaten a man's life, Mister Rolston? Explain yourself damned fast, boy."

"Sir, I—"

"Did you accuse Rolston of causing Gibbs' death, Mister Lewrie?"

"No, sir, I did not."

"Did he give anyone reason to think Rolston did it?" Swift asked the general mess. He was quickly informed that he had not; though the common opinion was against Rolston and his temper, Lewrie had refused to countenance such a thought.

"He's a clever liar, sir. Don't believe him!" from Rolston.

"Are you going to tell me that that is not your dirk, Rolston? Are you going to deny drawing it and attacking Mister Lewrie?"

"I . . ."

"Ashburn, was there a physical attack in these quarters with a weapon?" Swift turned to his trustworthy senior midshipman.

"Aye, sir, there was," Ashburn said reluctantly, knowing

he was sealing Rolston's fate. He described the events, gave Lewrie a fair report, and quoted Rolston's avowed purpose of murder.

"Master-at-arms, I shall have Mister Rolston taken aft to the captain at once. Charge of striking a fellow junior warrant and fighting with steel," Swift said, specifying a charge less than murder, or the attempt at it, which would automatically qualify for hanging.

"Mister Swift, sir," Rolston gasped, realizing what was to fall on him. "Please, sir, *no.*"

"Now get this place put to rights," Swift said. "This mess looks like a pigsty. I shall expect all of you to be ready to go aft when the captain summons you."

"Aye aye, sir," they mumbled in a rough chorus as Swift took the evidence from Finnegan and strode out.

"Sufferin' Jesus," Chapman breathed after Swift was safely gone. "That's all for that little boss cock."

"Rolston be damned," Shirke said. "Just look at my breeches. Idiot."

"What?" Chapman asked.

"I meant Rolston," Shirke replied quickly, trying to wipe food from his clothing with the table cloth.

"What's going to happen to him?" Lewrie asked. The whole joke had gotten way out of hand. He had not expected Rolston to come for him like that and was badly shaken.

"You notice the first lieutenant didn't say attempted murder, so I doubt they'll scrag him for it," Bascombe said. "I've never seen anything like that."

"Disrating most like," Chapman said. "Flog him raw and pack him off home soon as we get to Antigua."

"For losing his temper?" Lewrie asked. "I mean...we go after each other all the time down here. We all have bruises from it."

"When's the last time I drew a blade on you and said I'd kill you?" Keith asked him.

"At least a week ago."

"Be serious for once, Alan. That man tried to kill you.

Not just wave a dirk about and shout at you," Ashburn said sternly. "He's for it, now. Just as well, before he got control over people. A man who can't control his passions is obviously not a gentleman."

"At least that passion." Shirke picked up some bowls. "Though a passion for the ladies is allowed by the Navy."

"If that's so, I haven't seen much sign of it," Lewrie sighed.

THE next day in the forenoon watch Rolston was paraded on deck. There had been a swift inquiry, with all involved hands testifying. It also included details of what had happened with Gibbs, with Hawkes giving the impression that while it may have been accidental, it pleased Rolston greatly. While Captain Bales could not hold a court-martial (that took a panel of five captains), he could assign a punishment for fighting and assaulting a fellow midshipman with a weapon. Sea officers had the power of life and death in their hands, for though the Admiralty might limit the number of lashes a man might receive, written reports exceeding those limits never brought even a peep of displeasure from Whitehall. Out of reach of land and senior authority, a captain could do pretty much as he pleased.

So, while the Marines were formed up with their muskets on the quarterdeck, the officers below the rail on the upper gun deck and the midshipmen to one side, Rolston was called to punishment. A hatch grating was stood up and lashed to the gangway, and the bosun and his mates stood by with a red baize bag which contained a cat-o'-nine-tails.

Bales read out the charges against Rolston and asked him if he had anything to say. Rolston bit his lip and did not have any words. Bales referred to his slim book containing the Articles of War, and read the specific passages aloud, to drum into the hands the folly of fighting or laying hands on one another, much less a senior.

"The Twenty-Third Article," Bales intoned in a loud voice. "If any Person in the Fleet shall quarrel or fight with any other Person in the Fleet, or use reproachful or provoking Speeches or Gestures, tending to make any Quarrel or Disturbance, he shall upon being convicted thereof, suffer such Punishment as the Offence shall deserve, and a Court-martial shall impose." Bales also made reference to the Thirty-Sixth Article, the "Captain's Cloak", headed "All Other Crimes Not Capitol. . . ."

Snapping the book shut, he ordered, "Seize him up!"

Rolston was clad in shirt and breeches. The shirt was ripped off his back and a leather apron tied over his kidneys and buttocks. They pressed him against the grating and tied him spread-eagled with spun yarn.

"Give him a dozen!"

Bosun's mate Ream took off his coat and took the cat out of the bag. The lengths were not knotted, since it was not mutiny, theft or desertion, but that was cold comfort. Ream settled himself and drew back. He delivered the first stroke.

Rolston was a boy, after all, a vicious, bullying sixteen-year-old boy, not made to take a man's punishment. The lash made his whole body leap against the gratings with a thud, and he gasped audibly. Regular as a slow metronome, the lashes struck home. By the end of the first dozen, Rolston's back was crisscrossed by angry weals and already turning blue and mottled yellow from the savage pounding. He was weeping silently and had bit his lip trying to be game about it.

"Another bosun," Bales ordered at the end of the first dozen.

Jesus God, I started this, Lewrie told himself sadly. They're half-killing the little shit and it's my fault. I truly do hate him but was it worth this . . . ?

The second bosun laid on his first stroke, and this time, Rolston screamed. Not a yell, not a plea for mercy, but a womanish scream of agony. The next stroke knocked the air from his lungs. His back was now streaming blood where further lashes had broken open the inflamed weals. The youngest midshipmen that Lewrie saw were either weeping openly, or staring as though the flogging had happened not a moment too soon to please them. Rolston would have been the oldest in the gun room, and would have made their little lives hell.

Lewrie looked at the lines of men, and he saw furtive gleams of pleasure. There was none of the swaying or shuffling they normally showed when they thought a punishment had found the wrong person. Perhaps it was an accident about Gibbs, but to the ship's people, the punishment fit the crime, or answered their sense of a final justice.

The punishment ended after two dozen. It was doubtful if Rolston would have survived a third, and was so lost in agony already that one more stroke would not have affected him, or served a useful purpose.

He was cut down and hauled off to the sick bay. The deck was washed down and the grating put back in place. The men were dismissed and chivvied off to prepare for morning gun drill and cleaning.

Rolston was officially disrated, deprived of gunroom privilege and dressed in slop clothing like a common seaman. He was also confined in the brig as soon as the surgeon was through with him, there to languish until they docked.

"Lewrie, quit mooning," Lt. Kenyon snapped as he saw him lounging by the bulwarks.

"Sorry, sir. I was thinking about Rolston just now."

"Don't waste your time," Kenyon told him. Lewrie gave it a long thought, then decided to come clean about his scheme to ruin his rival, but Kenyon forestalled him.

"I still do not think he caused Gibbs to fall, but the captain had enough suspicion to give him chocolate. And the way he went after you was the end."

"Yes, but—"

"So you crowed about it in the mess. Believe me, I know what it's like to see a rival confounded, and Rolston was not the most popular man aboard, either. How often have I seen him having men up on charge to satisfy his petty grudges, or just to see a flogging? No, he is no loss to us. He was a brutal little monster, and would have been a real terror as an officer, God help us, as a captain. That kind we don't need in the Navy."

"I feel as if I precipitated the attack, sir."

"So what?" Kenyon shrugged. "So might any of the others who had a reason to wonder what happened aloft. Let Hawkes and Blunt stew on it long enough and it might have been Rolston who came down from the rigging next, and then we'd have to hang two good topmen for the sake of one bad midshipman."

I doubt if he'd let me admit rape of his only sister, Alan told himself. Maybe I did do something right, after all?

"You're shaping devilishly well as a midshipman, Lewrie."

"Er...thank you, sir."

"Even though you thoroughly detest the Navy, we're better off with your kind than his. And don't tell me you love the Navy like Ashburn does, 'cause I've seen you when no one was looking. I was not exactly enamored of going to sea when I was a boy, either, but there were reasons why it was necessary. I still do not *love* it, but I have a future in it. You'll make your way."

"Thank you for telling me that, sir."

"I said nothing, Mister Lewrie...Now, I expect you to make sure to inspect the mess tables and report which mess has not scrubbed up properly. And check the bread barges, too."

"Aye aye, sir."

FOR the next couple of weeks of their passage the world seemed incredibly sweet to Alan. The weather was fresh and clean, with deep blue skies and high-piled clouds with no threat in them. From the usual disturbed grey green color, the ocean changed to a spectacular shade of blue that glittered and folded and rose again under a balmy sun, so that it was as painful to look upon as a gem under a strong light. In the steady trade winds, *Ariadne* shook out the reefs in her tops'ls and hoisted her t'gallants for the first time in months, even setting studdingsails on the main course yard, and except for sail drill each day, there was less cause to reef and furl. Free of convoys and sluggish merchantmen, she proved that she could fly.

With better weather and steadier foot and hand holds, Alan practically lived aloft in the rigging as they traded their heavy storm sails for a lighter set, lowering tons of strained and patched flaxen sails to be aired and folded away, the new being bent onto the yards and stays.

Clearer skies also allowed better classes in navigation and the measuring of the noon sun's height with their quadrants, or the newfangled sextant that was Mister Ellison's pride and joy. Alan found himself becoming pleasingly accurate at plotting their position.

Dry decks and a following wind also gave better footing for small arms drill—musketry firing at towed kegs, pistol practice, pike training, tomahawks or boarding axes, and Lewrie's favorite, sword work. Kenyon let him borrow a slightly curved hunting sword, or hanger, and he became adept with it, for it was much lighter than a naval cutlass to handle, but was meant to be used partially in the same way, stamp and slash.

Ashburn's tutor had been Spanish, so he knew the two-bladed fighting style of rapier and main gauche, while Alan knew the fighting style of the London streets, smallsword and cloak, lantern or walking stick for a mobile shield. They delighted in practicing on each other. It was good exercise, and taught raw landsmen how to survive at close quarters, though once in action it was pretty much expected that they would forget most of what they had been taught and fall back on their instincts, which were to flail away madly and batter someone to death rather than apply any science to the task.

The master-at-arms was not a swordsman, and as Lewrie had proved months before, neither was the lieutenant-at-arms, Lt. Harm, so Marine captain Osmonde had been summoned from his life of ease in the wardroom to instruct at swordplay.

Lewrie was not exactly sure that a Marine officer had any duties to perform, except for looking elegant and lending a measure of tone to what was a minor squirearchy gathering aft. His sergeants did all the work, and he supposedly served as some sort of catering officer to the other officers, which might have taken an hour a week. Yet Osmonde was lean to the point of gauntness, always immaculately turned out in snow-white breeches, waistcoat and shirt, his neck-cloth perfect, his silk stockings looking brand new, his red tunic and scarlet sash without a speck of tar (or even dust) and his gold and brass and silver fit to blind the unwary. Lewrie was quite taken with Osmonde, for his skill with a sword, his gorgeous uniform, his egalitarian way of talking to the petty officers and midshipmen at drill (he did not talk to his own Marines, ever) and mostly with the fact that the man did not appear to ever have to do a lick of work and got paid right well for it, even getting to sleep in every night with no interruptions.

"I see you still sport Mister Kenyon's hanger," Osmonde said to him one sweaty day on the larboard gangway at drill.

"Aye, sir. And short enough to get under guard."

"You would benefit with hefting a regulation cutlass. Put that away and do so," Osmonde said, carefully phrasing each word.

"Aye, sir." Lewrie sheathed the wonderful little sword and dug a heavy cutlass from a tub of weapons. He looked around for an opponent and found everyone already engaged.

"Here, we shall face-off each the other," Osmonde said. "This shall be good for you. I notice you are a wrist player. Do you good to learn to hack and slash and strengthen your whole arm."

"Seems such a...clumsy way, sir. And inelegant," Lewrie said, taking up a middle guard.

"So shall your opponent be, should we ever be called upon to board a foe. Some common seaman." Osmonde said, clashing blades with him. He began to backpedal Lewrie across the gangway with crashing blows, while continuing to speak as if he were seated in a club chair. "You shall advance so gallantly and with such grace as to make your old pushing school proud, and some hulking brute like Fowles there will chop you to chutney before you can shout *'en garde'.*"

Lewrie fetched up at the quarterdeck netting, backed into it by the fury of the attack and the weight of the opposing blade.

"The damned thing has no point worth mentioning, so quit trying to frighten me with it," Osmonde said. "Try a two-handed swing if it helps."

They went back down the gangway toward the bows, Lewrie still retreating and his arms growing heavier by the minute.

"The idea is to hack your opponent down, not dance a quadrille with him," Osmonde said, his swings remorseless and the flat of the blade he wielded bringing stinging slaps on Lewrie's arms.

Lewrie tried to respond with some wittiness, but could not find his voice which was lost in a bale of raw cotton, so dry was he. He was nearing the foredeck, and planted his feet and began to swing back with both arms, clanging his blade against Osmonde's.

His arms were so tired they felt nerveless, though engorged with blood and heavy. Each meeting of the blades made his hands sting, and he found it more difficult to keep a grip on the wooden handle. With an air of desperation, he thrust the curved hilt into Osmonde's shoulder and shoved him back, then aimed a horizontal swipe at him with all his remaining strength that should have removed a month's worth of the officer's hair. But Osmonde's blade was just suddenly *there*, and his own recoiled away with a mighty clang, almost torn from his grasp. And then Osmonde thrust at him, which he barely countered off to the right. Then Osmonde brought a reverse stroke back at him and when their blades met this time, Lewrie's spun away from his exhausted grip. Osmonde laughed and tapped him lightly on the head with the flat of the sword.

"Not elegant, was it?"

"No . . . sir," Alan replied between wracking gulps of air.

"Humiliating experience?"

"Fucking right . . . sir."

"Such language from a young gentleman, but better being humiliated than killed by someone with bad breath and no forehead. Fetch your cutlass and we'll get some water."

In warmer climes a butt of water was kept on deck with a square cut, or scuttled, into the upper staves so that a small cup could be dipped inside without spillage. It was too long in cask, that water, and tan with oak and animalcules, but in Lewrie's parched condition it was sparkling wine.

"Most men are afraid of blades, Lewrie," Osmonde told him as he sipped at his water, making a face at the color and taste. "That's why people were so glad that gunpowder and muskets and cannon were invented. You don't have to get within reach of a blade or a point to get rid of the other bastard. I am glad to see you are not one of them."

"Thank you, sir." Lewrie replied. "I think."

"Most men these days wear swords the way they wear hats." Osmonde sighed, handing the cup back to Lewrie. "Or to give them a longer reach at the buffet table. Yet society, and the Navy, require us to face up to the enemy with steel in our hands. Fortunately for us, the Frogs and the Dons are a bunch of capering poltroons for all their supposed skills as swordsmen and swordsmiths. But there are a few men who are truly dangerous with a sword."

"Like you, sir?"

"Do not toady to me, Lewrie."

"I was merely asking if you thought yourself dangerous, sir."

"Yes, yes, I am. I am because I like cold steel," Osmonde said with a casualness that sent a chill down Lewrie's sweaty back. "I can shoot, I can fence prettily but I can also hack with the best of 'em. Axe, cutlass, boarding pike, take your pick. Ever duel?"

"Once, sir. Back home."

"Ever blaze?"

"No, sir. Smallsword only. I pinked him."

"Huzzah for you. How did you feel?"

"Well—"

"Was he skilled?"

"No, sir. He was easy to pink."

"And you were properly brave."

"Well..."

"You were both frightened. Hands damp, throat dry, trembling all over. Probably pale as death but you stood up game as a little lion, did you not?"

"Yes, I did, sir," Alan said, getting a little tired of being humiliated.

"It was only natural. And until you are really skillful with steel you will always feel that way, trusting to luck and hoping the foe is clumsy. Like going aloft, which I sincerely thank God I do not have to do, one learns caution but goes when called by facing one's fear and conquering it."

"I think I see, sir."

"Most likely you do not, but you shall someday. You do not know how many young fools have rushed blindly into danger and died for their supposed honor, or for glory. Those two have buried more idiots than the plague. Heroism cannot conquer all. You'll run into someone better someday. Better to be truly dangerous and let them come like sheep to the slaughter. Let the other fool die for his honor. Your job is to kill him, not with grace and style, but with anything that comes to hand."

"I suppose I'd live longer if I were that sort of man, sir?" Lewrie asked, not above placing his valuable skin at a high premium.

"Exactly. So I suggest you find the oldest and heaviest cutlass aboard and practice with that, until a smallsword or hanger becomes like a feather in your hand. Keep fitter than the other fellow. Not only will you tire less easily, but the ladies prefer a fit man."

"Aye, sir," Lewrie replied, now on familiar ground.

"Practice with all this ironmongery until they each become an instinctive part of you. I shall let you know if you are slacking."

"Aye, sir," Lewrie said, not looking forward to it. It was a lot of work, and he had to admit that the sight of a pike head coming for his eyes was most unnerving. "I shall try, though the ship's routine does take time from it. It must be easier to devote yourself to steel if one were a Marine officer, sir."

"Tempted to be a 'bullock', Mister Lewrie?"

"The thought had crossed my mind, sir."

"Prohibitively expensive to purchase a commission, you know," Osmonde said by way of dismissal. "Certain appearances to maintain in the mess, as well."

"Well," Alan said, turning to go as seven bells of the forenoon watch rang out and the bosun's pipes sounded clear-decks-and-up-spirits for the daily rum ration. Osmonde's Marine orderly was there with a small towel and Osmonde's smallsword and tunic, as the Marine sniffed the air from the galley funnel.

"Bugger the snooty bastards, anyway," Alan muttered, going below to his own mess, soaking wet from the exertion. He dropped off Lt. Kenyon's hanger and vowed that before the voyage was over, Captain Osmonde would rate him as a dangerous man.

DAYS passed as *Ariadne* made her westing, running down a line of latitude that would take them direct to Antigua as resolutely as a dray would stay within the banks of a country lane. There were two schools of thought about that; it made navigation easier to perform, and could almost be done by dead reckoning with a quick peak at the traverse board to determine distance run from one noon to the next, but it was a lazy, *civilian* way of doing things. Or, it was quite clever, since lazy civilian merchant captains would do it, and that put *Ariadne* in a position to intercept enemy Indiamen, or conversely, those privateers who might be lying in wait to prey upon British ships. But since the ship had not distinguished herself in the past as a great fighting ship, the latter was a minority opinion. Gun drill and some live firings were practiced, but it was undertaken with the tacit assumption that *Ariadne* would never fire those guns in anger—spite or pique, perhaps, but not battle, and it showed.

What a happy ship we are, Alan thought, stripping off his coat and waistcoat as he sat down for dinner following one of those morning gun drills in the forenoon watch. Lt. Harm had yelled himself hoarse with threats and curses to the gun crews on the lower deck, and the mechanical way they had gone through the motions. And when Lewrie had told some of them to remember to swab out so they would do it for real in action, Harm had screeched something like "a midshipman giving advice, by the nailed Christ?" and for him to shut the hell up, if he knew what was good for him.

There may have been a war raging in the Colonies, all around the world as France, Spain and Holland joined to support the rebels and rehash the Seven Years' War, and ships may have fought in these very waters; somewhere over the horizon British vessels could be up to close pistol shot with the broadsides howling, but the general idea was that *Ariadne* was not part of that same fleet, and never would be, so drilling on the great guns was make-work, sullenly accepted.

The pork joint in their mess was half bone and gristle, and the real meat was a piece of work to chew. Their peas were lost in fatty grease, the biscuit was crumbling with age and the depredation of the weevils. Lewrie watched his companions chew, heard the rapping of the biscuits on the table like a monotonous tatoo. He was sick to death of them all, even Ashburn. Shirke was telling Bascombe the same joke for the umpteenth time, and Bascombe was braying like an ass as he always did. Chapman chewed and blinked and swallowed as though he was concentrating hard on remembering how, and in which order, such actions of dining occurred. The master's mates smacked like pigs at a trough, and the surgeon's mates whispered dry rustlings of dog Latin and medical terms like a foreign language that set them apart from the rest. Brail fed himself with a daintiness he imagined a gentleman should, and maintained a silence that was in itself maddening.

I'd love to put a pistol ball into this damned joint, just to have something new to talk about, Lewrie decided. It might wake old Chapman up, at least. No, probably ricochet off the pork and kill one of them...

"And was our young prodigy all proficient at gun drill today?" Shirke asked him.

"What?" Lewrie said, realizing he had been asked a question.

"Were you a comfort to Lt. Harm?" from Bascombe.

"I'm sure the foretopmen heard it," Ashburn teased. "'By the nailed Christ', I think the expression was."

"Did big bad bogtwotter hurt baby's feewings?"

"I see you have reverted to your proper age and intellect, Harv," Lewrie said. "How refreshing. For a while there, I thought counting higher than ten at navigation was going to derange you."

Bascombe was not exactly a mental wizard when it came to the intricacy of working navigation problems, and had spent many hours at the masthead as punishment. The insult went home like a hot poker up the arse.

"You're a right smart little man, ain't you, Lewrie?"

"Smarter than some I know. At least I can make change."

"You bastard—"

"That's educated bastard to you."

"For twopence I'd call you out." Bascombe leaped to his feet with fists clenched.

"You want me to pay you," Lewrie said calmly, looking up at him with a bland expression. "Funny way to make a living. I didn't know you were that needy."

"Goddamn you—"

"And a parson's son, at that!" Lewrie was enjoying himself hugely. This is the best lunch we've had in days.

"'Ere, now," Finnegan said, waving a fork at them. "There's a midshipman awready wot's been rooned this voyage. Now shut yer traps."

Bascombe plumped back down on his chest, his hands still fisted in his lap. He stared at his plate for a long moment.

"Who ruined Rolston?" he asked softly. "Lewrie was the one that ran on about him, and swearing so innocent he meant nothing by it."

I didn't know he was that sharp, Lewrie thought. Have to watch young Harvey in future.

"Rolston ruined himself, and we all know it," Keith said, as if he was the only one to lay down the law. "And I think his case is example enough for all of us. We are here to learn to get along with each other. Alan, I think you owe Harvey an apology. And you owe one to Alan as well."

My ass on a bandbox, Lewrie thought, but he saw that the others were waiting on him to start. "Well, perhaps Lt. Harm made me raw, and being teased about it didn't do my temper any good. Sorry I took it out on you, Bascombe. What with this morning, I lashed out without thinking."

"For my part, I'm sorry for what I said as well," Bascombe said after taking a long moment to decide if Lewrie had actually apologized to him.

"Now shake hands and let's finish eating," Ashburn said.

They shook hands perfunctorily, Lewrie glaring daggers, and Bascombe thinking that he would find a way to put Lewrie in the deepest, hottest hell.

"Better," Ashburn smiled and picked up his knife and fork. "Did I hear right? Did Mister Harm really intend to put Snow up on a charge and see him flogged?"

"Mister Harm got hellish angry when two men slipped, and when Snow told him they couldn't help it because of the water on the deck from the slow match tubs, Harm thought it was back-talk and went barking mad.'"

"*Mister* Harm, mind ye," Turner said.

"Aye, sir," Lewrie corrected, waiting for Turner to tell him that commission lieutenants don't go barking mad, either, but evidently they sometimes do, for Turner went back to his meal. "Snow's a good quartergunner, been in forever, I'm told."

"Won't stand," Ashburn said, smearing mustard on his meat and hoping the flavor was improved. "Captain Bales will take it into account. Come to think of it, I cannot remember Snow ever being charged."

"Ten years in the Fleet and never a lash? My last captain would have had him dancing," Shirke said.

"Taut hand, was he?" Chapman asked, now that he remembered what came after chewing.

"Best day was Thursday forenoon." Shirke told them. "Looked like the Egyptians building the pyramids...whack, whack, whack."

"I fear the cat is a poor way to keep order," Brail said. "I should think grog or tobacco stoppage would be more effective."

"Nonsense," Finnegan said, digging for gristle with a horny claw. "Wot's better, d'ye think, hangin' fer stealin' half a crown, er takin' a dozen lashes fer drunk on duty?"

"Well..."

"I'd take the floggin'. It's done, it's over, yer back hurts like hell, but yer still breathin'. Ashore, they hang fer everythin'."

"Flogging is a brutal way to discipline," Brail maintained.

"Bein' on a King's Ship ain't brutal enough awready?"

"Exactly my point," Brail said. "The hands would do anything for tobacco or grog. Deprive them of it for a few days and they'll learn their lessons."

"Aw, Able Seaman Breezy lays Ordinary Seaman Joke open from 'is gullet ta the weddin' tackle, an' you'd stop somebody's grog?" Turner gaped at this dangerous notion. "Somebody says 'no' ta me when I tells 'im ta do somthin', an' you'd take his baccy from 'im?"

"Nothing like the cat ta make 'em walk small about ya," Finnegan said firmly.

"I had a captain who had a hand who could not stop pissing on the deck. Learned it in his alley, I've no doubt," Ashburn told them. "Grog, tobacco, nothing helped. Had him flogged, a dozen to start. Nothing worked. Finally tied him up in baby swaddles, itchy old canvas. Had to see the bosun whenever he had to pump his bilges and be unlocked. That cured him."

"Shamed 'im afore 'is mates, too," Finnegan said. "Felt more like a man iffen 'e'd got two-dozen an' they learned him the right way."

"Flogging is not always the best answer," Ashburn said with a saintly expression. "Some intelligence must play a part."

In the middle of their discussion, they heard the call of the bosun's pipes. Then came the drumming of the Marine to call them to quarters, bringing a groan. "Damme, not another drill," Lewrie said. "I know we were terrible this morning, but do we have to go through it all afternoon?"

He raced up to the lower gun deck, where the crew had been having their meal. It was a mass of confusion as hands slung food into their buckets and bread barges, stowing everything away out of sight and slamming their chests shut. Tables had to be hoisted up to the deckheads out of the way so they could fetch down the rammers, crows and handspikes to serve the guns, grumbling at their lost lunch.

Ariadne turned slightly north of their westerly course as the gun captains came up from the hanging magazines with their tools of the trade. By then, chests and stools and eating utensils had been stacked on the centerline out of the way of the guns, and the tompions were being removed. Ship's boys arrived with the first powder cartridges borne in flashproof leather or wood cases.

"Another drill, sir?" Lewrie asked Lt. Harm.

"No, you fool. We've sighted a strange sail."

"Oh, I see, sir..." This could be a real fight, a chance to do something grand...maybe even make some prize money. No, what am I saying? This is *Ariadne*. We'll lose her or she'll turn out to be one of our packets...

Little Beckett came scuttling down from the upper deck and went to Lt. Roth. "The captain's respects, Mister Roth, and would you be so good as to attend to the lowering of a cutter for an armed party to go aboard the chase once we have fetched her," he singsonged.

"My compliments to the captain, and I shall be on deck directly. Wish me luck, Horace," he said to Harm. "If she's a prize, I may be the one to take her into port. What an opportunity!"

Roth fled the deck as though devils were chasing him.

Horace Harm? Lewrie thought, stifling a grin with difficulty. No wonder he's such a surly Irish beau-nasty.

"Arrah now, fuck you, Jemmy Roth," Harm muttered under his breath. His associate could parley the strange ship into an independent command, first crack at fresh cabin stores, and a good chance at a promotion into another ship, while Harm languished aboard *Ariadne,* moving up to fourth officer, but still stuck in her until old age.

"Lewrie," Harm said, spinning on him and following the old adage that when in doubt, shout at someone. "Check to see that sand is spread for traction. And look to the fire-buckets. Can you stretch your little mind to handle all of that, Lewrie?"

"Aye aye, sir," Lewrie replied sweetly, which he knew galled the officer. *Horace!*

By the time Lewrie had finished his inspection, had ordered more sand, told some crews to clear away their raffle and gone back to report, the guns had been loaded with quarter weight powder cartridges, eight-pounds of powder to propel a thirty-two-pound iron ball. An increase in powder charge would not impel the shot any farther or faster, since all the powder did not take flame at once. It was good enough for random shot at long range, about a mile. As they closed with the chase, they might reduce the charge for short range, especially if they double-shotted the guns. Then, a normal charge would likely burst the piece.

"Should we not clear for action, Mister Harm?" Lewrie asked, seeing all the mess deck gear stowed on the centerline, and the partitions still standing for the midshipmens' mess.

"Should the captain require it, we shall," Harm said. "And if he does not, then we shan't. Now shut your trap and quit interfering with your betters, Lewrie, or I'll see you bent over a gun before this day is out."

"Aye aye, sir," Lewrie chirped again, full of sham eagerness to serve, and wondering why he had expected a sensible and polite answer from such a man. It must be one of ours, he decided. There are recognition signals. We'll most likely stand around down here until we're bored silly and then be released.

Once more, there was nothing to do for a long time as the day wore on and Ariadne bore down on the chase, plunging along with the wind on her starboard quarter and her shoulder to the sea. But it was still an hour before Beckett came below and told the crews to stand easy. They drug out their stools and sat down. Lewrie took a seat on a chest. In his heart, he knew it was wrong not to strike all the assorted junk below into the holds, take down those partitions and get rid of the chests and stools, but what could a midshipman do about it? And even if he got Harm to send a message with a respectful suggestion on the matter, what shrift would a lieutenant's advice receive from a post captain intent on the whiff of prize money?

Some of the older hands had tied their neckerchiefs about their ears, making them look decidedly piratical. When he asked a quartergunner, old Snow in fact, he was told that it would keep him from going deaf from the sound of the guns.

By four in the afternoon, the order came down to open the gun ports, and blessed sunlight flooded in, along with sweet fresh air.

The hands were called back to attention by their guns but they still ducked to peer out the ports at their possible prize.

"Full-rigged, boys!" a rammer man whispered to a sidetackle mate. "Maybe a French blockade runner full a gold."

"Have ta be a rum 'un ta get took by us!" a handspike man said.

"Silence, the lot of you," Lt. Harm shouted. "Watch your fronts!"

And it was another half-hour by Lewrie's watch before the strange ship was near enough to hail, about two cables off their starboard bows. A chase gun barked from the upper deck and a feather of spray leaped up right under the other ship's bowsprit. A flag broke from the chase's gaff —it was Dutch.

Everyone sighed with a hiss of disappointment. They weren't at war with Holland yet. They had wasted their whole afternoon.

"Damme," a hand cursed, rubbing his hands together with a dry rustle. "Thort she were a beamy one, woulda been a good prize."

There goes the start of my fortune, Alan thought, easing his aching back from long standing by the guns. He could have almost felt and heard those yellowboys clinking together, good golden guineas.

Beckett appeared on the companionway. "Mister Harm, the captain wishes you to run out, sir."

"Right," Harm crackled. "Run out yer guns." And fourteen black muzzles trundled up to the port sills with a sound resembling a stampede of hogs. "Point yer guns, handspikes there, number six!"

Harm had drawn his smallsword and stood with it cocked over his shoulder, and Alan wondered just exactly what good the officer thought a blade was going to do to a ship more than four-hundred yards away.

"But she's neutral, is she not?" Alan asked.

"Might be smuggling," Harm said. "I'd have thought ya'd have brains enough to realize we'll board her and check her papers anyway. Might pick up a few hands to flesh us out. Damn Dutchies always have a few English sailors aboard hiding out from the press gang under a foreign flag."

The Dutch ship took a look at that menacing broadside pointing at her and took the path of sanity. Her flag slowly fluttered down the gaff.

Alan hoped that she was indeed a smuggler, loaded with contraband goods destined for some American port, or had papers that would make her liable to seizure. If so they could take her into Antigua and sell her, cargo, hull and fittings. "Um, how much do you think she might be worth, if she is a smuggler, Mister Harm?"

"Hull and rigging'll fetch near ten thousand pounds," Harm told him, a gleam coming to his own eye. "Now, if she's carrying contraband, it'll be military stores and suchlike, and that may double her value."

Davit blocks squealed as the large cutter was lowered over the side directly in front of their midships guns, the main course yard being employed as a boat boom. Their prize had let fly all instead of bringing to into the wind, and her canvas fluttered like a line of shirts on wash day.

"Dutchies can carry right rich cargoes," Harm went on half to himself, almost pleasant for once in his greed. "Maybe fifty thous—"

The late afternoon was torn apart with red-hot stabs of flame and the lung-flattening booming of heavy guns. The side of the Dutch ship lit up and was wreathed in a sudden cloud of smoke as she fired a broadside right into *Ariadne*, two full gun decks of twenty-four- and eighteen-pounders. The air seemed to tremble and moan with the weight of iron headed their way, and another flag was shooting up the naked gaff. But this time it was the white and gold of Bourbon Spain!

"Bastard Dons," Harm shouted. "Prime yer—"

Once more Lt. Harm was interrupted as the lower gun-deck exploded. Heavy balls slammed into the ship's side at nearly 1,200 feet per second, and Lewrie could hear the shrieking of their massive oaken scantlings as they bulged and splintered.

The cutter that was dangling before their gun ports was demolished, and a cloud of splinters raved through the open ports, striking down men. One ball struck a gun and upended it, hurling it free of sidetackles, breeching ropes and train tackles and sending it slewing to the larboard side. Another loaded gun was hit right on the muzzle, which set

off its charge, and it burst asunder with a great roar! A little powder monkey standing terrified by the hatch to the orlop had his cartridge case explode in his arms, and was flung away like a broken doll, his clothes burned off and his arms missing!

There were screams of pain and surprise as though a pack of women were being ravaged. There were howls of agony as oak and iron splinters ripped into flesh, and guns turned on their servers and crushed them like sausages.

Lewrie had been blown off his feet by the explosion of the powder cartridge, and lay on the deck, still buffeted by the noise and the harsh thump of each cannon ball striking deep into *Ariadne*'s hull. He saw and heard throaty gobbling and sobbing all about him as men clawed at their hurts and burns. In a split second, the ordered world of the lower gun deck had become a colored illustration from a very original sort of hell. He got to his feet, unsure what to do or where to go, but certain he wanted to go anywhere else, fast. A hand touched him on the shoulder and he jumped with a yelp of fear. He turned to see who it was.

Lt. Harm had been struck in the face by a large splinter. Half his face, the side nearest Lewrie, had been shaved off to the bone. One eye was gone, and in its place was a splinter nearly a foot long and nearly as big around as Lewrie's wrist. Harm's mouth opened and closed a couple of times like a dying fish before he toppled forward like a marionette with the strings cut. He fell on top of Snow, the quartergunner, whose entrails were spread out in a stinking mess on the deck. Just beyond him, Lewrie could see a side-tackle man lying beneath the overturned gun, and still screaming at the ruin of his legs.

"Oh," Lewrie managed to say, gulping in fright. The fear that seized him made him dizzy, turned his limbs to jelly and took him far from the unbelievable sights and smells of the deck. He tried to take a step but felt like he was walking on pillows, and fell to his knees.

That's an eye, he decided, regarding the strange object

before his face. He threw up his lunch on it. Overhead, but no business of his, he could hear the upper deck twelve-pounders banging away raggedly, and the roar of the trucks as they recoiled. It sounded as if *Ariadne* was being turned into a pile of wood chips.

A second broadside from the Spanish ship slammed into them. More screams, more singing of flying debris, and a muffled explosion somewhere. He got back to his feet, clinging to a post.

Lt. Roth came skidding down the hatchway with his hat missing and the white facings of his uniform and breeches stained grey with powder smoke. "Harm! Lewrie, where's—"

And then someone jerked Lt. Roth's string, or so it seemed, for he left his feet and *flew* across the width of the gun deck to slam into the larboard side where he left a bloody splash, cut in half by shot.

Got to get out of here, he told himself, considering how dark and safe it would be in the holds below the waterline snuggled up by the rum kegs. He seemed to float to the hatch, but Cole, the gunner's mate, stopped him by hugging his leg in terror.

"Zur," Cole pleaded on his knees, clutching tight. "Zur."

"Not *now*." Alan was intent on salvation, but there was a Marine sentry at the hatch using his bayonet to disincline others who had already had the same thoughts, and he looked over at Lewrie as one more customer for his trade.

Couldn't make it with this bastard anyway, Alan decided, unable to move without dragging the mate along with him. "Goddamn you, you're a mate . . . tell *me* what to do!"

"Zur!" the mate babbled, shuffling on his knees with Alan.

"I want out of here, hear me? *OUT.*" Alan yelled.

"Run out, zur?" the gunner's mate asked, eager for any sane suggestion. "Run 'em out? Right, zur!"

"Let go of me, damn you, and do your job! Get up and do your job! Stand to your guns!" and he hauled Cole to his feet and shoved him away. "Corporal, run those shirkers to their guns!" Right, he told himself, I wouldn't believe me, either, seeing the Marine's look.

"Ready, zur!" Cole was wringing his hands in panic.

"Fire as you bear!" Lewrie ordered, hoping to be heard in all the din. The thirty-two-pounders began to slam, rolling back from the sills and filling the deck with a sour cloud of burnt powder. This isn't happening to me, he thought wildly. I refuse to be killed. I shall not allow myself to believe that this is real...

Lewrie staggered to a port which no longer contained a gun and peered out to see through the smoke cloud. He was amazed to see some ragged holes punched into the enemy's hull. The range was less than a cable as the two ships drifted down on each other.

"Beautiful! Hit him again!" He shouted, happy that he might take a few of the bastards with him. "Swab out, there, charge your guns..."

"Git yoor ztupid foot atta the bight a that tackle er yew'll be Mister Hop-kins," the gunner's mate told someone. Just to be sure it wasn't himself, Lewrie stepped back to the centerline of the deck. Knew we should have struck all this below, he thought, studying the wreck of chests and stools and spare clothing.

As they were ramming down round-shot, a rammer man beside him took a large splinter of oak in his back and gave a shrill scream as he toppled over, scattering the terrified gun crew.

"Clear away, there! Wounded to the larboard side! Run out your guns!" Lewrie was glad to have something to do besides shiver with fright. He had not thought it would be that cold below decks.

"Prime! Point!" He saw fists rise in the air as each gun was gotten ready and he felt the hull drumming to hits, but he also felt the scend of the sea under *Ariadne*. "On the uproll ...fire!"

This was much more organized, a twelve-gun broadside fired all at the same time. An avalanche of iron seemed to strike the enemy. She visibly staggered, and three waist gun ports were battered into one, whole chunks of scantling blown apart by the impact. Surely there was a cloud of splinters on *her* gun deck this time.

"Kick 'em up the arse!" Lewrie sang out, which raised a ragged cheer from the men. "Sponge out your guns!"

"B...better, zur!" the mate said as *Ariadne* was struck deep in the hull but not on the gun deck. He looked at Lewrie like a puppy who had lost his man in a crowd.

"They're not sullen about gun drill now, are they?" Lewrie said with a manic smile. "We'll take a few of the shits with us, hey?"

"Aye, zur!" Cole said, finding his courage and gazing at him with frank admiration, which Lewrie found disconcerting in the extreme.

"Have we fired twice or three times?" he asked. "Should we worm the guns? Don't want a charge going off early."

"I'd worm, zur!" Cole said. "Worm out yer guns there!"

He must think I've gone mad, Lewrie thought, getting away from Cole as far as possible. In doing so he stepped over the body of a boy, a tiny, young midshipman who had lost a leg and bled to death, his dirk still clenched in a pale fist. Odd that after eight months in the same ship together Alan could not place him at all. Fuck me, I'm dead or deranged already, he told himself. If I have to go game, I wish I could stop shaking so badly. I'm ready to squirt my breeches. He clung to a support beam amidships and tried to get a grip.

Within a minute fresh charges had been rammed down, wads, ball and sealing wads, and the guns trundled up to the ports. God, they're close now. At this range, we ought to shoot right through them...

"Prime your guns, point...on the uproll...fire!"

Another solid broadside, a blow beneath the heart.

"Sponge out!" Lewrie shrilled. "Gunner's mate, reduce charges and load with double shot...double shot and grape..."

Powder monkeys scampered like panting rats as they

came up from below with lighter powder bags, eyes widening in their blackened faces at the sight of the gore.

"No wonder they paint everything red down here," Lewrie told a handspike man as he levered his charge about. "Like the cloaks that the Spartans wore, I suppose, what?"

The handspike man was too busy to talk to him, or even to listen, and Lewrie chastised himself for beginning to sound like one of those Hanoverians at Court with their eh, what, what's.

"Gunner's mate, on the downroll this time, rip the bottom out from under them!"

"Aye aye, zur!" The gunner's mate stood in awe as he watched Lewrie take out his pocket watch, consult it, then pace about.

He knows I'm off my head . . . "On the downroll, fire!"

Below the level of the enemy's lower gun ports, star-shaped holes appeared. The range was a long musket shot now with hardly a chance for a miss.

"Lewrie, where's Lt. Harm?" Beckett yelled up at him.

"Dead as cold boiled mutton," Lewrie told him conversationally. "So is Roth. He's over to larboard someplace. Need something?"

"The Spanish are closing us, we must cripple them now—"

"Oh. Right. We'll give it a shot, pardon the play on words. Double shot the guns again. Or do you think, if we reduce to saluting charges, we could triple shot the damned things?"

Beckett and he had strolled aft through all the carnage, until Beckett spotted the dead midshipman, gave a shrill scream of disbelief and began to spew. "Striplin! Oh dear God, it's Striplin!"

"Wondered who that was," Lewrie said. "Ready? Run out your guns."

The enemy ship was evidently in trouble with her larboard battery, and was painfully tacking about to point her bows toward *Ariadne* to bring her undamaged side to bear.

Her turn could also cut across their stern, and round shot fired down the length of the gun deck would be like a game of bowls through the thin transom wood. But for that instant the Dago was vulnerable to the same thing.

"As you bear...fire!"

It was too much to ask for a synchronized broadside, but he could count on a few steady gunners to let fly as they readied their pieces. One at a time the thirty-two-pounders barked, no longer rolling back from the ports but leaping back and slamming to the deck with a crash as loud as their discharge as the breeching ropes stopped them.

The forward bulkhead aft of the jib boom burst open. The boom and the bowsprit was shattered, releasing the tension of the forestays that held the rigging tautly erect. Forward gun ports were hammered to ruin as they swung into view. Splinters and long-engrained dust and paint chips fluttered out in a cloud from each strike. With a groan they could hear below decks the Spaniard's foremast came apart like a snapped bow, royal and t'gallant and topmasts sagging down into separate parts and trailing wreckage over the side, or leaning back into the mainmast, ripping sails apart and creating more havoc.

"Yahh...fry those shits," Lewrie heard himself say.

Ariadne struggled to swing to starboard to keep the enemy on her beam, for there was still half that waiting broadside in reserve that could still do terrible damage. Lewrie pounded on people, rushing the swabbing and the loading and the running out. But they could not bear, and the enemy was drifting astern more and more.

"Point aft! Hurry it up!" Lewrie demanded, seizing a crow and throwing his own weight to shift a gun. "Quoins in! Prime your guns as we shift!"

"Done it!" the gunner's mate sounded off.

"Stand clear...fire!" someone yelled as a gun recoiled over his foot, and a cloud of smoke rushed back in the ports. Lewrie went halfway out the nearest port for a look. "Sonofabitch! Marvelous!"

There would not be a return broadside. There was not

one port showing a muzzle that did not tilt skyward, and close as they were, he could not see anyone working in the gloom.

Damme, it's nearly dark ... is it over, please, God?

Ariadne could not stay to windward, for she had taken much damage aloft from chain and bar shot that had torn her rigging to rags. She sagged down off the wind, while the Spaniard drifted away, going off the wind as well, but far down to the south, able to beam reach out of danger, and *Ariadne* could not follow.

"Think it's over fer now, zur," the gunner's mate told him.

"Water," Lewrie said. "Organise a butt of water."

"Right away, zur."

Lewrie sat down on what was left of a midshipman's chest and caught his breath. Now that the gunsmoke had been funneled out by fresh air, he could see a stack of bodies to the larboard side, and a steady stream of screaming wounded being carried below to the cockpit and the dubious mercies of the surgeon and his mates. The sound from below on the orlop was hideous as they sawed and cut and probed, mostly sawed, for badly damaged limbs had to come off at once.

"There was a gun dismounted," Lewrie said suddenly, aching at the effort of communication. "Has it been bowsed down?"

"Aye, sor," a quartergunner told him. "Got her back on her truck an' lashed snug ta larboard."

"Good. Good." He nodded. "Organise a crew from larboard to rig a wash deck pump and begin cleaning up. We may not be through yet." He could see that once the guns ceased to speak, the men were sagging into shock, and that sneaky bastard might come back. They would be useless the next time, and he did not know what to do.

"Water, zur," the gunner's mate said. "Have a cup."

"They're falling apart. What do I do?" Lewrie demanded.

"I'll see to keepin' 'em on the hop, zur. Yew take a breather. Yew done enough fer now," Cole said, making it sound like a reproof.

I must have screwed this up royally, Lewrie sighed. Well, who cares? I never wanted this anyway! I wonder if all this was famous or glorious? What would Osmonde say? Is he alive to say anything?

Bosun's pipes shrilled and the bosun yelled down. "D'ye hear, there? Secure from quarters!"

"Iffen yew want, zur, I'll finish up here," the gunner's mate said. "When ya zees the first lieutenant, the word is twenty-four dead an' thirty-eight wounded an' on the orlop."

"Jesus," Lewrie breathed. "Sweet Jesus."

"Aye, zur. Damned bad, it was."

Anything to get away from the screams from the surgery, he decided, getting to his feet with a groan and slowly ascending to the upper deck and the quarterdeck.

"Good God, are you wounded, Mister Lewrie?" Swift asked him as he reveled at the coolness and sweetness of the evening winds.

"I don't think so, Mister Swift," wondering if he had been struck and did not yet realize it. Perhaps that explained his weakness and the trembling of his limbs.

"You gave me a fright with all that blood," Swift said. Lewrie looked down and saw his trousers, waistcoat and facings blotched black in the gloom with dried blood as if he had been wallowing in an abbatoir.

"I beg to report that the lower gun deck is secured, sir. One gun burst, one overturned but righted. All lashed down snug. The gunner's mate said to tell you twenty-four dead and thirty-eight on the orlop with the surgeon."

"What about Mister Roth and Mister Harm?"

"Dead, sir. Mister Harm had this big baulk of wood stuck in his face. And Mister Roth came below and just...went splash across the deck."

"Who ran the gun deck, then?"

"Me and the gunner's mate, sir."

"Wait here, Lewrie," and Swift tramped off across the splintered deck toward the binnacle, where Lewrie could make out the sailing master and the captain.

"You look like death's head on a mopstick," Kenyon said as he strolled up.

"Who won, sir?"

"Draw, I'd say. Those Dons are off to the suth'rd making repairs. We'll have to work like Trojans through the night, or they'll be back at dawn and finish us off. Where are Roth and Harm?"

Lewrie recited his litany of woe once more, leaving Kenyon at a loss for words. "I shall need you to assist replacing the maintopmast with the spare main course yard."

"Aye aye, sir."

"Lewrie, come here," from Lt. Swift.

Standing before Bales, he had to explain when Harm and Roth had fallen, and what had happened following their deaths, what the state of the lower gun deck was, how many wounded and killed. It felt like an old story that he couldn't dine out on for long.

"And you did not think to report your officers fallen?" Bales asked.

"There wasn't time, sir." Lewrie was feeling faint again, ready to drop in his tracks. "Could I sit down, sir? I'm feeling a bit rum."

If they want to cane me for not sending a messenger, then they can have this bloody job. I quit, he told himself, leaning on the corner of the quarterdeck netting.

The captain's servant offered him a mug of something which he said would buck him right up, and Lewrie took it and tipped it back, drinking half of it before he realized it was neat rum. No matter, it was wet and alcoholic, whatever it was. He smiled and belched contentedly at all of them.

The gunner's mate was there, pointing at Lewrie, but he could not hear what he was saying...Probably telling him what a total poltroon I was. I should've been taking orders from him, not the other way around...

"God bless you, Mister Lewrie," someone very like Captain Bales said to his face. "From the most unlikely places we find courage and leadership in our hour of troubles. I shall feature your bravery in my report most prominently, believe you me."

Here, now, you can't be saying that, Lewrie goggled at him, unable to feature it. He could not speak, merely nod dumbly, unable to remove his weary, drunken smile.

But then he had to go aloft to clear away the raffle of all their damage, which sobered him up right smartly but did nothing for his aching weariness.

CHAPTER

6

NGLISH harbor at Antigua was a bit of a letdown, after yearning for it, imagining the joy of it, and struggling so hard to reach it. Once round Cape Shirley into the outer roads, the land was all dust and sere hills, sprinkled with dull green flora. They were told it was the dry season, even though it was also the start of the hurricane season. There were island women in view, loose-hipped doxies in bright dresses and headclothes ready to provide comfort and pleasure for the poor English sailors, but the ship was not allowed out of discipline. They were much too busy for that.

First, they had to keep from sinking at their temporary moorings. *Ariadne*'s bilges and holds were deep in the water, and the orlop hatches had been sealed tight; even then at least an inch of dirty water sloshed about on the orlop. Since their battle with the disguised Spanish two-decker the pumps had gushed and clanked without pause while carpenters slaved to patch holes. The upper deck damage could wait; gilt and taffrail carvings were moot if *Ariadne* foundered.

Along her waterline, ravelled sails could be seen, hairy patches fothered over gaping wounds to slow the inrush of water. Discarded bandages, bloody slop clothing and floating personal possessions seeped from her like pus.

Rowed barges towed her down the tortuous channel to the inner harbor and the dockyard, where she was buoyed up with camels, barges on either beam supporting thick cables that slung under the hull. As the camels were pumped out, they rose in the water, bringing *Ariadne* with them so that laborers could get into her holds and begin plugging the many shot holes.

Above decks, she was in much better shape; damaged yards and topmasts had been replaced, snapped rigging reroved, torn canvas taken down and replaced with the heavy air set, or hastily patched. But the poop, starboard side and the starboard gangway still bore shot holes, especially around the waist. Light shot was still embedded in her thick scantlings, the decks were still torn from splintering, and no amount of scrubbing could remove the huge bloodstains, especially on the lower deck.

And *Ariadne* stank, though she had been scoured with vinegar or black strap, smoked with tubs of burning tobacco, or painted with her slim stocks of whitewash and red. She reeked of vomit, of gangrenous wounds from her tortured men who had been killed but had not yet been allowed the final release from agony. She smelled coppery-sickly from the smell of decaying bodies, and the island flies found her and made a new home so they could feast on her corruption, on all the blood that had been spilled and seemed now a part of her framework.

She was a worse environment than the old Fleet Ditch, Dung Wharf or the worst reeking slums Lewrie could remember hastily passing. He was an Englishman, which meant that he was used to stinks, but he had never imagined anything that bad.

Dockyard officials had been aboard and had ordered the removal of her artillery to lighten her. They had poked and probed, measured and calculated, noting her new tendency to "hog", to bend down a bit at bow and stern, a sure sign that the keel structure was badly strained, some of her key midships beams weakened. It was supposed that once she could float on her own without aid, she would go into the dock for permanent repair.

The wounded were taken off to the hospital; the dead had been buried at sea. Altogether, they had suffered sixty-one men discharged dead, and another seventy severely wounded, and half of those stood a good chance of dying yet. That was a quarter of the entire ship's company, and did not count those lightly wounded that had been returned to light duties.

There were gaping absences in her crew. Turner had been killed on the riddled starboard gangway. The master gunner, Mister Tencher, had been killed up by the bow chasers. Harm and Roth, of course, were gone from the officer's mess. Two young midshipmen had died, as well as little Striplin, and his friend Beckett had lost a foot on that last broadside. Shirke was ashore with a broken arm, but looked likely to mend. Chapman, on the other hand, had lost a chunk out of his right thigh from a grape shot ball, and his future held in a precarious balance, for they thought the leg might have to come off near the groin.

Finnegan and another of his mates had been made acting lieutenants, as had Keith Ashburn, since no officers could be spared from the other ships in port. Indeed, no captain would willingly give up a competent commission officer into such a ship, and no lieutenant would consider such an appointment, since if she were condemned he would be left high and dry without employment.

Captain Bales, once he had made his dire report to the admiral, had kept his own silent counsel aft in his quarters. Lt. Church was nowhere to be found, and no one would admit knowledge of his whereabouts. Rolston also had gone, in custody of Marines, from the flagship.

The remaining midshipmen had been run ragged in the days that followed, standing watches, ferrying groaning and crying wounded ashore and bringing back fresh supplies to feed the survivors, lumber to plug shot holes, emptying the magazines and hoisting out the great guns and their trucks, and the tons of round shot to lighten the ship. They were also involved ferrying the dockyard officials, flag officers, the idle curious and the morbid who wished to come and gawk and marvel, praise or damn, inspect and condemn.

Lewrie clambered up the ship's side and through the battered entry port, chafing in his uniform. The day was hot, and there was no wind in the harbor. He let Bascombe take his place and went to the scuttlebutt for a measure of fresh water, grateful for the shade of the old scrap canvas that was rigged over the quarterdeck as an awning.

By God, I know it's dangerous to bathe too often but I'd admire a dunk in a creek or something, he thought. With so much fresh water coming aboard, no one would miss a gallon in which he could take a quick, cooling scrub and put on some clean linen.

"Mister Lewrie?" the captain's clerk said to him.

"Aye, Mister Brail?" Alan noted that even Brail wore his arm in a sling, fortunately not his writing arm.

"The captain would like to see you."

"Me? What have I done?"

"I have no indication that Captain Bales is displeased with you, Mister Lewrie. He would be, however, should you keep him waiting."

Lewrie straightened his sweaty clothing and went aft.

"Midshipman Lewrie reporting, sir."

The captain stared at him, scowling with those huge eyebrows, and Alan was sure he had committed some grievous and punishable offense without knowing what.

"Mister Ashburn has informed me of your mess's request that I release some of your money for the purchase of fresh cabin stores. I have summoned you to take charge of it, since the others are away at their duties at present."

"Whew..."

"I will allow each of you no more than five pounds apiece, as the prices here in the islands are higher than normal. That shall have to be sufficient. And I'll not have it all spent on spirits, mind you."

Lewrie was mystified that Captain Bales sat there, in a

ship that could still sink right out from under him, and took care of a small chore that his clerk or coxswain could have handled easily. Had he lost his senses, or could he no longer bear to face the larger issues?

"With the artillery removed, you may consider livestock. Sheep or pigs are your best bet. Island bullocks are too lean and stringy, and usually overpriced. Hard-skinned fruits are plentiful, as are the onions hereabouts. You'll find cheese dear, as well as tea, but coffee is fairly cheap."

"We shall try to spend it wisely, sir," Lewrie said, knowing that Ashburn was ashore trying to get rooms and a private dining area for a long overdue shore leave, as well as some women.

"As I said in my report, and I shall say it to your face, Lewrie, you did extremely well when put to the test," Bales said, fingering a stack of guineas on his desk. "Eight months ago I despaired that you would ever amount to anything, and now here you are, the one bright bit in a dismal report. Had you not reorganised the lower deck guns and gotten them firing again there is a very good possibility that every man jack in this ship would now be dead or a prisoner of war, and *Ariadne* sunk or a prize."

"Thank you for your good opinion, sir..." Damme, did I really do all that? And did you really put it that way in your report? If you did, I'm a bloody hero!

"Of such good beginnings are great careers and reputations made in the Fleet. And you have worked diligently at your studies as well. I predict that you may do very well in the Navy, Mister Lewrie. But watch the course you steer well. There're a hundred pitfalls for the ambitious officer. No one can rush about blind to hazard, or forget to cover his back. I'd advise you to make caution your watchword and not let this fleeting fame be the high-water mark for you."

"Aye aye, sir," Lewrie said, not knowing what the hell Bales was talking about, and a little unsettled at seeing such a stern man muttering to himself between phrases.

Once dismissed, Lewrie went back on deck, just in time to

see Keith Ashburn coming through the entry port, and went to join him. His friend was now half a commission officer at least, clad in breeches and stockings, and had replaced the round hat with a cocked one. He wore a new smallsword on his hip instead of a dirk, but his tailor must have been a slow worker since he still had to move about in a midshipman's short coat.

"Twenty pounds, Keith," Lewrie said. "Excuse me, Mister Ashburn. Ours, Bascombe's and Shirke's, though I don't see what a parson's son and a man with one arm in boards is going to do with a bareback rider."

"He forgot Chapman," Ashburn said.

"Who wouldn't." Lewrie shrugged. "What have you gotten for us?"

"A good dinner for a start, and a suite of rooms, a dozen of wine. That's fifteen shillings apiece. Only two girls so far, but they have friends. A guinea apiece for them."

"What are they, blood royal? There must be a whole island full of mutton that'd do it for half a crown, and that's a whole night of it."

"These are gentlemens' doxies, not common trulls. Won't go for anyone less than a lieutenant, usually. The two I met are quite fetching," Ashburn promised. Since his promotion to acting lieutenant, he had been *acting*, all right, acting much more superior, reclaiming those languid airs he had grown up with in rich society. Lewrie was getting a bit peeved with his attitude. It was not a week ago that Ashburn was not above borrowing money from him until his packet arrived.

"There's a boat comin' offshore, sir," a bosun's mate told Ashburn, pointing over the starboard rail. "Headed fer us, I thinks."

"Very well. Hail him, Mister Lewrie."

"Boat ahoy!" Alan shouted.

"Aye aye!" Came the answering hail, meaning the boat was for them and from the fingers stuck in the air by the bowman, there was a full captain aboard.

"Bosun's mate, muster the sideparty," Lewrie ordered.

"Another ghoul come to marvel, I expect. I feel like the gatekeeper at Bedlam. Poking sticks, sir? Stir 'em up? Water squirts? Only a penny more."

A youngish post captain came in through the entry port and did a long survey of the splintered and stained decks, the lack of guns, and the many repairs still being done to the bulwarks. He carried a large canvas bundle of papers tied up with many fluttering ribbons.

"Welcome aboard, sir," Ashburn said.

"Stuyckes, flag captain to Rear Admiral Sir Onsley Matthews. I am here to see your captain."

"This way, sir, if you please," Ashburn smiled smarmily. "Here, you. Inform the captain of Captain Stuyckes' arrival. You know, sir, I was looking forward to coming to Antigua. Sir Onsley is well-known to my family in London."

"Here, you, indeed," Lewrie grumbled as he ran off to inform Bales that he had a visitor, he being the 'here you' in question *I don't think this is going to be one of those friendships that lasts for generations, Keith. And if I ever have a daughter, God help her, your son can go hang before he marries her.*

But it didn't seem as if Keith's toadying was getting him anywhere with Captain Stuyckes, since that worthy wore an expression more in keeping with a funeral, and whatever his business with Captain Bales was, it didn't look like it was to be a social call.

News of the visit did not take long to circulate through the vessel, so quite a few interested parties made it their business to take the air either on the quarterdeck, or as close as they could get to it.

"The flag captain, was he?" Ellison asked the general vicinity.

"A Captain Stuyckes, sir," Lewrie volunteered. "With a bundle of papers all bound in ribbons."

"Then it's bad news, no doubt of it," Ellison said bitterly. "Poor old girl, shot to pieces."

"You mean they might not be able to repair the ship, sir," Alan said.

"She's bad sprung. Twenty-years-old, she is, and only brought out of ordinary because we need ships bad. You ask 'Chips', she's half rotten, and now too bad gut-shot to be repaired. Not out here, not in the tropics. Might make a powder hulk."

"So there might be a possibility I could end up in another ship?" Lewrie speculated with a tingle of hope for better chances.

"Aye, a lot of us, most like," Ellison said, considering his slim chances for future employment. Another sailing master would have to die before he could be taken aboard a ship already in commission. He could be temporarily derated to master's mate "for the good of the Service" and spend years trying to get his pay straightened out after stoppages.

"Shore duty for me, then, and my Marines," Osmonde said. "Some garrison work would not go amiss."

"I'd love to get a frigate," Lewrie announced.

"Wouldn't we all?" Ellison snarled.

"A chance to see more action, eh?" Osmonde asked Lewrie.

"Aye, sir. As long as I have to be in the Navy, what better duty is there?"

"Amazing what a taste of powder smoke can do for a boy."

"You were right, Mister Osmonde," Lewrie said. "I almost ran and hid, but I didn't. Or couldn't. And then I didn't have any time to think about it, I just did it. It was terrifying, and I thought I had gone mad. But never more alive."

"And you did extremely well," Osmonde told him. "In fact, you may be the only one to garner any credit from our encounter. One word of advice?"

"Aye, sir, your advice has been good."

"Don't go dashing madly after more fame and glory. They are always bigger than you are and will eat you right up."

"The captain said much the same thing, sir. At least, I think he did," Lewrie replied, repeating Bales' admonition.

"Hmm, I fear Captain Bales and I do not mean the same thing at all. Of course, he is right, in a way. This service is very political. Whig, Tory, City interests, country interests. Anyone who makes a name will always be desperately envied, and there's a hundred people ready to run you through for your position. You must be cautious about the people you anger on your way up, and the people you espouse. But in your actions, too much caution can get you killed, or ruined. It's a fine line to walk, like the edge of a sharp sword."

The sideparty formed again as Captain Stuyckes took his leave of them. He was even grimmer in aspect than when he had come aboard, and most conspicuously, was without his bundle of papers.

"Lewrie," Kenyon called as they were breaking up the sideparty. "Pass the word to all the midshipmen to be sure to wash and dress in their best uniforms in the morning. You'll be called to the flag," Kenyon ordered sternly. "You and a few of the others shall be called upon to testify at the court-martial."

"Eh?" Were they going to try Rolston?

"*Ariadne* has been condemned," Kenyon said bleakly, his own hopes for the future seemingly dashed. "Since she has been lost to the fleet, the captain and the first lieutenant are to face charges in her loss."

JUST after breakfast, at one bell of the forenoon watch, a gun boomed from the flag of the Inshore Squadron which *Ariadne* had been to join, the fifty-gun 4th rate *Glatton*. A court-martial jack went up her masts, and boats from several ships in harbor converged on her, boats bearing the five captains that made a court-martial panel, and boats from shore bearing wounded witnesses, as well as two cutters from *Ariadne*, with her sorrowful looking party. Once aboard, Bales and Swift were called aft to the admiral's cabins while Lewrie and the rest were led below to *Glatton*'s wardroom and told to wait. Shirke was also there, his arm encased in a set of boards and wrapped with leather.

"I understand we are unemployed," Shirke whispered to Lewrie as he gave up his chair to him.

"Accommodations ship, they tell me," Lewrie said softly.

"We may be kept on. But I expect the fleet here in the islands is in sore need of people, what with sickness and all."

"Pray God they've just had the plague," Shirke said, then grinned. "What about our party?"

"I have five pounds of yours," Lewrie told him. "But with you laid up—"

"Just get me a gentle one and I'll take my fences as well as anyone. What's my share?"

"Three crown, say a pound total with tip for supper, rooms and wine. A guinea for the whore."

"A guinea? For a guinea she'd better be Salome!"

"Quiet, you two!" Kenyon was audible from across the room.

One at a time they were called upon as the morning wore on. First Kenyon as ranking officer, then the warrants. Ashburn went and was back in minutes.

"That was quick," Lewrie said as a cabin steward circulated a tray of fresh coffee about the wardroom and he used it as an excuse to get close to Ashburn. "How was it?"

"It doesn't look too good for them," Ashburn muttered. "There wasn't much I could tell them, except that I was on the quarterdeck, and never heard a word about clearing for action. Um, good coffee. First real article I've had in weeks."

"Passing the word for Midshipman Lewrie," a Marine called.

On his way up to the admiral's cabins to testify, Lewrie saw two faces that he had not expected to run across again. The first was his disrated enemy Rolston. He stood by the larboard entry port with a small chest and canvas bag at his feet, going with a draft of men to one of the ships in harbor. He was dressed as a common seaman in slop trousers, checked shirt and neckerchief, with a flat, tarred hat on his head, and his feet bare. Evidently the needs of the fleet were such that there would be no further punishment for him, and he was a trained hand able to hand, reef and possibly steer. Rolston saw him and gave him such a black look that Lewrie was afraid for his life for a second. Then the irony of it struck him and he waved hello gaily.

The second face was their silent Lt. Church. He was in the company of a Marine Lieutenant, dressed in normal uniform but minus his sword. Lewrie attempted to speak to him, but Church turned away with a cut direct.

"You'd think he could speak . . ."

"Not likely," his guide, an elegantly turned out midshipman on the admiral's staff, told him with a wry grin. "He's due in there himself tomorrow."

"What for?"

"Court-martial. Cowardice under fire," the boy took pleasure in informing him. "Seems you lot from *Ariadne* have no luck at all, eh?"

Lewrie was announced, led in to face the assembled court and shown to a witness chair. Captain Bales and Mister Swift sat to one side, and he nodded to them as he was sworn in.

He was led through his name, his date of joining, his duties, and all the mundane things. Then came the day of their fight.

"My station at quarters was on the lower gun deck, sir," he said, in response to the first serious question, and he tensed up, not knowing what would help or hurt Bales and Swift, and if he should even bother.

"And what occurred, Mister Lewrie?"

"We were finishing dinner, sir, when we were called to quarters. We had been at gun drill all morning."

"Did you think it was another drill?" a sharp featured captain asked. It was hard to figure out if he was a lawyer or a member of the court.

"At first, sir. Just before one bell of the day watch."

"What was done on the lower gun deck, Mister Lewrie?"

"We turned to the fourteen thirty-two-pounders to starboard, sir. The larboard guns had three men each. Sand was cast, the gun tackles were cast off, tompions removed and the starboard battery loaded with eight pound charges and single round shot."

"You did not run out?"

"No, sir."

"I see. What else did you do to prepare for battle?"

"That was it, sir." Lewrie squirmed in his hard chair as he said it, unable to look at Bales or Swift.

"You did not strike the mess tables? Take chests below?"

"Tables had been raised to the deckheads, sir. But everything else was placed on the centerline away from recoil."

"What is everything else?"

"Seamen's chests, sir. Stools, plates, mess kits and bread barges. The gunroom was still standing and so was the Marine quarters and the officer's mess."

"You were on the lower gun deck. How could you know about the other?" another captain asked.

"I think what this young man means is, that if those quarters had been struck below, they would have come past him, is that right, Mister Lewrie?" the sharp featured one put in.

"Yes, sir."

"Did that strike you as odd?"

"Excuse me, but what a midshipman of so little experience holds as an opinion is of no interest," a much older captain grumped.

And God save me from serving under you, Lewrie thought.

"Did your officers find it odd? Did they say anything about the fact that *Ariadne* would be full of dangerous sources of splinters should the ship be called upon to fight?" the sharp one pressed.

"I asked Mister Harm if we should not clear, sir. But he did not like me asking questions."

"What did he say?"

"To keep my trap shut, sir." Which raised a laugh from the court.

"Yess," the sharp captain drawled, "so you went to quarters at one bell of the day watch. And you did not engage until one bell of the first dog. Is that your recollection?"

"Aye, sir. We stood easy for a long time."

They got to the point when the Spaniard was only two cables off and struck her false Dutch flag, that awful first broadside, and the revelation of their foe's true identity.

"And what happened on the lower gun deck?"

"Mister Harm was killed immediately, sir," Lewrie replied, seeing again that shaved skull and the huge splinter in the man's eye and in his brain. "Splinters from our cutter came through the gun ports, one gun was dismounted, one burst and a powder charge blew up."

"The cutter had been lowered from the boat tiers?"

"Aye, sir."

"What about the other boats?"

"At divisions that morning, sir, they were all on the boat tier. But after we went to gun drill, I cannot say, sir."

"I would like to point out," the sharp faced captain said, "that Midshipman Lewrie and gunner's mate Cole took over at this time and did exceptional service with the lower deck guns."

"Well, not exactly, sir."

"You did not?"

"I was blown to the deck, sir, and it was an absolute madhouse. Mister Roth did join us but he was also killed almost at once. It must have been two or three minutes before we got sorted out."

"But you *did*, after that, take charge?"

"After I had gotten over being terrified, sir."

"Mister Cole tells me he took orders from you. Did you find that strange, a warrant gunner obeying a midshipman?"

"Aye, sir ... but we got the job done."

"What was the final toll from the lower deck?" another officer asked, one who had been sitting silent for most of the testimony.

"Two officers and twenty-four men killed, thirty-eight wounded, sir. And five more have since passed on."

"Lots of splinter wounds, I suppose."

"Yes, sir. A lot."

They conferred among themselves for a moment, then turned to face their court once more. "I believe that is all for this witness," the president announced. "Unless you have anything, Captain Bales?"

"I think Mister Lewrie will bear me out that we held regular gun drills, did we not?" Captain Bales said, looking sharper and more aware than in the past few days.

"Aye, sir, we did," Alan agreed.

"And was the starboard battery of the lower deck run out and ready to fire when that Spaniard fired into us?" Bales added.

"The guns were run out...sir, yes."

"And ready to fire!" Bales repeated, thumping his chair arm.

"Um, no, sir. After Lt. Harm believed our chase to be a neutral Dutchman he forgot to order the guns primed."

Bales' exuberant defense crumpled. "But...ah...the gunners and crews were thoroughly competent, were they not?"

"There goes someone again asking an *opinion* of a newly," the old captain muttered.

"I shall let this one stand," the president of the court said.

"Aye, sir, I felt we were competent," Lewrie lied, knowing that they had been terrible shots, grudgingly adequate at best, men who had never considered gun drill a serious business; who could go through the motions but had found fighting for their lives to be a horror, not even used to the sound of their own gunfire.

Poor Bales is fucked, Alan thought. And I've put one of the nails in his coffin. The least I can do is soften the blow for him... *God, where did I get so noble suddenly?* Then Alan also realized that anything he said in Bales' defense would look good for him as well before the members of the court. After all, he too was soon to be unemployed.

"If I may say something about Captain Bales, sir?" Lewrie said, and received a nod. "If I have learned anything in my short time in the Navy it's that Captain Bales is a good officer, and a fine captain. When we were on convoy duty he was the one we all looked to when it was blowing a full gale. No matter what happened when that Spaniard tried to ambush us, and we did do him more damage than he did to us, I was glad to have Captain Bales as our commanding officer. I'd sail with him again, sirs."

"Ah, well, I think that's all. You are dismissed, Mister Lewrie," the president said, all but piping his eyes.

"Aye aye, sir," Lewrie said crisply, rising from his seat. God, you are such a toadying little shit, Lewrie, he told himself, turning red with embarrassment. Did I lay it on a trifle thick? Maybe it will even help the old bastard a little bit in the end. But if I'd been on the listening side I'd have spewed and then kicked my young ass out...

"God bless you, Mister Lewrie," Captain Bales whispered to him as he passed him on the way out. "I'll not forget that."

"I meant it, sir," Lewrie said, knowing that he hadn't meant a bloody word of it and eager to get away.

ARIADNE was condemned. Her topmasts were struck for the last time, and she was warped alongside a stone dock, there to be a receiving ship. Most of her hands were dispersed to the hungry vessels that still had a job to do. Without them, she felt eerily empty.

Captain Bales, found guilty by the court of Article Ten, and Lt. Swift being found guilty of the same charge, were dismissed from the service, to be sent home to England. Lt. Church was found guilty of Article Twelve, Cowardice and Neglect of Duty; he was liable to the death penalty, but also dismissed from the Navy.

Lewrie thought that if they all went back home in the same ship it would make a cozy little gathering in the passenger's mess—Bales, Swift, Church, Chapman now minus his leg and doomed to a life of poverty and being chased by children in the street calling him 'Mister Hop-kin's, and young Beckett, minus a foot at twelve years of age, all ruing the day they had joined the Fleet, and *Ariadne*, for she had been bad luck for everybody.

Lewrie was moved into the old officers' wardroom but still had to sling a hammock. Some form of ship's routine still went on; rising to scrub decks, stow hammocks, sail drill with the courses, anything to keep the newly arrived hands busy before they were assigned ships. He also supervised a lot of working parties at the dockyard and stores warehouses. All his friends left. Osmonde went to an eighty-gun ship of the line whose Marine Captain had been cashiered; Ashburn attended the flagship and passed his examination for lieutenancy, and took his place as sixth officer in *Glatton*, which was easy duty since it had been months since that ship had seen the seaward view of Cape Shirley and was rumored to be resting on a reef of beef bones. Shirke was on the mend in hospital while Bascombe went into a fine frigate. All the senior warrants and mates disappeared, except for the oldest and slowest. He languished for weeks in limbo, waiting for his call.

A very old lieutenant had charge of *Ariadne*, a man so old that he made Bales look like a spry young topman. When Lt. Cork drank, Alan drank. In fact, everybody drank. Cork knew he wasn't going anywhere important for the rest of the century, so he drank a lot, which meant that Lewrie had to sit and drink with him almost every night.

On those nights when Lt. Cork had started early, or simply forgot that he had a ready-made audience for his maunderings, Lewrie had the chance to slip ashore and caterwaul. He checked out the whores, he ate the spiciest foods he could find which were such a change from the Navy's idea of what to do with rock-hard salt meat.

But it was an expensive island, and wartime wasn't helping to hold down prices, and he found himself in the miserable position of *having* to go ashore to get away from the drudgery, but not being able to afford doing it more than once a week. His hundred guineas were going fast, and there was no guarantee that his father even intended to honor their agreement, now that he was thousands of miles away. He had sent Pilchard a letter so his new guineas would catch up with him, but he wasn't holding his breath waiting for them.

He found himself in the miserable position one night of really wishing he were at sea, if just to cut his expenses, and he knew that he was going mad even to consider it. Once Lt.

Cork went face down in a puddle of claret (Lewrie had to give the man credit for supplying a good vintage, and free to boot) he went on deck to thin out the fumes in his head with fresh air, and leaned on the railing, wondering what was going on aboard all the ships in harbor.

"Mister Lewrie?" a familiar voice called from the darkness.

"Aye?"

"Lewrie, you're cup-shot!"

Lewrie could not make out who it was and stepped closer before he made the wrong answer to someone more senior. "Mister Kenyon?" he said, once he could make out the uniform and a hint of the face.

"It's me, right enough. How do you keep?"

"Like a ghost, sir. I think I'm the only soul left from the old crew," he said, happy to see his favorite officer and hoping that it wasn't just a social call.

"Too much idle time on your young hands, if you ask me, Mister Lewrie."

"Too true, sir."

"Then how would you like something that would keep you out of mischief?"

"I like mischief, sir, frankly. But this is getting boring."

"So you wouldn't turn down a chance to be a midshipman in an independent command."

"Mischief be damned, sir, where do I go?"

"Admiral Matthews has just given me command of HMS *Parrot*. She is a big fore n' aft schooner, American built and English took. I'm allowed two midshipmen and I was delighted to find that you were available. Matter of fact, Matthews was quite taken with the report about you and was saving you for something good."

"Lead me to her, sir."

"We'll be doing some interesting things, running fleet mails and orders all up and down the Leewards, over to Jamaica now and then, maybe as far as the Bahamas or the Colonies."

"I'll go pack, sir," Lewrie told him, aware that he was

much happier than the last time he had uttered those words.

"We're lying off the far side of the dockyard. Report aboard by the end of the forenoon watch. Sober and clear-eyed, if you know what's good for you." Kenyon said it goodnaturedly.

They spent some time catching up on old times, then Kenyon had to leave for his lodgings before taking command in the morning, and he wanted to pack. Lewrie knew that his chest was ready to go, except for a few loose ends and laundry. His head was as clear as a bell now, and he quivered with excitement at the thought of being not only employed once more, but having been held in reserve for a choice assignment such as *Parrot* by Rear Admiral Sir Onsley Matthews.

There had to be twenty, thirty midshipmen who were more senior and deserving, just dying for a berth such as *Parrot*. He thought of Keith Ashburn as a new lieutenant, pacing back and forth and aching for sea time on the flag, and he knew he had the better berth, after all.

This calls for a celebration, he told himself. There was going to be a lot of work in the days ahead, if his new ship was fitting out, and no more chance to go ashore with the ease which he enjoyed presently. Perhaps he did not have to drink himself blind to celebrate, but that did not mean he could not visit a girl one more time.

CHAPTER

7

PARROT was big as schooners go, not like the smaller island-built types. She was over sixty-five feet on the range of the deck, American-built of pine and fast as the very wind. Except for a small raised area aft to improve the headroom of the master's cabins, she was a flushdeck, and carried eight small four-pounder cannon, four on each beam, and with lighter swivels fore and aft as chase guns. She could fly three fore-sails, or jibs, two huge gaffed fore-and-aft sails on her fore and mainmasts, and when at any point of sail from a close reach to running before the wind could also add two smaller topsails on crossed yards. Since she would be running despatches, it was not meant for her to carry the usual four months of food and water required of rated ships, so the crew had much more room in which to stretch out. But she still had a large crew of eighty men, including officers, warrants and stewards. Enough to make sail, and enough to fight her, if pressed into a corner. But her principal defense was to be her greater speed—she could do nearly twelve knots.

She could also point up much higher to windward than

most ships such as brigs, which was a final form of salvation against being taken.

As soon as Lewrie saw her he was in heaven, since she did not rate a sailing master, chaplain, school master, no Marines and only one master's mate, a stocky individual with thinning hair named Claghorne.

Kenyon was master and commander, and was given the deferential title of Captain, and was responsible for her navigation and safety, with only Claghorne to help him. There was a bosun and only one mate, and though she rated a surgeon, did not have one, but only a surgeon's mate to serve in lieu of a more experienced man. But since they never would be far from some port, it was thought that he would suffice until they could drop anchor where there was medical help.

Kenyon had a tidy aftercabin which had a private quartergalley privy, and a hanging locker to the other side, a day cabin which held his settee by the stern windows, a desk, a sleeping cabin with a hanging bed box, small chart cabin and a dining space. And the furnishings the former owners had been deprived of were of good quality. Mr. Claghorne the master's mate, Boggs the surgeon's mate, Lewrie and the other midshipman, a fifteen-year-old named Thaddeus Purnell, berthed in the wardroom forward of Kenyon's quarters. *Parrot* had been meant to be a privateer, so she had carried prize officers, who had been given small private cabins. They weren't much; canvas and lath screens for partitions, stationary bunks, and a washhand stand and bookshelf, with room for a chest (barely) and a row of pegs for a locker, but it had a door, and it was more privacy than he had seen in months, even if every noise penetrated the insubstantial walls.

They also had a good quality dining table, and trestle seats down each side instead of using their chests. After the cockpit in *Ariadne* it was approaching luxury.

There were some familiar faces from *Ariadne* in the crew. The rest were those "volunteers" who had hoped to escape a bad officer or a bosun in their previous ship, or those men that any captain would offer up first to the needs of the Fleet, and would gladly get rid of at the first opportunity. There were also a great many hands fresh-arrived in Antigua who were barely seamen at all. Ten of the men, and all the boy servants, were West Indians, cheeky runts who spoke a dialect that Alan had a great difficulty understanding as the King's English.

The first item of business was stocking the ship. A man was chosen to be a cook, another West Indian who swore he knew how, and supplies began to arrive aboard, ferried by Lewrie and Purnell in their eternal role of water taxi men. Since there was no purser or assistant, the Jack in The Bread Room, Kenyon's clerk and Lewrie had to take over the role, but since Leonard wished to eventually save enough to purchase a place as a purser, it was much easier than Lewrie thought. And *Parrot* was already armed and stocked well with good French powder and small arms, though the guns were English, as was the shot. Their task was to bring firewood, coal, rum, livestock, flour, fruit, paint, extra slop clothing and naval stores for the bosun, Mr. Mooney.

After two days of stocking, Kenyon summoned his mates and petty officers to the aftercabin, which crowded that space severely. Kenyon sat behind his desk while Mooney, Claghorne and Leonard had the settee by the open stern windows. Also on hand were Lewrie, Purnell, Docken the gunner, Bright the gunner's mate. Kenyon had had the cook squeeze some fresh lemons and limes to make a cooling drink for the meeting. Lewrie's first duty was to help the captain's servant, a West Indian named George, fill everyone's mugs.

"Let's get down to business, shall we?" Kenyon said. "Now, normally with only me and Mister Claghorne, and only Mister Mooney and his mate to tend to things, we should be watch and watch in rotation. But I propose that we go to three watches and take advantage of the midshipmen. Mister Purnell has a good report from his last captain, and has served on prizes with a bosun's mate, which is why we got him. And I know Mister Lewrie's qualities from our last ship, *Ariadne*."

Purnell snuck a look at Lewrie to size him up, and Lewrie gave him equal treatment. Obviously Purnell had money, he was very well turned out and obviously someone's favorite for him to be here. He was a gawky fifteen-year-old with red hair and freckles. Hardly looked harmful. Yet.

"Mooney tells me that Bond, one of the quartermasters, wants to strike for bosun's mate, and we shall let him do so, and appoint one hand to serve as his replacement. Mister Mooney, you might have some name to suggest?"

"Aye, sir," Mooney rumbled deep in his barrel chest.

"Might pick another man for acting quartermaster for the tiller as well, so we have a chance to train as many people as possible," Lt. Kenyon went on, sipping at his lemon water.

"That will do for the men aft, at any rate. The hands will stay in their familiar starboard and larboard watches. I doubt if their conservatism would allow else."

"Aye, sir," Claghorne said, thinking on the superstitious and habitual nature of their seamen, who would balk at anything that smacked of newfangled notions.

"We shall place an experienced bosun's mate with the lads, and the acting bosun's mate with either me or Mister Claghorne. I expect we could put Purnell and Lewrie on the middle watch and first or second dog watches, where they could not get into much trouble, and give us a chance to sleep somewhat peacefully. They could nap in the forenoon, subject to the requirements of the ship, of course."

Lewrie grinned over the edge of his mug. It was tantamount to being appointed an acting lieutenant, and would look good in his record to be so honored, perhaps shortening the time he would have to be a midshipman. And there was also the prospect that *Parrot* just might take a prize and he appointed to command of it...

"I also want to take advantage of Mister Purnell's experience to assist the bosun and his mates in the general condition of the ship, and I wish Mister Lewrie to be seconded to the gunner and his mate, as he has a great fondness for artillery. Sail tending in the forenoon watches, exercise the guns during the day. We have a stout little vessel in *Parrot*, well built and clean of rot. We have guns sufficient to protect us against any light vessel that could catch us, and enough turn of speed to outrun or outpoint anything heavier. We have some people who need training, and some that need reminding that they are still in the King's Navy, so we have hard work ahead of us. Use your starters as you will for now, but try to avoid flogging incidents until we have shaken down into a crew, unless totally unavoidable."

Soon after that they were dismissed. Lewrie went below to the magazine to check up on things and do an inventory. Bright, the gunner's mate, went with him.

They counted their linstocks, lengths of slow match, sand, powder horns, firing quills and their condition, gun tools and the general condition of the four-pounders.

"Spankin' new, they are, Mister Lewrie," Bright told him, unsure how much authority Kenyon had given him. "Took off one of ours, I guess. Not a year old by the proof marks an' hardly fired."

"How accurate is a four-pounder?" Lewrie asked.

"Random shot at a mile, good chance of a hit at four cables. Not as accurate as a nine-pounder. Might wanta get rid a this junk."

"What is it?"

"She's fulla Frog tricks, Mister Lewrie. Canister—cases a musket balls ta clear a deck or a fightin' top. That's star shot," Bright said, picking up a round. "Comes apart inta four pieces held tagether like this. Good for takin' down riggin' and cripple a prize first. No stomach for a good fight."

"I see we have more swivels."

"Aye, eight more. I guess they were gonna mount 'em on each beam."

"We shall have to get the hands used to them. You might make up some cartridges, and some canister for the swivels. We might get some target practice at kegs or something with them."

"Aye, we could." Bright frowned, thinking how much work it was.

"What are these?" Lewrie asked, picking up an unusual rod of some kind from an entire case of them. It resembled a large iron dart but was wrapped with a tarred cap of cloth and seemed to have small springloaded arms attached, neatly folded up behind the head along the shaft.

"Easy with that, them's fire arrers," Bright said.

"What do you do with them, Bright?" Lewrie asked, turning to look him square in the eye and establish that he was on at least an equal footing with the gunner's mate. Being rated a watch officer didn't hurt, either.

"They's nasty stuff, Mister Lewrie. Ya shoots 'em outa the swivels. That sets 'em afire, an' when they hits, they snap open so's they can't go no farther. Sticks in the sails and burns 'em up. I'd feel a lot safer without 'em. They're touchy as hell. 'Sides, it ain't Christian to do that, even to an enemy. It's a damn pirate's weapon, not fit for a King's ship."

"But they have been found to be most effective?"

"Sir?" Bright asked, not understanding the word and taking the deferential air of an inferior by force of habit.

"Do they work real good." Alan rephrased.

"Devilish good, sir."

"Let's hang on to them, then. Bring in a tub of water and make sure they are closed up, and unable to rub and take fire on their own. We just might find a use for them."

"Aye, sir," Bright said, almost touching his forehead in a salute.

The rest of the inventory went swiftly, counting the French model 1763 muskets, boarding pikes, cutlasses, tomahawks and pistols, and the gun tools and grindstone that went with them. Since *Parrot* had no master-at-arms, Lewrie would be filling in in that capacity, and was happy to have so much to play with. The days ahead looked very promising.

* * *

A week later, *Parrot* was in all respects ready for sea. Lewrie was happy with his duties, and with his responsibilities. He had the guns painted, all tackles and breeching ropes snug. There were enough cartridges made up for a good battle, and still a quarter ton of powder below decks in casks. The round shot had been filed and sanded and painted and laid out in shot garlands, while the slightly imperfect hung in net bags ready for practice use. All the small arms were oiled and sharpened, and he had gotten two watches in which to hold arms drill and change the allotment of who got axes or pikes or muskets.

Finally, a gig had flown out to them from the flag, and a stuffy lieutenant had handed over to them several weighted bags of mail or orders, along with their first sailing orders. For the first time the jibs were hoisted, and the anchor broken out of the bottom. The huge fore-and-aft sails rose up the masts and the booms swung out as they filled with wind. Water began to chuckle under *Parrot*'s forefoot as she tacked her way out of the narrow channel to the outer roads and past the shipping anchored there. Once past Cape Shirley they turned southeast for an offing, going hard to windward.

And then, with the island a smudge to the nor'west, they came about to the starboard tack with the wind abeam and began to thrash to the north, hoisting topsails as well, and winging out the gaff sails to use every ounce of wind. By the time they cast the first log they had gotten up to nearly ten knots, and it was glorious, since *Parrot* could go like a Cambridge Coach with her larboard side down slightly and cool spray bursting in sheets from her bows and creaming down her flanks, spattering the decks and wetting the jibs and fores'ls high over the beakhead.

By evening quarters at sundown Antigua was out of sight, and other islands were silhouetted against the sunset far away to the west as they drove to pass Barbuda to their lee side. They were bound for Road Town in the Virgins on the island of Tortola, thence to Nassau in New Providence, with a final stop at Bermuda. It was a risky voyage, prime hurricane season, but for then, the sea was kind, and the very best of the tropic weather prevailed.

They reefed down for the night and took in tops'ls, but even in the middle watch with Purnell a pale ghost near his side, Lewrie was taken by how fast they were going, and how much glorious fun it was.

"I think I am going to enjoy this immensely," he told Purnell over the sluicing noise and hiss of their hull cleaving the ocean.

"The freedom," Purnell shouted back. "God, no line of battle, no admirals, no post captains. We're free as the wind!"

"No sailing master. No screaming first officer," Lewrie added.

"Good food everytime we anchor somewhere," Purnell went on, making circling motions over his stomach. "Like tonight."

Lewrie had to agree that their dinner had been very good, boiled mutton cut fresh from a carcass, and seasoned with God knew what by the West Indian cook, but the old man had created a substantial meal that stuck with you, by God, and was snappier on the tongue than neat rum or plug tobacco. There had been new potatoes and strange red purple onions and a decent French red wine that was a lot more pleasing than Black Strap could ever hope to be.

"Tell you what, I'll be senior for the first two hours," Purnell said. "You be my junior, and then at four bells we'll change round."

"Fair enough. I suppose you want the windward rail?" Lewrie asked, referring to the senior officer's right.

"Yes, if you don't mind."

Lewrie really didn't mind. The night was too full of stars, of moonlight shimmering on the ocean, of the pleasing motion and the cool humidity of the night to be enjoyed.

By God, this is more like it, he told himself at the larboard rail as he stared out at the ocean that glittered like a fairyland. If the rest of the Navy could be like this....

Kenyon had allowed them to forego heavy broadcloth uniform jackets. Now Alan rolled up the sleeves of his shirt, dressed in waistcoat, slop trousers and shirt. And since it was the middle watch he soon did away with the waistcoat and neck cloth as well, opening his shirt to the winds so that it fluttered and billowed out as it filled. Spray flew over the rail and smacked him now and then, and he found he looked forward to it each time, leaning far out to intercept it. He was in charge of a ship; maybe not much of a ship, but she was his for a while.

Even if he had to share her with Purnell and the bosun's mate.

When it came his turn, he was amazed to see a dark smear to the nor'west that was Barbuda. He left the windward side to cross to the binnacle and look at the chart by the tiller. By the feeble glow of the binnacle light he could see that they had already fetched Barbuda. Far inshore there were some faint lights, perhaps houses on the Atlantic side, or fishing boats working offshore. They would pass well to seaward of them, as long as the wind held steady. He closed his eyes and tried to measure the strength of the wind on his cheek. Had it shifted a point? Backed on us, he decided. *Parrot* seemed to slow a bit. He could order the quartermaster to adjust his helm, but was afraid to upset the settled order of the night. No, there was something else to do that would allow them to hold the course that Kenyon had ordained.

"Bosun?" he called, and Mister Kelly, the experienced bosun's mate who was their watcher, was there in a moment.

"Wind's backed a point. Summon the hands of the watch to veer out a piece on the braces and heads'l sheets," Lewrie ordered, hands behind his back and looking up at the set of the sails like a real watch officer would. He also found it hard to match Kelly's eyes as he issued his first real order.

"Spect it's about time fer that, Mister Lewrie," Kelly replied, touching his hat with his fingers and turning away to call the hands.

Damme, that wasn't so hard after all, Alan told himself—after they had let out and allowed the sails to stay full at a proper angle. "That ought to be enough, Mister Kelly. Belay all that."

Lewrie made an entry in the log, also his first, noting what he had done, and then they slogged along into the night with the wind now more on the quarter, but still holding their compass course, and *Parrot* giving no sign that she was going to do anything dire after being meddled with by amateurs. And when the end of the watch came, and Mister Claghorne took over for the morning watch, Lewrie was almost sorry to have to cede him the deck. As he doffed all his clothing and rolled into his bunk he pondered how fast people seemed to get promoted in wartime, as people got sick and had to be replaced, got killed and had to be replaced, or, like *Parrot*, the fleet grew in size and had to spread her substance thinner. Six years as a midshipman could be circumvented, if he were lucky enough, and in the right place at the right time. It felt like *Parrot* might be that place, and he swore that he would knuckle down once more and shine.

ALL during the hurricane season, *Parrot* dashed about the islands on her duties, putting in when a real storm threatened, but mostly out in full gales and riding it out, or running ahead of them with waves crashing into her bows and spraying the full length of her decks. In those times when it was clear, she flew from one port to another, from one command to another, with all the drama and panache of an actress making a surprise entrance.

By the time hurricanes had ended for the winter, *Parrot* was a well worked up and fairly happy ship. The crew had settled down, the new men trained well enough and salted by their experiences, and the old hands brought up to

scratch as they realized that *Parrot* was different from the
Navy in which they had so recently suffered. They had a
good cook, which went a long way toward making a happy
ship, and they had fresh food more often than most because they were never more than a week or two at best from
a new anchorage.

Kenyon was firm but fair in his punishments when
called upon to hand out disciplinary measures, and a taut-
handed captain always seemed to do better than a lax one,
or one who could not be relied upon to be fair. And as
often as possible Kenyon let the ship out of discipline and
allowed the doxies aboard to entertain the hands. With
the regularity of their stops the men looked forward to
seeing their favorite trulls on a steady basis, which provided a measure of stability and homelike consistency to
their lives.

Lewrie began to enjoy naval service. The food was fresh
and spicy, the wine palatable, the hours of work reasonable,
as were the hours available for a good long rest at the end
of them.

There was also the matter of their duty; it was indepen-
dence, dash and speed, and everyone reveled in it. He knew
that every lieutenant that saw them had his teeth set on
edge in envy at their freedom from convoys, from plodding
patrol duty, from rocking along in the wake of a flagship in
rigid order under the pitiless eye of senior officers. Other
midshipmen he saw envied him as he climbed through the
entry port with orders, for they knew that he had more
responsibility than they, more chances to gain experience
they could never have on larger ships, more opportunity to
practice his skills they only could read about.

The days were so full of work, and the nights so full of
learning how to lead, to steer, to be *in charge,* that he didn't
have much time to think about it; he just did it, and, to be
honest, it was satisfying.

Parrot went to so many interesting places. They might run
over to Nevis and St. Kitts, then run with a landsman's
breeze for Kingston, Jamaica. They might go down to St.

Lucia, or up to Road Town. There were despatches from the senior admirals that had to go to rustic little Savannah in the Colonies, where the recently vanquished civilians gave dirty looks to anyone wearing the King's coat, but their women had to make a living, regardless. They might go into Charleston, where a tiny Tory minority made the most of their recent victory, and wondered how long they could hang on, and their parties for visiting officers were frantic with tension that translated into eager ladies whose men were away with Cornwallis and Tarleton.

They might work their way into St. Augustine in the British Floridas, and wonder why anyone bothered with such a malarial, homespun sort of a place, more Spanish than anything else, a wilderness outpost with one foot in the grave already.

They might dash north from there to tiny Wilmington, up the Cape Fear River, and enjoy the pleasures that the place offered, as planters gathered at the shore for fear of their inland cousins.

Once, they even got to carry messages as far north as New York, and finally went ashore in the great city, which turned out to be less impressive than Portsmouth back home. That was a city that could turn anyone crooked, Lewrie decided. You could hear cannon fire at night, and the women pulsed to its sound, and the monetary speculation that rode the latest omens for good or ill, and the general background of graft and cupidity with military and naval stores could turn a saint into a stockbroker or pimp.

Alan Lewrie learned that war could be a powerful aphrodisiac, and that a well-set-up young man in a uniform was able to take advantage of it. And when he had time to think back on his time before the Navy in London he no longer found an aching emptiness but merely vague regrets that he hadn't had more time there to enjoy what he was enjoying now.

Sometimes he was shocked to find, in the middle of some duty, that he had risen gladly to that duty, and was satisfied with the crew's progress at small arms, gun drill, sailtending, or his own skill at leading them, or performing those personal skills such as longsplicing, position plotting and ship-handling. He knew he was a different person. The Alan Lewrie of December, 1780, in no way resembled the one almost press ganged in January. His skin was bronzed by the sun, his hair a lighter shade of brown from constant exposure, hands tougher, muscles leaner and fuller and able to carry him aloft or wield a sword with ease. His uniforms needed alteration to make room for the bulk he had added in those months of hard work, hard play and good food.

He had some money in hand, too, for those pleasures of their port stays, for *Parrot* had been lucky with prizes, though taking ships was not their primary purpose. But they had come upon a Spanish packet brig in the Straits of Florida after a gale, and took her without a shot being fired since she was still repairing damage and could offer no resistance.

On passage to St. Lucia they had run into a native lugger that was manned by a crazed pack of Creoles, Spaniards and poor French who were intent on a little practical piracy. Without a letter of marque, they were totally illegal. The leaders were later hanged, the lugger sold, and the blacks sold at auction, plus the head money from taking her.

They were chased once by a big privateer, and had the good fortune first of all to outrun her in a long stern chase, and the even greater fortune to run across an English frigate off Anegada, which promptly went to quarters and took the privateer. Since they were the only other naval vessel in sight they shared in her prize money.

Altogether, Lewrie had accrued nearly 160 pounds, or at least, Prize Court certificates for that amount, which he could sell off to a jobber for at least half their true value or hold on to the largest until he returned to London, where he could be paid off.

Had someone forced Lewrie to delve into the reasons for a certain smug look of satisfaction on his face, he could discover that he was well-fed, had access to a goodly supply of decent drink, got enough sleep, was being treated like a real person without being shouted at, could play with God's own amount of artillery, and what amounted to a yacht, and never went more than a fortnight without a chance to get beastly with all the willing mutton within reach.

CHAPTER

_____

8

"STAND by, the anchor party," Claghorne yelled through a brass speaking trumpet from the afterdeck by the tiller.

"Aye aye," Lewrie replied, raising his fist in the air. *Parrot* ghosted along in light air inside the harbor, barely raising a ripple under her bows since they had passed the forts on the Palisades. They had handed all but the outer flying jib and mainsail.

"Helm's alee." The tiller was put over and *Parrot* rounded up slowly into the light ocean breeze until her sails shivered, and her forward progress came to a halt.

"Let go!"

Lewrie lowered his arm briskly, and the best bower anchor was cast loose, and cable rumbled out the hawsehole. "Loose the outer jib halyard and lower away handsomely," he ordered. *Parrot* coasted on for a piece, until reaching the end of the anchor cable veered out. She snubbed, then drifted back slantwise for a way before streaming back from the cable with the light wind straight down her decks.

By the time the sails had been handed and furled, the gig had been brought round from being towed astern, and

Purnell and his boat crew had tumbled into it, ready to carry Lt. Kenyon ashore with his bags of mail and despatches. They had made good time from English Harbor to Kingston, Jamaica, this passage. The weather had been sparkling clear and mildly sunny, and they had not seen one other sail.

The bumboats began to swarm *Parrot* almost before Lt. Kenyon was away from the side, the island blacks offering up tropical birds, rum, fresh fruits, cheap shirts and hats and neckerchiefs, and women of just about every color. Mooney and his mates were busy trying to fend them off goodnaturedly and to stop any furtive trading for rum or other liquors.

"Not yet," Mooney shouted down to a piratical black entrepreneur. "N' keep yer cussed rum fer other ships, ya hear?"

"De Boh-sohn, he wan no rum, Lord," the man grinned back. "Dis be de King's Navy heuh?"

"Sheer off, ya shark. We might be outa discipline later, but not now."

"Then I see you later, Mistah Boh-sohn," the woman in the trader's boat promised, sliding her dress up to her waist.

"Gawd." Mooney was staring at what was offered.

Lewrie was standing at his side and marvelling along with him.

Mooney licked his lips in anticipation and dug into his slop trousers to see what silver he had to offer the woman if she was let aboard.

Kenyon returned about two hours later after his visit to the flag, looking happy and sated from a good lunch and a bottle of wine. He was in a very good mood, beaming at everyone.

"Mister Lewrie, summon 'Chips'," he said. "I shall need him."

"Aye aye, sir. Pass the word for Mister Bee."

Within moments the elderly carpenter was there.

"Mister Bee, we shall be carrying passengers to Antiqua, a lord and his lady and two servants," Kenyon informed him.

"Arrange me some sleeping accommodations in the dining space. We shall shift all the furnishings to the day cabin, and I shall need a larger bed box in the cabin as well. There will be a maid berthing in the chart room, and a servant in the wardroom. Mister Lewrie, since your ears have grown long enough to hear, perhaps you could give up your cabin for the duration of the voyage?"

"Aye, sir," Lewrie replied sadly, "I shall fetch a hammock from the bosun."

"Have everything ready by Wednesday sundown, Mister Bee."

"Aye aye, sir."

"Mister Purnell," Kenyon shouted. "Take the cutter ashore with Mister Leonard to collect fresh supplies. We'll get a bullock for the men, plus some fresh meat for our passengers. Mister Claghorne?"

"Aye, sir."

"As soon as stores are aboard, we shall take the ship out of discipline for a day. We cannot depart until Thursday."

The hands standing closest by grinned happily and spread the word through the rest of the crew within seconds. They had all lately been given pay-certificates and even though they would get cheated badly in transactions for perhaps a quarter of their certificates' worth, they would have money to spend for their pleasures. So they turned to with a lusty will. The boat fairly flew across the harbor to the stores dock and returned laden in short order. A bawling lean steer was slung aboard and slaughtered on the spot. A coop full of chickens appeared, several tender piglets and lambs, a boar for the hands later in the voyage, fresh cabin stores for Kenyon and the wardroom, and several crates of wine. Hammering sounds could be heard aft as Kenyon's request was fulfilled. George the servant and several of the West Indian ship's boys busied themselves polishing and scouring the guest quarters so *Parrot* could make a favorable impression on whoever their prestigious passengers might be.

By the end of the forenoon watch, the crew's major work

was done, and at a signal from Kenyon the pendant for easy discipline was hoisted, which brought the bumboats swarming back.

Mooney and Leonard stood by the entry port, along with the surgeon's mate, to witness the exchange of certificates for cash, so that the men were not too badly cheated. They also made sure that drink did not make its way below decks in major quantities, though some smuggling of small bottles was inevitable. Lastly the surgeon's mate performed his duty of checking the boarding polls for the more obvious signs of the pox. He rejected several, turning away the oldest and most raddled whores. The crew did a good job of sorting as well, booing down the arrival of some women that Boggs could find no fault with.

"Wot a monkey-face, throw 'er back, somebody..."

"'Oo shall 'ave this'n, then?" Mooney asked.

"Nobody," several men called out.

"On yer way, twickle-bum."

"Yair, go fook a Marine!" Someone laughed.

Awnings were spread over the deck, and canvas chutes for ventilation, while hammocks were slung below in the crew's mess area, and crude blanket partitions were hung for some semblance of privacy for their rutting. The women would work hard to earn their few shillings, paired off for a day or night to a lustful seaman who would feed her and ply her with drink out of his earnings like a temporary wife. Her man had duties to attend to, still, but she would be waiting below for him once he was released.

Once the sun had lost most of its heat, the awnings were taken in and stowed and supper was served along with the second rum ration. Lewrie made a quick tour of the lower deck to see if all was in order, then attended to his own meal.

He lounged at the mess table in the wardroom, half his uniform removed for comfort and sipping at a very decent hock just brought from shore. Their Creole cook had come up with roast chicken, fresh bread and butter, boiled onions, carrots and peas. There had been some new Stilton and a small apple apiece, too. Had it not been for the occasional squeal of delight or a husky grunt of transport coming from the crew's quarters he could have fallen asleep, pleasantly stuffed.

"A bumper with ya, lad," Boggs said happily cup-shot, and his scruffy white bag wig askew on his head. "Give us heel taps on the last of yer hock and have port with me."

He accepted a full measure after draining his glass, and clinked glass with Boggs.

"Goddamn me, we're close to losing British Florida," Leonard told them as he read a newspaper nearly three months old but new to them.

"Good riddance," Claghorne said. "Whole lot of colonies south of the Chesapeake is nothin' but swamp and bugs and sweat."

"But, I mean, the Rebels'll never hold 'em against the Spanish. They'll take 'em right back, and then we're in a pickle," Leonard went on, waving the paper at them.

"But if the Spaniards lost their fleet in that storm last year," Tad Purnell asked, "what have we to worry about?"

"Hark the younker," Claghorne said.

Purnell and Lewrie shared a look between them. If one were a midshipman, every one of your questions was greeted with ridicule, and every one of your answers was usually wrong, according to the older men. Samuel Johnson as a midshipman would have been caned for even opening his mouth.

"DeGuichen has a Frog fleet back in the Windwards," Leonard said. "Rodney and Parker tangled with him all summer but couldn't finish him off. They provide the ships, the Dons provide the troops, we could have trouble somewhere. Then the closest American port open to us would be Charleston, and you know they'd try to take that back. Cornwallis has enough on his plate as it is."

"Let the French come out," Boggs said loudly. "Let them come, I say, and the King's Navy will square their yards for 'em."

"Gentlemen, the Navy," Claghorne shouted, raising his

glass, and they all had to knock their wine back and refill.

Claghorne dipped a taper into the lamp hung over the mess table to get a light for a long clay pipe, and was soon happy to lean back with a wreath of tobacco fumes about his head. Leonard, crossed in his opinions by the others, withdrew from the fray and put aside the paper to peruse his account books, making clucking sounds now and then as he either found some expense he deplored, or didn't think he could get the Admirality to believe. Boggs began to rock and sing, but the exact tune was hard to make out, and the words slurred together, until his wig fell off. As he bent to retrieve it he slipped to the deck and stayed there in a heap, beginning to snore loudly.

"Thank God," Purnell said. When most men considered it a gentlemanly accomplishment to be a three-bottle man, Boggs was more like a half-dozen man, and that on top of his rum or Black Strap issue. The suspicion was strong that drink had run him to sea, and God help the hand who really needed a surgeon if only Boggs was available...

Claghorne got to his feet and dragged their surgeon's mate to bed, and Alan and Tad slipped out on deck for some fresh air. There was none to be had. The harbor was as smooth as a millpond and not a capful of wind stirred. *Parrot* could almost roll on her beam-ends under bare poles in a stiff breeze, but she now lay as calm as a stone bridge.

"Damned hot for December," Purnell said quietly beside him, studying the many riding lights in the harbor.

"We'll have some weather. Maybe a late storm. It's unreal for it to be so still and airless," Alan replied.

"My, how salty we've become, for one dipped in brine so little time."

"I still say we'll get a shift of wind out of this," Alan insisted. "You mark my words."

"Think enough to put up half a crown on it?" Tad pressed.

"Done. But you should know better. Pity to take your money so easy. Your brothers would know."

Purnell's family were from Bristol, shipowners, traders,

importers, and his older brothers were already merchant captains. Their clan was so absolutely stiff with the chink that Purnell clanked when he did a turn about the decks, but for all his money, he was all right as a mate. He did not compete with Lewrie for favor, and each had their own specialty. For Purnell, it was sail-handling and navigation—Lewrie was capable, but more at home with artillery and small arms. Tad Purnell was also a good fellow to know, fairly upright and honest in their dealings but still possessed a sense of humor and a streak of deviltry that his family, and now the Navy, sat upon to keep from running riot.

Claghorne emerged from the hatchway, his pipe still fuming, and a newspaper clutched in his hand for a long, contemplative visit to the heads. "Damn still," he said to them. "We'll get half a gale out of this right soon, I swear."

"Sorry about your half a crown," Lewrie whispered, delighted to hear his opinion confirmed by an old tarpaulin man.

"And I'll bet our live-lumber will be casting up their accounts as soon as we get beyond the breakwater," Tad said happily.

"Just who is this Lord Cantner?" Lewrie asked Purnell after hearing Lt. Kenyon drop the name to his clerk Leonard earlier that afternoon.

"Rum old squint-a-pipes, tries to see six directions at once. He used to be a very big planter and trader out here before the war started. As big a cutthroat as a Mohawk. I heard he'd become one of Lord North's creatures, come to see if the war is still winable. But most like to collect what he can from his old estates."

"Thing that amazes me is that he'd bring his wife out here to this place," Alan said. "It's a sickly climate for a woman."

"Well, I hear she's much younger, and her dowry was worth a duke's ransom. Probably couldn't stand the thought of her being left back home with time on her hands."

"Or someone else's hands on her."

"Look, Lewrie," Tad began, suddenly unsure of himself,

"if we get ashore this time I was wondering...you seem to know a bit about the fairer sex, and I..."

God help me but I really should become a pimp, Alan told himself. Everyone seems to think I'm so very good at it...

"And the sound of our crew slaking their lust is driving you mad, is that it, Purnell?"

"Well, I am fifteen now, almost sixteen, and I've spent the last three years of my life afloat. This ship seems my best chance."

"Probably cost you one guinea for a good bareback rider," Alan warned him with a grin, "and you have to be careful that you don't get a poxy one."

"I don't know how to tell," Tad said, turning red at his own words, "but if you sort of gave me a fair wind, and a course to steer..."

"And you don't want to just hop on and hop off."

"I don't know..."

"Whores can be right nice, if they know it's your first time," Alan said. "Kind of like the press gang. If I had to go, why not you, too? Best way is to spend some time with her, have a stoup or two, get rigged properly, bear down and board her, and not have to run for the door after. Take a dog watch to enjoy watching her move."

"God almighty," Tad breathed heavily, "that would be marvelous."

"Bloody right it is," Alan heartily agreed, getting the itch himself.

"Could you do it?"

"I promise I shall."

They went below for more wine, the only thing that seemed to cool the night. Boggs was snoring, and Leonard had retired to his cabin to do some writing. Claghorne came back down through the hatch and poured himself a drink, preparatory to turning in.

"Shit," he said, pawing the air.

"Sir," Lewrie asked. Was it an order, or a comment?

"Bloodsuckers have found us," Claghorne said, waving off a mosquito. Lewrie heard a whine and looked down to see one ready to perch on his wrist. He brought his other hand down and smashed it, leaving a tiny smear of blood.

"Well-fed little bastard."

"I've seen 'em down on the Spanish Main, thicker'n a Channel fog, and each one hungry as a rolled leech," Claghorne said groggily. "Seen 'em suck a man white..."

"Aye, Mister Claghorne," Tad said with an angelic expression that almost made Lewrie snort port up his nose as he tried to stifle a laugh.

"Shows how much *you* know," Claghorne said. "But I'm sleepin' with a net tonight to keep 'em off me. You should, too, if ya had any sense, but I 'spect midshipmen could do with a rash a welts an' all the itchin', so we'll see who caulks down quiet an' who tosses all night." So saying, Claghorne took his mug of port and went off to his cabin to slam the insubstantial door.

"Seen 'em suck a man white down on the Spanish Main," Tad said in a soft whisper, and a fairly accurate imitation of Claghorne.

Eight bells chimed from the belfry, and the ship's corporal began to make his rounds to make sure that the galley fire was out, and all glims extinguished below decks. The wardroom could keep their pewter lamps burning for another hour, but after more port neither one wanted to stay up and read. Tad Purnell had the deck watch, so he dressed properly and left, and Lewrie turned in, making sure his door was shut tight and that no flying pests lived in his space to disturb his rest.

IT was the next morning while the crew were at Divisions that a boat came out to *Parrot*, bumping against the hull. A mulatto man in livery stood waiting patiently until the men had been inspected and released back to their morning duties, and their pleasures.

After all the wine, and a night on deck, Lewrie felt that

his eyes were ready to glaze over and wished he had had more time in his bed box.

"Mister Lewrie," Lt. Kenyon called. "Could you join me?"

Lewrie crossed to the hatchway to the after cabins, where Kenyon stood with a piece of paper in his hand that had just been handed to him by the mulatto servant.

"I have just been given an invitation to a dinner party this evening at the home of ... an old acquaintance of mine, now Sir Richard Slade. He requests that I bring some of my officers as well. Do you think you could be presentable enough to represent *Parrot* properly?"

"Aye, sir!"

"Good. Purnell as well. Mister Claghorne might be a bit too rough for that sort of company so I shall leave him in charge."

"I should be delighted, sir."

"I thought you would be. See to making the gig presentable. We shall go ashore at the end of the first dog. This could be quite important. Our passengers shall be there, as well as the lieutenant-governor and other luminaries from these parts. I shall hope that you and Purnell are on your absolute best behavior, mind."

"We shall endeavor to please, sir," Lewrie said earnestly, but thinking that it would be a splendid opportunity to please himself, and possibly initiate Thaddeus to the pleasures of strumming a bawd.

An extremely handsome coach had met them at the boat landing, and they rode in comfort through the streets of Kingston as night fell. The coach ascended a hill overlooking the army camp north of the town, then spiralled down to a pleasant valley at the foot of the hills that rose to the east into the Blue Mountains.

The house they came to on a shell drive was huge, island-built imitation Palladian but with a veranda all about it. Light gleamed from the front rooms and over thirty carriages already stood in the shadows of the trees.

Once in the foyer Lewrie began to almost purr in delight. There was a large salon aglow in candlelight as large as any he had seen in London. Perhaps the trim work was not as fine, but the drapes and the furnishings were top quality and in impeccable taste. And the salon was crowded with people, civilians in their finery, naval officers in blue and white, army and Marine officers in red, planters in velvet and silk and broadcloth. And women. Women of every imaginable type, done up in silk, lace, velvet, satin and damask, their bell-shaped gowns all trimmed with flowers and embroidered panels, their bosoms hitched up in tightfitting bodices, lace sleeves and fine wigs. Jewels shone in the flattering candlelight, and eyes were already flashing.

The butler introduced them to no special notice from the crowd, which was intent on their own conversations, or the delights of the groaning buffets or wine tables.

"James. How good to see you after all these years," their host said upon spotting Kenyon.

"Richard," Kenyon replied. "Rather, Sir Richard, now!"

"Pox on that, it's still Dick to you," Sir Richard Slade said. "And who are these two scamps? Yours?"

"My midshipmen, Dick," Kenyon said. "Thaddeus Purnell."

"Not Alexander Purnell's boy?"

"Aye, sir," Tad said.

"Knew your father well, used to do a lot of trading through Bristol."

"Midshipman Alan Lewrie."

"Your servant, Sir Richard," Alan said, making a leg. What a Macaroni, he thought. Must be fifty guineas for his duds but he's too old for them by half...

Sir Richard Slade sported heavy dark blue breeches made of velvet, and an extremely flared coat of powder blue satin, sprigged with fanciful gilt braids and button trim, gilt buttons everywhere, tight sleeves and huge pockets. His waistcoat was gold silk with elaborate floral embroidery. In spite of the heat he wore a huge floured wig. His shoes were even high-heeled in the French style, and his buckles seemed paved with brilliants. Altogether, the image of a man with too much money and not enough clothes sense.

His handshake was also as limp as a dead halibut. Lewrie felt an instant revulsion and wondered where Kenyon had made friends with such a coxcomb. Reminds me of Gerald and all his Molly friends.

"The pleasures of my house are yours, gentlemen," Sir Richard told them. "James, come, let us catch up on things. It has been too long since we've talked."

"Enjoy yourselves," Kenyon told them. "Within reason."

"If you are allowed, why do you not all stay over tonight and accept the hospitality of my home?" Sir Richard asked. "I'll have Cassius arrange some rooms for you."

"Aye, but let me send a message to my mate," Kenyon said. A servant was there in a moment, and another younger boy in livery to steer Kenyon to a study, where he could pen some orders for Claghorne. This left Lewrie and Purnell alone, so they wandered off toward the buffets and the wine tables.

"Odd sort," Lewrie said. "Knows your family, does he?"

"I suppose. But there are so many traders out here we deal with. I'll have to write father about him."

"Well, let's get some wine aboard and see what the buffet has to offer. Oh, Lord, look at the cat-heads on that woman."

Purnell stared open-mouthed at a slim woman in her thirties who sported a pair of breasts that looked as large and firm as apples, half her globes swelling above her gown and thrust forward proudly. They almost could make out a hint of her rosy aureoles.

"My, yes," Tad breathed, close to fingering his crotch.

"Don't do that, they'll all want some," Lewrie warned him, seeing his strangled expression.

"Do you . . . think tonight has possibilities?"

"Definitely."

"I see no young ladies my age."

"And damned lucky you are, at that. Last thing you want is a young girl. Hold hands, giggle, and that's all."

"Oh?"

"Half these ladies are escorted by officers or husbands

who could have you flogged to death if you even breathed on 'em. Now that leaves about half to choose from. Older ladies have a great fascination with younger men, Tad," Lewrie said, piling tasty morsels onto a plate. "And should one of those take a fancy to you, while her husband is off doing something grand for King and Country, and discover that it's your first time, I swear you may not survive her kindness."

"Oh, I didn't consider a married lady, Alan. That would be a sin. I thought we'd find a young whore. I mean, doing it with a married lady would be a mortal sin."

"Would it be a sin with a widow?" Lewrie asked, nibbling on some shrimp as they grazed their way down the long food-laden table.

"Well... I'm not sure."

"There are all kinds of widows, Purnell. This hock is iced, By God. Marvelous."

"You were talking about widows," Tad said, taking a glass of wine without caring what it was.

"Well, some have lost their mates to the Grim Reaper, naturally," Lewrie said, leading him to a quiet corner where they could munch and drink without being trampled by the crowd, "but there are some widows who have lost their husbands who have become enamored of someone prettier, or younger, or they have chased after their careers or money or a peerage to the total exclusion of their wives' happiness. They have committed the greatest sin you can inflict on a woman still ripe and comely, Tad. They have shunned them, ignored them, denied them."

"Well, I suppose, if the husband was really tired of her..."

"Consider a woman who enjoys a romp, and affection and loving and all the folderol being cast aside like an orange that has been sucked dry. There is a woman who is as much a widow as the natural kind, mourning the loss of everything she staked her life on, and some of them are just aching to get their own back. Somewhere here, tonight,

Tad, there are women exactly like that, just waiting to find a strapping little chub like you."

Purnell's eyes cut about the room. He finished his wine in two sips. "But what if she doesn't find me attractive, or I don't like her, or something?"

"We shall do our best for you, Tad. Now go slow on the wine. You need oysters and some of those spicy kickshaws to raise the heat of your blood. And we can chat up a few now, 'cause we're going to get seated way below the salt at this party."

THEIR end of the long table was definitely below the salt. The rich, the high-ranking and the glittering were near the head of the dining room on either side of Sir Richard and Lord Cantner in plum satin, and his wife, who was a raven beauty with an adventurous look to her eyes. No wonder the old monkey brought her, Lewrie thought. Were she my wife I wouldn't let her out of the room by herself...

Their closest dinner companions were less impressive socially, an older couple from the Customs, a magistrate and his wife, a matron named Gordon with her daughter, both of whom would serve, if one didn't mind country-puts.

Purnell was seated next to a sleepy old gentleman said to be some sort of banker—it didn't matter much because he could barely open an eye to survey his plate. But on Purnell's other side was a lean older woman named Mrs. Hillwood who at one time must have been a great blonde beauty. During the course of conversation it was learned that her lawful blanket was off in the wilds inland doing plantation-type things, and had been for some months. To Alan's left was a woman named Haymer, a short, plump and fetching woman in her late thirties, Lewrie guessed, done up nicely in white taffeta with burgundy ribbons and flounces. It seemed her husband was also off on business in the Americas.

Halfway through dinner Lewrie had to nudge Purnell to

open his mouth and speak to Mrs. Hillwood instead of feeding like a beast. He felt a kick back under the table, and looked up to glare at Tad, but instead met the steady gaze of Mrs. Hillwood.

"That looks such succulent pork before you, Mister Lewrie," Mrs. Haymer said to his left. "Do be a dear and carve me a small slice."

"Delighted, Mrs. Haymer. In fact, I may assay a bit myself." As she offered her plate to him, she leaned toward him, pressing her bosom against his arm. We're aboard, he exulted.

"How clumsy of me," she said, dropping her napkin.

"I'll fetch it. Allow me," he offered, bending over and wondering if he should attempt a small squeeze right away. But in reaching for it Mrs. Haymer's hand brushed his thigh and stayed to linger.

"Such a wonderful texture," she sighed, after chewing a bite of her pork. "I think it is dreadful that poor young sailors such as you never get any fresh food."

"It is a great trial, ma'am," he sighed right back. "And then there are Banyan Days, when not even a morsel of meat is served, no matter how long in the cask."

"Scandalous," she replied, locking her gaze firmly on his eyes. "How relieved you must be to dine well when ashore."

"Indeed, ma'am," he told her softly, shifting his gaze to her ample bosom, "the mere sight of all this bounty has raised quite a passion in me to eat my fill without inhibition."

That bosom heaved deeply at his words, and a fine sheet of sweat broke out on her upper lip. She hoisted her glass and drank deep.

"We were happy that our captain received Sir Richard's invitation," Lewrie went on. "Poor sailors are dependent on the generosity of others for such a feast."

Lewrie glanced about the table to see if his wooing was making any comment, but the sleepy old gentleman had succumbed to wine fumes and sat snoring with a clawed hand about the stem of his empty glass. The Gordons did seemed mildly shocked and were busy looking elsewhere, as though Mrs. Haymer was "no better than she ought to be" and had tried this on before. Mrs. Hillwood across the table gave him a barely noticeable shrug, then turned her attentions to Tad. Her left hand went below the table, and young Tad suddenly looked as though he was about to strangle.

"You must rejoin your ship tonight, Mister Lewrie?" Mrs. Haymer asked in a very soft voice.

"Sir Richard and my captain are old friends, ma'am. He has offered us the hospitality of his house for the night."

"How generous of our host. I am told that he is scandalously rich and has the most blessed luck at getting ships across the ocean without loss. I admire generosity."

"In the giving or in the receiving, ma'am?"

"Both," she said, dimpling prettily and blushing. "The gardens here are most beautiful. Too bad you could not see them in daylight."

"A cool stroll in a fresh garden would be delightful, no matter the hour, ma'am . . ."

WITH dinner over, the ladies retired for first shot at the jakes, then coffee and cards, while the men shuffled down to the head of the table to talk and drink and smoke. Waiters produced an ocean of port, and opened the sideboards to place chamberpots below the table within range of those gentlemen who felt the call.

Lewrie and Purnell stayed long enough for a glass of port, then snuck out. Being nobodies, none of the company would miss them. Alan was almost reeling with the bounty they had been offered—he had not seen a dinner like that in a year: spicy soup, fresh green salads, beef, chicken, pork, two kinds of fish, rabbit, veal, geese, hot bread, native yams, local kickshaws and made dishes for removes, corn, potatoes, beans and peas, a wine with each course, lovely fresh cheese and extra fine biscuits and nuts. Even limiting himself to a mere sliver of everything, following Captain Osmonde's advice, he felt uncomfortably tight around the middle.

Thankfully, once they joined the ladies there was strong coffee or tea with fresh milk and sugar.

Mrs. Haymer was happy to join him on the veranda with a cup of coffee as the older couples made their good-bys and clattered off in their carriages. The younger bucks and their girls were also going, but many people were staying on for the music and cards and the chance of a cold supper later with more wine.

"You said something about the gardens, I believe, ma'am," Lewrie prodded, and Mrs. Haymer allowed him to offer his arm and lead her off the veranda into the fragrant night air. It was really much cooler in the gardens, once past the glow of the house lights in the darkness of flowering shrubs and bushes and planters.

"I do believe there is a maze hereabouts, with some stone benches where we may rest, Mister Lewrie. If you would allow me to lead?"

They eventually discovered a cul-de-sac surrounded by flowers, and a small grove hidden by the turn in the path. In the center of the grove was a large round stone table, surrounded by curved stone benches. They seated themselves in the companionable darkness, Lewrie offering his coat to protect her dress from the bench. He put an arm behind her on the table and leaned toward her, able to smell her. Their thighs were touching through the vastness of her skirts, their shoulders were touching. She turned toward him slightly.

"Is it not a beautiful night, Mister Lewrie? The stars in these climes are so clear and lovely."

"I see enough stars at sea, I'd much rather gaze at your beauty."

"Mister Lewrie, I cannot imagine what you can be thinking of!"

"Of the glory that is you, Mrs. Haymer," he said, leaning

closer, which she did not seem totally to object to.

"I must protest, young sir," she said, but not too loudly. "I am a married woman, and you are such a boy—"

"Call me Alan," he whispered.

"All right...Alan. But had I known that you intended to woo me when we set out from the house I would not have allowed you. Why, what must people think of my good name? And my husband is a most jealous man. He would most likely kill you if he discovered you had even gotten me alone."

"I shall risk your husband's temper, Mrs. Haymer. And we are quite alone and private here. What is your name, my dear?" he said, putting his arm along her shoulders.

"Margaret, if you must know, but—"

"Margaret, so womanly, so lovely, soft..."

"Alan, I fear you have misjudged me," she said, making no move to break away. "I could not hazard your young life, and we must not tempt each other like this...my husband would shoot you dead—"

"I must taste your lips, and hang the danger," he said. He brushed her mouth with his, kissed her eyes, cheeks, then took possession of her lips and felt her tremble a little. She raised her face to him, a hand came up to hold the back of his head. She began to moan and make cooing sounds. He brought up his free hand and caressed a restrained breast.

"God, we must not do this," she said harshly against his neck as he bent to kiss her shoulders. "I forbid you!"

And so saying, her arms encircling him and she leaned back against the edge of the table as he slid and squirmed to press more of himself against her. A leg came up to caress him as he slid his free hand down to her buttocks.

I'm going to snap my spine or hers like this, he thought, getting to his feet and pulling her with him so they could fit together for their full length. She stood on tiptoe to match him, and ground her belly into him as he squeezed down through all the material of her gown, trying to find flesh to press on her backside.

"Alan, I demand that you cease now." She shuddered. "We must not persist in this, I...I shall resist you, with force, if necessary—"

His reply was to free her breasts and bend down to press his face into her apple-dumpling shop, noting that her nipples were rock-hard and her bosom all warm and soft.

He seated her on the table and knelt on a bench before her, and she parted her thighs for him. His fingers were busy with the back of her sack gown while hers opened his waistcoat, and their lips ground against each other, bringing a salty taste. She gasped as he lifted her gown and all the petticoats and stepped closer, struggling with the buttons of his straining breeches.

"You will witness that I was forced!" she said in a soft voice as he slid her forward toward him and found her wet and slick and open for him. She gasped and squealed as he entered her deep, and clung to him fierce as a new bride as he began slowly pumping away. After a while she began to sob and gnaw on his shoulder, and lifted her legs about his waist to hold him closer to her.

"Oh God, my husband shall surely kill you for this, oh God, yes he shall, oh...*Alan,*" and much more in the same vein. A moment later she squealed in delicious transport and melted to him as he stood between her thighs until his own release exploded into her.

She insisted he was a heartless ravisher, but helped as they explored the cool surface of the table, knelt on a bench before him as he stood behind her ahold of her hips; she cried softly for mercy as she drew him down on the grass in only corset and stockings, or rode Saint George above him, her heavy breasts dangling in his palms while she galloped as frenzied as a huntsman riding hell-for-leather for a distant steeple while he looked up at the stars and her crumpled face. Between bouts she fought him without strength, swore he was sure to be killed for ravishing her, that he had tempted her weak and vulnerable nature...

It was midnight before they felt sated enough to dress and head back to the veranda. The dinner and card party was still going strong as people got drunker and louder. Music played and some danced.

"I must go now," she said, attempting to adjust her wig and hat. "Don't see me in. I would die of shame, I must look ravaged."

"Use my room to rearrange yourself, dear," Alan said, still eager to use her more, "we can send down for cold wine, perhaps a bite of supper. You can't go home like this, or face the company so mussed."

"You must swear that you shall not abuse me further. What you have done is mortal sin enough. Oh, I *must* make myself presentable...only to save my honor, will I go upstairs. Promise me—"

"I promise." He looked about for Kenyon, Tad, or their host, but they were not present. The servant Cassius approached.

"I shall be retiring shortly, Cassius," Lewrie said. "I'd admire some cold hock and something from the supper. Before that, light us up. This lady tripped and fell while taking the air in the gardens and she would like to freshen up before going home."

"Yas, sah," Cassius said with a knowing expression. He summoned a tiny linkboy with a candelabra who led them toward the side stairs as Margaret went on. "I thank you for the kind offer of your room so I can rearrange myself, Mister Lewrie. I promise I shan't delay your retiring any more than I can help..."

The room was small but pleasant, fitted with a wash-hand stand and mirror, chest, armoire and a table and two chairs by the veranda doors. The bed was high, curtained with thin cloth to keep insects off during the night. The linkboy lit two candles and stepped out into the hall, Lewrie following to complete the sham as Margaret began to attend to her makeup and dress.

The boy went down the stairs with the candelabra, leaving Lewrie alone in the dark hall, listening to the sounds of the house. Within a few minutes the boy was back, as Cassius ascended the stairs with a tray bearing a chilled bottle of hock, glistening and dripping dew, a covered server redolent of tongue, ham and roast chicken, two plates and two glasses. Cassius knocked on the door and was admitted. Margaret blushed even further when she saw the tray and its contents, and glared at Lewrie in the doorway.

"I shall not discommode you further, Mister Lewrie," she said.

"Take your time, madam. I am quite happy to wait in the hall until you have completed your toilet," he offered to her dignity.

"I wait n' light the lady down, sah?" Cassius asked.

"I shall do that, no bother," Lewrie told him, and the servant gave him a slight nod on his way out. Lewrie stepped out into the dark hall to protect her reputation, at least until the servants had made their way down the stairs. Once they were out of sight, Alan started to reenter the room but was taken by the sight of a dark lady at the end of the hall, clad in a thin gown, making her way surreptitiously from one room to another, and from the stealthy way she handled the doorknobs and avoided creaks, she was most practiced at country-house games. In the shadows he was unseen, and grinned with delight as he saw that the lady bore a striking resemblance to Lady Cantner.

He scratched at his own door, and not hearing any answer, turned the knob and entered. Mrs. Haymer had seated herself in front of a small mirror re-doing her makeup, and still wore her wig and hat.

"I really am going to go, Alan," she said. "I am not a guest in this house. We must end this charade. You have done enough..."

He stepped up behind her and put his hands on her shoulders and began to massage her neck. She relaxed and leaned back against him. He bent down and kissed her shoulders. "Like hell we have."

"No, Alan...do not tempt me further, please."

He raised his hands and lifted her wig off, hat and all. She had cut her hair short for the heat of the tropics, little longer than his. He pulled her to her feet and linked his arms around her from behind, massaging her breasts through her corset and gown.

"I mean to have you in a real bed, so I can look at all of you, so I can get at all of you—"

"No, there isn't time, I must go—"

He hoisted her gown and pressed his aching groin against the pillow-softness of her buttocks, fitting between the mounds.

Take your time, spoon 'em up with kisses and cream and they'll sit on it like it was the crown jewels. Give 'em half a choice an' you can whistle before they'd let you. But tell 'em, and they melt. Some of 'em, anyway...

One hand held a breast, one hand pressed at the base of her belly, twining in the mossy growth still damp with their passion. It was a matter of moments to have her out of her gown, to shuck his own rags, to peel her stockings off, unlace her corset and tumble into bed on top of her. As though mesmerized, she allowed herself to be opened, to be molded and kissed and stroked into panting ruin once more, and then again, and again...

The candles guttered down in puddles of tallow before he allowed her to insist, and win, that she must depart. By his watch it was nearly three in the morning, and the house was dead quiet as he lit her down the stairs with a stub of a candle. She pressed a note with her address into his hand, told him that the only servant had the day off on Thursdays, which was soon, that he must not even consider ever seeing her again, and that there was a garden gate entrance to her lodgings on a quiet side street, but that he must desist in his passion before her husband shot him dead. She slunk into her coach, practically the last one still on the grounds, and plodded away at a pace that would not draw undue attention as birds began to twitter in the trees.

"Now maybe I can eat that bird," Lewrie said aloud.

He found another candle by a cardtable as his own guttered out, then tread softly back up the stairs in his stockinged feet. Once in his room he slid out of his clothes and went to the tray. The wine was enough for a full bumper and still cool. And the cold meat and crusty bread went down pleasantly. He was sitting at the small table stark naked and chewing lustily when he heard a tiny noise in the hall. It brought a grin. Somebody sneaking back to their lawful blanket, I'll warrant . . .

A shadow stopped outside his door. A moment later a folded note was pushed with some force under the gap of the door, sliding three or four feet into the room across the polished boards.

"She's surely not come back for more," he thought, rising to pick it up and read it. He almost spilled his wine when he realized what he held. Evidently Mrs. Hillwood, the faded blonde lady, had not been pleased by his choice of Mrs. Haymer. If she herself had slipped the note under the door, then she had stayed as someone's guest for the night—he hoped it was Tad Purnell. But she was inviting him to attend her if the Navy did not require him.

Damme, I love the Navy, he thought happily. Where else can I get into so much mischief so quickly?

"I trust you both enjoyed Sir Richard's dinner party," Kenyon said as they rode back through town in the coach.

It was much too early for Alan. He had barely gotten to sleep when a servant had arrived with hot coffee and sweetened rolls and practically pushed him into his clothing. He had scarcely had time to shave, not that that was yet a daily necessity.

"Oh, aye, sir," he said, worn down to a nubbin. He could not have felt much worse if he had emptied the punchbowl down his own gullet and retired a puking corpse.

Purnell, on the other hand, glowed in silence with a mystified expression, all youthful innocence. Evidently he had had a restful sleep after his introduction to the Alpha and Omega of pleasure. But his beatific pose was betrayed by the lace-trimmed handkerchief that peeked from a waistcoat pocket. As soon as they had gotten into the coach, Purnell had grinned so hugely that Lewrie was sure that Mrs.

Hillwood had been most generous with her favors. Now, Alan's main concern was if he wished to avail himself of those same favors, and just how he would go about it if he did.

The somber heat and stillness of the day before had gone with the approach of clouds from the east, and a cooling wind blew dead foul for Antigua, perhaps delaying their sailing. It was only Wednesday, and their distinguished passengers would not board until evening, with a dawn departure planned on the land breeze Thursday, but if the Trades did not back to the sou'east it would be a hard beat just to clear Morant Point, clawing off a lee shore. They would not risk their passengers to that, surely.

"I don't think we're going to get a fair wind by morning," Lt. Kenyon said, surveying the harbor and the wind indicators.

"Too much easterly for a storm, isn't it, sir?" Lewrie said. "And too late in the year for a hurricane, I'd have thought."

"Perhaps, oh nautical one." Kenyon laughed. "I shall send Mister Purnell to the flag with a message concerning this wind shift. I doubt if they wish to hazard our lord and lady. We may be delayed."

"Oh, good," Alan said without thinking.

"Have you some ulterior motive for wishing to stay in Kingston, Mister Lewrie?"

"Well, there are my pay-certificates, sir. Now I have them, I...have wanted a sextant, like Mister Ellison had in *Ariadne*. They are more accurate than a quadrant, and if we have to thread up the Bahamas again I would feel more secure in my reckoning. I hear they are fifteen guineas but I may find one for less with something to pledge for credit."

Kenyon only stared at him, and Lewrie dropped back in his seat, suddenly intent on the view.

But their departure *was* delayed; the flag did not wish to send a lord to his death on a lee shore, nor did the local admiral desire to have his career end suddenly by losing an important government official. The Cantners would not board *Parrot* until Thursday evening for a Friday departure. The mail was not a priority, nor were any orders they carried of an urgent nature that would allow no delay of transmission.

Lewrie went below to change into fresh clothing after sweating up what he had worn at dinner and sport. He also had the wardroom servant haul up a bucket of salt water so that he could sponge himself somewhat clean in the privacy of his tiny cabin.

"Mister Lewrie," Kenyon called from the hatch to his cabins. "I believe you have some shopping to do?"

"Aye, sir," he said, halfway into a clean shirt.

"So do I, and Mister Claghorne does not begrudge remaining in charge for a while longer. At the end of the day watch I will allow you to go ashore with me. We'll leave Mister Purnell here to pursue his own endeavors."

"Aye aye, sir!"

Lewrie scribbled a quick note and passed it to a passing bumboat with a shilling for delivery and the return of an answer, taking care that no one noticed.

Within two hours, a message was returned to him. Mrs. Hillwood would be at home for tea, and would be delighted to have him join her.

"Alan," Purnell said, once they were aft by the taffrail deep in the flag lockers for inventory. "It was wonderful!"

"I thought you did, you little rogue! How does it feel to be a buck of the first head?"

"Great, she gave me her handkerchief. It still has her perfume..."

"Next time you're back in Kingston you'll have a place to go," Alan told him, cringing a bit that he was soon to be coupled with the same woman. "How was she?"

"Well, she was very slim, as you might have noticed. Not bad, though. I thought she was going to eat me alive for a time there..."

"How grand for you," Alan said, smiling at the news that Mrs. Hillwood enjoyed devouring midshipmen.

He was aching with anticipation by the time he and Lt. Kenyon were dropped off at the boat landing a little after

4:00 P.M. as the town began to awaken from the hottest part of the day, and cooling shadows lengthened.

"I shall sup at the Grapes, yonder," Kenyon said, pointing to a modest and homely Georgian style inn. "I wish you back here before midnight. May I trust you, Mister Lewrie?"

"Aye, sir," Lewrie said, wondering if Kenyon thought he was going to take leg-bail from the Navy.

"Then leave the lady's address with the doorkeeper at the inn, should I need you before then," Kenyon said, making Lewrie gape at Kenyon's powers of observation.

"How did you know it was a lady, sir?"

"That is for masters and commanders to know, and for rutting midshipmen to discover later in their careers. Now off with you, and if you truly do find a sextant for less than fifteen guineas let me know if they have another."

"Aye, sir." Lewrie was continually amazed by Kenyon and his attitude toward him. It was much more lenient than he had come to expect from a sea officer toward a lowly midshipman of so little practical experience. He thought that Kenyon truly liked him, and he knew that he had made great progress in gaining nautical skills as a result of it, but the exact reasons why it was so nagged at him. Who else would be a co-conspirator in his designs on a lonely grass widow? It was almost beyond credence, and there were times that Alan felt that there was a debt building up which might someday have to be repaid.

He found Mrs. Hillwood's building, a great walled enclosure with a central court and front double iron gate that opened off a quiet side street. On the alleys there were discreet servants' entrances. Normally, he would be scratching at one of those, but this afternoon he was an openly invited guest, so he entered the court and was faced with several apartments. Mrs. Hillwood's number was on the second floor overlooking the court and its garden and fish pool.

The door was opened by a black maidservant, and he heard the tinny tinkling of a harpsichord and the murmur of several voices. At once his expectant erection became a distinct embarrassment as he realized it was truly a tea, with other guests, and not the sly invitation to strum the damned woman he had thought it was.

"Ah, our other guest," Mrs. Hillwood said, rising to greet him. "This is Midshipman Alan Lewrie, from *Parrot*, the despatch boat. Mister Lewrie, allow me to introduce you to the Reverend Robinson."

"Your servant, sir," Alan said, adjusting roles and making a graceful leg to the man, a young, chubby, and obviously poor, sort of curate.

He met the reverend's wife, a blubber-booby who had difficulty even bowing from a seated position, a planter and his wife, and an army officer from the local regiment with a young woman of his acquaintance.

The tea's good, anyway, Alan thought sourly, sipping from his cup and gathering a small plate of baked trifles to pass the time. It was an agonizing hour and a half of small talk of privateers, prices in the Indies, prospects for crushing the rebellion in America, facing up to the French and the Dagoes, the state of the church, the latest poems, and a screed against those damned Wesleys and Methodism.

Lewrie got to put his oar in about life in the Navy and hoped he was amusing about some of his first experiences, but he could not hope to match broadsides with the Reverend Mr. Robinson or an opinionated young army major who was barely two years older than himself and sure that he was the last word on military affairs.

Only reason he's a major is that he could buy a subaltern's commission, and then buy his way up as people chucked it, Lewrie told himself. And he wasn't too sure that he really didn't know more about small arms and musketry, and most especially artillery, than the young man in the red coat with the scarlet sash and gorget and epaulet.

Mrs. Hillwood finally began to break up the tea party as the others began to stir in mutual boredom. The major gossip had been delivered, their bladders were full and it was getting on for sundown. Lewrie sighed and looked for his hat while Mrs. Hillwood gushed over the reverend and his chick-a-biddy wife at the door.

"Yo hat, sah," the maid servant said softly. Lewrie had not had many island women, most of them were sure to be poxed if they dwelled anywhere near a harbor, but this one was tempting. She tapped the brim of his hat, forcing him to look down. There was a folded note in the inside of the crown. Aha. Now we're getting somewhere. Must be from Mrs. Hillwood. I doubt if the servant can write.

Furtively, he stood to one side, adjusting his neckcloth in a mirror with his hat resting on the small table below it, and opened it to read without the others seeing. He was gratified to see that it was short and to the point: "Return in a quarter hour." Alan made his good-bys publicly with the others and set off at a brisk pace to town.

When he was readmitted to the apartments the second time after a short detour to allay suspicion, the maidservant was now dressed in a hat and lace shawl. She let him in, then slipped out the door herself, leaving him alone in the front parlor. There was no sign of Mrs. Hillwood but there was now a serving tray on the tea table that held several bottles. Alan helped himself to some claret.

"Mister Lewrie," Mrs. Hillwood said sweetly, entering the room from the back rooms. She had changed her more formal sack dress for a loose morning gown and now sported her own hair instead of a floured wig. She walked up to him and gave him a light kiss on the cheek, as one would greet an old friend, before breezing out of his hungry reach to cross to the array of bottles.

He was amazed to see her pour herself a healthy measure of Blue Ruin. "After the tedium of such guests I have need of gin, Mister Lewrie. I am very happy that you could accept my invitation to return."

"I would not have missed it, I assure you, Mrs. Hillwood."

"Come sit with me," she said, alighting gracefully on a sofa and patting the brocaded fabric next to her. He obeyed. "Those people say the same things time after time but it is my duty as a woman of some consequence here in the island to allow them to pay their respects. Though they cost me my time and my patience."

"At sea we have no choice of our messmates, either," Alan said, sipping at his wine. "They can become... predictable."

"And you dislike tedium, do you not, Mister Lewrie? As I?"

"I like adventure," he said, turning in his seat to her.

"A direct young man, how delightful!" Mrs. Hillwood said, waving her empty glass at him in silent request for a refill. She had the look in her eyes of a predator, and Alan noticed that her nose was long and hawklike, the only mar of her still considerable beauty, though she must have at least been in her mid-to-late forties.

He took her glass and went to the table to pour her another dose of gin, and to top up his claret as well.

"Your captain allows you ashore for how long, Mister Lewrie?" she asked, tucking her legs up on the sofa and leaning over one arm.

"If the wind does not shift suddenly I have til midnight," he said, carrying her drink back to her.

"How generous he is," she said, "and such a good friend of Sir Richard Slade?"

"So he told me, ma'am, though I don't know the connection." He handed her the glass. There was now no place to sit next to her so he stood easy, one hand behind his back like a deck officer and the other at high port with the glass. She seemed amused.

"So you like adventure," she said after a healthy slug of her gin. "Were you adventurous last night?"

"A gentleman never tells," Lewrie said with a tight grin, and took a sip of his own drink.

"Nonsense, gentleman always tell. Why else do they linger so long over the port while we poor women have to retire to cards and coffee and talk of tatting lace?"

"You sound like someone who enjoys adventure yourself, ma'am."

"Oh, I do. And I was, I confess, disappointed that you

found that tawdry little dumpling more preferable. Your friend was amusing, even so, for all his clumsiness."

"It was his debut, ma'am. But I trust that your kindness and generosity treated him well," Lewrie said, feeling somewhat out of his depth. He had never run into a woman of her wealth and position that wasn't a little sniveller and simperer, always swearing that they had never done anything like that before and that he was the ravisher that broke down their resistance. Yet here was a woman ready to admit to desires of the flesh as strong as his, and from Tad's description of his night with her, she would be as aggressive as he.

"He was smiling peacefully when I left him," she said, finishing her drink and waving for him to serve once more.

"That's good," he said, going back to the table for more gin. "Poor Tad smiles so seldom."

"And poor Mister Lewrie?"

"I am always seeking amusements to lighten the soul, ma'am."

He stood close with her drink, but instead of reaching to take it from him, she put out a hand to his crotch and ran light fingers over his evident excitement through the cloth of his breeches.

"Never send a boy to do a man's job," she said. "You look so stifled in the uniform of yours. Take it off and be comfortable." As he struggled out of his coat and waistcoat she undid his breeches, and as his neck cloth and shirt went flying across the room, she bent down and kissed his manhood.

"So strong, so upright. And you taste of ocean salt."

"Oh God," he said, throwing his head back to look at the ceiling as she clasped his buttocks and drew him into her.

"Bring our drinks," she ordered, breaking off and swaying off to the back rooms while he tried to shed his shoes and breeches and follow.

Mrs. Betty Hillwood was, as they said, a man-killer. She sobbed and she groaned deep in her throat, flinging her head back and forth and gasping, riding him rantipole with her hands clawed into his shoulders, and when she hit the melting moments she sounded like someone being flogged at each warm stroke. She was incredibly slim with much smaller breasts than Alan preferred, but her nipples and aureoles were large and dark. Her hipbones dug into him harshly, but her flesh was incredibly fine and soft over her thin frame. The down of her legs was maddening as she stroked his buttocks with her legs and clasped him tight to her, and she loved to have his fingers twine in the sopping wet hair of her underarms as she gripped the headboard and thrust back at him stroke for stroke.

They broke for more drink, for a cold supper that they ate in bed, still tangled in the linen. They stood in a large tub of cool water that had been standing all day and sponged themselves, then went to the edge of her high bed and made love seated. Followed by more to drink.

Frankly, Betty Hillwood could put gin away like a grenadier, and it only made her more passionate, more animal in her actions, and in her desires, which already seemed insatiable.

She complained about her dried up stick of a husband, who liked island boys out at the plantations more than her, of how hard it was to find suitable satisfaction for her own desires in so proscribed a society as the islands, where there were so few true aristocrats who had a freer code of conduct than the squirearchy that made up most of the traders and planters of her own association.

She then took on another load of Blue Ruin and proceeded to make up for lost opportunities on Alan, who was wearing out. Once he was spent, she dandled him and kissed him into performing once more, just once more...

"Don't flag on me, Alan dear," she pleaded, half-drunk now and her hair hanging slattern-loose about her face. "I need a real man to spit me and split me, oh God, I need your hard prick deep inside me so hard and strong."

He lay on his back on the piled up pillows, almost hoping that it was time to leave. She lay between his outflung legs, idly trying to get his interest up once more, clutching his member with one hand and her eternal glass of gin in the other. She now reminded him of a one-shilling whore, eyes red and rheumy with drink, face flushed and mottled, and the marks of age more prominent. He snuck a look at his watch—God, only nine-thirty...

"I'm hungry, Betty love. Let me go to the jakes and have some food," he said softly. As long as she's got hold of my prick, damme if I want to get her mad.

"Then will you love me?"

"Absolutely," he said. "But even cannon have to reload."

He rolled out of the bed and went to the necessary closet, then came back and wrapped a sheet about him. He picked through the supper dishes to find some cold beef, cheese and bread. He fed her dainty bites while he wolfed most of it down. She stood up and walked nude to the nearest bottle of gin, which was empty.

"Oh, damn," she said, flinging it into a corner. With a noticeable list, she tacked her way out of the bedroom, made some alarming clinking noises in the parlor and returned with a fresh bottle.

"I must tell you, Alan my sweetling, that you are the most impressive man I have played balum rancum with in ages," she slurred as she crawled up his body to lay her head on his chest.

"And you, Betty, are a tigress," he said, which seemed to please her. "Also, your husband is a fool."

"Aye, he's that and more." She laughed, spilling gin on his ribs, which felt cool. She licked at his side and he squirmed. "Ticklish, my chuck?"

"Felt good."

"Then I must do more of it," she said, tipping her glass and making a small pool of gin in his belly button, which she proceeded to lap like a tabby, running her tongue all over his stomach and chest.

"Yes, my husband is a fool, and a backgammon player, always looking for a new black boy to play with. If I'd known that I'd have never married him and moved to this disgusting island," she said between applications. "Were it

215

possible to divorce him I would and go back to London where I belong, where the right sort of people don't begrudge a woman her needs. There're so many of them, you know."

"I know," Lewrie sighed as she treated his nipples with gin and tender care.

"So many Mollys out there," she muttered.

"My half brother. Disgusting little shit."

"But not you, sweetling," she smiled, reaching down to dandle his penis, which was showing signs of life. "You know, at first I thought you might be, being houseguests of Sir Richard's..."

"Me? Keep doing that and I warrant I'll show you... again...that I'm not..."

"Sir Richard tries to be discreet but he's most infamous for it," she said, sliding down toward his groin and parting the sheet.

"Are you sure?" he asked, sitting up. "I mean, I wondered about him. Such a coxcomb."

"Of course, I'm sure. And I'd watch out for my captain, too, were I you, dearest Alan. Shall I tell you a secret?"

"Yes."

"Last night, on my way upstairs with your eager little friend...God, I felt like a matron leading her youngest son ...I saw Sir Richard and your captain."

"Upstairs?"

"Entering a room together. It was quite late. Isn't that just delicious?"

"Good God, woman, it can't be! He's a real taut hand, a real sailor man. There's nothing Molly about him—"

"Remember, there's an Article of War against it," she said. "Now let me improve your taste a little."

Betty proceeded to dribble gin over his member, which stung after all the exertions he had demanded of it over the last two days. Then before he could complain, she slipped her warm mouth down over it, her tongue sliding and flicking. Without conscious will, he became erect deep between her lips as she raised and lowered her head over him, making him as rigid as a marlinspike, as tumescent as a belaying pin.

He gripped her head between his hands and lay back on the pillows, half his mind on what she had implied about Lt. Kenyon. Never mind, he decided, giving himself over to the intense pleasure she was giving him. I'll think about that some other time. Even Drake had time for a game of bowls, didn't he?

ALAN let himself out into a dark and nearly empty street at eleven that night. Betty Hillwood had demanded, and he had risen to the call of duty, until she had cuddled up to him, reeking of gin and her sweat and the aroma of their lovemaking. He had sponged off, gotten dressed properly and had tucked her in for the night. He had also left a note in her hand that expressed his joy at their coupling and a promise that next time he was in Kingston he would be sure to spend three days sunk deep into every part of her. After her conversation of the evening he was sure that she would be aroused and titilated at his choice of language. The woman has a Billingsgate streak to her, he assured himself happily. She may play the great lady but she's a damned great cracking tuppenny tart with a mouth like a fishwife.

He strolled loose-hipped down the hill to the Grapes, feeling peckish once more, and in need of sustenance and a pot of coffee if he was to pass Kenyon's sharp eye. Most of the stores were closed, but he found a small chandlery open at that late hour and their light drew him in. They had a used copy of a Smollett novel, *Peregrine Pickle*, and he remembered that it was a good long read so he parted with three shillings for it. They did not have sextants, and if they did they were twenty-five guineas—"They's a war on, sor, an' everythin's short, they is"—so he loafed his way into the Grapes and took a table by the window overlooking the boat landing.

"Yer servant, sir, this fine evenin'," the publican said.

"Still got your ordinary?"

"All gone, sor, but if yer partial to pork I can still slice ya some. Got some nice figgy-dowdy fer yer sweet tooth, too," the moonfaced man said, wiping his hands on his blue apron.

"That and bread, and coffee."

"Right-ho," the man replied smartly, fetching a candle from a vacant table so he could see better. The Grapes was half-empty, the crowd made up of naval officers for the most part, none too senior to put a damper on things. The few civilians seemed there on sufferance.

Alan got his coffee and began to sip at it, enjoying it black and rolling the bitterness about his mouth to kill the odor of all the claret he had downed. He was about to crack his book in the ample glow of the candle when he heard a coach rattling up outside. He glanced out the window with idle curiosity. The coach looked familiar, as did the mulatto man in livery who got down from the boot.

The coach occluded the lamps at the boat landing and threw a deep shadow toward the inn, but the torches by the door of the Grapes relieved that opaqueness enough for him to see that it was Sir Richard Slade's coach and that the coachee and the footman were the same ones who had driven them out to the house party. He twisted in his chair the better to see, and to lean back against the homey brick wall above the wainscoting so that he himself would not be seen framed in the window.

There were people in the coach, two hats and a flash of some sheened material; one hat was trimmed with feathers and white lace.

The other showed only a gold loop and the flash of a button. Very like a naval officer's cockade. Very like a lieutenant's plain black cocked hat, with only a dog's vane of ribbon held in place by the gold loop of braid and a fouled gilt anchor button.

The hats leaned close together and stayed that way for a long moment, then the mulatto opened the coach door and flipped down the steps. One passenger prepared to depart, but before he did so he leaned back in and Alan could clearly see two men pressing their lips together, not in the fond farewell kiss that childhood friends might bestow upon each other at parting but in the writhing, practiced kiss of two men who were both of the same inclination. Was it his imagination, or had he given Betty Hillwood such a fond farewell just minutes before, with the same sweet-sad spark of remembered passion? He felt sick at his stomach.

"Pray God, it's someone else," he whispered, clenching his fists hard and ignoring the arrival of his cold supper.

"Holy shit on a biscuit," he said bitterly. The man in the coach was the effeminate Sir Richard Slade, down to the very suit. The man departing the coach was Lt. James Kenyon, master and commander of HMS *Parrot*!

"If yer not wantin' anythin' else right away, sor, that'll be two shillin's," the publican repeated.

"Yes," Lewrie said, fumbling out coins blindly. "Here."

"Righty-ho, then."

Lewrie spun away from the window and propped the book up with fumbling hands in front of him. He took a scalding sip of coffee, and wiped his eyes with the back of his hand. He dug into his cold pork and pease pudding, as though he had been at for some time, though each bite threatened to gag him on the way down, and sat queasy as a lump of coal once in his stomach.

Kenyon entered the inn's public rooms a moment later, sharing a cheery greeting with the other officers of his rank at the other tables. He spotted Lewrie by the window and came over to join him.

"And what are you having, Mister Lewrie?" he asked jovially.

"Spot of cold supper ... sir."

"And a whacking thick book," Kenyon said, picking it up to read the title. "*Peregrine Pickle*, is it? Just the thing for you, a roguish adventure, and long as a Welsh mile. Mind if I join you?"

"Not at all, sir," Alan replied, taking back the book and marking his place at random, as though he had read part of it.

"No sextant, I see?"

"Twenty-five guineas. If they had one, sir."

"Will you be havin' anythin', sor?" the publican asked.

"Brandy for me," Kenyon said briskly, "and a pint of stingo to wash it down...Other than that, did you enjoy your time ashore?" Kenyon asked casually, flinging a leg over the arm of his chair.

"A cat-lapping party with a lady I made acquaintance of at Sir Richard's, sir," Lewrie said, forced to smile at the unintended double-entendre of a tea party and what Mrs. Hillwood had done with her gin and her tongue. "Devilish boring, though. Went all over town looking in the stores, then paid down some socket money for an obliging wench."

He stared at Kenyon directly, not as adoring midshipman to older brother or superior officer, as if daring him with an account of some *manly* endeavor.

"No, I think Smollett has no lessons to teach you, Mister Lewrie." But it was a bit more forced than before.

"And you, sir?" Lewrie asked, getting intent on his meal.

"A gentleman never tells, me lad," Kenyon said as his brandy and strong beer arrived, and he took time to wet his tongue. "Frankly, there's a willing enough tit I have been seeing. Just got back from seeing her home. Parents are chaw-bacons made it rich out here and she'd be a good enough rattle, but she's such a country-put, and her family is so eager for a good match they're hotter than a false justice with suggestions of marriage."

"I didn't think marriage and the Navy went well together, sir," Lewrie said. "What with the long separations, and all."

"You're right there," Kenyon said, still not tumbling to the fact that Lewrie knew more than he should. "Why tie yourself down to a termagant little mort when you can have a wife in every port for half the cost, eh?"

"Or just take it to sea with you," Lewrie said, knowing that many ships allowed women aboard all the time, and that there were many captains who traveled with their wives or mistresses.

"Now that's something I don't hold with, women at sea,"

Kenyon said firmly, thumping down his pint of stingo to exchange it for the glass of brandy. "And there's many a captain I've known that will tell you that it's bad for morale and discipline."

I'll bet you have, Lewrie thought. Here was the man he wished to emulate, the only officer who had been in any way kind to him since he had been forced into the Navy, acting bluff and hearty as the biggest rogering buck, and secretly a sodomite! Was that why he asked for me to join *Parrot*, because he thought he'd have a go at my backside someday? By God, if he ever lays a finger on me I'll kill him! Just being around him makes me sick...

That did not stop him, however, from eating every bite of his rich, sweet figgy-dowdy, knowing there would be nothing like that once they had sailed.

CHAPTER

9

FRIDAY noon found *Parrot* due south of Morant Point, beating her way offshore for Antigua. The wind had backed to the sou'east, and with her jibs and gaff sails laid close to the centerline, she clawed for every yard to windward, bowling along with her lee rail slanted close to the bright blue sea, and leaving a creaming wake bone white behind her.

Their passengers were no trouble. Lord Cantner was a minikin of a man, not above five feet tall, but obviously much taller when he sat on his purse. His wife, Lady Cantner, was indeed the raven beauty Alan had seen sneaking down the dark hallway at Sir Richard Slade's, and she recognized him as well, and blushed prettily when introduced. She was not quite thirty, while Cantner was a stringy sort pushing sixty, and a colt's tooth for marrying such a younger woman who had such a roving eye. Lewrie was irked that the manservant had his berth space, and was reduced to swaying in a hammock over the wardroom table again. But so far, they had been no bother.

For all the first day, *Parrot* labored hard to make her easting without losing ground to leeward, but she was putting up a steady eleven knots, and sometimes striking twelve, and it was such a joy to be on deck in the mild winter sunshine with the wind howling and the rigging humming and crying and spray and foam flying about her like dust from a thundering coach that Lewrie could find solace from his disappointment in Lt. Kenyon. Still, he found it hard to be properly civil to him, so he reduced himself to duty and did not seek out the sort of friendly chats they had enjoyed before.

By the second day the wind had veered more east, and they turned and tacked so they would not be set upon Hispaniola, angling more to the sou'sou'east half east, which would bring them below Antigua but in position for another tack direct for English Harbor, and the waiting winter convoy for England.

It was on the second day that the acting quartermaster went down sick, complaining of severe headaches, and Boggs was at a loss as to the cause. The man quickly got worse, pouring sweat, retching and vomiting, and running a high fever. Boggs began to look worried when the man cried that he was blind and raved in the fever's delirium.

Bright, the gunner's mate was the next man to be struck down. He stumbled to the deck in the middle of gun drill, almost insensible. Next was one of the carpenter's crew, then a ship's corporal. After him, it was an older topman, and then the forecastle captain. The acting quartermaster had meanwhile turned the color of a quince pudding, and began to bring up black bile.

"It's the Yellow Jack," Boggs told them shakily.

There was no more horrifying name that could have been uttered in the tropics, other than Plague. Yellow Jack was the scourge of the West Indies, and all those scrubby coasts of the Spanish Main and up into the Floridas. Whole regiments could go down sick in a week, and the survivors would not make a corporal's guard. The most complex objects of the age, the huge and powerful 1st and 2nd rate line of battle ships, could be turned to dead piles of timber and iron as their crews died by the boatload.

"What can we do?" Leonard asked, plainly scared to death.

"There's bad air aboard," Boggs told them. "Some feverish vapor trapped below. Tropic land gives off sickening ethers at night as it cools, you've seen the mists. Ventilate immediately. We must pump our bilges, flush 'em clean, and scour with vinegar belowdecks."

They rigged wind scoops. They pumped the sea below through the washdeck pumps until the chain pumps brought nothing from the bilges but bright sea water. They scoured every surface with vinegar. The acting quartermaster died. Gunner's mate Bright died. Two gunners came down with the fever, moaning and shivering. One of the little West Indian ship's boys went sick, as did Lord Cantner's manservant.

"We must smoke the ship to drive the bad air out," Boggs prescribed, and they took plug and leaf tobacco and burned it in tubs, waving smouldering faggots of the stuff in every compartment and nook and cranny, like shamans ministering to an aboriginal sufferer. But the old topman, the forecastle captain, and the ship's boy, died, and had to be interred to the mercy of the ocean, and one could feel the jittery tension in the air like a palpable force.

By evening Docken the warrant gunner had fallen ill, as had five more hands and the cook's native assistant.

"We must keep all the sick on deck in fresh air in a patch of shade, and give them all the water and small beer they can drink," Boggs said. "Cut down the grog ration, and stop issuing acid fruits that bring on biliousness. Thin soups and gruels instead of fresh or salt meat."

The two gunners died. Lord Cantner's manservant died. During the night, six more hands began to stagger and sweat, complaining of raging, blinding headaches. Those already stricken turned shocking yellow and began to throw up a black bile.

Vomito Negro, the Spaniards called it: Yellow Jack.

Boggs and Leonard made a project of inspecting the galley and rations on the chance the native cook's dirty habits might be to blame, but could find nothing they could fault in cleanliness.

By dawn Lady Cantner's maid dropped in a swoon and cried in terror as she realized she was afflicted. Everyone began to walk the decks cutty-eyed, wary of being too close to another person, and one could smell a miasma of sweaty fear amid the odors of the sickness.

They threw the island animals overboard on the suspicion that they might have carried the fever aboard, along with their coops and pens, and the manger was hosed out and scrubbed with vinegar or wine.

The wind veered dead foul, forcing them to face a long board to the suth'rd, which would take them closer to the French island of Martinique. Regretfully they had to tack and stand nor'east as close to the wind as possible for Anguilla, the nearest British settlement.

Boggs was by now half-drunk most of the time in sheer panic at the thought of dying and his inability to do any good for anyone. He made up bags of assafoetida for everyone to wear, and the crew eagerly seized their bags of "Devil's Dung" like a talisman.

Docken died. The acting bosun died, along with three more men. Two of the youngest victims seemed to recover, though they were weak as kittens and all their hair had fallen out, so there was some hope.

"We are seven days from Anguilla," Kenyon told them aft on the tiny poop by the taffrail. "Lewrie, I shall have the starboard guns run out and the larboard guns hauled back to the centerline to ease her heel. It will make her faster through the water."

"Aye aye, sir."

"Mister Claghorne, we must drive this ship like Jehu for the nearest port. Nevis or St. Kitts, if Anguilla will not serve. It is our only hope that we reach a friendly port with medical facilities greater than our own." Kenyon seemed foursquare and dependable amid all the suppressed hysteria, but Lewrie could see the tension around his eyes, the desperate glance as he realized just how powerless any man was in the face of the unknown—Yellow Jack.

ON the third day in late afternoon they spied a merchant ship. They hoisted their colors and recognition signal. When she was close enough to hail they discovered she was a packet brig, the *Black Friars,* bound for Kingston.

"Have you a doctor on board?" Kenyon yelled across the surging water that separated them.

"Yes. Have you no surgeon?" the master called back.

"We have many sick aboard."

"What is it?" the man asked warily.

"We have fever," Kenyon had to admit.

"I cannot help you," the master said as *Black Friars* sped out of reach on an opposite course.

"Goddamn you," Kenyon shouted. "Bring to or I shall fire into you!"

Lewrie sprang to one of the after swivels and hastily loaded it. He placed a pound ball right in her transom, but *Black Friars* did not stop for them, but began to loose t'gallants for more speed. Lt. Kenyon looked ready to weep as he watched a possible salvation tearing down to leeward but he could do nothing. No one would turn a hand for them for fear of the Yellow Jack...

Leonard went down sick. Boggs decocted a foul-tasting brew of quinine bark and forced the hands to drink it, but no one had faith in his cures. The maidservant died at sundown.

It made no sense. Kenyon, Mooney, Claghorne and Lewrie and Purnell discussed it aft, avoiding Boggs, who by then could not raise a cup to his own lips, much less offer help to the sick.

Men had sickened who had not gone ashore into the tropical miasma. They should have been safe. Men who had spent the night ashore did not get sick, but members of the gig's crew who had only been to the boat landing in broad daylight had sickened and died. All ate the same rations, drank the same grog and Black Strap and small beer, breathed the same air ashore, on deck at anchor or below decks.

Had it been the whores? Mooney wondered, something you could get from native women? Yet hardly any of the West Indians in the crew had gotten it, and only one of them had died of it. They were on the mend, or immune somehow. When questioned, most admitted to having the *Vomito Negro* when they were very young, and surviving.

"The salt rations?" Lewrie said, wondering out loud. "Sir, we were ashore and we ate fresh food and drank clean drink. We have not been stricken with it. But the crew on salt rations and biscuit for the most part have."

"Then how do you explain the maid, or the manservant?" Kenyon asked.

"He was much older, and a woman's constitution is not a man's, sir," Lewrie said, making rationalizations for his own funk... I don't have to die, he told himself grimly, aware of the sour reek of fear on his body and in his clothes. Some of the hands are getting better, the younger ones, mostly. It's the old and the weak that are dying. Oh God, why not in battle, but not like this. I swear to you I'll offer you anything you want, but don't let me die...

Purnell's breathing made him turn his head. Tad was all covered in sweat, his neckcloth and shirt already soaked with it, and his hands on the tabletop trembled like a fresh-killed cock.

"I am all right," Purnell rasped. "Really, I am..."

"Oh God... take Mister Purnell to the surgeon," Kenyon ordered.

Around midnight Leonard, the captain's clerk, died. When they held his burial at dawn after quarters one could hear the hands weeping and snuffling, but it was not any affection for their departed acting purser; it was pity for themselves in the face of the Yellow Jack.

Lewrie was on deck in full uniform to enforce orders, also armed with a pair of pistols and his dirk. The crew was trembling on the edge of panic, and if the officers lost control the men would run wild, get to the rum and spirits and destroy any chance they might have had to work their way into a friendly port.

Lord and Lady Cantner stood nearby, holding their small bags of Devil's Dung to their noses to allay the stench. Lewrie went to them.

"This wind is holding, milord. Six more days should see us fair into Anguilla," he said, doffing his hat.

"Pray God it does," Lady Cantner said.

"You can still work the ship?" the lord asked, working his sour little mouth as though eating a lime. "Your captain does nothing to assure me. And that mate is so inarticulate he seems half-witted. Pagh, I hate the smell of this..."

"Perhaps one of milady's scented sachets would serve as well, milord. The assafoetida seems to have had little affect."

"Gladly," Lord Cantner said, throwing the foul-smelling bag over the side. "There's not much to choose between that stuff and the odors from the sick men up forward. Stap me, what a foul stench it is. I'd rather sniff a corpse's arse."

You can take your pick of assholes up forward, Lewrie thought.

"Your surgeon is a fool."

"Only a surgeon's mate, milord. An apothecary, mostly. But I doubt if a surgeon's skill at cutting would avail us."

"No one will tell us anything, and who the hell are you? Your name escapes me."

"Midshipman Alan Lewrie, milord."

"You look like you might know something. How long you been wearing the King's coat?"

"One year, milord."

"God's teeth," and Lord Cantner turned away in misery.

"It is not his fault, my dear," Lady Cantner said. "Is there anything I could do to help, Mister Lewrie, perhaps help tend to the sick, or read to them?"

"Delia!" Lord Cantner was shocked at her suggestion.

Tending the sick was for the worst sort, those so already degraded that the odors and sights of sick and injured people could have no further influence. It was a job for abbatoir workers, not titled ladies . . .

"I doubt if anyone could appreciate a good book just now, milady," Alan said gently, sharing an astounded glance with Lord Cantner that his lady would even consider such a thing. "The loblolly men shall suffice for the hands. Though I wonder—"

"Yes?"

"The other midshipman, Mister Purnell, was taken ill last night."

"And he is your friend," she said, full of pity.

"Aye, milady, he is."

The thought of Tad lying helpless and puking scared him silly, and Tad Purnell lying sick could have been him so easily, still might be . . .

"I shall go to him at once," Lady Cantner said, "if you would approve, my dear."

"A gentleman, is he?"

"Aye, milord. Of a good trading family from Bristol."

"I suppose." Lord Canter relented sourly.

"Mister Lewrie?" Claghorne called from further forward.

"Excuse me, milord . . . milady."

Claghorne stood by the quartermaster at the tiller head, his hands behind his back and his feet planted firmly on the tilting deck.

"Mister Lewrie, the captain's took sick as hell," he said in a low mutter. "I'll be dependin' on you an' Mister Mooney ta see us through."

"Oh, Christ," Lewrie said, turning cold all over with another shock to his already shattered nerves. "Has Boggs seen to him?"

"Boggs stands more chance o' dyin' o' barrel-fever than Yeller Jack. Drunk as an emperor down below. Keep that quiet. We don't want the people gettin' scared."

"They're not already, sir?"

"Aye, true enough," Claghorne said. "Knew I could count on ya to buck up an' stay solid. Must be the only person not scared out a yer boots by this."

"You misjudge me badly, Mister Claghorne."

"Then keep it up, 'cause so everyone else misjudges ya, too."

"May I suggest, sir, that you inform Lord Cantner of Lt. Kenyon and his distress?"

"I can't talk his break-teeth kinda words," Claghorne said. "You do it. I've a ship ta run and he can go hang before I let him shit on me again. Stuck up squinty-eyed little hop-o'-my-thumb fool!"

"Aye, sir, but he is very influential. A word from him in the right place and the officer who brought him safe into harbor could gain a commission overnight."

"I'm a scaly old fish, Lewrie. Not one o' yer bowin' an' arse-kissin' buggers. I'd be a tarpaulin mate forever before I'd piss down his back, nor anyone else's, fer *favor*."

Lewrie shrugged, knowing that Claghorne was out of his element in the face of a peer and was throwing away a sterling opportunity to gain influence because he lacked the wit and took such a perverse pride in being a tarry, self-made man of his hands, beholden to no one.

I must be healthy, Lewrie assured himself wryly. I can still toady with the best right in the middle of shrieking hysteria . . .

THE wind held steady for hours as they drove nor'east. They were still five days from harbor, if the wind held. Thankfully no one else had gone down ill in the last few hours. Perhaps something they had done had worked against the fever. For all the fear and grief, it had so far been a remarkably fast passage to windward.

"God, give us just a little luck . . ." Alan felt weights slough from his shoulders each time they cast the log. He could get ashore, away from whatever was causing the Yellow Jack.

Tad could get a doctor, and he would get credit for standing as an acting officer.

"Sail ho!" The lookout cried from the mainmast gaff throat. "Four points off the weather bow."

"Aloft with you, Mister Lewrie, an' spy her out," Claghorne ordered. Alan seized a glass and scrambled up into the rigging to hug the mainmast alongside the lookout.

"Brig," Alan said, studying the sail through the telescope.

"Aye, zur," said the lookout. "An' a Frenchy, I thinks, zur."

"French? Why?" Lewrie asked, afraid he was right.

"Jus' looks French ta me, zur. Can't rightly say."

"Keep us informed," Alan said, heading down to report to Claghorne. "A brig, sir, coming north with a soldier's wind. The lookout thinks she's French."

"Goddamn, what would a Frog brig be doing so close to Anguilla or Nevis?"

"Looking for morsels such as us, Mister Claghorne?" Lewrie offered, drawing a withering glare from the master's mate.

"An' goddamn you, too, sir," Claghorne shouted.

"Aye aye, sir." Alan shyed, backing away.

An hour passed. By then the strange sail was hull down over the horizon, both ships doomed to intersect at a point off to the east with no way to avoid meeting. *Parrot* was going as fast as possible but could not get to windward. Neither, in their pitiful condition, could they run. They had already been seen, and any course of evasion would only take them that much farther away from safety and help for their sick after getting so tantalizingly near. And neither, reduced in manpower, could they fight well if the brig was indeed French.

"Goddamn me, she's French, all right," Claghorne said after returning from the lookout perch himself. "Privateer outa Martinique, most like. Maybe not heavy-gunned but loaded with men for prize crews."

"So they'll try to board us, sir," Lewrie said, wondering if their luck could possibly get any worse.

"They might not, if they see we have Yeller Jack aboard. Them Popish breast-beaters is superstitious as hell. We hoist the Quarantine flag, let 'em see our sick, an' they might let us go fer safer pickin's."

"And if they don't?"

Claghorne did not answer him, but walked away to the windward rail and began to pace. As close as they were to death from Yellow Jack, it was preferable to being taken a prize and led off to some prison hulk or dungeon on Martinique. With Kenyon down sick, the burden of running, fighting or striking their colors devolved on him, as if he didn't already have enough to worry about.

"Mister Lewrie," Lady Cantner called from the hatch to the wardroom. "I think you should come..."

Tad was slung in a hammock below the skylight, where there was a chance for some breeze below decks, and Lewrie thought he looked as dead as anyone could that still breathed. He was yellow, the skin stretched taut over his skull, while his eyes were sunk deep in currant-colored circles of exhaustion.

"Tad, how do you keep?" Alan asked softly.

"God, Alan, I am so sick...when I'm gone do write my parents and say I fell in action, will you do that?"

"You'll be fine, you silly hobbledehoy." But Tad's hand was dry as sunbaked timber and hot as a gun barrel, and leaning close to him Alan could smell the corruption of the blood in the bile Purnell had been bringing up.

"I can taste it," Tad was saying. "I can taste death, Alan, I'm going to die—"

"Nonsense," Alan said, realizing he was probably right.

"Thanks for...that night," Tad managed so softly that Alan had to lean ever closer, and it was like bending down over a hot oven. "It was wonderful, not so hard, after all..."

"Just like riding a cockhorse," Alan said, trying to plaster a smile on his face. Tad tried to smile back but began coughing and retching and choking, fighting for breath.

Alan tried to lift him but he was drowning in his own vomit. Tad gripped his hand with all his strength, going rigid, eyes wide open. After a final gasping try for a breath, he went limp, eyes blank and staring at Lewrie.

"Goddamn it," Alan cursed, tears burning his eyes. "Just Goddamn sweet fuck all!"

Lady Cantner came to him and held out her arms, tears on her face, and he sank into her arms gladly. "Damme, he was such a decent little chub. Oh, Goddamn this..."

"He was your friend," she said, stroking his hair, "but his sorrow and pain are ended. God harvests the flowers early, and leaves weeds such as us to suffer and try to understand."

That's a hellish sort of comfort, he thought miserably. "Half a dozen worse people could have died except him. God, what a terrible thing this is! Tad, half the crew sick or dead, Lt. Kenyon like to be on his own deathbed, maybe a French privateer ready to take us. What next, for Christ's sake? God, I'm so scared..."

"There, there," Lady Cantner continued to comfort.

God stap me, but she has a great set of poonts, Alan thought inanely, appreciating the tender and yielding surfaces against which his face was now pressed as she gentled him.

"You must have faith, Mister Lewrie," Lord Cantner said from the door to the after cabin, just a second before Alan decided that dying would not be so bad, if he could grab hold of Lady Cantner's bouncers for a second. "I'm sure the other officers shall see us through."

"Aye, milord," Alan replied, stepping back and wiping his eyes. Lady Cantner offered a handkerchief and Lewrie applied it to his face. It was Mrs. Hillwood's... still redolent of lovemaking. Alan found it hard to keep a straight face, or stifle an urge to begin howling with laughter. He finally managed to say, almost strangling, "We shall do what we can, me and Mister Claghorne. Right now, we are the officers, milord."

Lord Cantner's look of annoyance at finding a snivelling

midshipmen on his wife's tits changed to a stricken rictus at that news.

"Was it his mother's?" Lady Cantner asked of the hand-kerchief.

"Er...not exactly, milady," Lewrie said, pulling himself together. He had to escape them before he burst out in manic laughter and they ended up clapping him in irons. "I thank you for your comfort when I had given way to despair, milady. I have to go on deck, now. Mister Claghorne will be needing me. Excuse me."

Fine bastard's gullion you are, he scathed himself. Your best friend just died, all hell riding down on us, scared so bad I wouldn't trust my arse with a fart, and you're ready to laugh like a deranged loon, and feel up the blanket of our live-lumber.

He took a glass from the binnacle rack and crossed to join Claghorne, who stood by the windward rail and gripped the narrow bulwark as he stared at their approaching stranger with a forlorn expression.

"About three miles off, now," Claghorne sighed heavily. "She'll be up ta us an' alongside in an hour, holdin' the wind gauge, dammit."

"French, sir?" Lewrie asked, hoping against hope.

"Yes, God rot 'em," Claghorne said. "See the length of the yards, cut shorter'n ours? No guts fer a stiff wind. Black-painted masts, an' the way they cut their jibs different from ours?"

"Then what shall we do, Mister Claghorne?"

"Might still fox 'em. Show 'em a body, tell 'em we have fever aboard. They don't want that.... Was it young Purnell?"

"He just died, sir," Lewrie said, getting ready to dive back down into a real session of the Blue Devils.

"Damn hard luck. Watch yer luff, By God..."

The wind had backed a full point to the east-sou'east, and had fallen in its intensity. To stay on the wind for maximum speed they would have to steer more easterly, which was now a perfect course for Antigua, their original destination.

"I do believe that God has a shitten sense of humor," Claghorne said, trying manfully to keep from raging and tearing his hair at his misfortune.

"Sir, if we have to fight—"

"Mister Lewrie, shut yer trap," Claghorne said, and stepped away from him to begin pacing the deck again as *Parrot* seemed to slow and ride a little heavier on the sea.

Lewrie eyed the French brig again, now hull up and aiming for that point of intersection of their courses. There had to be something they could do besides beat up to the brig and surrender, he thought. If Claghorne could convince them that *Parrot* had fever aboard, they just might be shocked enough for *Parrot* to surprise them. Lewrie began to inventory what they had below in the magazines that would serve.

"Goddamn you, you poltroon," Lord Cantner was shouting from aft at Claghorne. "There must be *some* idea in your head."

"The wind is dying, milord," Claghorne said, close to giving into despair. "He has a longer hull, an' with this wind I cannot outrun him. He has more guns an' most likely nine-pounders that can shoot clean through our hull. If they board us they'll not leave a man jack alive, an' what they'd do ta yer good lady, I shudder ta think about—"

"Well, I shudder to think about what happens to the Indies if I am captured by those frog-eating sonsabitches," Lord Cantner raved.

"I can give you a weighted bag ta drop yer secret stuff overboard, milord, but I can't guarantee yer freedom an hour from now."

"If I could suggest something, Mister Claghorne?" Lewrie said after clearing his throat for attention. Lady Cantner had been attracted to the deck at the sound of the argument and stood by, waiting to hear what would happen to her.

"I command this ship now, *Mister* Lewrie," Claghorne said, "and I'll thank you ta remember yer place."

"No, let's hear him out," Lord Cantner said, clutching at even the feeblest of straws.

"They want to come close aboard and demand surrender. Let them. Put them off their guard with the Quarantine flag and the sight of our sick and dead. Then give them a broadside of double shot and grape, with star shot and langridge and fire arrows to take their rigging down and set fires aloft. They'll be so busy at saving their own ship we may have a chance to escape and make it a stern chase. We shall be going toward our own bases after dark. Would they pursue that far? Could we lose them after sundown?"

"One sign o' resistance an' they'll shoot us ta pieces," Claghorne said wearily. "Then you'll be responsible fer milord's and milady's deaths."

"Then what would you do?" Lord Cantner demanded. And both of the Cantners and Alan realized that Claghorne had no plan. He was riding the back of the tiger with no idea how to get off, or how to even change the course of events. Perhaps he could have responded to a lesser set of circumstances like a dismasting, a hull leak, fighting *Parrot* through a hurricane, even storming another ship's bulwarks with sword in hand, if ordered by someone else. But this, on top of the fever and all the deaths, and losing Kenyon's sure hand to guide him was too much for him to handle, and he would be damned if he was going to admit it even if it meant losing *Parrot,* striking the colors. What little pride he had left would probably force him to consider striking the best possible decision he could have made until the end of his life.

"May I call the hands to quarters, Mister Claghorne?"

"You wish ta make yer *gesture,* Mister Lewrie, then go ahead," Claghorne said, thinking it a small point with no real purpose. "But you'll not fire a shot unless I directly tell you to, hear me?"

"Aye aye, sir."

Claghorne turned away, and Lord Cantner restrained Lewrie with a hand on his arm. "Let's pray it works, Mister Lewrie. I cannot abide the idea of striking to a pack of Frogs without at least trying."

"It may cost us our lives, milord," Lewrie told him, "but at least we shall retain some of our honor. If I may suggest gathering your papers in a weighted bag, just in case? And in placing your good lady below decks?"

Once free, Lewrie went to his men amidships. "She's French, boys. And we're going to sink her or burn her," he said, trying to look confident. "We shall fetch up all the spare swivels and charges. I'll want some men to go below to the magazine and break out the canister and star shot and gun cartridges. Lay out boarding pikes and cutlasses out of sight by the bulwarks. Mister Kelly?"

"Aye?" the bosun's mate said, wary of Lewrie's intentions.

"Hands to quarters, handsomely, so the Frogs won't notice. Load with reduced charges for double shot. Star shot, canister and langridge as well. We'll give them a surprise, a big one."

"Handsomely," Kelly said. "Aye aye."

The French brig ran up her colors, and there was a groan from several hands at the sight of the pure white banner with the gold *fleur de lis* of Bourbon France.

"We'll show 'em who they're dealin' with," Claghorne said. "Run up the colors," and their own red ensign soared up the leach of their mains'l to the peak of the gaff yard, which brought a thready cheer from a few die-hards on deck.

"Swivels in every socket," Lewrie ordered. "Number-one gun, load with double star shot. Quoin out and aim for the rigging and give those French bastards some of their own medicine. Number-two, double shot and canister. Quoin half-in and aim for their gangway, got it?"

He went from gun to gun, giving them their load and aiming point, sent a hand to fetch up the case of fire arrows from the magazine and had them loaded in the swivels.

"Swivel men, aim for the sails and rigging, get it? Set fire to the bastards and give them something to gripe on instead of taking us. Once we open fire you've got to load and fire fast as you can without orders. It's that or die in chains, got it? Damme, Crouch, quit mooning! What did I say?"

Crouch was the slowest hulk he had, hairy and beetle-browed and incapable of concentrating on anything for long.

"Ah aims fer 'is sails an' keeps at it til 'e burns ta hell, sir."

"Good enough. Now, this is most important. We shall be standing by the windward rail, but not crouched down by the guns. Nobody lays a hand on a swivel until I say. Keep your matches out of sight. They think we're going to be easy. Keep your small arms out of sight, too. Don't let the gun ports swing open or we're dead before we get a chance to hurt them. *They* think they're going to take us without a fight and throw us into their hulks on Martinique, so you think on it and look gloomy, for Christ's sake!"

Considering the victim was French, the men fell into their roles well enough. Indeed, Lewrie had to threaten flogging for overacting to keep a couple of them from wailing and wringing their hands a little too histrionically.

The brig was up within seven or eight cables by then, turning to open her broadside to point at *Parrot*. There was a sharp bang, and the sound of iron moaning through the air. A ball struck short ahead of them, raising a pillar of water.

"Nine-pounders," Lewrie said out loud. He stepped aft to see Claghorne.

"They'll stand off an' shoot right through us with nine-pound shot," he said. "We haven't a chance—"

"How close do you think they'll come to demand our surrender?" Lewrie asked, gauging the distance between them to be six cables and closing slowly. He saw the brig let fly her tops'ls so they would not pass ahead of *Parrot*, adjusting their closing rate so that they would end up rounded into the wind parallel to them.

"About a cable, most-like." Claghorne sighed. "Maybe closer."

"It would be best if we had them at pistol shot, sir." Lewrie said, knowing that Claghorne had ceded him the initiative as sure as that panic-stricken gunner's mate had done in *Ariadne*.

"No, no! They'd blow us apart at that range if they fired. I'll not have it, Mister Lewrie. You'll obey my orders an' not do anythin' rash. You hear me, sir?"

Another bang from the privateer. This time the ball droned over the deck low enough to part people's hair. All the enemy's gun ports were open, and a line of ten guns were visible. The brig's crew crowded the bulwarks and gangway, seemingly hundreds of them that provided the crews to man enough prizes to send them back to their island lair rich men, enough to overpower a frigate if they got lucky.

Three cables off, now. A third gun fired from the brig, and this ball struck *Parrot*, thudding into the wale of the hull below the gun ports.

"Damme, the game's blocked at both ends," Claghorne said, collapsing against the railing. "I am goin' ta strike, Mister Lewrie. I order you to stand yer gun crews down."

"We can't just surrender, sir..."

"Damme you, get forward! Mister Mooney, I want you ta strike the colors."

"Mister Claghorne!" the husky bosun objected, shocked to his bones.

"I said strike the colors."

"Aye, sir, but I'll tell ya this, Mister Claghorne, sir, yer a shiverin' coward, sir!"

"I'm a realist, damn yer eyes!"

Lewrie went back forward to his gun crews. "Boys, we're going to strike. That'll get the Frog in closer so we can hit him. Don't anybody be alarmed."

How much worse can it be? he thought wearily, his eyes aching from his earlier jerking tears and the glare of the sea. A band of pain circled his head from staring so intently across the water, and the tension. If we're prisoners, nobody's going to hang me for disobeying orders. The French may shoot me, but there's still the Yellow Jack to consider first. If we fail I can die right here on my own deck, in my own way, and go hard and game...

The Red Ensign sank to the deck and was gathered up in

a limp bundle, which brought cheers from the privateer brig. Claghorne ordered the fore course lowered and the jibs backed so that *Parrot* cocked up into the wind and fetched to. The brig began taking in sail and sidled down alongside, no longer making headway as they let fly, but being brought down to *Parrot* to her lee by the dying wind.

"Do you strike?" a leather-lunged voice called to them.

"Aye," Claghorne shouted back. "We have fever aboard."

The Yellow Quarantine flag was hoisted, and the French laughed. Their gun ports were still open, and Lewrie could see men standing by them with burning slow match, but the majority of the much less disciplined privateer crew was standing in the rigging or on the bulwarks with muskets or swords, jeering happily at a foe that would strike without even a shot fired for honor's sake.

Claghorne hoisted a dead man up onto the rail, a man yellow as a custard, the stains of his bloody dark bile still streaking his bare chest. "We have Yeller Jack, *comprend? Vomito Negro!*"

The brig was close now, a musket shot away, less than fifty yards. Lewrie could see the men crossing themselves, gesticulating in their lingo, eager to be away from the fever and the pest ship that carried it. Their officers aft were standing in a knot arguing and waving their arms in broad gestures. Hands were going aloft to lower yard and stay tackles or clew jiggers for boat tackles to hoist out a launch so they could stand off and investigate. The privateers did not want to give up a prize so easily gotten, but neither did they want any fever in their own crew.

"Stand ready, lads," Lewrie told the uneasy hands. "Easy, now, get ready for it, don't blow the gaff on me, now."

The brig was now twenty-five yards off, a very long pistol shot, and men were laying down their weapons to bear a hand on the boat tackles, while others were lifting out long sweeps to fend *Parrot* off from the hull so they would not become infected.

"Now!" Alan ordered. "Fire as you bear!"

"Damme you, Lewrie," Claghorne howled as though

stabbed in his guts. "Our word of honor! We *struck!*"

The rest of his ranting was lost in the din as the gun ports were flung open and the guns were run out the last few feet. The swivels were already banging away. Fire arrows sizzled into life and flew in short arcs for the brig's yards and sails. The first four-pounder fired, flinging a double load of star shot at the brig's masts, bringing down braces, sheets and blocks, shattering her fortops'l yard.

The packed mass of jeering boarders, the teams of men ready to walk away with the stay tackles, or snub the yard tackles, the men aloft taking in sail, and the men in the rigging for a better view, they were all seemingly scythed away as the four-pounders spewed their wicked loads of langridge and canister, rough bags of scrap iron bits, nails, broken plates and ironmongery, or light tin cases that contained hundreds of small musket-caliber balls.

"Kill them," Lewrie raved. "Kill them *now.*"

The swivels were barking again. Even Crouch was loading, ramming and aiming as rapidly and accurately as he could. Fire arrows darted out, flaming dots trailing greasy black smoke. They jammed point-first into masts, bulwarks and the hoisted boat. The spring-loaded bars snapped open as they struck sails, jamming into them so their flames could feed hungrily.

"We gave our word of honor!" Claghorne ranted from aft, but no one paid him much attention in their fighting frenzy. After days of terror at the invisible, their fear came out in an orgy of hatred and destruction against a real foe they could fight, maybe even conquer.

"Larboard men, fores'l halyards!" Mooney cried like a bull. "Off heads'l sheets n' run 'em ta larboard. Smartly, now, laddies."

Sails made of flax, tanned and dried by tropic sun, shivered and thrashed until powdery with broken fiber particles...Masts and spars brushed with linseed oil, to keep out rot. Tarred standing rigging holding the masts erect...Running rigging coated with slush; beef and pork fat and rancid butter, the skimming of the galley boiling pots (that the cook didn't sell to the hands on the sly) so that the lines stayed supple and didn't swell in the rain and would run true through all the blocks aloft that controlled the jeers, halyards, lifts, clew lines, buntlines, braces, jiggers and tackles... And ships are made of wood; painted, tarred, oiled wood—baked as tinder dry as galley pine shavings—given a chance, all of it would burn.

Now the French crew saw the small points of fire aloft that quickly were fanned into large fires. Her sails flashed into sheets of flame that flagged in the wind, lighting the rigging, carrying flame to her spars and her topmasts. The lower masts began to work and groan.

"Sheet home!" Claghorne cried as he saw what was happening. The fire could blow down on *Parrot* if she did not get away quickly. "Helm up, you farmer. Mains'l haul. Now belay on heads'l sheets. Now belay on the foresheet. Thus!" he ordered, indicating a course.

Parrot began to move, creeping away to the east from the burning French privateer brig, whose masts were now well alight. As *Parrot* got a way on her the brig suffered a shower of flaming debris raining down on her decks. Her fore-topmast came down like a blazing log.

They continued to fire at the French ship until their guns would no longer bear. They passed her bows, out of danger of burning, or of being fired upon except with bow chasers, gaining speed and headway. The brig had an inner fore-stays'l still standing that pulled her head downwind to the north, and turning her broadside to the wind so the fire could rage her full-length unchecked. Thick coils of dark smoke plumed from her up forward where her foremast had collapsed on the deck. Her boat tier was also well ablaze, shooting flames as high as her main course yard, now bare of canvas. There were some dull explosions lost in the rush and roar of flames as guns cooked off from the heat, or scattered powder bags burst like grenades on her decks.

"Cease fire, cease fire," Lewrie shouted to his jubilant men, having to knock gun tools from their hands. "Crouch, leave off. Drop it, dead 'un, Crouch," he shouted, using the terms of the rat pit.

"Aye, sir," Crouch breathed, his dumb face flowing with pleasure. "But jus' looka the fuckers *burn*, sir. God almighty!" He was leaping up and down in thick-witted victory.

"Ya done 'em proper, sir!" someone shouted to him as he made his way aft through them, telling them to secure from quarters. They were cheering themselves, slapping each other on the back in glory at what they had done.

Claghorne was waiting for him on the quarterdeck, face red and sword drawn. "Damn yer black soul ta the hottest fires a hell, Lewrie! You disobeyed me, you motherless bastard. You fired after we had struck like a lowdown lying Barbary pirate. I'll see you face a court for it, I swear I'll see you hang!"

Alan had not considered their chances of success so great as to have reckoned fully on the consequences of victory. The reality of Claghorne's threat hit him like a bucket of cold water. They had won, hadn't they? He realized that he had disobeyed a direct order, even if it was wrong; had violated a major article of gentlemanly conduct at sea. But weren't they free?

What Claghorne was really mad about was that he had been shamed before the men, and that was what could get Lewrie scragged.

"Dammit, Mister Claghorne, we're alive and free, and *they'll* not be telling anybody about it," Alan said.

"I'll know, you little bastard. I've a mind ta strike you down right now fer what you did—"

"You shall do no such thing," Lord Cantner said, coming on deck with his wife. "God stap me, just look at that, Delia. *You* look on it, Mister Claghorne. It's salvation, and victory. Honor be damned!"

He was transfixed by the burning brig, and a hush fell over the deck as the men turned to see the end, silencing Claghorne as he, too, turned to stare.

It was a terrifying and heartbreaking sight for sailors to

see a ship burn, even an enemy. The brig had been especially pretty, long and lean and fast, golden oak hull with a jaunty red stripe, black wale and bold figurehead, picked out with gold leaf on her rails and entry port and transom carvings. Now she was a smutty lamp bowl of a hull that served as the vessel of a raging conflagration.

Men could be seen tossing over kegs and hammocks, coops and hatch gratings, anything that would float...their boats had burned. Crewmen were splashing into the sea and calling out as the heat became unbearable, and a hot glow could be seen through her open gun ports. Over the loud whooshing roar of the fire they could hear thin screams as men were roasted to death, or pleaded for mercy on their souls as they hung on for just a moment more of life before going into the sea—few sailors of any nation could really swim, and *Parrot* could not approach that raging furnace to save them without risking her own safety.

The fight drained out of Lewrie, sucked dry now by all the terror and the tension, and Claghorne's heartstopping prediction of a court-martial. He had been wild with passion, leaping and screaming obscenities at the French, raving with all his strength in a berserk release. His headache was back with a vengeance, after all the waiting and hoping that the French would come close enough to be hurt, staring hard over the glittering ocean and hurting his eyes trying to see everything at once. His limbs seemed to have turned to water.

Just like after that fight in *Ariadne*, he reminded himself, so tired he could barely stay erect. Is it always going to be like this?

"Well done, my boy," Lord Cantner said, his voice cracking with emotion as he pumped Lewrie's hand. "Goddamn wonderful job."

"Thank you, milord, thank you."

"God bless you, Mister Lewrie," Lady Cantner added, looking at him with open adoration, that roving look back in her dark eyes. Her chest heaved magnificently.

Once they were ashore on Anguilla, and her lord asleep

some night before they sailed, her eyes told him it could be arranged, but at the moment it didn't seem to matter much to him.

He also knew, or felt, or hoped that Lord Cantner's influence would stop any court-martial. After all, he was alive and still free to sail for England. The less said about Claghorne's lack of wit at finding a way to avoid or defeat the privateer the better. A court-martial would be as much a condemnation of his striking the colors as Alan's disobedience, and striking before doing your utmost to fight was also a hanging offense. Had he not learned, even in his short career in the Navy, that a victory has a hundred parents, but failure none?

A rich and influential peer could have things done his own way, as they usually ended up doing. If Claghorne was possessed of any wit at all he would write his report taking credit for the idea, excusing the breach of honor as necessary to save the lord and his lady and all the secrets in his head, giving Lewrie grudging allowance for being a brave little fellow who followed orders well.

"Mister Lewrie?" Lord Cantner asked in a faraway whisper. Alan could not hear him through the ringing in his ears. Too much noise of the guns, he thought. But he seemed so far away, and it was hard to focus on the lord's phiz. It also seemed to be getting dark awfully early...

He realized he was seated on the deck, shivering all over.

Why are they looking at me like that, he wondered. Haven't the bastards ever seen a hero? But there was no answer.

CHAPTER

10

THERE were many strange and awful dreams that bothered him as he swam in the delirium of a raging fever. He and Mrs. Hillwood romped in the maintop while Marines threw buckets of seawater on them by the numbers and Captain Osmonde called the pace with a fugleman's cane. Tad toasted cheese on burning sails for him and asked if he wanted his shoes blacked. Keith Ashburn and Shirke bought him a half dozen bottles of claret, but he couldn't drink with them, for their heads were skulls with clacking jaws and the wine ran down their chests like black ink.

Lt. Harm and Mr. Pilchard and Margaret Haymer danced together, comparing wounds. His sister Belinda was a figurehead on a ship of the line, and the sailors fondled her bare breasts as they sat on the beakhead rails to relieve themselves. Chapman hopped one-legged down the Strand with a beautiful young girl in a blue gown in search of a bookseller's, and he could not catch them no matter how hard he ran. Sir Hugo and Sir Richard Slade chased him down an endless work gangway, waving their pricks at him.

He found himself flying low across sparkling wavetops

with a crowd of pelicans who knew how to do spherical trig-onometry in their heads, and he jeered with them at the seagulls, who had to use slates. Captain Bales was served at dinner by a nude Lady Cantner with an apple in his mouth. Alan was made post, but his ship was a hundred fathoms down off Nevis, and the wind kept shifting all about the compass. Kenyon and some admiral stood together in full uniform but no breeches and told him what a brute he was to harm the French, who were only two inches tall and crawled all over him. He was in a cart on his way to Tyburn to be hanged, and with his jeering friends telling him to die game, there was an elfin face framed in honey gold ringlets staring up at him and telling him to keep his wig on straight, while a fiddler did a bad rendition of "*Portsmouth Lass*" and Claghorne and seaman Crouch shoved on the capstan bars, and some very ugly old woman sold poking sticks to the gentry who wished to have at him.

He dreamed he had Yellow Jack and had turned the color of a Quarantine flag, all his hair falling out in his eyes and a beautiful young girl tenderly bathed his face, softly saying "you sonofabitching bastard" over and over, and he had an erection because her eyes were the color of the ocean in a shallow island harbor, and Cassius rang a tiny silver bell so everyone could come and marvel.

Then there was a dream of a cool room, dim and quiet and still, with some kind of bars slanting one wall, and that one lasted for a while. The walls looked like plaster instead of the lathed partitions of a ship, and there might have been pictures on the walls but they were hard to make out because there seemed to be some kind of fog about him.

I'm in a house, he told himself dreamily, after pondering it a long time. I'm in bed in a house. So what happens after that? Slow sort of dream, compared to the others...

He could not move but he could blink and shift his vision to discover what seemed to be two sets of louvered doors on one wall at the foot of the bed he occupied. The light from outside was what was making the bar patterns on the wall.

They are not prison bars, he decided, shifting his eyes to

a closer vantage of his body. He could see his arms on the sheets, so Boggs had not cut anything off. He tried to raise his arm but it would not move, and he sighed as he realized he had little control over this dream. He tried to shift a leg, and felt cool linen pressing down lightly all over him. I am in bed, in a house, nude, and not in jail. Lots of possibilities to this...

It was such a pleasant prospect that he dreamed he went right back to sleep to mull things over. When he dreamed that he awoke, it was much lighter. Then he saw that the fog about him was an insect net of very fine gauze around his bed, that the louvered doors led to some sort of veranda or patio. This time, he could move a hand and reach down to feel his groin. Yep, still got my wedding tackle. Nice room. Nice furnishings. Too good for a debtors' prison, and it's too quiet for a hospital. It was cool, and a hint of breeze came through those louvered doors, bringing the sound of surging waves on a beach, and he didn't think it was Brighton. There was a decided salt-and-iodine tang to that breeze, and it was so bright beyond the louvers that he thought he might be somewhere in the tropics, maybe the West Indies.

His mouth fell open and a foetid odor rushed out. He tried to make words but all that came out was "gracck". But he thought, with a joy that was almost sexual, My God! I'm alive!

He looked at his hands and his arms against the cool white linen sheet and saw that he was a lot more yellow than he remembered.

I survived Yellow Jack, he crowed silently, almost weeping in happiness. I'm as yellow as a quince but I'm alive!

He listened to his heart beat, took deep breaths and rejoiced to the sound of air rushing in and out. The taste in his mouth was positively vile but he thought it nice to be able to taste something.

There was a sound to his right. A door was being opened, a swish of clothing could be heard. He caught a flash of white cloth and thought it might be some sort of mop-squeezer. But he saw that elfin face that was so incredibly young and lovely, those bright blue eyes and the honey gold hair set in ringlets, and he became afraid that he had seen her somewhere before being hanged or something. If she were here, was he really alive? Was she some tantalizing angel or devil? Did he have his wig on straight?

She crossed to the double-doors and threw the first set open. A flood of painfully brilliant sunlight exploded into the room. The second set opened, and he blinked in pain, until he could make out a bar of cerulean blue framed by intensely green bushes, bright green grass and the hint of dune grass and sandy soil beyond the green. Was that a ship out there, a three-masted Indiaman? The girl took a moment to stand in the second door, arms still holding the doors apart like a figure on a crucifix in some Romish church.

Once his eyes had adjusted and been blinked clean of tears he could surmise that it was early morning, for there was a hint of sun just at the top of the door, and the girl was silhouetted against the bright light. She must have been wearing a morning gown instead of a more formal sack gown, and without stays or corset, because he could see how slim her back was through the fabric, how tiny her waist, how slim her hips, almost like a boy's but for the gentle continuation to the curve of her behind.

With the doors open the breeze hit him with a gentle rush, and it was cool and clean, heavy with tropical flowers, the astringent tang of deep ocean that came to him as lustily as the steam from a smoking joint of meat. He could hear birds singing, birds he did not recognize.

The girl still stood against the light, and he could see that her shoulders were not too broad. She had long legs, slim thighs that left a gap between them at her cleft, shapely calves and trim ankles. She turned and did something in the shadows on tiptoe, and he could see how full and high her young breasts were above a flat belly, how snug and trim her buttocks were. Then she stepped out of the light into the shadows, and a bird was singing quite loudly.

There was another rustle of cloth in the room, and he shifted his eyes to that direction. He saw an incredibly ugly woman in a mobcap and morning gown. She bore something with her. Where had he seen her before, selling something at Tyburn or Bedlam? She brought something forward; long, thin, made of wood and ... Poking stick! I'M DEAD!

"Hanggankk," he said, eyes wide in fright, and the woman gave out a harpy's shriek and disappeared in a twinkling.

"Mister Lewrie," the woman said, reappearing with a glass of something in her hand. "You spoke! Lucy, he spoke!"

"I heard him, yes, thank God, oh thank God," a young voice cried.

"Agghk," he went on, his heart pounding hard enough to shake the bed. The woman's shriek, and the sight of that broom handle he had thought was a poking stick had nearly frightened him out of what few wits he still possessed, and he had not made much inventory yet as to that.

Hands were there to lift him up in bed and pile pillows behind him until he was almost sitting up. A black maid appeared to help out. A glass was thrust under his nose and he opened his sticky lips to accept whatever was offered. It was water: not stale ship's water, but fresh and sparkling clear water, and he gulped it down greedily, hoping to sluice away the vile taste in his mouth. He wasn't much for water if one could get beer or ale or wine, but at the moment he thought the water a marvelous discovery.

"Thank you. Thank you," he rasped, licking his dry lips.

"We feared the fever had curdled your brains, Mister Lewrie."

"Thought I was dead. Dreaming. Where?"

"Antigua," the soft young voice said, and he looked into that elfin face, at those high cheekbones, that narrow chin and high forehead and still felt like he was dreaming.

"You are on the Atlantic side, Mister Lewrie," the old woman told him. "We brought you here when the surgeons had despaired of your recovery in hospital in English Harbor. After the brave thing you did, it was the least we could do for you."

"God bless you, ma'am," he breathed in her direction. Here, did she say I'd done something brave? That sounds promising...

"This is the shore residence of Admiral Sir Onsley Matthews. I am Lady Maude and this is the admiral's niece, Miss Lucy Beauman, from Jamaica."

"God bless," he said, gazing at the girl. "She was there."

"Lucy?" Lady Maude asked. "Where?"

"Tyburn. The Strand. I saw her. I think I did."

"Just dreams, Mister Lewrie," Lady Maude said. "Fevers do that to you."

"Followed her," he insisted weakly, "couldn't catch up."

"Auntie, he's still so weak," the girl whispered, concerned.

"Aye, and will be for some time longer. Mister Lewrie, could you take a portion of a nourishing broth?"

He nodded slowly.

"Andromeda, go tell cook to prepare a thin meat broth and be quick about it," Lady Maude told the mop-squeezer, "and put some red wine in it for stoutness."

"Yassum."

"*Parrot*," Lewrie asked, wondering what he had done that was so brave and wonderful, and concerned about his ship.... "Is she safe?"

"Indeed she is, Mister Lewrie!" Lady Maude beamed down at him. "Lord and Lady Cantner have sailed to Tortola to meet the winter convoy, and *Parrot* still swims proudly. And you can be proud of doing such a brave duty for the Crown, young man. Very resourceful indeed..."

"The privateer brig," Lewrie said as the memory of what he had done came back in a rush.

"As Sir Onsley said, 'burnt to the waterline and Frogs' legs in a flambe'," Lady Maude tittered.

"Serve 'em right," Lewrie muttered, ready to fall asleep once more.

"Still thirsty, Mister Lewrie?" Lucy asked.

"Yes," he replied, realizing that he was.

"Lucy, fetch a bottle of brandy from the wine cabinet," Lady Maude instructed. "A pinch of that in his water will put color in his cheeks."

"Any color but quince," he said with a happy sigh, and they began to laugh heartily, a giddy sound of relief, and Lewrie drifted off to the sound of it.

WHEN he was adjudged strong enough to hear the news Rear Admiral Sir Onsley Matthews stopped by to visit him. Lewrie had been sitting up in bed, bemoaning the loss of his hair and eyebrows to the fever when the man entered. Sir Onsley was corpulent, big all over, balding and looking strangled in his neckcloth.

"Sir Onsley." He nodded in lieu of a bow.

"You look like death's head on a mopstick, but I hear you're going to recover, lad," Sir Onsley began, sitting down on the edge of the table by the bed, which fortunately was square and heavy enough to support his considerable bulk.

"I am feeling much better, Sir Onsley. Still weak as a kitten, but better."

"Damn close thing, you and the Yellow Jack. Not many survive, but if you do you stand a good chance of being acclimated to it and won't come down with it again." Sir Onsley crossed his arms on his chest. "Have some news for you."

"Aye, sir?"

"Your captain recovered as well, and about a third of your sick."

"I am gratified to hear that, Sir Onsley," Lewrie said automatically, but thinking that he wasn't so sure, after discovering that Lt. Kenyon preferred the windward passage.

"*Parrot* is under another officer and has departed for Nassau. We needed her badly. Had to appoint two new midshipmen to her, so I'm afraid you're without a berth for a while."

"Oh," Lewrie said, feeling a sadness that he would not

have expected six months before at such news. What would become of him? What sort of berth would he get, once he recovered fit to stand duties? Would he have to go back to the sullen abuse of the regular Fleet once more? "I understand, Sir Onsley."

"I understand, too, lad," the admiral said, clearing his throat. "Happened to me once, my first time in the Indies, for the same reason. Now look here, you're not to worry about anything but getting well for now. You shall be my wife and Lucy's project until you're well enough to get around, and I'll find something for you to do."

"You are too kind to me, Sir Onsley."

"Until then, you have the hospitality of my house."

"I am most grateful to you, Sir Onsley. But I am probably well enough to go back to hospital to recover," Lewrie ofered, hoping that it was *pro forma* for him to say that and be denied. He liked it there, and the girl was gorgeous . . .

"Nonsense. Healthier over here on the windward side, anyway. If a ship could tack out of what passes for a harbor here, I'd move the whole damned base. That's your chest over there, by the way. And I have some of your things, pay certificates and such. There're some letters for you when you feel up to reading them. And, a present or two."

"Presents?" Lewrie asked, finding it hard to believe.

"Andromeda," Sir Onsley bellowed in his best quarter-deck voice. "Fetch those packages for Mister Lewrie."

The girl entered the room with them and placed them on the bed. There was a small ivory box such as used in gambling houses like White's or the Cocoa Tree to hold guineas in set amounts. Lewrie opened it and beheld a double row of glittering guineas. He dug one out and discovered that it was real. A hundred guineas, at the very least.

"That's from Lord and Lady Cantner. Reward for your bravery, and your nacky ruse to sink or cripple that privateer. Mind you, not my idea of a truly honorable *ruse de guerre*, but to save the life of a high government official and his lady, it was the only thing you could do to fight a stronger ship and get away with a whole skin," Sir Onsley told him. "If there are no Frogs to complain about it, then I'll not. Old colt's tooth puts a high price on his skin, it seems."

"Aye, sir, indeed," Lewrie said, unable to feature it.

There was a second small package from Lady Cantner. It was a gold locket that when opened sported a miniature of her countenance on one side, and under a wafer of glass on the other, a lock of her dark hair. Lewrie snapped it shut, and met the admiral's raised eyebrows.

"Lord Cantner asked me to review the report your mate Claghorne wrote on the action, to see that you got proper credit at Whitehall," the admiral went on. "And I submitted my own as well. Your family will be proud to read about you in the London papers. Won't do your career any harm, either, to be an eight-day wonder. Though if the Lord North government is turned out, Cantner will no longer be much help to you."

"This is heady stuff, all the same, Sir Onsley," Lewrie said with a shyness he did not exactly feel. "I am quite overcome."

"This is from your Lt. Kenyon," Sir Onsley said, handing him a cloth-wrapped bundle. Lewrie unfolded it to reveal a sword, a hunting sword, or hanger. It was bright steel, chased minimally with nautical detailing on the blade, slightly curved, flat on top but razor-sharp from narrow tip to within an inch of the hilt. And the hilt was a double sea-shell pattern with a tapering hand guard that ran back to a lion's head pommel, all gleaming silver. The grip was silver wire wound over blue sharkskin for a firm, dry grip. The scabbard was a dark blue leather with silver drag and upper fitting, and the belt hook was a smaller replica of the sea-shells of the hilt.

Not only was it utterly lovely, but it was a Gill's, reputed to be the strongest blades in all of Europe, harder to break than a Bilboa or Toledo or Solingen blade, even when struck with great force on the flat of the blade. It was a handsome gift, nearly a hundred guineas in its own right, and he actually felt guilty to feel such animosity toward Lt. Kenyon for being a miserable Molly after he had given him such a magnificent present.

"God, it's beautiful..."

"He believes that you earned it, saving his ship for him, even if he lost her due to his illness," Sir Onsley said, rising to pace the room. He glared at the chirping bird in the cage by the louvered doors, a black and brightly banded local bird called a bananaquit that doted on jams and fruit. "Damn silly creature. You can let dogs in, but never birds. Trouble has a way of following you about like one of those hounds of Hades or something, know that, Mister Lewrie?"

"Aye, Sir Onsley," Alan scarcely able to tear his eyes from the beautiful bright sword.

"First *Ariadne*, now *Parrot*, and you have the devil's own luck not only to survive, but come out covered in credit."

"I don't know what to say, Sir Onsley," he said with a shrug of nonunderstanding. Was he being criticized?

"Resourceful," Sir Onsley mused aloud. "Courageous. Crafty. Not much of a tarpaulin man yet, but that'll come. That'll come."

Lewrie studied him intently, waiting for the *bad* shoe to drop.

"I'm off for dinner and bed. You rest up and recover, and we'll see what comes open after that. Delighted to have met you at last, my boy."

"And I you, Sir Onsley," trying to bow from a sitting position as the admiral stomped from the room.

Damn, am I famous for what I did? he asked himself after the admiral had left the room. One thing is for certain, I'm rich. A pair of ponies for saving Lord Cantner, and it's gold, not certificates. If he's that grateful, maybe I should make a career out of saving lords, and I'd be rolling in chink!

He stood the sword and its scabbard by the bed and opened his mail. There was a letter from Lord Cantner, full of fulsome praises and charming compliments, expressing his gratitude for his life and freedom, and a promise to keep an eye on his career once he was back in London. Alan vowed to write him as soon as he was able, to keep in touch with someone who could turn out to be a benefactor, knowing that the Navy admired nautical skills, but the officer who succeeded was often the recipient of exactly such favor and unofficial maneuverings at Whitehall.

If the first letter had pleased him, the second had him ready to tear at his hair (had he any remaining). It was from Kenyon. While he had given him the sword, it was in the nature of a parting gift, and they would not consider themselves as associates in future. Kenyon was shocked and saddened that Alan had disobeyed Claghorne, even more outraged that he would have violated the time-honored usage of striking the colors as a subterfuge against an honorable foe, even a ship full of privateers. Scum or not, they were blessed with a letter of marque giving them quasi status as a naval vessel.

Kenyon went on to inform him that Claghorne had been promoted to lieutenant, and given *Parrot*, not as a due reward for his skills and knowledge, but more as a peace offering to keep him quiet.

Kenyon, and Claghorne, were deeply saddened that a man who should have found joy in an earned promotion found only shame, due to the reprehensible behavior of someone he had once thought full of promise.

"Oh so holy bastard," Lewrie muttered angrily, crumpling up the letter. "Raving on about honor when he'd bare his own backside to any of his kind who'd ride him. Gifting me with a sword—what does he think I should do, fall on it like a Roman senator? 'Be prepared for when your lack of honor is called to question, so you'll have something to duel with, as you cannot escape that fate if you continue as you are'," he quoted to himself from the letter. "Well, the admiral didn't think what I did was evil or reprehensible. Sneaky, perhaps, but he didn't want to hang me for it. Deep down, under all his manly talk and bluster, Kenyon's an old woman. Should have been a vicar, so he could preach about honor and all that, instead of a sailor. He doesn't like the Navy anymore than I, maybe less...so what's he so exercised about?"

Once he had composed himself (and hidden that accusatory epistle safely away from prying eyes), he helped himself to Lady Maude's special decoction, cold tea and the rob of lemons with a pinch of sugar, and opened the third letter.

"Now this is more like it!" It was from Keith Ashburn, still sixth lieutenant to Sir Onsley on *Glatton*. It was chatty and newsy about previous messmates, and an open invitation to spend some time roving English Harbor's pleasureable pursuits once he had gotten stronger. It was also full of a teasing, but basically envious, accounting of how his heroism had been received in the flagship, and in port, which was most gratifying to peruse.

Without knowing all the intimate details of the fight with that privateer, it was assumed by one and all that some hard and plucky *bottom* was shown by Claghorne and Lewrie as the only two officers still well enough to not only face up to a better-armed brig, but to burn her to the waterline and win the day. All honor and glory to Claghorne, now a commission officer with an independent command, the recognizable mark of favor usually shown a first lieutenant after a spectacular victory. And all honor and glory to a plucky, courageous midshipman named Lewrie that any captain would be damned glad to have in his gun room.

Aye, give even a cur like me a good name, and it'll be harder to get rid of than cowshit on riding boots, Alan agreed to himself, secretly and totally delighted. *Kenyon can stick his nose up at the smell, but I'll bet most of 'em would still think I was heroic even if they knew the whole truth.*

His jubilation was disturbed as the maidservant entered with a dinner tray, followed by Lucy Beauman, eyes glowing with the admiration she clearly felt for him.

"We must not allow news from the wide world to upset you, Mister Lewrie," she said. "Your main concern is recovery. Now here's your dinner. A nourishing soup," she said brightly, indicating various dishes on the tray, lifting the lid of his dinner. "Old Isaac caught this lobster this afternoon, and there's drawn butter, carrots and peas. And Auntie... Lady Maude believes a small amount of hock will strengthen your blood. Do you need another pillow? May I fluff up that one? There you are, more comfortable."

"You are too kind to me, Miss Beauman."

She tucked a large white napkin into the top of his bed gown and spread it over his chest. Andromeda placed the tray across his lap and began to pour him some white wine.

"There's enough for two glasses tonight," Lucy informed him, taking a seat in a chair by the bed that left her seated below him, from where she looked up at him like a prepubescent elder sister would regard the arrival of a new offspring. "I know how you Navy men enjoy your wine. And if you're very good, and gain your strength, Lady Maude shall allow you more."

"I shall try," Alan promised her, taking a welcome sip.

"Is this your sword?" Lucy asked, touching it but not attempting to pick it up. "How marvelous. Did your captain give it you?"

"Yes, he did. Sir Onsley just presented it to me."

"So he should reward someone that saved his command as he lay ill." Lucy nodded firmly, shifting her adoring gaze back to him. "That will be all for now, Andromeda."

"Youah dinnah be ready soon, Missy," the black girl said on the way out.

"You really look much better, Mister Lewrie," Lucy said as he cracked a claw open, spurting hot juices across the napkin. "May I assist you?"

"I believe I may manage, but thankee just the same, Miss Beauman." He cut a portion and dunked the meat in the hot butter, brought it to his mouth and chewed, thinking how regal a good fresh lobster could be. And how messy.

But the girl was there with another napkin to help daub at him.

"Is there anything else you would require, Mister Lewrie?" she asked, eager to fetch for him. "Perhaps a nice heel of bread?"

"This shall be sufficient," he told her, spooning up some of the soup. It was hot and spicy, loaded with chunks of some local fish and various pot vegetables. "I fear I am making a mess."

"Then allow me to assist. Really, I don't mind at all," she assured him. "Give me your spoon and rest easy."

"How much longer shall I be confined to bed, Miss Beauman?"

"I believe a naval surgeon visits tomorrow. He would know better, Mister Lewrie." Delicately she brought the spoon to his lips. "I love island soups and stews, don't you?"

"I feel so useless lying here," he said, "and I must get back aboard a ship."

"Not until you are perfectly recovered, I pray," she said quickly, then blushed at her sentiment. "I mean—"

"Well, if I am to recover fully I can think of no better place in which to do it, and no better company, Miss Beauman," which brought another stronger flush to her cheeks and shoulders. "My Christian name is Alan."

"Alan," she repeated, tasting the strength of it. "I am Lucy."

"May I call you that?"

"I am sure that Lady Maude would not mind. Nor would I."

"Wonderful." He smiled. "Then I shall, with all respect, and all gratitude."

"I did nothing," she said shyly. "It was all Lady Maude's idea. But I must say you have richly earned her hospitality and concern."

"Words cannot express my thanks, Lucy," he said softly, glad the tray covered a hopeful stirring at the sight of how fresh and adoring she was, and how beautiful.

"Your return to duty in full health shall be our reward, Alan," she said right back, showing a tremulous boldness for a second.

If I had died, heaven could not have been half this grand, he told himself as she cut him another bite of lobster.

A week later, he still lingered at Lady Maude's house, able to rise from bed and get about without assistance. With Lucy as his companion, and Old Isaac as a chaperone, he was encouraged to take exercise to rebuild his shattered strength. Mostly they walked the beaches, going down the gentlest inclines to the sea.

Alan was painfully thin after his ordeal, a trace of quince still remained in his complexion, but was content to puff and blow as he climbed up or down the slopes to the sandy beaches where he could stroll for hours, with many a rest stop under the trees and flowering bushes that fringed the strand.

To protect his bald pate from the sun he wore a floppy sennit hat that was much cooler than using a tightly curled white wig to disguise his bare scalp. There was a down coming back in now, a sign that he would recover, and within a week more would have a head of hair no shorter than most people had it cut generally under their own fashionable wigs for coolness and the easy detection of pests.

Once out of sight of the house he would peel off his stockings and shoes and undo the knee buckles and buttons of his oldest, tarriest breeches. He would open his shirt and roll up the sleeves, then revel in the warm winds that blew steadily off the Atlantic, would wade in the surf sometimes up to his waist, in the crystal clear inrush from the ocean. When he got too hot and sweaty he would plunge into the shallows, or squat and duck himself, to come up snorting and refreshed.

There were plenty of crabs to watch and chase after at a fast walk. There were shells to discover and wash clean in the shallows. There were seabirds to admire, the little sandpipers that dug in the wet sand as the waves hissed to nothing and the hiding places of small morsels plopped and bubbled before the waves rolled back in, and the sandpipers ran away from a soaking on a blur of spindly legs. There were seagulls that hung motionless against the steady breeze and cried for bits of bread.

And when they wished to rest there was always a bottle of ale or beer in Old Isaac's bottomless leather sack, a stone jug of Lady Maude's cold tea, fruit to peel and eat, a rusk or a slice of something sweet and special that Lucy had packed as a tiny gift to him, which he always insisted they share.

Old Isaac kept a wary eye on him. He was, after all, a slave that Lucy's father had sent along with her from Jamaica when the latest slave revolt had broken out, an old family retainer with specific instructions to protect her from just such a potential danger as Lewrie. Alan speculated on how big the knife was that Old Isaac might have in the bottom of that sack of his, should he make a move on his lovely young charge.

Old Isaac swore he was part Caribe, the ancient Indians of the West Indies, but he looked as blue-black as any import from Dahomey—even his gums were blue. But he did know a lot about the shells they found, the birds, the fish, the sea urchins to avoid, what trees were unsafe to take shade under, such as the manchineel, which continually misted a sap like acid. He had been a fisherman for the Beauman family for years at their plantation on Portland Bight on Jamaica, until too old to work so hard at the oars and deep nets.

Lucy said that Old Isaac was making him a juju bag that would keep him safe from the dangers of the sea, but he was never to inspect the inside of the bag, and wear it forever. It would save him from drowning, Old Isaac assured him. Lewrie told him of the belief that a tatoo of a certain cross would do the same, but Old Isaac had only laughed at how gullible white people could be. He could not say anything such as that, but from the way he had tittered open-mouthed and walked off, muttering to himself and laughing, he said volumes.

TWO weeks later, one bright and sunny and pleasantly cool morning on the beach, basking barechested under a mild sun, Lewrie began to realize that his idyll might come to an end. He looked up the beach at Lucy, walking barefoot in the surf, a fashionable sunshade in one hand to retain her paleness, the other holding up the skirt of her gown. She wore no stays and no petticoats, like a poor country wench, and the gown was old and shabby enough to allow her to wade if she wished. The bottom two feet of hem was soaking wet and clinging to her bare legs, and he felt his groin stir pleasantly at the sight.

If he felt well enough to think about bedding a wench, and Lucy was the only dell in sight, then he was well enough to go back to the harbor and resume his duties. In a way it would be a relief, for she was openly fond of him. But she was only sixteen years old, coltish and lovely, but not his sort of pigeon, and being the recipient of so much open adoration, without being able to take advantage of it, was driving him to distraction.

I'm just a toy to her, anyway, he thought. Young girls like to play with dolls to feed and nurse, and all I am to her is a doll that can talk back. And if I did get into her mutton, Admiral Matthews would have me flogged round the Fleet...

He stood up and walked into the gentle surf at low tide, wading out until he was waist-deep, then ducked under and splashed up and down several times to take his mind off how virginal she was, and how much he'd enjoy ending that condition. Damme, she's built for sport, though...

"Sah," he heard Old Isaac yell as though in command.

Lewrie took time to see three pelicans rise from the water, and a boil of fingerling fish break the surface perhaps a musket shot away farther out, and began to wade back

ashore immediately. He had seen sharks on this beach, rolling open-mouthed and hungry in the face of a wave, black
eyes seemingly aiming at him. Perhaps it was nothing, but it
was better to be safe than sorry, and supposedly Old Isaac
thought so as well.

"You must be careful, Alan," Lucy told him as he gained
the dry sand. "It might have been a shark out there!"

"Thank you, Isaac," he said as the old man settled back to
rest.

"Except for the sharks, this would be ideal," Lucy said,
angling her parasol against the morning sun. Old Isaac had
resumed his reclining position at the top of the beach in the
shade of a tree, and Lucy led him down the beach by her
very presence.

"Would it not be idyllic, Alan, to stay here like this forever," she went on. "It would be just like the tale of the
lotus-eaters from the *Odyssey*."

"Sand and sun. Fish to eat..."

"Wine...goats and cheese, and all the fresh fruit and
nectar one could want forever. Never too cold, never too
hot, time never passing," she enthused on her theme,
swinging her skirt more boldly as they left Old Isaac further
behind.

"Now that would be boring," Alan scoffed. While in his
delirium, he had turned eighteen, and Lucy was sixteen.
While such a fantasy was nice, that meant she would remain
a feckless child forever, and instead of a good romp in the
bushes she would most likely want to stroll hand in hand
and get orange juice on her bodice from all that damned
fruit!

"It would not," she said. "There would be music and
books, and interesting people to talk to. Perhaps even someone such as your Mrs. Hillwood?"

"What?" He spun to face her.

"One raves during a fever...just imagine what I heard
you say."

He followed her up the beach as she twirled and skipped

ahead of him, teasing him on. "So what did I say?"

"Lots of silly things," she replied, seeming cross. "Hateful things. I believe you really must be a very bad person inside, to have done so many sinful acts so young."

God, I hate perceptive women, he thought. "Where did you hear all this, Lucy?"

"You were raving, I told you. I heard you when we washed you."

"Andromeda told you, didn't she?"

"She did not!"

"Your good aunt wouldn't let a little girl like you see me naked. They keep people like you under toadstools until they're grown—"

"I am not a little girl, Alan Lewrie..."

"I doubt if they let you even come to balls, yet," he went on. "Most likely you listen from the top of the stairs with your nurse."

She dropped the parasol to her side and stepped up to him. She flung her arms around him and kissed him most expertly, raising the sunshade to screen their activities from Old Isaac up the beach.

Damme, they train 'em right in the Indies, Alan told himself, taking her into a close embrace that brushed his groin against the front of her thin gown. There were no underpinnings or petticoats to soften the impact of a trembling young body against his, and his newly restored power to be excited made him positively ache with sudden want.

"Did Mrs. Hillwood kiss you like that?" she whispered, stepping back from him. Her bright blue eyes were twinkling.

"Often," he said honestly, rattled badly.

She flung herself on him again for another long and passionate kiss, arms twined about his neck possessively.

"Did she kiss you like *that*?" Once more she broke away as he dropped a hand to a firm buttock.

"No, not exactly," he said, feeling weak.

"And no one else ever shall." She squeezed his hand and began to stride back up the beach toward Old Isaac, leaving him standing as though he had just been struck with a quarterstaff.

"Holy Christ," he whispered, watching her walk away, so fully pleased with herself. With a groan he turned to the surf and flung himself into it once more, his clothes barely dry from his last immersion. He bobbed and ducked until he could walk erect without getting the old man suspicious, then made his way down the beach.

Old Isaac had a cloth spread in the shade. His shirt was there, and a towel that he used to dry himself and remove some of the sand that had stuck to his feet and legs. Isaac reached into his leather bag and pulled out an orange, which he bit like a horse with strong yellow teeth. He spat out the plug and began to suck. Lewrie helped himself to a pewter mug of cold tea, watching Lucy prowl the sand further up the beach in search of shells.

"You gettin' bettah, sah," Old Isaac said softly.

"What's it to you?"

"Maybe 'bout time you go back to sea, sah," Old Isaac said, turning to look at him.

"And that is what you shall tell Sir Onsley and Lady Maude?"

"Ah doan tell nobody nothin, sah. But it be time."

He's right, Lewrie nodded in silent agreement. If I lay a hand on her, there goes all that good influence, and my good name hereabouts. Only way I could have her is to marry her. God, what a thought!

"If I stay any longer, I hurt her, right?"

"Not for me tah say, sah."

"I hope it will not please you too much if I agree with you, you old fart." Lewrie smiled as he said it.

Old Isaac gave him a toothy grin, nodded and went back to eating his fruit.

ADMIRAL Matthews dined with them that evening, free for once of his flagship and her responsibilities, though Alan wondered what he did that was so important that would not require *Glatton* to be at sea. Once the cloth had been removed, and the ladies had withdrawn, Sir Onsley waved Lewrie down to join him by the port bottle.

"As I remarked earlier, you have recovered well, Mister Lewrie."

"Thank you, Sir Onsley. I feel very able to join a ship. And I cannot with good conscience prevail on Lady Maude's hospitality any longer."

"Yes," Sir Onsley said, eyeing him. "One can only stand to be mothered and fussed over so long before one begins to feel like a lap dog. The surgeon suggests light duties for a spell. How would you like to serve ashore for a while?"

"While I would dearly love a sea berth, Sir Onsley, I would of course be happy to serve in any capacity, and be grateful to be alive to do so."

"Hmm, yes, I expect you would be. I could take you into *Glatton*...but I see that you do not wish to idle in a harbor when you could be more use at sea, perhaps."

"I am good with small arms, and artillery, Sir Onsley."

"That is very true," Sir Onsley said, reaching for the port. He poured himself a full bumper, and topped Alan's glass as well. "I shall be going back to English Harbor before dawn. Have your chest packed and ready and we'll find you something to keep you busy."

"Thank you, Sir Onsley. I am pleased you would find me useful."

"You can handle a boat? Ride? Know something about stores?"

"Aye, sir."

"Excellent," Sir Onsley said with a firm nod. "Well, heel taps, and then I'm for bed. I shall leave word for you to be wakened."

"Aye aye, sir."

FOR the next month, Alan was busy, up at dawn and out on the roads on a strong little mare, carrying messages and orders from the flag to the dockyard, to the batteries and the other military encampments on the island. And when not in the saddle he was given charge of a finely trimmed and manned rowing boat.

His launch visited each ship in harbor as it arrived, went aboard just before departure with last-minute orders, plied between flag and the dock. He was seconded to the dock-yard superintendent as well, and got ink stains on his hands from inventories, from supervising working parties, from visiting warships due supplies to see that they got what was authorized and no more.

Frankly, he looked on it as loathsome quill-pushing, but he did what he was told since it gave him a certain freedom. He berthed on old *Ariadne* once more, now full of arriving or transient officers and men, and since he knew the island better than the arrivals he turned into an evening guide to the better entertainments, confirming once more his belief that he would make a topping pimp. It continually amazed him how little warrant and commission officers much older than he did not know about women and how to get them.

There was also a certain delight to be taken in being the Voice of Authority. He was one of Admiral Matthews' bearers of bad tidings and glad tidings. Even if it was proxy power, it was power. Lordly post captains tensed up when he was piped through the entry port, especially if they had been remiss in their duties. Lieutenants tried to milk him for information almost from the moment he headed aft, and he enjoyed dropping the most obtuse hints for them to ponder while withholding the true import of the messages he carried in enigmatic silence, going about his duties in a splendid new uniform with the supercilious air of a flag lieutenant.

But after about a month it all began to pale. There was no chance for him to make any profits from the lucrative trade in naval stores such as the dockyard people reaped in bribes and graft. He could not visit the deck of some seedily main-tained and poorly run warship with her round shot rusty and her rigging hanging in untidy bights, without wishing to jump in and start kicking a bosun's mate's arse, or giving the quartergunners hell for neglecting their guns. He could not go aboard a smartly run ship just in with prizes, full of tales of derring-do, without envying the shabby but competent demeanor of her midshipmen, who looked upon him as a toy grenadier painted up like a tart.

There was no future ashore for an ambitious, somewhat competent and resourceful fellow such as he, and he was being rubbed up against the fact like a puppy in his piddle.

He went for long rides, until the little mare would breathe as hard as one of those steam machines he had heard about, and his legs ached and grumbled. He continued to practice swordsmanship every time he had free until an old naval cutlass could be swung about like a toy sword and his new hanger did indeed feel light as a feather.

He taught the intricacies of gambling at cards to other midshipmen with a steady income from home, increased his purse. He found himself a doxie in town and paid for her room and his frequent visits, warning her that if he got the pox from her he would have her nose off before the disease did, and was about three-quarters' sure that she did not entertain others when he was gone, which was about as good as could be expected from a bawd.

He was not exactly bored. But he was not exactly happy, either.

The crowning humiliation of being a shore sailor, no greater than a whip jack, was when Lady Maude decided to sponsor a ball and dinner.

Alan was loaned by Sir Onsley to be her clerk and had to suffer the twittering idiocy of Lady Maude and the other naval wives as he did up their shopping lists, their dinner plans, their music choices, and then issue the invitations, copying the same words over and over again in his best round hand. No midshipmen could be spared from the flagship or the dockyard for that duty—it was all his, since he was no loss to the demands of the Navy.

Lucy was there in the background, ignoring him for departing in the night like a thief without so much as a farewell note. Which made it much more pleasant to get away once the invitations were finished and go galloping or rowing to deliver them. The only sop to his feelings was that he was at least invited to attend.

HE was tricked out perfectly in his best new blue coat, snow-white shirt and waistcoat and breeches that had never known tar or slush, fine silk stockings and new gold plated buckles on his well-blacked shoes. He might be a low addition to the ball but he thought he glittered properly. Very few other midshipmen had been invited, except for those that could sport "The Honorable" before their names. In the mob of lieutenants, commanders, captains and a commodore or two, civilians took him for some sort of staff person, which was good for his ego; or a servant, which was not.

Admiralty House atop the hill was a sea of candlelight, a rich amber aura most flattering to all, especially the women. The men in their floured wigs looked bronzed as golden oak from the sun, even if half of them spent their lives in counting houses.

Alan strolled about, sipping at a cold hock. There was still plenty of Greenland ice down in the storm cellars packed in chaff and straw to last the summer. His hosts had even been so profligate with it as to float large blocks in the punchbowls.

He could see Lucy, the center of attention from a host of young admirers, and some not so young. There was even a pop-eyed commander with the face of a frog off a sloop of war courting her. Lewrie had to admit that she looked luscious. Instead of her own hair she wore a high-piled white wig, a reddish gold satin gown faced with pale yellow filigreed and embroidered silk undergown, making her seem older.

"Devilish fine looking young thing," Keith Ashburn said at his side. Lewrie turned to him. "Hallo, Alan, how do you keep?"

"Main well, considering...yes, yes, she is."

"Must have been a trial to be around her, knowing you, even if you did have the Yellow Jack."

"That's why they ran me off. Thought I was looking a tad too robust to be near such a sweet young tit."

"Ever try to get into her mutton? Sorry."

"No, I didn't," Alan glowered, irked that he, of all people, would speak of her so casually.

"My apologies. But you wouldn't mind if I danced with her?"

"Not at all." Alan shrugged as though it made no difference to him, but was suddenly queasy with jealousy at the thought of someone else paying court to her, or discussing her like some cheap merchandise.

He knew there was no future in it for his career, and knew that her sort of affection would involve marriage. What's more, he knew she was being ravishing to her circle of courtiers to get back at him, just as she had snubbed him earlier, and that his best course of action was to ignore her and spark someone else for the evening so he would not appear to her to be a foolish cully over a chit of a girl. But he found himself drifting nearer, as though drawn into a maelstrom.

"I throw myself on your mercy, Miss Beauman," Ashburn was pleading in mock seriousness. "Allow me just the one dance this evening."

"For such gallantry, Mister Ashburn, I shall make it two." She laughed lightly. "Have you met Lt. Warner of the *Dido* frigate? Commander Ozzard of *Vixen*? Lt. Wyndham of the 12th Foot? Lt. Ashburn of *Glatton*...and Midshipman Lewrie of my uncle's staff?"

He was drawn into the conversational circle against his will, having stood close enough to Keith to look as if he was with him, and had to suffer the looks of the commission officers at his affrontery to poach on their private preserve. But when she needed a fresh cup of punch it was Alan that she drew to her and linked arms with to escort her to the buffets, leaving the others fuming.

"Is it not a beautiful evening for a party, Alan?" she asked as he fetched a fresh cup for her. "It's so exciting..."

"Indeed. Everything is lovely," he agreed with a smile.

"And does my new gown please you?"

"I believe that you are the most beautiful young lady present. The gown is magnificent, as you are."

"Why, thank you indeed, Alan," she said, seeming really pleased. "I should not expect such a pretty compliment from someone who would toss me aside so easily."

"Your uncle, and the Service, required me to leave."

"But without a word, not a note, not even a hint..."

"As I said—"

"You can dissemble so well, Alan," she told him sweetly. "Was I not desirable enough to tempt you to stay?"

"How tempting you were was the prime reason I had to leave. Do you think Sir Onsley and Lady Maude, Old Isaac, or those other servants who came from Jamaica with you would allow me to pay court to you without your family's approval? I have more respect for you than to do anything to harm your good name."

"While Mrs. Hillwood, and that gorgeous Lady Cantner have no good name to lose?"

"What do you think I should have done, sneak into your room to bid you good-by?"

"Not at all!" But he had half an idea that she might have entertained just such a fantasy. "You could, however, have considered my feelings at your lack of manners."

"I shall in future. I should also wish to ask for a dance or two, if you are not too promised already."

"Ah, Alan..." she said with a wistful adoring smile. "You are so...of course, I shall dance with you. In fact, I would be most cross with you if we did not. I might remind you that I shall soon be seventeen, not such a little girl to you."

"Believe me, I have noticed your maturing."

"I shall not always be a gawky girl, and you shall not always be interested in trivial..." She turned away from him to avoid him seeing her distress.

"I am very fond of you as well, Lucy."

"You shall be a post captain," she said proudly. "Perhaps even knighted for some act of great bravery." She turned to him and smoothed a lapel for him. "But perhaps when you become a lieutenant..."

"And the war is over," he added, almost piss-proud at what he was hearing from her.

"Pray God it is soon," she agreed hotly. He took her gloved hand and brushed her fingers with his lips.

My God, she loves me, he thought wildly. Now there's a new thing. There've been trulls enough glad to see my shillings, but here's an admiral's niece as good as saying she wants to marry me!

Not that he was that anxious to marry, but she had the best prospects he had seen since leaving London. Nor was he anxious for the war to end, for how else could he earn prize money, make more of a name for himself, gain that commission that would assure his future? And there were a hundred obstacles in the way; she was a girl, therefore fickle in her affections. Her father could go barking mad at the thought, and most likely had a better-suited young man of her own set in mind already, and it was never up to the girl to choose.

Oh, fond daddys might indulge the whims of a favorite daughter, but if a better match was in the offing in land, entitlements, opportunity for mutual profit or (fond parents' hope of hopes) a link to the peerage, then a salty young swain could go sing for his supper.

I'm being led by my prick, he realized, but also noted that love had to start somewhere, and she did seem genuinely fond of him. She was sweet and gentle, well-spoken—so much more so than most of the squirearchy chaw-bacons in the Indies—and would make a good wife for him, dowry or no. I really am fond of her, too. But Pray God I get a ship soon. She can wait, as I shall have to...

They browsed the buffets, nibbling at the rich and spicy titbits proferred. He could not monopolize her and did not try. She was young and delighted with all the attention she was receiving from even the oldest male guests.

She was seated about midway down the long table at dinner with the middleranking folks while Alan was once more down far below. He shared table with a silly blonde, chicken-breasted noddy whose sole social skill seemed to be stuttering "how fascinating" whenever anyone else paused for comment. There was a dark girl named Aemilia, daughter of a pair of Country Harrys who peered about the available men with the eyes of hungry ferrets for a suitable match. Had she been by herself, and was he not almost but not quite pledged to Lucy, Alan would have been fascinated by her, for Aemilia was a sleepy young brunette with a chest like a pouter pigeon that put him in mind of a younger edition of Lady Delia Cantner. She was a bit crude for his taste, though, a hearty Midlands girl with a Mumbletonian accent.

He tried to let an infantry ensign take the lead, but he was more interested in the blonde noddy, whose parents owned a whacking chunk of Hampshire, it seemed, so while trying to maintain a silent dinner conversation with Lucy uptable by eye and shrug and smile, he also found himself down for three dances with Aemilia Country-Get without knowing just how he had managed it. Her buttock-brokering parents looked most pleased.

Lewrie always enjoyed dancing. His French hopmaster had convinced him that women dearly loved a man who could dance well and carry himself gracefully, and would eventually show their gratitude. Most naval officers, having been prenticed at age ten or twelve, could not dance a courtly step and only rumble about like a loose cannon in the country dances, so he had a leg up on most of them.

He and Lucy always came back together, after she had been amused by Lt. Wyndham, by Ashburn, by Warner and Ozzard and a platoon of panting admirers. Her hand lingered on his arm longer, their fingers held their touch longer, their smiles were shyer and more pleasing. But it was her night, and the most ardent finally got her to go to the card room to wager pennies at loo or hazard, and Lucy gave him a backward glance of mock-despair and he was left alone.

As he fortified himself with a cup of claret punch Ashburn came across the room to join him.

"I see we have been both outranked and outmarched by those bastards from the Army," Keith said, mopping his sweaty brow.

"There's an ocean of mutton here tonight, Keith. Why complain?"

"Do you and Miss Beauman have some sort of an agreement?" Keith asked, finishing off one cold cup of punch and dipping another. "The sighing and peeking have been making Commander Ozzard's teeth grind most wonderfully hard."

"We have established that we are fond of each other," Alan admitted. "And there is hope for after the war, perhaps. But in this life you may bank on little."

"God stap me, but you have the best shitten luck," Keith said. "Prize money, some fame, and now Miss Beauman."

"I was envious of you when you gained your commission."

"Want to trade?" Keith said sourly. "We shall never stir up the anchors unless the French sail past Cape Shirley, please God they do!"

"Sir Onsley's a friend to you. You've already moved up to the fifth officer from sixth."

"But we're not at sea," Keith said.

"Aye, I could use a berth myself. Oh, God, Aemilia Chaw-Bacon," Alan muttered, spying the dark girl approaching him from the other side of the salon. "Like to meet a very obliging girl, Keith?"

"Oh, nice poonts," Keith said. Alan tried to introduce Keith but it was no go, not the fact that he was a commission officer, not the fact that his family was rich as the Crown, not that he was related to just about everyone who mattered. She had Alan down to dance with her at the country dances, and that was that. She was civil, but never took her

274

gaze off Lewrie. He had to take her out onto the floor as the band struck up more lively airs, though he would have much preferred going to the card room to see how Lucy fared.

After half an hour he pushed another claret punch into her and set out to deposit her in the paws of her family, but they could not be spotted.

"Oh, they retired," Aemilia said matter-of-factly. "There was a nice old captain was to see me home but he's had too much to drink. Perhaps you could..."

"Well, perhaps. Where do your folks live?"

"On the other side of the island."

"I would admire that, Miss Aemilia, but I am on the admiral's staff and have strict orders to stay close should he need me," Alan lied quickly, listening to the happy cries from the card room as Lucy won a small pot. Unfortunately, Aemilia had laid her plans too well. Sir Onsley was nearby and saw no reason that Mister Lewrie could not safely escort a young lady home, once Aemilia had wiggled against him pleasantly. One look at her straining bosom and it was a close thing as to whether he would have traded his flagship for a chance to fondle her bouncers.

"If I could presume upon you to pay my respects to your niece, Sir Onsley," Alan said, almost strangling in his neck-cloth at the thought of having to leave, "and to your good lady for a most enjoyable evening."

Sir Onsley assured him that he would, and there was nothing for it but to escort Aemilia out onto the veranda. The family coach was already gone, but a hired coach was whistled up, Aemilia insisting on a closed one to avoid the cool night air on her shoulders.

Damn the Navy, damn, damn damn, he thought miserably as he handed the girl in and took a seat on the front bench facing her. The coachee whipped up, but was obviously a cautious man on the steep hill road with his team. And once at the bottom he would not force the horses faster than a brisk walk. It would be two hours to get the girl home, and most likely the same returning.

"Come sit by me so we can talk," Aemilia ordered, patting the upholstery by her side. "The coach will sway on these roads so, we'll be safer wedged in together."

He slid over to lump beside her as the coach left the cobbled town streets for a country lane with an uneven surface. There was only a hint of the moon, and the interior of the coach was dark as a boot.

"I know about you midshipmen . . ."

"Oh?"

"Won't do nothing to hurt their chances."

"Um. I suppose so . . ."

"My parents're pushing for a good match."

"I believe I had noticed that at dinner."

"So if I wanted me a good match, I'd be having a young captain see me home, wouldn't I have?" she said, turning to press against him.

"Most like," he said in the dark, trying to slide away.

"Nobody wants a midshipman with no prospects."

"I hardly rate myself as one with no prospects," he fumed, in a pet that he had to be there in the first place, and for being told he was a nobody in the second by some island-born . . .

"Being a good little girl is such a bore. Ever do it in a carriage?" she whispered, leaning close and laying a kiss on his cheek.

"Now look here, that's all fine for you, but if you turn up with a Jack-In-The-Box, where am I?"

Damned if I haven't had my fill of these island women. Leading you into promises or pushing you into the bunk like you have no say about things.

"Well, don't you know that the blacks know how to stop babies?" she said, stroking his cheek. "There's half a dozen men with better prospects I could blame it on, anyway."

Well, if that's so, the whole evening won't be a waste, he told himself.

"I'll have to marry one of 'em sooner or later, but for now, why can't we have some fun?" she said into his ear. She took hold of one of his hands and forced him to seize a breast. It promised to be as full and heavy and round as he had imagined. "I like doing it in a coach. Ever so nice. So dark and cozy, and the coachee not knowing what's going on, or if he does, he can't do a thing about it, can he? And the people by the side of the road who can't see in while we're having our fun?"

Lord, you will remember I was ordered, he sighed. He tossed his hat on the opposite seat and turned to her. Within a minute he had his waistcoat and coat off, and his breeches down. He unbuttoned her gown and played with her truly magnificent breasts as she hauled up her gown and petticoats.

She spread herself open for him and propped her feet on the opposite seat while he half-knelt before her, his knees precariously perched on the seat between her legs, and gripped her buttocks.

"Oh, God, yes!" she whispered happily as he slid into her deeply. His knees slipped off the upholstery, but his feet were firmly planted against the front of the opposite bench, giving him purchase so he could thrust into her. Once engaged, he became excited and drove hard, partly for the enjoyment, partly to take his anger out on her for press ganging him into leaving Lucy at the ball. Aemilia didn't care if he was performing with a knife at his throat, lost in her own joy and delighting in crying out just loud enough to tantalize their black coachman on top of the box. That also excited him, and he forced her to turn and present to him after her first pleasuring, still iron-hard and eager to gain revenge. He exploded into her, hoping that she was impregnated and forced into an unhappy marriage with one of her "better prospects". Wants servicing does she? I'll give the bitch service!

She was nimble and eager for more after some cooing and sighing, and he bulled her all over the coach for the rest of the trip, slamming into her hard, and ending with her head down into his groin as he sat on the seat and watched the suggestion of a planter's house loom up from the darkness. He ordered the coachee to stop for a while as he filled her once more, even though she was beginning to protest by then. She was shaken by the time he handed her down, and scurried into her home without looking at him. He shut the coach door and climbed up by the coachee, snapping the whip to speed their passage back to English Harbor.

"THE things one is forced to do for one's admiral," Alan said as he entered a dockside inn and found Ashburn still up, dozing over a pipe and a glass of wine.

"With that little country-put?" Keith asked, jealous.

"Just got back. Damn trull like to have had the skin off my back," Alan said, motioning for the waiter. He was dehydrated by his exertions, and badly in need of ale. "How was the rest of the ball?"

"Wonderful," Keith said. "Ozzard got stinking drunk and had to be carried home. Lucy stayed 'til about one and then went home with her aunt. Far as I know, Sir Onsley is still tippling port with the dockyard captain and that ugly old general."

The door slammed open and a roistering party of Army officers staggered in, hooting loudly, calling for drink, service and spare women. Lt. Wyndham was with them, as well as the little Ensign Ames who had been at table with Lewrie at dinner, plus two more lieutenants and a captain of some years named O'Boyle.

"We want your best, not common swill," O'Boyle said as he swayed over a table. "Not the usual stuff you trot out for sailors an' whores."

"And we'll only pay for what we like," Wyndham added to the cheers of his mates. "Here, I don't like this glass." It went into the fireplace, raising another cheer. Several naval officers began to look for their hats.

"Sufferin' Jesus," Ashburn said. "There goes a fairly nice public house. Behold our Army, the Drury Lane Fencibles!"

"Wonder what got them out of Hyde Park?" Alan speculated. "Gambling debts?"

278

"That was good enough for Admiral Rodney."

"This will do, barely," the ensign told the publican. "Though it's piss compared to the cases we brought with us."

"I don't need no trouble with the watch, now, sirs," the publican told them, grovelling and trying to watch all of them at the same time. "Maybe ya might be findin' yer own better ta drink at this late hour."

"There's a cod's-head I know," Wyndham shouted, pointing at Keith and Alan. "Ashburn, and little Cap'n Queernabs... Lewrie or something, isn't it?"

"Your servant, sirs," Keith said, raising his glass to them.

"Come have a drink on the 12th Foot," Wyndham said, which set the officers off on a regimental ditty that made no sense at all, set to a nonsensical tune that resembled "The World Turned Upside Down".

"They look like they can pay," Keith said. "Want to?"

"Free wine. Never refuse a treat."

It seemed that they were all from London, or close thereabouts, so they spent a lively half-hour reviewing plays, raree shows, gossip and comparing mutton they had bulled. The 12th Foot had given up a half-battalion, a grenadier company and two line companies, which were to transship to St. Kitts to upgrade the defenses. The rest were still enjoying the pleasures of London, and this batch was mortally offended that they had been thought dispensable. The captain was Irish, which meant that he felt disposed of by the more fashionable officers, and was morose as a Paddy could be after having been sent to fight a war while his English compatriots still rogered and swaggered through the towns back home.

More wine was called for, and the empties went smash into the fireplace. Gradually, the noise drove most of the other naval sort of customers away into the night.

"Lewrie," Lt. Wyndham said suddenly. "Now I remember you. You were at the ball this evening."

"Yes, I was."

"With that tasty little dish Lucy Beauman. Gentlemen,

you remember the blonde tit I taught cards to?" Wyndham asked, and received their drunken and heartfelt assent. "A lovely piece, was she not?"

"Admiral Sir Onsley Matthews' niece, yes," Alan said, looking at Keith, who was beginning to sense trouble as well.

"I'm told you've been dashing, Lewrie," Wyndham said. "Particularly dashing, I believe was the lady's term for it. Burned a privateer all up with your own little hands. Saved a ship of the line, too."

"Alan has been busy since coming to the Indies," Keith interposed quickly. "I was in *Ariadne* with him, both midshipmen at the time. Let me tell you—"

"In fact, that was *all* I heard from that bitch," Wyndham broke in. "And I don't want to hear any more of it."

"Here, now," Alan said evenly.

"I shall make it a point to taste her pleasures, even if she is a lowbred island trull. Gentlemen, charge your glasses. Let's drink to my next mutton!"

"Warren," the Irish captain warned. His mates had gone silent at the provocation.

"No, I want us all to drink to Lucy Beauman," Wyndham insisted, swaying to his feet. "I'll play the upright man and break that little dell, though she wouldn't be fit company at home without half a crown for socket money. Unless Mister Lewrie here has already strummed with her, then I won't go over a shilling."

Alan tipped his wine glass and spilled it on the table. Keith did the same and they both rose together. "I shall speak for both of us, sir," Keith said, almost grinding his teeth. "Such billingsgate about a fine young lady we would never drink to, even if she were unknown to us. That you slander a lady of our acquaintance is a shameful example of your lack of wit and manners. I trust your regiment is not known for it." Keith kept a firm hand on Lewrie's wrist as he spoke after seeing the flush of anger on his face.

"Good night, sirs," Keith finished, almost dragging Lewrie off for the door. "Come on, damn you! I am ordering you, lieutenant to midshipman, not as your friend, you little idiot!" he whispered.

"I should have known the Navy would go all pious on us," Wyndham sneered, flinging his wine glass at them. "Tawdry lot of Bartholomew Babies! Aye, drag his cowardly cooler out of this place before he might have to blaze with me. What he says he did, and what he really did, are two different things. Just like the Navy—"

"Warren, I am ordering you to sit down and shut up!" the captain said, grabbing Wyndham's arm while the other lieutenants and ensigns looked on.

"Are you calling me a coward, sir?" Alan turned abruptly and shook off Ashburn's hand.

"Talk of the wine table is no reason for meeting," the little ensign said. "I am sure Warren does not really mean—"

"Don't tell me anything, Ames!"

"Being ill-received by the young lady in question is no reason to provoke a duel, either," Ashburn said. "Perhaps his pride is pinching him. Let's allow him to sleep it off, shall we?"

"Fuck you, you cod's-head!" Wyndham said. "Yes, I think that Mister Lewrie is a coward! A coward and a liar and a man-fucking Molly, just like everybody else in the Navy is a bugger in disguise—"

"Warren!" from the ensign named Ames.

"And I think his precious Lucy Beauman is a poxy whore..."

"We need to meet, sir," Alan replied icily in the shocked silence that followed Wyndham's accusations. The on-lookers gave a groan, whether of pain or delight it was hard to tell.

"Alan!" Ashburn barked in his best quarterdeck voice.

"No, Keith. There's been enough," Alan said, stepping back up to the table. "I, sir, consider you a piss-proud cully. You're a butcher's dog with no nutmegs for a *real* fighting regiment. You're a bastardly gullion with a Cambridge fortune, and a great damme-boy with your fellow bucks, but you're the pig-ignorant get of a threepenny upright..."

Alan had always been able to wound with the choice word, and he must have stung something in Wyndham's background. The young man blazed up and, without thinking, slapped him hard across the face.

"Excellent," Lewrie said. "A slur on my character, a slur on the innocence of a young lady, and striking a gentleman. The sooner the better, as far as I am concerned, gentlemen."

"You will witness that he scoured me beyond all temperance," Lt. Wyndham declared. "Captain O'Boyle, I shall request that you arrange this for me."

"I must talk to the major, Warren," O'Boyle muttered. "But I'll tell you you're a God-cursed fool for doing this."

"Lt. Ashburn, would you negotiate for me?" Alan said.

"Aye, and what weapons would you prefer, Mister Lewrie?"

"Naval cutlasses," Lewrie decided after a long moment.

"That's no weapon for a gentleman to use. Why don't we blaze?"

"A man who would strike another can have no objections, can he?" Ashburn said. "Captain O'Boyle, your party has issued a mortal and grievous series of slanders, sir. The choice of weapons, and the place, is ours, is it not?"

"Aye, even by the Irish Code," O'Boyle admitted.

"I shall communicate with you further, sir, after my principal and I have informed our commanding officers," Ashburn promised.

"I shall await you, sir."

THERE are 365 beaches on Antigua, one for every day of the year for a sybarite intent on enjoying the gifts of sun and wind and water. Lewrie's coach rolled up to the low overlook at one of them on the north end of the island two days later, just at low tide, when the sand would be firm under foot. He had with him Keith Ashburn, a naval surgeon, and Captain Osmonde of the Marines, formerly of *Ariadne* and now captain of Marines in the eighty-gun *Tele-*

machus. Osmonde had drilled Lewrie hard for those two days to get him in shape.

Wyndham and his party were already waiting; O'Boyle his second, a regimental surgeon and his friend Ames. There was also an Army officer from the garrison, a Major Overstreet, who would referee. There was a small fire burning, and the regimental surgeon's tools and instruments were already boiling to lessen the shock of cold steel to the flesh of the loser.

"Admiral Matthews gave me a message, Mister Lewrie," Osmonde said as he flicked some invisible dirt from his uniform after they had stepped down.

"Aye?" Alan asked, icy cold and already very thirsty.

"While he deplores the idea of dueling, he deplores the insult to his niece even more. I doubt if your feelings matter to him but he told me to tell you that his hopes are with you."

"That was kind of him, sir," Alan said, disappointed. "For a while I thought he would not allow us to meet."

"I think their commander tipped the scales, smug little bastard. Thought Miss Beauman was a common dell, no matter who her uncle was." Osmonde laughed without humor. "The lad's built like a young bull."

He indicated the enemy below on the beach—Lt. Wyndham was a thick and stocky fellow, bluff and hard looking.

"Somewhat of a duellist. Fought two with pistols, killed his man both times. Only once with a blade, won it but no fatality."

"You do little to reassure me, sir," Alan said. A servant offered him a mug of small beer, which he drank at greedily.

"Keep nothing on your stomach," Osmonde advised. "It will sour on you soon enough and turn heavy as lead."

"Aye, sir."

"Wet your lips and tongue but don't swallow much. I know that thirst, boy, but you can have all you want to drink once this is over."

"Aye, sir," nodding, hoping and praying that was so.

"One thing in your favor I have learned," Osmonde said

as they descended the overlook to the beach. "Your foe is very fond of the bottle. Puts it down like small beer, and he's spent the last five weeks aboard ship doing nothing but getting cup-shot and laying about. He's been ashore less than a week, and the heat is affecting him. Now you're recovered from the Yellow Jack, you've been riding hard, fencing hard, kept yourself fitter than him. I'd wear him down. Fend him off until he begins to drag. Were you fencing with the usual choice of weapon, he might still have the stronger and quicker wrist, but a navy cutlass will wear him down fast enough."

"Yes," Alan intoned, barely hearing Osmonde for the rush of blood in his head and the sound of his breath rushing in and out so full of life. Why did I want to defend the silly mort, he thought queasily. I've no honor, and everybody seems to know it.

"I trust that you have become a dangerous man, Mister Lewrie," Captain Osmonde said, pumping his hand. "And my best wishes to you."

Lewrie shed his uniform and undid his neckcloth, tossing it aside. He took a deep breath and enjoyed the sight of the gulls wheeling over their cove-sheltered beach, the play of sun on the bright green water. He shook himself all over to loosen his tenseness. This is what comes of getting involved with a chick-a-biddy young girl. I should stick to whores.

"Gentlemen," Major Overstreet called them together. "That a blow was struck, and grievous insults exchanged notwithstanding, they were brought about by strong drink, and can be excusable. I charge both of you now, is there no way to settle this quarrel without recourse to steel?"

"Only if Lt. Wyndham publicly recants his slurs on the lady in question, his slurs on me, and apologizes for striking me, sir," Alan stated as calmly as he could, feeling trapped and knowing in his heart that it was not going to be that way. He could see the swaggering, superior way Wyndham glared at him.

"I stand by my statements, sir," Wyndham replied.

Overstreet sighed. "Then it is my sad duty to allow you to proceed. The weapons chosen by the aggrieved party are naval cutlasses. You shall both draw a weapon which your second shall offer you. You shall separate to the red pegs, which are five paces apart. You shall salute each other at my command, then take what guard you will and advance to touch blades. On my count you shall begin. I shall say one, and two, and three, begin. The duel shall continue until such time as one party has received his third cut. At that time I shall call you to cease. Should honor be deemed satisfied, the duel will end. Should you not feel that your cause has been redeemed, your seconds shall inform me and the duel shall continue until such time as one or both of you has fallen. A disarm shall be considered a touch. Should either of you advance threateningly before my count, or fail to halt after the third cut at my call, or if one of you attempt to strike the other after disarming the other, the second of the offended party and I shall shoot him down. Do you understand?"

They both nodded, grim and pale.

"Then take your weapons, please."

Lewrie went to his peg, where Asburn stood. He offered him a cutlass hilt-first. "Pray God for you, Alan," Keith whispered. "Now why don't you cut the swaggering duck-fucker up!"

Lewrie nodded to him and touched him on the shoulder with his free hand, then turned to face Lt. Wyndham, who was getting the feel of the heavy cutlass as though he had never handled one before. It was a plain weapon, heavy as sin, a simple chopping weapon with a wide blade and only one edge and a point of sorts at the end of the upward curve, like a caricature of an infantryman's hanger. The hand guard was of flat steel with a ring guard and a wooden handle, which had been rubbed with dust to staunch the expected sweat.

"Salute," Overstreet called, raising a long double-barreled pistol at half-cock.

Wyndham took up a graceful, balanced pose with one hand over his shoulder, perfect as a French sword instructor, his blade in *quarte*.

Lewrie brought his own blade to *octave* and he had to smile at the incongruous sight of someone posing with a cutlass as though it was a foil.

"I shall begin the count," Overstreet intoned. "One... and two... and three... begin."

They advanced with small steps, blades trembling with anticipation. First beat rang hesitantly as they explored. The army man opened with a thrust, which Lewrie beat aside, and then Wyndham responded with a cut-over. It was obvious that the lieutenant was a point man. They fenced in school style for a while, Lewrie trying Wyndham's disengage and parry style, eyes on Wyndham's own, his point, and the set of his feet.

Wyndham exploded with a sudden lunge. Lewrie parried it off high to his left, stepping aside the thrust in *quartata*, then swung at the unbalanced man and came a toucher of disemboweling Wyndham, who leaped back like a cat, eyes wide with surprise. Lewrie went to the attack with a feint thrust, beating aside the parry and lunged himself. Wyndham gave a grunt of alarm and stumbled backward to fall on the firm sand beach, while Lewrie spun past him and took up guard, waiting for him to regain his feet.

Lewrie understood what Osmonde had meant. What little small beer he had drunk was sloshing around in his belly like a sack of mercury, and his thirst was hellish. The exertion felt debilitating, and they had barely begun. But he found time to whirl his cutlass in mock salute and raise one eyebrow in a cocky grin as Lt. Wyndham got to his feet and began to advance once more.

Wyndham began thrusting low with feint thrusts, stamping to distract Lewrie's attention, or throw off his timing, forcing him back as their blades rang in engagement and light parries. Lewrie gave ground half step for half step to maintain distance before shifting to a low guard and point-parrying Wyndham wider and wider. The soldier wanted to step back and regain his advantage, so he ended with his blade at high first, and whirled it suddenly in a killing swing that Lewrie met with a cross-over to fourth. The two blades met with a great clang and the shock stunned his arm and hand, but Lewrie cut across, his own blade ringing off Wyndham's hilt guard, which lowered the army man's weapon below his waist. Lewrie feinted a cut to the head backhanded, which made him duck back off-balance. Lewrie drew his elbows back and disengaged, then whirled his cutlass under and around to spin Wyndham's guard over his head. He then struck down the blade and lay the heavy cutlass on Wyndham's scalp with a firm tap that cut through hair and skin and thudded off the bone. The infantryman tried to bind, but Lewrie shoved forward with his hilt and pushed hard, jumping back at the same time from the mad, angry swing that followed.

There were murmurs of alarm or pleasure from the witnesses as they saw the blood on Wyndham's head and face running down into his eyes. Humiliated, Wyndham was on the attack at once, taking the hint of their brief practice and using the point less, wielding the cutlass more like one would a hanger to attack edge to edge. Lewrie gave ground, seeing the energy Wyndham was putting into his efforts, and knowing that sooner or later the man would go back to the pointwork he was used to, once he began to flag.

Wyndham began to execute flying cut-overs fairly well, which Alan was parrying off, but he suddenly went back to the point and faked Alan out badly. The straight-armed lunge grazed his left cheek with steel, and he felt a sudden pain in his face. But he responded with a counterthrust under that made Wyndham hop to save his nutmegs, then an upward parry and a rapid double, which forced Wyndham to leap back once more.

Lewrie took a long pace forward to attack, changing tactics to the full naval cutlass drill—stamp, slash, balance and return, slash—right and left, up and down, whirling the heavy blade in a whistling arc that brought grunts of effort from Wyndham each time he parried, the blades smashing together with the hefty clang of a farrier making a new horseshoe. Lewrie added flying cut-overs to break the pace, going from high to low before making a swing with his wrist that almost put his point into the army man's chest. Wyndham's parry was weak, and he almost dragged himself backward to escape, his chest heaving.

Lewrie thought it a trick, but was not sure. He himself was tired...God, he was aching, his wrist and his arms heavy as lead, and his legs juddering props that threatened to go slack at any second and drop him to the ground. But Wyndham did look finished. His body was streaming sweat, thinning the blood that ran down his face and coating it with claret. And his eyes that had been so mocking and so sure were now squinted with concern and doubt. He was tempted to leap forward and finish it but remembered Captain Osmonde's advice to go slow and wear him down.

They met again, blades still ringing, but now softer.

Wyndham thrust low, using the point to come up with a ripping slash at Lewrie's stomach, but he beat it aside at the last instant, driving Wyndham's guard low, met the next blow with a two-handed swing that forced Wyndham's blade wide to the left and almost into the sand. Lewrie stepped forward into his guard sideways and swung back to the right two-handed again with all his flagging might. He felt a thud like sinking an axe into a chopping block, and leaped back, centering his guard against a reply. But it was over.

Wyndham stood before him with his feet together, his face as white as his snowy breeches. They both looked down at the sand to see Lt. Wyndham's right arm lying there, still clutching the cutlass and the nerveless fingers curling and drumming an irregular tatoo on the hilt.

Wyndham looked back to him in surprise before his eyes rolled back into his head and he pitched forward to the sand, a fountain of blood gushing from what remained of his shoulder with each beat of his heart.

Lewrie stumbled backward, unable to feature it, the tip of his blade dragging a furrow through the sand. Ashburn came up to him and he dropped his cutlass and turned away from him. Wyndham's party came forward, and both surgeons worked on the infantry officer, cauterizing a great cut in Wyndham's side, and hands slipped in gore as they tried to seize the spurting arteries and sear them shut, while the sea birds cried and wheeled at the smell of blood steaming on the beach.

Lewrie sat down on the step of his coach, watching the drama below. The naval coachee gave him a large glass of brandy to drink.

"Gawd almighty, sir..."

"Indeed." Alan nodded in shock. "Another please."

This brandy he sipped more slowly, becoming aware of how sore he was all over after being so tensed up for God knew how long, how his arms ached and throbbed, and the pain pulsed in his ravaged cheek. His thigh muscles were jumping and his calves and ankles hurt as though he had strolled twenty miles across country.

Captain Osmonde climbed up the sand slope from the beach to him. "I believe you shall make a dangerous man, after all, Mister Lewrie."

"I meant but to cut him..."

"I believe you could consider that intent most successful," the Marine officer said.

"Will he live?"

"Lt. Warren Wyndham is now *late* of His Majesty's 12th Regiment of Foot," Osmonde said. "Totally exsanguined of his life's blood and dead on the field of...*honor*. Was it worth it?"

"At the moment, yes, sir," Lewrie said, studying his shoes. "I don't know about tomorrow."

"An honest answer, at any rate," Osmonde said, kneeling down in front of him. "Don't develop a taste for this, boy. War is gloriously obscene enough without turning into a man-killer."

"I want no more of it," Alan confessed.

"Best have the surgeon sew that up," Osmonde said, touching his cheek to examine his wound. "Won't spoil your looks for the ladies, I doubt. Hungry?"

"Yes," Alan realized.

"Ashburn had the good faith in you to reserve rooms for us for a late breakfast at an inn on the way back. I, for one, am famished."

"There's one good that will come out of this," Lewrie said as he got to his feet at the approach of the surgeon with his bag. "There is no way they'll keep me as a messenger and errand boy ashore after this. If I'm not at sea within a week, there's a dozen of good claret for you and Ashburn on it..."

CHAPTER

11

"YOU were fortunate, Mister Lewrie," Commander the Honorable Tobias Treghues said, seated behind his glossy mahoghany desk in the day cabins of the 20-gun frigate *Desperate*. "I am told the officers of the 12th Foot detachment have talked of a syndicate to challenge you one at a time until you are bested. They were not enamored of your choice of weapons, or how you won."

"Aye aye, sir," Lewrie said, studying his new lord and master. Treghues was in his late twenties, slim and brown-haired with grey eyes. His uniform was impeccable, as were his cabin furnishings. He showed no signs of poverty, though it had been rumored he was the eldest son of a lord gone to sea to improve the family fortunes with prizes.

"Fortunate also that I had a suitable berth, after losing one young gentleman drowned, and another to the bottle," Treghues went on.

"Aye aye, sir." When a midshipman had no better answer, that usually struck the right obedient note without committing to anything.

"You are, for your own safety, to remain aboard until we

have sailed. You are not even to place foot in a rowing boat. By the time we return from a cruising patrol the 12th shall have gone to St. Kitts and the problem shall have been resolved."

"Aye aye, sir," Lewrie said, trying to find a new way to do it.

"I do not hold with dueling," Treghues warned. "Or hotheaded bucks who cannot resist taking offense at the slightest reproach like some swaggering Frog duke, Mister Lewrie. Usually bad officers, too."

"I do not wish to give that impression, sir, but I had—"

Treghues waved off the rest of his answer. "Spare me your innocent and honorable motives. Sir Onsley informed me as to the circumstance. He also gives you a glowing report, so I am aware of your services to the Crown of late. You may be useful to this ship, but all I want to see from you is duty done in a cheerful and efficient manner. Spare us your blood-lust for the foe."

"Aye aye, sir." Lewrie parroted himself.

"Admiral Sir George Rodney has taken over from Admiral Byron, thanks be to God, so we should see some action soon. Hood and Rodney together and we'll see an end to these French and Spanish combinations. So, you see what is needed. Get below and into your working rig. I allow you to forego the waistcoat in these climes, but I expect a midshipman to look like a proper officer at all times, no matter how junior you may be. That means a regulation dirk instead of that pretty hanger of yours. And I prefer a cocked hat to the usual one. I took you on sufferance—don't give me reason to regret it."

Lewrie nodded and left the cabins, emerging on the upper deck. *Desperate* had no poop but a long quarterdeck over the captain's cabin. Her first (and only) lieutenant had quarters below the captain with the surgeon, purser, Marine lieutenant and suchlike worthies. The wheel stood over the captain's cabins on the long quarterdeck, unprotected by binnacle bulwarks. The lower deck was not a gun deck at all, the artillery being sited on the upper deck where the captain lived in solitary splendor. Hands berthed forward on the lower deck, then petty officers, Marines, warrants and midshipmen, and then the officer's gun room right aft. The orlop and hold were too crammed with supplies to let anyone berth there.

"What a crosspatch he is." Lewrie sighed. From the way Treghues regarded Rodney, he must be one of his—not a good sign, Rodney was famed for incredibly bad judgement in appointments.

But the cobbing he had received could not dampen his joy to be aboard any sort of ship once more, and *Desperate* was magnificent. She was 110 feet on the range of the lower deck, a bit over 30 in beam, of 450 tons burthen. Piercing her upper deck bulwarks were eighteen nine-pounder cannon, with two of the new eighteen-pounder carronades on her foc's'l, short guns mounted on swivelling slides that fired bursting shot at no great range—"Smashers"—he was dying to try them out.

Desperate carried Treghues, a first lieutenant named Railsford, Mr. Monk the sailing master and two mates, one bosun and mate, one warrant gunner, one gunner's mate and a yeoman of the powder room, a surgeon named Dorne and a mate, five quartergunners, one carpenter and mate, one armorer, one master-at-arms, two quartermasters and mates, a yeoman of the sheets, one coxswain, four carpenter's crew, one ship's corporal, a sailmaker and one sailmaker's assistant, one captain's clerk, the young purser named Cheatham and his steward, four midshipmen, four young boy fifers and drummers, eighteen boyservants, and fifty-six men rated as either ordinary or able seamen, or landsmen. She also carried Marines; a lieutenant named Peck, one sergeant, one corporal, and thirty private soldiers.

She was a 6th rate, the smallest type of ship-rigged frigate in the fleet, and with Lewrie joining her, was fortunate to be only six hands short of full complement.

Desperate was too light for the line of battle with her four-inch oak scantlings and beams on twelve-inch centers. She was too fast to be tied to a squadron, but also too well armed to waste on despatches like *Parrot*. *Desperate* was what was coming to be known as a "cruizer"; she was a huntress on her own in the most likely places to seek out, take, or burn enemy merchantmen, privateers and light naval units.

Lewrie entered the midshipmens' berth to find his new mess mates lounging about the small compartment, sandwiched in without air by storerooms and the mate's dog boxes. The total space was about twelve-by-ten, with barely five feet of headroom between the beams. There was a polished table down the center for dining, chests for seats, and pegs for storage of handy items.

"Hullo. I'm Alan Lewrie," he said to them, reliving that scene long ago when he had reported below in *Ariadne*. But there was a difference; he had nearly fifteen months in the Navy, and knew what sort of drudgery and folderol to expect now. He was introduced to the others. There was Peter Carey, a ginger-haired boy of thirteen with the usual modest squirearchy background. There was a gotch-gutted sixteen-year-old pig named Francis Forrester. He was quick to point out that it was the Honorable Francis Forrester, and his elegant manners and his drawling, superior voice made it abundantly clear that he looked on Lewrie's arrival as another mark of the reduction in tone of their mess.

Lewrie's other companion was also sixteen, a dark and merry Cornish boy that Lewrie had known slightly long before when posted to the *Ariadne* after it had become a receiving ship. He and David Avery had gone roaming English Harbor together, and had enjoyed each other's company, before Avery had joined an armed transport.

Alan carefully removed and folded up his fine new uniform. He packed the waistcoat away for Sunday Divisions, slipped out of his snowy breeches and dug out a ragged pair of slop trousers. He exchanged his silk stockings for cotton, wrapped his best shoes and donned a cracked pair. His worst faded and stained coat he hung up on a peg. Sadly, he packed the hanger away in his open chest and fetched out his dirk, now showing signs of wear around that "best gold plate pommel".

"Pretty hanger." Forrester pouted like a sow, picking it up and studying it. "But your parents should have known better."

"It was a recent gift," Alan said, meaning to get off to a fair start, if allowed. "For saving my last captain his ship."

"Yess," Forrester drawled. "Avery has been regaling us with the heroism of your derring-do." He sheathed the hanger and tossed it into Lewrie's chest like a poor discard at a secondhand shop.

"Did you really kill a man in a duel?" Carey asked wide-eyed.

"Yes. Dead as cold, boiled mutton. He insulted a young lady of my acquaintance."

"Carey, we must remember to tremble before the anger of our new man-slaughtering Hector," Forrester said. "Even if he is, by length of service, junior to you. How long at sea, Lewrie?"

"A year. Fifteen months total."

"Then I am still senior," Forrester said, pleased to hear it. "June of '76."

"We're not lieutenants, Forrester," Avery replied. "I actually predate you by a whole month, if the truth be known. We're all equal here."

"Ah, the rebellious Adamses and Thomas Paines have been after you again," Forrester said in a way that Lewrie could only think of as greasy. "Remember that I have the signals and you don't, so that makes me senior. And I trust that any new errant newlies shall remember that."

"We had a man who said much the same thing in *Ariadne*," Lewrie said, taking a pew on his closed chest. "He died."

"Would be having the gall to threaten me?" Forrester's piggy eyes were squinted.

"Now why should I do a thing like that? I'm but stating a fact. You remember me mentioning him, don't you Avery?"

"Oh, you mean Mister the Honorable...what was his name?"

"Fotheringfop," Lewrie said. "Ferdinand Fotheringfop."

"Choked on his beef bones, didn't he?" Avery said.

"No, that was Mister the Honorable D'Arcy DeBloat."

"And what, pray did he die of?" Avery was playing along, to the great delight of young Carey, who was already stifling a grin.

"Fotheringfop was so elevated an individual, with such an airy opinion of himself that his head swelled one morning at dawn quarters. We tried to save him and got a gantline to him, but he pulled the maint'gallantmast right out of her. Last seen drifting for Panama. Crew did a little hornpipe of despair at his passing. Sad, it was."

Forrester snorted at the foolishness and left the midshipmens' berth for the upper deck, while Carey dared to laugh out loud and Avery pronounced Lewrie a fellow that would do.

"What a fubsy, crusty thing it is," Lewrie observed of their mess mate. "What does he expect us to do, carry his scepter for him, or just be his fags?"

"Just a puffed up dilberry." Avery shrugged. "Probably afraid we know more than him and show him up before his lord and master."

"Fat pig," Carey said, softly.

"Carey, what were the other midshipmen like?" Lewrie asked.

"Dodds was twenty or so. But I've never seen anyone drink so much all the time. The captain finally threw him out, said he'd never make an officer or live long enough to take the exam."

"Good relations to the captain?" Lewrie probed.

"I think he was a cater-cousin." Carey frowned. "The other...Montgomery, he was real smart, and nice. He was a year older than me but he knew everything. He got washed overboard in a gale last month north of St. Lucia. He was my friend."

Lewrie shared a look with Avery. They could imagine

what the mess had been like for Carey, with one raging sponge in his cups all the time, the brutish Forrester lording it over all the others, and only Montgomery to shield the younger boy. Carey gave no sign that he was a mental giant, or in any way assertive. Just a scared and homesick child, mediocre at best when it came to duty and too small and weak to perform like a real sailor.

"Well, there's a new order here, by God," Avery told him with a rap on the shoulder. "Just let that cow's ass try to push his weight around..."

"Of which he has considerable," Lewrie added.

"Aye, and we'll fix him," Avery said. "Right, Lewrie?"

"Amen to that," Lewrie intoned with mock piety.

"You can't go too far, though," Carey said. "I mean, Treghues and Forrester...they're not related, but you'd think Forrester was his brother."

"Plays the favorite, does your captain?"

"I shouldn't say it, but he—"

"A wonderful berth," Avery sighed. "And I thought that rotten armed transport was bad."

"Hell with it," Lewrie said. "I hear she's made her people a pot of prize money, and she goes her own way looking for fame and fortune. We're in the right place. Now all we have to do is to convince our captain that we're the right midshipmen for him."

"That shouldn't be too hard," Avery said. "Here, Lewrie, you wouldn't have a neckcloth that would pass Divisions, have you?"

JUST before departure, mail came aboard, and Lewrie was surprised to have two packets. Sir Hugo was actually living up to his end of the bargain and had sent him a *rouleau* of one hundred guineas. Well, actually, the solicitor Mr. Pilchard had sent it. There was no letter attached and that was no disappointment, but the money was most welcome.

The next was from Lucy Beauman. He had been isolated aboard *Ariadne* following the duel, then rapidly transferred to *Desperate* and had not been allowed to see her, though he had sent her a letter that he was not sure her aunt and uncle would allow her to see.

There was belated fear for his life, wonderment at his courage, a recital of prayers said for him, a brief screed against Wyndham, who had not struck her as a trustworthy gentleman, a denial that she had encouraged him in the slightest manner (which Lewrie doubted...she was a girl, wasn't she?), profound relief at his victory and survival, deep despair at being denied his presence, grief and tears at their cruel separation (but more prayers for success at his new endeavors in *Desperate*) and fond hopes of a quick reunion.

She enclosed an embroidered handkerchief for him, scented and splashed with her tears, binding up a generous lock of her honey gold hair. There was also Old Isaac's completed juju bag, which he was to hang about his neck immediately and never remove. Lewrie was leery as to that instruction; the bag had a redolence of badly cured goat skin, tidal effluvia and perhaps the slight admixture of chicken guts. She wrote:

> I shall wate with constant Longing for your Safe Retern, that we may avale ourselves once more of that mutuol Pleasure in our companyunship, and may agane strole without Cares on that particular Strand I have cumm to regard as a most Blesed and Speshul Place.

> Awl my Fondness Goe With You, Lucy

Someone should teach the little mort to spell, he thought, but was touched by her sentiments, and by her evident love for him. He took time to pen her a proper but passionate reply, the sort that would turn a young girl's head for a while. As a fillip, he enclosed a lock of his own hair (still fairly short). Then it was time to sail.

* * *

ADMIRAL Rodney had plugged one hole in the dyke against all the supplies from Europe that reached the rebellious colonies by taking the island of St. Eustatius, a major smuggling and transshipment port for naval and military stores and a convenient outlet for American produce and manufactured goods with which they partly paid for all the French, Spanish and Dutch largesse.

By keeping the expected flags flying, and with secret recognition signals, Rodney kept the island open, luring in ships that had no chance to be apprised of the change of ownership. It was resulting in scores of captures.

Desperate was sent north with a roving commission to hunt down ships hoping to use St. Eustatius.

Barely ten days after coming aboard, Lewrie emerged on deck one fine brisk morning sated with a good breakfast of thin sliced fried pork, boiled egg and crumbled biscuit in treacle. He was still smacking his lips and regretting not being able to enjoy a second cup of coffee when the lookout gave a loud hail to the deck below, ending any thoughts of sail drill for the forenoon watch.

"Sail ho!" he bellowed. "Three points off the larboard bow!"

Lt. Railsford chose Avery to dash aloft to confirm the sighting, and Avery handed Lewrie his hat, brushed back his black hair and ran for the mainmast crosstrees.

Treghues came on deck in breeches and waistcoat and went to the wheel, waiting for a report. Peck, the gangly young blond Marine officer came up, eager for action.

"Two sail, sir," Avery said. "Schooner and brig. Headed due north under all plain sail."

"Mister Monk," Treghues called. "Alter course to chase, and we shall crack on all sail she can stand. Stuns'ls, too."

"Bosun!" their stocky dark sailing master relayed. "All hands aloft and make sail. Trice up and lay out for stuns'ls."

The single night reef in the courses and tops'ls was shaken out, and Lewrie went aloft to the t'gallant mast as the yards were raised up by the jeers. Below him on the main course yard, hands were extending the stuns'l booms, bending on canvas to spread every stitch their ship could fly. *Desperate* leaned her shoulder firmly to the sea and began to soar across the moderate seas, smashing into the odd wave, but slicing clean through the regular set of rollers, her wake boiling.

By ten in the forenoon she had run the schooner hull up before her, and the brig beyond showed all her sail plan; clearly they were overtaking handily, which suggested ships too heavily loaded to run. *Desperate* was already towing one boat, and put another down from her quarter davits to be ready with boarding parties. Lewrie hoped that he would be entrusted with one of those parties.

Just after Clear-Deck-And-Up-Spirits at seven bells of the forenoon they beat to quarters and manned their guns. Lunch would be delayed but with the prospect of prizes ahead, no one minded.

Treghues had gone below to catch up on paper work with his clerk, interview the purser and pretend that there was nothing to get excited about, while Lewrie fretted and stewed in impatience. And when their captain did emerge he was close-shaved, dressed in a good coat and cocked hat, his small sword hung just so from his belt frog.

When they had the schooner within range of a nine-pounder, just about six cables off, she took one look and raised her rebel colors to satisfy honor, then quickly hauled them down and rounded to into the wind. Mr. Feather, a burly master's mate, and Midshipman Forrester went over in the first cutter to take charge of her with a dozen hands.

"Good man, Forrester," Treghues commented to Railsford by the quarterdeck nettings. "He'll keep our prize safe."

"Aye, sir," Railsford agreed dutifully but without much enthusiasm. Lewrie stood close by and heard this exchange and weighed it for what he thought it was worth. In his short time aboard he had found that young Forrester had a reputation much like Rolston in *Ariadne* when it came to discipline and tautness.

Then they were off again in pursuit of the brig. Treghues ordered stand-easy for the gun crews, but unlike old Bales he had had the ship properly cleared for action, though their chase might be a mere smuggler and not a privateer or warship. He was taking no chances, and Lewrie approved. Their captured schooner fell in line astern far back, so loaded she was barely able to stay in sight.

Water and cheese and biscuit was brought up to the gun crews as they stood easy for a cold dinner with the galley-fire extinguished. Lewrie stood in the waist of the ship by the mainmast, idling on the jeer bitts and chewing his dry dinner. The cheese was a navy-issue Suffolk, more like crumbling rock than cheese. Giving up on making a meal on it, he brushed his hands and stood on the jeer bitts for a better view.

The brig was now well hull up, perhaps a league off and still being overhauled. Lewrie imagined that she was badly laden besides being heavily loaded. Her bow seemed to slough and make a large wave even with her forecourse spread taut for the lifting effect. Had her bow ridden higher, lessening her resistance, she might have made a knot more. And as low in the water as she looked, her shallower draft would be of no avail in the maze of islands ahead to the nor-nor'west, where she could normally expect to lose the frigate with her deeper draft.

"Got a good view, Mister Lewrie?" Treghues asked, hands behind his back and staring up at him as he paced the gun deck to inspect his hands.

"Aye, sir." Lewrie climbed down to doff his hat.

"Learning anything?"

"Aye, sir. She draws a foot deeper forrard," Lewrie said. "He'll have to shift a pair of guns, or some cargo, or he's ours before two hours pass."

"Indeed," Treghues said, shocked to hear such talk from a midshipman. "But he can always get a favorable slant of wind. Get into those islands."

"Aye, he could, sir," Lewrie persisted. "But the Trades hereabouts drop off around the first dog, sir, and he's too deep to risk shoal water. We're balanced, more sail aloft and have a longer waterline."

"So you are confident." Treghues smiled, using the moment to put life into his crew.

"That I am, sir."

"We'll have him, lads. Our new midshipman believes so, so we must, eh? A little more gold in your pockets would not go amiss."

Treghues passed on to trade joshes with the quartergunners, mostly of the squire-to-tenant "how do your sheep keep old un" variety with the expected reply of bright smiles and much tugging of forelocks, leaving Lewrie abashed. He had tried to make a good impression on the captain concerning his skill and nautical knowledge so that he would think of him as competent and equal to Forrester, but now he was the silent butt of the crew's humor.

Goddamn him, Lewrie fumed, busying himself with looking at train tackles. I didn't deserve that.

Before another hour had passed, the brig wore to larboard slightly and opened fire at extreme long range with a six-pounder gun, the ball dropping far short but good evidence of her intent to fight.

I'd get the stuns'ls in, Lewrie thought, peering aloft. If I were the chase I'd wear hard onto the wind, lay her full and by to the nor'east and beat up toward St. Barts. Maybe gain a league before we got ourselves sorted out...A Molly or not, he had to give Lt. Kenyon credit for a superb education in ship-handling and how to draw out a stern chase, as they had once off Anegada pursued by that privateer.

"Bosun, hands aloft and take in stuns'ls," Treghues called. "Mr. Gwynn, stand by to try your eye with the number one gun."

Desperate turned off the wind as mastergunner Gwynn fussed over his foremost starboard cannon. Once the quoin was out and he was satisfied, he put up his fist and stood clear, looking aft. Treghues must have waved to him, because the linstock came down to the firing quill in the vent, and the gun lurched inboard with a flat bang. The ball splashed short but directly in line with the brig's bowsprit. The brig responded with a full broadside of six guns, aimed high. Lewrie could hear the shot as it moaned overhead through the rigging. A sail twitched, and a block and halyard snaked down to thud onto the larboard gangway.

"Stand by the starboard battery!"

Alan looked aloft again. The stuns'l booms were still rigged out, though the sails were mostly furled. Now would be the time to wear, he thought grimly, and this broadside will be wasted. It's nearly five cables' range, anyway. This is just what they want of us...

"As you bear...fire!" Treghues shouted.

The guns began to belch and roll back to the extent of the breeching ropes, and the well-drilled crews leaped on them to sponge out, to clear the vents and begin ramming down fresh powder and shot.

Thought so, Lewrie told himself. The smuggler brig had hardened up her braces and sheets and was wheeling to present her stern to them, wearing through at least ninety-degrees to the nor'east.

"Goddamn and blast the bugger," Monk called out as though he had just had his purse cut loose, and Treghues chafed him for blaspheming.

"Hands to train and sidetackles!" Lewrie shouted. "Snug 'em down tight and prepare to come about!" A second later that same command was shouted to them from Railsford on the quarterdeck. Waisters ran to the braces to cast them off the delaying pins while the forecastle captain prepared to heave on his heads'l sheets. But they had to wait until the men aloft had laid in from the yards after securing the stuns'ls, and the brig was gaining time to windward, no matter how the officers aft shouted for the topmen to speed their work.

"Hands wear ship!" came finally. "Put yer helm down!"

"Haul, you people, haul!" The bosun roared.

"'Vast hauling and belay!"

Desperate turned up into the wind as steady as a needle on a pin and settled on her new course. The chase was still on her starboard side, now settled just over their windward cathead, and had regained at least half a league of distance on them. It would take the frigate at least two more hours to beat up to windward against that more weatherly brig, at which point it would be near the start of the first dogwatch.

"Gun crews stand easy."

Lewrie climbed onto the jeer bitts once more to look to the suth'rd for their first prize. If Forrester had two brain cells to rub together he would wear onto the wind now as soon as he saw what was happening. A schooner, even a loaded one, could go to windward much better than either the brig or *Desperate*, could cut the corner off and with even one gun manned, could threaten their chase into heading north once more.

There was no sign that Forrester had the requisite number of brain cells, for she plodded along for long minutes on her original course. A signal went up *Desperate*'s mizzen, which went unseen.

"Blind fucker," Lewrie muttered just loud enough for the nearest hands to hear. "He'll not stand a chance now."

By the time the schooner came about she was not just downwind of the chase but downwind of *Desperate* as well.

Desperate stood on for three hours before coming within range once more. The captain of the brig must have been a nacky man himself, because he hauled his wind to head due north, and as soon as *Desperate* began to parallel her course and open fire once again, he tacked, this time crossing the eye of the wind. He ducked out of the way of the broadside and headed off into the gloom of late afternoon to the sou-sou'east, back the way he had come. Forrester stood no chance even to get close. And the brig was not as unhandy on the wind as Lewrie had thought, for she pulled up half a point higher than the frigate, and was actually very slowly drawing away.

The hands were stood down from quarters and the galley fire was lit. Lewrie looked at his watch. It would be dusk in forty-five minutes. They would stand to evening quarters, then, without a prize.

This evening Lewrie was in what was left of the second dogwatch, so he left the gun deck and went up to the quarterdeck to stand by the wheel, where Monk and Treghues and Railsford were conferring.

"Still so confident, Mister Lewrie?" Treghues said irritably.

"He was mickle-crafty, sir," Lewrie replied, searching for something safe to say to a captain who was livid inside. "Most likely a Jonathan captain—"

"What makes you think *that*?"

"The French and the Dons don't handle ships that well, sir. He may have been Dutch, but I doubt it. American-built brig with a rebel captain. She was smartly handled, sir."

"Next thing you know, Mister Lewrie shall be giving us lessons in ship-handling," Treghues said. "Jesus Lord."

"I would not presume, sir."

"Don't take that tone with me, young sir, or I'll have you bent over a gun before you can say Jack Ketch..."

"Aye aye, sir."

"Get off my quarterdeck."

"I'm in the watch, sir?"

"Then get down to loo'rd and out of my face."

"Aye aye, sir."

Welcome back to the real Navy, Lewrie thought, gazing off to the north as it got darker. There was a spectacular sunset astern, all reds and golds and layers of clouds painted pink and amber and blue grey, and the seas were bright as glittering rubies. At least he could appreciate that without harm.

Lewrie idled his time until evening quarters thinking about that brig. She would most likely run to windward until after full dark, then come about north once more, probably wear on a reciprocal course because she did not want to get tangled up with the inshore patrols near St. Barts and St. Maartin. She could go due north outside the island chain. She could not set west—that would take her back into the arms of *Desperate* and the prize schooner. And on the map engraved in his head, Lewrie saw the Saba

Bank. No, she would turn nor'west and run the gap for the other smuggler's holes in the Danish Virgins, St. Croix as the best bet, Spanish Puerto Rico if she was set to westerly. Lewrie was not sure what Commander Tobias Treghues had planned, but he knew where he would have waited to find her again. But then, nobody was asking him about it, were they?

IF he could not dazzle his new ship with his brilliance, he could at least succeed at appearing competent, and that was what he did in the weeks of cruising that followed. He re-quested that Railsford let him assist in small arms. He let it be known at lunch to the captain's clerk that he had assisted an acting purser and had worked in the English Harbor stores warehouses. He chatted with Mr. Gwynn and dropped a hint that he loved artillery and the great guns. At navigation practice with his new sextant (thanks to Lord Cantner's reward) he displayed to the sailing master his skills naturally, and Mister Monk let it be known that he was a dab-hand at navigating. In the course of this endeavor he casually revealed that Lt. Kenyon had let him stand middle-watch with a bosun's mate, and had filled in as an acting master's mate in *Parrot* during her time with fever.

To each of these worthies he also showed a false front, that of a young man lately run to death by duties and happy to be once more a junior petty officer with no major respon-sibilities. Having been in the Navy long enough to know how hatefully any senior warrant or commission officer re-garded idle hands, and knowing that when a midshipman was working some officer was well-pleased (and cannily un-derstanding the perverse nature of his fellow-man), Alan soon found himself exactly where he wanted to be.

He assisted the master-at-arms and Marine lieutenant at small arms. He assisted Mr. Cheatham with the ship's books and expense ledgers. He and the gunner's mate and yeo-man of the powder room became coequal authorities on the upkeep of the great guns and all their ancillary gear.

Avery found his niches as well, and they drilled young Carey in terminology and lore until he could spout technical lingo with the ease of a bosun twenty years at sea. Carey also learned how to curse most wonderfully well.

As the weeks went by, Treghues and Railsford learned that there was indeed a new order aboard—midshipmen who were useful instead of the usual snot-nosed younkers-in-training they had grown accustomed to. There was less snarling from Treghues. In fact, there was a grudging acceptance, then a secret delight in having thoroughly salted and tarred midshipmen who could be trusted to carry out an order smartly.

Forrester, however, began to pout more, to purse his lips and squint his porcine eyes and curse them roundly. He was being threatened, and he knew it. Oh, he still had Captain Treghues' favor, since he had long been the man's star pupil, and their families were obviously cater-cousins. He was one of the original crew when *Desperate* was commissioned, and it would take an act of incredible stupidity or craven cowardice to break that bond. But when it came to something prestigious to do, his name was no longer the first on Treghues' lips.

Nor could he hold his superior social position in their mess, because if he struck out at Carey, he had Avery and Lewrie to contend with, and he could not push his weight around with either of them. He did try, but Avery was a most inventive fellow when it came to filling the young man's shoes with molasses during the night, nailing his chest shut when he was on deck, starting small rips in his hammock with a shaving razor that would tear open and leave his large ass hanging out in the air by the start of the morning watch, substituting smaller sizes of slop trousers so that Forrester had to appear on deck with a distinctly pinched look about the middle. With all of them on deck during the day at exercises and drills, Forrester found it hard to respond with his own brand of trickery, since they all watched him close in a cabal sworn and dedicated to drive him to distraction.

Lewrie was a little more direct. When Forrester was caught trying to sabotage Avery's chest one morning, Lewrie simply told him that if he caught him at it again he would kick him in the balls. And when he caught him trying to open his own chest the next day, Alan made good on his threat, which made Forrester crouch for a week.

After the loss of the smuggler brig, *Desperate* made up for it... there were still dozens of islands engaged in illicit trade and hundreds of ships crossing the Atlantic on the Trades. Not a fortnight went by that they did not send a prize crew into port with the Red Ensign flying over the striped colors of the Rebels, the flag of Spain or the golden lillies of France.

Their prizes were small—brigs and snows, brigantines and schooners, luggers and cutters, but the value of the cargoes and bottoms lost to the American Rebellion mounted steadily. Powder, shot, carriage guns, stands of arms, crates of swords and uniforms, blankets and camp gear for Washington's army—rice, pitch, spars, indigo, molasses and rum, log wood and bales of cotton—it all piled up in Admiralty Prize Courts warehouses in British hands.

To Lewrie it was as much like a legal form of piracy as any he had ever read about (with not the slightest idea that he would ever be involved), piracy with the right to have a bank account.

And while Article Eight of the Articles of War specifically stated that all contents of a seized ship was property of the Admiralty, *Desperate* could continually feed herself on casks of salt meat "condemned" as unfit, firewood, water, coffee and cabin stores from the officer's messes, "split" flour sacks, "rat infested" bread bags, crates of wine that no one thought to list in the prize manifests, livestock that had "died," spare cordage and sailcloth and yards and spars... everything they needed to continue cruising. They ate well, they drank well and they maintained their ship in prime condition at their enemies' expense, and the prize money piled up for eventual payout.

After two months *Desperate* was becoming seriously undermanned for fighting, much less for working the ship. One at a time she had been forced to part with quartermasters and mates, bosun's mates, both master's mates, half a dozen hands into this prize, ten into that one, until all the midshipmen, including Carey, had been called to stand a deck watch with no supervision.

The turnover in an active frigate that spent so much time on the prowl, and had had such good luck with prizes, was nearly fifty percent a year, but it made grand chances for able men. Able seamen constantly rose to more demanding acting positions. And they could always hope that the man they replaced was not languishing ashore, waiting to be recalled, but had been appointed into another ship, leaving them the possession of their new berth and extra pay.

The man sent off could not expect to return to his own ship, and stood a good chance of rising in the service in a new vessel, but perversely, they usually preferred to return. *Desperate* and her ways were a known quality, with a firm but fair captain and for the most part decent officers. Who knew what the next ship would be like?

Finally, *Desperate* was forced to put about and head for Antigua, as miserly manned as the seediest merchantman with a skinflint for a master.

CHAPTER

12

THERE was more bustle in English Harbor when *Desperate* arrived. Admiral Hood and his flagship *Barfleur*, along with his fleet of larger ships of the line, filled the outer roads, and the port worked alive with rowing boats and supply ships.

Treghues was rowed over to *Glatton* to report to Admiral Matthews, and then was taken to *Barfleur* to dine. Forrester accompanied him, to everyone's disgust, while Lewrie and Avery were handed the cutter and the pinnace and told to start heading for the inner harbor.

It was promising to see that all their prizes had arrived safe, anchored in a huddle of shipping far out of the way. That meant that there should be a share out of prize money soon. Maybe not the whole sum due each man, but enough pounds and shillings to make his life a little interesting, buy him a woman, some liquid refreshment, new slop clothing, tobacco, shares in some fresh meat or imported delicacies, or pay off his outstanding account with the purser, who could loan money against future pay for slop purchases.

Lewrie was also happy to note that at least half of *Desperate*'s missing people were still ashore waiting her arrival;

happy that her most capable mates and inferior petty officers and able seamen were available once more; the ship would not be deprived of their experience any longer.

It was something of an embarrassing shock to see how happy their sojourners were to see him. He had thought they would be glad to be back aboard among their own mates, but here they were, making much of the sight of *him*. They sounded genuinely pleased to say hello to him and asked him joshing questions about those who had remained behind; how things stood with their acting replacements, was a certain ship's boy bearing up and behaving, had a piece of gear been overhauled in their absence, had the goat foaled yet, asking him how he kept and had he and Mister Avery been looking after Carey, abusing Forrester and bragging about what they had done in their free time ashore.

I don't know these people that well, Lewrie thought, at a loss to explain their seeming affection from people in his subdivision, his watch. I know names and faces, who works and who hangs back. Maybe I've gotten some of them a rating and they think I'm due. I haven't tried to be popular. Don't tell me they have any real love for me...

He tried to be cynical about it, but it was touching all the same, running another delusion about the Navy squarely on the rocks. He had to admit that, for the most part, they were good men, able and well-trained, but not the sort he'd have in for a joint and a bottle and a yarn if he were back home in London. Pressed or volunteer, one could no longer tell. But then he wasn't back home, was he?

Lewrie soon gave up wondering about it as *Desperate* restocked. While the dockyard supplied most of the labor, stable men were picked to help out for extra pay in ferrying out fresh food and replacements for their depleted stores of bread, spirits and consumables.

Lewrie took Dr. Dorne and Mr. Cheatham ashore to select several bullocks for fresh meat while *Desperate* was in port, along with fresh flour, raisins, sugar and fixings for plenty of figgy-dowdys or duffs.

Dorne was also to make sure that Cheatham purchased cases of fresh hard-skinned acid fruit. Commander Treghues was of the opinion that the rob of lemons, limes and oranges had been the best anti-scorbutic the late Captain Cook had found against scurvy on his worldwide voyages. Dr. Dorne clung to the theory that bad air from the bilges caused scurvy. Had the rate of the disease dropped once Hales' Patent Ventilators had been installed to air the spaces below the waterline? Yes, it had. But Dorne was not about to question a commander's decision.

Dr. Dorne was an untidy little man, fussy about his appearance, and was one of the few men Lewrie had seen who normally wore a wig in the tropics as a matter of course. Perhaps because he was vain about going bald, he was never seen without his horsehair appliance. But he was considered a good surgeon, able to take off a limb in seconds, never causing unnecessary pain in the process, though he had little call for his skills so far. He could lance a boil, tend to ropeburns, fit a truss, provide ointment for saltwater rashes and swore his fifteen-shilling mercury cure for the pox was devilish fine. He was also an easy touch for a late night drink or a good book to read.

Cheatham, the purser, was a real puzzle. First of all, why should someone leave the Kentish fruit trade for the uncertain life of the sea where the profit margins were so low on issued stores, where any cheating beyond the Victualing Board's fourteen ounces to the pound would be noticed by the men and complained about right smartly? Even slops at twelve percent profit could not sustain him, and Lewrie had yet to find him listing discharged men as big users of tobacco or sundry other items. Yet Cheatham always smiled, had no more complaints than most, and his books balanced nicely. He had a "lay" somewhere that was paying handsomely or he had a wish to die poor. Only time would tell the truth.

Lewrie came back aboard littered with chicken feathers after ferrying the last major items on the gun room's shopping lists, and was told to wash up and muster aft in the captain's cabins at the beginning of the first dogwatch. He was welcomed in by the officers and senior warrants. Commander Treghues' servant was circulating with claret and pouring liberally.

"Gentlemen, I have summoned you aft to announce some good fortune that has come our way," Treghues began, glass in hand. "Good fortune for every hand, every man jack."

Railsford sat nearby, already in on the secret and smiling at his ease for once now that the ship was anchored and nothing could go wrong to upset a first lieutenant's peace— for a while, at least.

"Admiral Sir Onsley Matthews has informed me that the Admiralty Prize Court has made a determination on some of our recent prizes. In their infinite wisdom they have found time for our tawdry little affairs instead of dealing exclusively with Admiral Rodney and St. Eustatius."

Bloody hell, quit being coy and get on with it! Lewrie had noticed that Treghues loved the sound of his own voice and wit.

"Since April we have taken two brigs, a brigantine, two schooners and two local sloops in these waters. That does not count our latest two prizes." Treghues went on to enumerate all the various war supplies denied the rebels, all the outward-bound products, until Lewrie was ready to scream.

"My agent informs me," Treghues said with the slightest glance to his right, which Lewrie spotted. It was Cheatham! He was the prize agent. There was five percent total in it for him. No wonder he smiled all the time. "We have amassed a total of £14,551, 8 shillings 9 pence. And...we shall receive a partial payout tomorrow...in gold!"

The tumult which resulted would have raised the hair of Mohawk Indians, and Lewrie was sure that the full news was already circulating on the lower deck barely before the words had drawled out of Treghues' mouth.

Sir Onsley would get an eighth. Two-eighths would go to Treghues. The officers—Railsford, Lt. Peck, Mr. Monk, Dr. Dorne and Cheatham—split an eighth; the senior warrants, master's mates and Admiral Matthews' secretary split an eighth; the midshipmen, petty officers, quartermasters and their mates, the bosun's mate and a few others took an eighth; and the rest of the crew received the final two-eighths.

Lewrie did some rapid calculations. He would get a little over seventy-two pounds, more than a lieutenant made in a 1st rate ship of the line for a year's work! Naturally, he would not see ten pounds of it in real money, but it was welcome.

"Now there's going to be about three pounds per man paid out in coin and the rest in certificates. I want you all to warn your men in your watches and divisions to watch out for the sharks who'll try to buy them out for twenty percent in ready money," Treghues warned. "I believe there'll be some few who have allotment papers on the books who'll want it forwarded all or in part to their parents or families. We're anchored far enough out to prevent someone going out a gun port, and Antigua is an island, after all. Each of you pick out the men most likely to run, and let the rest go ashore for a two-day leave. Mister Lewrie, you have a good copperplate hand. See my clerk and begin writing out blank leave-tickets. Mind you, any man who runs, or overstays his leave, ruins it for the rest of his subdivision or watch, and I'll have him run the gauntlet when he's fetched back aboard. I want to see liberty lists tomorrow in the fore-noon."

Another idea foundered, Lewrie thought, amazed at what he learned from Treghues, for all his coyness and preachi-fying. No one had talked to him of leave. He assumed the men stayed aboard from the beginning of the commission til the ship paid off, without a chance to go ashore except in a supervised working party. But if the man was owed back pay and prize money, it made sense to let him have his fun ashore, especially on an island. How could he walk away from two years' wages, and enough in prize-certificates to set him up for life? And the crew had been together for a long while; they were used to each other, less eager to change their situation for something new. How much had poor Harrison sacrificed back there in Portsmouth when he took leg-bail and ran inland with his skinny little wife?

"Admiral Matthews also informs me that whatever we lack in manpower shall be made good at his personal selection," Treghues told them after they had calmed down from the momentous news. "This is quite an honor for us to receive, possibly the last people personally spoken for by our squadron admiral before he hauls down his flag."

What? Lewrie thought, almost choking on Treghues' excellent claret. Hauling down his flag? How soon? God, there goes my one source of interest in the West Indies. Now what the hell's going to happen to me?

He had been in the fleet long enough to know that petticoat influence in London did not count for that much—civilians could not get into naval affairs. Petticoat influence was only good when the petticoats controlled naval influence.

Officers normally gathered to them in their ships, and in their squadrons and fleets and staffs men they could count on, from able seamen to post captains, and were judged by how wisely they chose proteges to sponsor and promote and aid throughout their careers. They also expected others of their close acquaintance to aid their followers, and were prepared to aid followers of others in a fair swap of "interest."

There was only one requirement that never varied—you could not advance a *total* fool, for the abiding needs of the Navy came first, last and always. And it took a certain political skill to play the game right. Admiral Rodney did not, had recommended poor choices and promoted unprepared people when in command of foreign stations beyond the immediate reach of Whitehall, abusing the system, angering friends.

"Do you need some water, Mister Lewrie?" Treghues asked.

"No, thankee, sir. I was already spending my share on a very tasty meal."

"Got carried away, eh? Remember to swallow first, that's always the way. A midshipman's stomach controls his brains, and then there's all hell to pay."

Lewrie did not in the least feel like smiling, but it was a social occasion and he had to show a civil face, so he grinned sheepishly, which was what midshipmen were good at...was what Treghues expected from his young gentlemen.

"Do you know how soon Sir Onsley will be going home, sir?"

"His replacement, Sir George Sinclair, is purported to be on his way already."

"Sir Onsley and Lady Maude have been most kind to me, sir. I shall miss him. Came as a shock."

Treghues nodded, remembering that Lewrie himself was one of Sir Onsley's followers. "Then you shall be relieved to know that Sir Onsley shall be appointed to the Admiralty Board upon his return to London," Treghues said, handing him the tacit reassurance that the admiral could still look out for him even thousands of miles away.

"There is also a scheme that Admiral Rodney wished to put into action regarding these so-called neutral islands," Treghues informed his gathering. "I cannot reveal any details as of yet, but you can be sure that *Desperate* shall play a part in it, and it may promise to be a most rewarding part, for the public good, and our private gain."

ONCE *Desperate* began to let her people ashore in manageable batches for shore leave, Mr. Monk and the bosun discovered a healthy crop of underwater growth on her bottom. She should have put to sea immediately once her people were back inboard, but it was thought a good opportunity to bream her.

This involved everyone in nearly a week of heavy labor, hoisting out all her guns, powder and shot, beef and pork barrels, striking her masts down to maintops and gantlines, and warping her into the inner harbor where she was careened at low tide on a sand bank so the dock workers could burn and scour her bottom clean, then coat her with a mix of sulfur, tallow and pitch to retard future marine growth. While empty, the carpenter and his crew inspected her for rot in her bilges and below-water beams and keel members. She was pronounced healthy for at least another year in the tropics, where any proud ship could be eaten down to hollow kindling once the teredo worms got to her.

With nearly a knot and a half restored to her best speed, they floated her upright and began to reload her. They had just begun to hoist topmasts once she was back at her moorings when the day's work was interrupted by the sound of a salute being fired.

Lewrie went up the shrouds with a glass, eager for a chance to take a breather, and watched a handsome thirty-two-gun frigate ghosting into harbor, firing a salute to Hood and the forts. At her mizzen truck she flew a broad pendant, the sign of a commodore or rear admiral.

"So that's our new commodore," Lewrie said, half to himself. "We won't sail right away, not if Matthews will be hauling down his flag. We shall all want to get to know the new man."

IT was a farewell ball for Sir Onsley and Lady Maude, and the introductory social event for Commodore Sir George Sinclair. The harbor gleamed in another of those splendid West Indies sunsets that Alan had come to enjoy so much, though there was not a breath of wind and the summer evening was close, hot and humid. By the time their party from *Desperate* had climbed the hill road on foot to Admiralty House, their shirts and waistcoats were glued to them by sweat. Fortunately there was, like a tops'l breeze, a cooling breath of the Trades once atop the hill, and servants offered towels so they could mop themselves down.

Admiral Hood was present, standing tall and slim and beaky over the normal-sized guests, surrounded by a set of admirers. Sir Onsley and Lady Maude were off in a corner with less of a coterie; he was now only a half-pay rear admiral of the red, and sycophants no longer had to be quite so attentive. The crowd had transferred their attention to the newest officer by the buffets, eager to get a first look at their new Commodore even if he was a jumped-up post captain. That was where the Dockyard Superintendent, the Master Attendant and the Prize Court Agents lurked and simpered.

Admiral Rodney had gone home with his fabulous prize fleet, so Treghues had to settle for lesser lights, and led them first to Sir Onsley. Their former admiral looked even fatter than ever, ever-strangling in a neckcloth too tight for him, and Lady Maude had chosen a bilious purple-and-grey satin sackgown, a poor comparison to her complexion. If it weren't for Sir Onsley's uniform they would have looked like servants.

"Sir Onsley...Lady Maude. Your servant, sir..."

"Oh, Alan Lewrie," Lady Maude said. "My, they feed you well in *Desperate*. You must have grown another inch since we saw you last."

"We have been living quite well for a cruiser, Lady Maude."

"Mister Lewrie," Sir Onsley said, offering his hand. "You are looking Bristol fashion, I must say."

"Thank you, Sir Onsley. I...I was most distressed to hear you and Lady Maude would be going back to England," Lewrie began, trying to make his prepared speech sound natural. "May I say that I shall always be grateful for your and Lady Maude's many kindnesses and considerations. I hope your voyage is tranquil, and your next post rewarding."

"Thankee, Mister Lewrie. Most kind," Sir Onsley said. "I'll miss the islands, damme if I won't. But, you have to make way for younger men."

"I am certain the islands shall miss you, too, Sir Onsley. I'm sure I speak for many who served under you." He smiled. Yes, they'll miss the sight of *Glatton* sitting out there like the Pharos, Lewrie thought.

"Be odd not to have a sea command after all these years," Sir Onsley maundered on, now well into his wine cups.

"Sir George Sinclair would have to be a most impressive officer to replace you, sir. Or match our record of success in reducing the number of privateers and all," Lewrie said, wondering if he really knew when to stop before even Sir Onsley noticed.

"We have stuck a dry bone in Brother Jonathan's throat, have we not?" Sir Onsley chuckled. Dead lazy or not, Sir Onsley was going home rich as Croesus from prize money reaped by his squadron.

"Only thing I regret is I'm going to miss the last act out here," Sir Onsley said. "Here, walk with me and we'll have some wine, boy. Do you know anything about DeGrasse?"

Something to eat? Lewrie thought. "No, sir."

"Damn crafty Frog admiral. Left Brest back in the spring and he got down to Martinique with a huge convoy and a fleet of line of battle ships. Sam Hood's crossed swords with him once so far, pretty much of a draw. But he's here for a purpose, and it won't be good when it comes. Met Sam Hood yet?"

"No, sir."

"Then come with me."

And before Lewrie knew it, he was bowing to that worthy, who looked down that long nose at him. Sir Onsley bubbled on about Lewrie's record and what ship he was in at present.

"Yes, Mister Lewrie," Hood said with a meager smile. "Believe I read something about *Ariadne*. Knew Bales long ago, you know. And it was *Parrot*, I believe, before *Desperate*?"

"Aye, sir," Lewrie said, almost quivering with excitement. The admiral had indeed actually heard something of him.

"Damn glad to meet you, Mister Lewrie. You keep up that sort of work," Hood told him, before shifting his eyes away.

"I shall, sir," Lewrie promised, allowing himself to be led off by Sir Onsley.

"Put in a word for you. Never hurts for him to remember

what you look like," Sir Onsley said, now firmly playing naval politics. "He must have a thousand midshipmen, but he'll know you."

And you'll be on the Board at the Admiralty, giving advice and support to Hood, so he's amenable to a good relationship with you, but at what price? Lewrie speculated, sipping his wine, noticing for the first time that it was champagne and as cold as mortal sin.

"Ah, I see Treghues has already found our new commodore," Sir Onsley noted, jutting his chin across the room to point at Alan's captain and a thin, reedy stick of a man in a coat a bit too faded to be fashionable at a ball. Still, it was laced as a captain's coat, but for the buttons set in threes. Sir George Sinclair wore a tight periwig with close side curls, emphasizing the skin as dark as any foredeck hand, making those sharp eyes and down-turned hook of a nose appear even more daunting.

"A real taut hand, is Sinclair," Sir Onsley continued. "Put up his first broad pendant when the French came in in '78, and was a real terror off Bordeaux, I'm told. Got knighted at Quiberon Bay in the last war and earned it three times over. We are not close, but I did have a chance to mention a few people by way of recommendation. I do not think you would mind if Sir George knew of my regard for you."

"Not at all, sir. Your thoughtfulness at a time like this is... I cannot find the words, Sir Onsley."

It was heady stuff to be endorsed as able by a man who now had distant control over the officers he would be answering to in future. Lewrie had not thought to wonder how well-regarded Sir Onsley was when it came to choosing followers. But he had yet to hear that he was as inept as Admiral Rodney, so it might be all right for his career.

He felt success falling like a laurel wreath in some fever dream, slow and catchable, right into his outstretched hands. He had won over Captain Bales, had convinced Kenyon of his ability—even if Kenyon was a Molly, Alan still respected his skills. He had caught Sir Onsley's eye as a comer, was well recommended to Admiral Hood (another comer), and now was most likely going to cap the evening by winning the same notice from his new admiral of the squadron!

Why had he not joined the Navy years ago, so that he then could have been entered on ships' books for six years? There was a commission in the offing, and he knew, from asking questions of other midshipmen passed for lieutenant that he could make a fair showing at the exam.

Sir Hugo may have done me the greatest favor of my life by making me go to sea, he realized.

But standing slightly behind and to one side of Sir George Sinclair was his flag captain, someone Lewrie had known under less auspicious circumstances, and the laurel wreath of success was snatched out of his fingers.

He almost snapped the stem of his wine glass. Not now, not him!

It was Captain Bevan, the very officer who had dragged him from his father's house. Captain Bevan, who knew enough of his background and the alleged reason for his banishment to ruin him forever. Captain Bevan, the man who had been his jailer in that damned post chaise to Portsmouth and had shoved him into *Ariadne*.

"That would not be Captain Bevan with him, Sir Onsley?" Alan said, ready to run or throw up or both.

"Aye, his flag captain. Know him?" Sir Onsley asked.

"We've met," Lewrie mumbled, sinking in a bleak despair.

Lewrie could not escape being led across the salon to Commodore Sinclair's circle. Up close, the man had that predatory look that Mrs. Hillwood possessed, but Lewrie felt he was not going to get the same sort of gentle treatment.

"Sir George."

"Sir Onsley." It was the sound of talons rustling.

"Here's another of your band, off *Desperate*. Midshipman Alan Lewrie," Sir Onsley said proudly. "Commodore Sir George Sinclair, Mr. Lewrie."

"Your servant, Sir George," Alan said, summoning up what was left of his nerves and trying to look plucky and direct.

"Ah yes, Lewrie." Sir George smiled thinly, which smile was as quickly gone. "I've heard of you."

"Another one of my promising lads, Sir George, like your nephew," Treghues said. "When he puts his mind to it, of course, ha ha."

"January of last year, was it not, Mister Lewrie?" Sir George asked with a sniff.

The Navy, the rape, the Gordon Riots, what? Lewrie fumbled at such a surprising question. "Aye, sir. January of '80."

"Is that your recollection, Bevan?" Sir George asked his aide.

"I remember it most distinctly, Sir George," Captain Bevan said, bestowing upon his chief a benign look, then turning to face Lewrie.

"Yes," Sir George said. "Poor old Bales."

Sir Onsley and Comdr. Treghues were mystified by this exchange, and Lewrie rushed to sort things out for them.

"Captain Bevan was the officer who obtained me my first berth in *Ariadne*. He was also kind enough to see me safely to Portsmouth and helped me stock my kit. I wish to extend to you my hearty thanks for doing so, Captain Bevan. I have learned so much in the Navy, first under Captain Bales in poor *Ariadne*, from Sir Onsley and now Commander Treghues. I feel so grateful for your assistance in discovering my new career. Having had a bit of success, and gaining so much knowledge has been an . . . an inspiring experience. Not to mention, uplifting."

They know I'm raving, he told himself. They'll get the leg irons first, and then the poking sticks. Lewrie, you can lie like a butcher's dog. Oh, you arse-kissing, vile wretch . . . Please God they eat this shit up like plum duff . . .

"Really," Sir George drawled, drawing the word out like a rapier.

"He is keen, and a fast learner," Treghues said offhandedly, not wanting to praise Lewrie publicly now that Sir George was reacting to him much as he would regard a drunken hand at the gratings.

"Well, I shall keep my eye on him, then," Sir George said with just the hint of a thaw, but it wasn't the sort of smile that would give a man much cheer. It reminded Alan of a judge finding a new way to pronounce "transportation for life" after a full docket.

The interview died after that as Lewrie stumbled off, trying to find a graceful way to say good-by to such an equivocal dismissal. He chased down a servant and loaded up on wine, fast.

The first went down in a rush and he began on the second.

"Merciful God in heaven," he declared. "I am so well and truly *fucked*—"

"'Ere, you watch yer mouth around a lady, ya dirty little Navy guttersnipe," a gentleman standing close enough to hear said as he shook his arm. His wife stood by, face pruned in pious outrage.

"I am so sorry for disturbing your good lady, sir," Lewrie said in surprise but thinking fast. "I have just had the most shocking news from home. Do forgive me but I was beyond all temperance."

"Oh, sorry, then..."

"Funny way of showing grief," the woman said.

Grief's the fucking word for it, he told himself.

He began to wander the salon, nodding to everyone whether he knew them or not, asking himself what he had done to bring down such a fate on himself. He had studied hard, he had worked hard, he had almost but not quite come to tolerate the Navy, he was not even a three-bottle man, and hadn't had any mutton for months, and could not understand why God could bring him so close to the edge of triumph and then dash him into the mud.

"Saving yourself for dinner, Lewrie?" Treghues asked him on his third aimless circuit of the salon.

"I'm sorry, sir?"

"This isn't a drum," Treghues told him. "There's a sit-down meal coming. Are you half-seas over?"

"Oh no, sir, I'm fine, really."

"Slow down on the wine and go have a bite from the buffet, or I shall send you back aboard ship and blast your supper, and your dancing," Treghues told him, not understanding what Sir George had against Lewrie but determined to find out.

"Aye aye, sir, I . . . I shall join Avery and Forrester at the buffet, sir. They look to be having a fine time at the moment."

The buffet was groaning under a load of wonderful looking and smelling food for snacking. Avery and Forrester were tucking it in like famished dogs, standing side by side and amiable for once in their greed, slowly grazing down the tables. If his nerves had not already suffered such a shock as to be terminal to his appetite, the sight of Forrester at trough would have done it anyway.

Feeling that Treghues was still watching him, he joined them and took a plate and utensils, spooning up the first thing handy with no regard for what it was.

"Do try some of this, Alan," Avery said. "Some local kick-shaw with honey and nuts on it. Could be rabbit. Forrester swears it's partridge."

"Um, yes," Alan said after chewing a bite. "Maybe duck?"

"What a palate," Forrester said. "Salt pork is more to your style."

"Spreading yourself a bit broader than usual tonight, Francis?" He shot back. "You'll be needing new breeches if you keep on loading cargo like that."

"You are so unbelievably common, Lewrie."

"David, did you ever notice right after eating, you can't understand a word he says?"

"Keeping his cheeks full, for later," Avery surmised.

"Sucks it right up like a washdeck pump," Alan said, studying Forrester closely. "But whatever does he do with the little bones?"

"Not sure, but it explains those low crunching noises in the middle of the night."

"Have your little laughs," Forrester said, "and then I shall have mine. You'll be all-amort..."

"Whatever did he mean by that?" Lewrie wondered as Forrester moved away from them.

"I suppose he thinks he'll be going into the flagship."

"Could we be so lucky?" Lewrie asked, feeling a ray of sunshine penetrating his gloom. "Treghues and Sinclair are as thick as thieves, are they?"

"His uncle will take care of him," said Avery.

"No," Lewrie said with a sudden chill. "Forrester..."

"And Sinclair." Avery was relentless. "I damn near cried."

"Sweet suffering God, this is hellish," Lewrie whispered. "I am ruined..."

"You?" Avery scoffed. "Think he has any more love for me? I was the one played so many pranks on him. But he stands a good chance of being out of our lives. He'll be passed for lieutenant a lot quicker than us, but then he's gone. Thank the good Lord."

Lewrie set his plate down and rubbed his forehead, lost in a vise-like agony trying to puzzle things out so they made sense.

"*Desperate* could be the post of honor," he told David. "He might stay with us until a suitable big prize needed a master, and he would go into her. Immediate promotion, bought in, at least a lieutenant's command below the rate."

"That makes me ill to contemplate."

Or Forrester could stay in *Desperate* and I go to the flag, where Sir George hounds me to ruin because of Forrester's lies, and what happened in London, he thought gloomily. But plenty of men go to sea under a cloud, and as long as you're good at your job no one gives a groat what you've done before. Alright, so Sir George doesn't like me—that's no reason he would harm me. What would it profit him? Oh, God, what else can go wrong?

"Alan!"

He turned to see Lucy Beauman dressed in a new gown of pale pink satin with an undergown of white lace, lots of ruched material on sleeves and bodice, her own hair in ringlets instead of a wig, all done up with flowers and maroon ribbons.

"Lucy... how truly magnificent and beautiful you look."

"Oh, Alan," she said, taking his hands. David coughed to break the spell.

"Excuse my manners... David Avery, Miss Lucy Beauman, Admiral Sir Onsley Matthews' niece. Lucy, this is my shipmate, Midshipman David Avery."

"Your servant, ma'am," David said, making a graceful leg, and dribbling food from his unattended plate behind him.

Thank God for one good thing that has happened to me this evening, Alan thought happily, flushing with pleasure at seeing her once more, and aching with sudden longing as well. Every time he was reunited with her he found her more womanly, more desirable, more lovely, if such a thing was possible.

"Alan, Mister Avery, I should like you to meet my father."

Right, thank you, God, Alan almost said aloud.

"Your servant, Mister Beauman, sir."

Père Beauman was squat as a toad, crammed into a bright green velvet coat, a longer skirted old style waistcoat awash in silver brocade, buff breeches and hose, with calves as thick as tillerheads. And the high-roached, elaborately curled bag wig he wore fairly screamed "Country"—of the worst huntin', shootin', ridin', drinkin', tenant-tramplin', dog-lovin' View Halloo variety.

This lovely girl is daughter to... that? Alan couldn't accept it.

"You're Lewrie, hey?" said Mister Beauman once they had both been bowed to. "Heard a lot about you."

He has much in common with Sir George, Alan thought unhappily. He has heard of me. I cannot imagine a more ghastly evening...

"Like a lad with gumption. Chopped that fella, hey? With good reason, o' course."

"I could not in good conscience let his remarks pass, sir," Lewrie told him, happy to hear that Lucy's father sounded approving of his duel. Nothing like defending a daughter to placate a daddy. "The less said about his scurrilous remarks, the better, though, with the ladies present."

"Onsley sez yer a comer. That so?"

"I am very grateful for Sir Onsley's and Lady Maude's good opinion, Mister Beauman. They are wonderful people."

"Aye, that's so. That's so," Mr. Beauman agreed, snaking himself a glass of wine from the buffet.

"And you come on business to Antigua, sir?"

"Hell, the Matthews' are sailing for home, lad. The slave revolt's been put down, and Portland Bight's healthier than Antigua in the summer. I've come to fetch Lucy home."

"I had not thought that far ahead about the consequences, sir," he said, sharing a heartbreaking look of confirmation from Lucy. "I am sure you're pleased to be able to receive her back into your family in safety and peace—"

"Aye, true," Beauman nodded heavily, changing glasses for a full one. "Bubbly Frog trash. Got your juju bag?"

"Yes, sir, I do."

"Sambo nonsense," Beauman Sr. chuckled. "Still, any luck's better than none, hey?"

Does this man ever speak in complete sentences? Alan wondered.

They were interrupted by the dinner gong, and the most important people began to pair off to file into the long dining rooms.

"Mister Beauman, if you are to fetch Lucy home, and I shall be sailing north in a few days, this ball may be our last chance to converse for some time. With your permission, of course, I should like to dance with your daughter."

"Me, too," Avery said in a barely audible mutter behind him.

"Aye, if she's willin'," Beauman agreed.

There were farewell speeches about Sir Onsley, welcoming speeches about Sir George, a word or two from Admiral

Hood, many toasts and much food. With her father beside her, Lucy could not indulge in one of those long-distance romances of eyes and shrugs, so Lewrie had to content himself with his table companions, and a damned dull lot they were. The food he could barely taste, and did little more than mangle what little he allowed on his plate. His appetite was quite gone.

Am I going to be ruined? And if I am, then what am I to do for a living? I could stay in the Navy, but if this war ends I'll have no chance of being retained. And they don't give half-pay to midshipmen. Hell, without Sir Onsley's help there's no way I can make my lieutenantcy. Even as a commission sea officer, I'd be turned out on the beach, and half-pay is more like quarter-pay, it's a joke. But, if I married Lucy Beauman I'd be a led-captain, a poor relation, but that's worth more than half-pay, even worth more than a post captain's command. Either way, bless her, she's the key to prosperity after the war...

After the ladies had retired, but before the port got going, he left the dining rooms to hunt up Lucy. He also badly needed coffee or tea. He had eaten little and had taken on a bit too much drink.

He got his coffee, dark and sweet the way he enjoyed it, drank one cup scanning the salon for Lucy, then got another cup and went out on the veranda. There she was, taking the air with some other younger girls. She left them quickly and came to him. They went around the corner for privacy, and once alone she buried her face in his shoulder and embraced him hungrily.

"Oh, Alan, I've been so miserable, and foolish...I never thought I'd have to go back to Jamaica and not see you again—"

"I've missed you, too, Lucy, and when I was told the admiral was hauling down his flag..."

"I wrote you so many letters."

"We spoke no friendly ships the last two months," Alan told her.

"I wrote you several, as well. Did you get them?"

"No we spoke no friendly ships. Did you get mine?"

"Oh, *yes*. There was always some sailor showing up with a letter saying he had just come in with news from you. I don't know how you managed it."

"They were our crew that came in with a prize," he explained, finding it hard to believe that she had thought he could arrange his mail to be delivered whenever he wanted it. Maybe there's a good reason she can't spell, maybe she's feebler than most women...

"And now I shall never see you again."

"I may sail to Kingston again, Lucy, we can still write each other, and I intend to ask your father if I may have his leave to call upon you when we put into port."

"Oh, Alan..." She looked at him as if he had just invented gravity. "Do you love me, Alan? Do you truly love me that much?"

"Aye, I do." Hold on here, do I? Yes, I must. But maybe I don't. How do you tell? I've only been in lust. She's such a beauty, and what I know of her body is enough to make anyone mad with passion. So, she may *not* be bright as a man. Who expects her to be...

"I love you, Alan," she said, squeezing him tight. "I have been in love with you since I first saw you, all weak and ill, when they brought you into Auntie's house. Oh, I think I shall die with happiness tonight..."

We're not going that far just yet, he thought.

"Your father has to allow me to call upon you—"

"Oh, father cannot deny us. No one could be that cruel. Alan, why must we wait? I had thought we would wait until the war was over, until you had become an officer, but if we feel so strongly, why do we not marry now?"

Her father will never go for that. Damn, she'll blow the gaff on me with her impatience, and then good-by security...

"I cannot, Lucy...there's my duty to the Navy, my oath to the Crown. And I doubt if your father will agree after just meeting me. Perhaps we should let him get used to the idea?"

"But, Alan, many people marry in time of war..."

"But they don't look kindly on midshipmen doing it. Lieutenants, perhaps. Right now the Navy is the only life I have, Lucy." And a right dirty one it is, too, he added to himself.

"You shall have a life with me," she said, pouting in the darkness of the veranda. Somehow Alan knew she was pouting. "Once the war is over, you owe the Navy nothing. If you wish a seafaring life, my father owns many ships. Their captains take their wives on trading voyages to so many exciting places... Or we could have a fine plantation of our own, thousands of acres to ourselves."

I have discovered the keys to heaven itself, Alan rejoiced as he held her close to him. God, to be a planter, a trader, with ships of my own and regiments of slaves. And dear Lucy to rattle every night of the week. We could go back to London in triumph. And then to hell with the Navy, and my family and anyone else.

"I shall speak to your father but I beg you, Lucy, don't be hasty. Let him consider me. He has no reason to dislike me as of yet, and Sir Onsley and Lady Maude can speak for me. And at home you can bring him round. How could he refuse his lovely daughter anything she desires once he has gotten used to the idea of me as a son-in-law?"

"You are such a slyboots, Alan," she said, kissing him. "I am so proud of you. So smart and clever. I love you so much."

"And I love you, Lucy," he echoed... did he mean it, a little?... kissing her back. "Now, we must go back in before someone comments on us being alone together. I would not give anyone the slightest reason to doubt your honor."

"Yes," she said, giving him one last hug. "I shall join Auntie and try to compose myself. And you will speak to father tonight."

"I promise."

They kissed once more, a lingering kiss full of promised passion to come, before parting and making tiny adjustments to their dress. He offered her his arm and they re-entered the salon just as the men began to leave the dining rooms to join the ladies for coffee.

Mister Beauman spotted her right off and came across the room to join them, a frown on his face.

Lucy evidently knew that look from many years' experience of his temper, and chattered with him briefly before hurrying to her aunt.

"Missed you over the port, lad," Mister Beauman said. "Wanted to get you alone for a while and have a chat. Veranda good for you?"

"Aye, sir..." The older man led him back out to the veranda. Alan retrieved his half-empty cup of coffee and sipped at it.

"Been gettin' letters from Lucy, from her aunt about you. You've turned the lass's head good n' proper."

"I have become fond of your daughter, Mister Beauman. At first I was grateful for all her concern and care when I was ill. But once I was well enough to get around and hold a real conversation with her, well..."

"An' you want to talk about somethin' more than dancin' with the lass," Beauman said.

"I would be most honored if I could come calling on her, sir, in the event that I get to Kingston."

"The shit you say!"

"Aye, sir."

"She's barely turned seventeen!"

"I am aware of that, sir."

"What are you, eighteen? Boy with a Cambridge fortune, just a midshipman, an' those're two-a-penny."

"Your brother-in-law, Sir Onsley, must have told you I have prospects, Mister Beauman. It's true, I'm only a midshipman now, but that is now, not what I hope to accomplish."

"Got lands back home? Rents o' yer own?" Beauman carried on. "You in line to inherit? Yer parents substantial people?"

"No, sir."

"Onsley sez there's gossip ya had to join the Navy to make somethin' of yerself. That true?"

Good God, I really am fucked . . . He nodded yes to that question, not trusting himself to speak.

"Don't rightly hold that against ya, lad." Beauman smiled. "Had to come out to the Indies to make a man of meself, make my own way. Woulda gone to hell on my own back home. But, see this my way, yer a pretty fella, pretty enough to turn the girl's poor head, but yer not the solid type o' match I'd trust to keep her proper. There's nothin' goin' to come of this. Sorry, lad. Nothin' personal."

"I may not be ideal now, sir. But I'm not asking permission to marry tomorrow. I mean to gain my commission first, and there is the war still to be fought. Allow me to write her, and to call. If she finds someone more pleasing in the meantime, then that is Providence. I would not press any sort of suit until I felt I could meet your standards as a suitor, or doom her to a shabby life to suit my pleasure."

"How often you think you might get to Jamaica?"

"Perhaps once a year, sir, at best."

"Hmm. Tell ya what, you make somethin' of yerself. I'll allow you to write. And if you get to Jamaica you can come callin'. But you'll not be doin' anythin' to disturb the peace o' my family 'til I say I'm satisfied with yer prospects."

"I give you my solemn word on that, sir."

I know what he's thinking, Lewrie thought. Creampot love I or Lucy will grow out of. Out of sight, out of mind, while he throws his sort of bachelor up to her. He may not know it, but we're as good as engaged right now . . .

"Good enough," Beauman told him. "Old Onsley's right, you've got bottom, boy. My advice to ya."

"Aye, sir?"

"Whoever ya end up married to, never have daughters."

"I'll take that to heart, Mister Beauman." Alan smiled in relief. "May I go tell Lucy the news?"

"Aye, run along."

Lucy was glowing with delight at his report, and Lady Maude was cooing and fanning herself in joy. Sir Onsley frowned a lot, said a bit how married officers were lost to the Navy, which got him a withering glare from Lady Maude, which he had to splutter his way free of by reminding her that he was a post captain when they married.

The rest of the evening was a glimpse of Paradise itself, for Lucy told all her girl acquaintances, they told all the young men at the ball, and everyone assumed it was a much more formal arrangement than it really was. Older couples beamed at them foolishly and remarked on what a splendid couple they would be.

On his part Alan completely forgot about his fears concerning Captain Bevan and Sir George Sinclair. With Lucy at his side they were no more than fleabites from a traveller's bed; nothing to get exercised about. His future was assured once the war was over, and the Navy was little more than a slight aggravation to be borne until then.

Once her father and Lucy left, Alan had no more reason to stay at the ball, so he visited the kitchens for a bundle of food to sate his now roaring appetite. The cooks and stewards remembered him from his previous stint of duty, so he left with a substantial basket of goodies and two bottles of champagne. This he and young Carey, who had stayed behind aboard, devoured happily in the quiet darkness of their mess.

Once in bed, he was so busy thinking on his prospects that he was still awake two hours later when Avery and Forrester staggered to their hammocks, tipsy and trying to shush each other like a pair of lamebrained housebreakers trying to smash through a wall without waking the house's owner.

They dropped their shoes, dropped their chest lids, clanked their dirks trying to find spare pegs, giggled, belched, farted, thumped into each other and apologized profusely, hummed their favorite tunes, slung their hammocks and tumbled out at least once with loud crashes and began to curse everything roundly. Carey found it so entertaining that he ended up shrieking with laughter at their bungling.

And once the mess area was filled by nothing but drunken snores, Alan still lay awake, closer to contentment than he had been in two full years, listening to the ship breathe around him, and the watch bell up forward chiming the half-hour, until he too drowsed off, quite pleased with himself.

CHAPTER

13

"**P**ASSING the word for Mister Lewrie," a marine sentry bawled.

Alan was aloft with Toliver, one of the bosun's mates, checking over the foret'gallant mast after it had been hoisted into place to see if the standing rigging was set up properly. He scrambled down to the gangway and jogged aft to answer the summons, passing Forrester on the way. Forrester grinned evilly at him as he passed and gave him a sniff that Alan had come to know as a sign of complete satisfaction.

Damme, what does that bacon fed thatch-gallows know that I don't? he wondered. He looked too happy for my liking. Oh God, is this when he starts getting his own back?

He instantly had visions of being transferred to the flagship and being triced up to a grating for daring to enter the Navy, or for offending Sir George or Forrester.

"Calling for me?" Lewrie asked the sentry.

"Cap'n wants ta see yer, sir."

"Aye, thank you."

There was little he could do to make himself more presentable in a stained working rig uniform. He straightened his neckcloth, tucked in his shirt so a large tar stain would not show, and went below and aft to the passage to Treghues' cabins.

"You wished to see me, sir?"

Treghues was seated in his coach, the dining space to starboard of his bed cabin. He was having his breakfast, neatly dressed, freshly shaved and surrounded by good quality furniture and plate. His cabin servant bustled to pour him a second cup of coffee.

"You may go, Judkin."

"Aye aye, sor."

Oh shit, I'm in the quag now, Alan thought as the servant left, closing the fragile door behind him.

"I had a most distressing conversation with Captain Bevan and Sir George last night about you, Lewrie," Treghues told him, frowning over his beef and eggs. "Is it true that you did not join the Navy willingly?"

"Aye, sir," Alan said after a long moment.

"I had heard talk of a young lady, so I naturally thought it was a star-crossed affair. But, now I am told that you were banished before a magistrate could have you up on a charge of raping your own *sister.*"

"That's... that's not strictly true, sir."

"Either it is or it isn't. There's no such thing as half-rape, boy. Anymore than anyone can be half-pregnant. Is it true?"

"If you would let me try to explain, sir... it's not a thing that is 'yes' or 'no'—"

"I can only believe that some money changed hands for Bevan to have allowed you to wear the king's coat." Treghues said. "I put that down to Bevan's cupidity. Too long in the Impress Service could ruin anyone. And no doubt he must have lied to your first captain, if not offered him money to take you on."

"Captain Bales was aware that I had been banished, sir. In my first interview he had a letter from our family solicitor, Mister Pilchard."

"Who are your people, anyway?"

"Sir Hugo Willoughby, sir."

"The one in St. James's?" Treghues appeared to be shocked.

"Aye, sir."

"And you're his get? No wonder you're such a black rogue. That's sweet. So they gave you a false name and foisted you off onto the first poor captain that was fitting out? That's a wicked sort of business."

"It was no false name, sir. Sir Hugo never married my mother, Elizabeth Lewrie. He adopted me but never really made me one of his."

"He and Lord Sandwich and Dashwood are all of a set. Hell-Fire Club, balum rancum bucks without the fear of God. Sacreligious bastards. And they push *you* on me!"

"Sir, I must explain—"

"How dare you stand there fouling the uniform with your evil stink," Treghues ranted with prim, outraged passion. "Trailing your false colors and hoping to avoid the gibbet by joining the Navy—"

"It's all a lying packet, sir," Alan said, raising his voice.

"Don't you dare sass back to me. I'll have you flogged for it. I've a good mind to do that, anyway, and send you in chains to the flag."

"How else am I to get to say my side of it, sir?"

"What side could you possibly present, after forcing your foul self on a gentle, virginal girl, your own flesh and blood?"

"Belinda Willoughby has the shortest heels in London, sir," Alan said loudly. "She spent two weeks luring me into *her* bed, and then up turns Sir Hugo, my half-brother Gerald, who's known for being a windward-passage fellow, our solicitor, the vicar from our parish, and a catch-fart with a pistol. Very damned convenient, if you ask me. And no justice was ever called, no constable of the watch, no one, except for a Navy captain."

"Don't you dare shout at me, damn you," Treghues said, rising.

"You have heard what I have said, sir?" Alan asked, numb

to the possibility that he was about to be lashed and disrated. "Does it not sound suspicious to you, sir?"

"What motive could they possibly have had?" Treghues said, showing that at least some of it had sunk in but still on a tear at the affront to him personally, as though the inventor of the original sin had just pissed liquid fire in his coffee.

"I was forced to sign a paper that pledged me to disavow any hope of inheritance from my mother's estate, sir, though they told me she had none and had died a prostitute in a parish poorhouse. There was never any talk of my mother or her family, so I have no way of knowing if her people were still alive, or if they had property."

"Then why should they go to such lengths? Why did Sir Hugo not just disown you and throw you out into the street?"

"I have no idea, sir. I have been thinking on it for nigh on a year and a half, and still can find no reason for such a deception."

"But you were caught. Not just in her room, I'm told, but bare as you were born, in the middle of..." Evidently Treghues could not bring himself to say the word.

"Had you ever met her, sir, you would be tempted yourself."

"But your own sister, the last of your *line*."

"No, sir. My half sister. Belinda *Willoughby*, not Lewrie."

Treghues sat down, flung himself into his chair and sipped at his coffee, brow creased, while Alan stood at attention, breathing hard.

"And you have been totally disowned? No allowance or any support?"

"Mister Pilchard sends me an hundred guineas a year, sir. And they gave Captain Bevan money to buy my kit. I am to never go back to London—"

"Does he! That does not sound like a man so ill-disposed to his son. No, Mister Lewrie, you've spun a pretty tale, but I fear you'd make a better novelist than Fielding. Thank God, the world is changing, and all the avarice and lust of the last forty years is being swept away by a new morality. There are now God-fearing people unwilling to put up with, or condone, the openly sinful doings that characterized our society in past years."

My God, is Treghues some kind of leaping Methodist? Alan wondered, listening to his captain rant.

"I cannot help who my father was, or in what environment I was raised, sir, but since joining the Navy I have put all that behind me. Am I not a better than average midshipman, sir?"

"I've a good mind to write Sir Onsley Matthews and inform him just what a total wastrel and Godless rake you really are," Treghues went on as though he had not heard a word. "Had I leave to do so, I would turn you out of this ship at once, at once, do you hear, Mister Lewrie?"

"On what grounds, sir?" Alan asked, mild as possible.

"Don't play the sea lawyer with me, boy. I do not want you in my command any more than the Navy should have wanted you. And at the first opportunity I shall make it my God-fearing duty to make sure that both *Desperate*, and the Sea Service, shall be a much cleaner place, without your foul presence. Until that time I shall want to see only the most obedient and circumspect behavior from you, or I shall make you sorry that you were ever born. Now get out of my sight."

"Aye aye, sir."

I was your pride and joy, you priggish bastard, as long as you thought you were making Sir Onsley happy, Alan thought miserably. But now you have a new master, you'll cut your cloth to suit Sir George.

Alan stumbled out the entryway and up to the quarter deck to the taffrail, as far away from everyone as possible. There was a fair wind that morning, and English Harbor sparkled.

The breeze that came to him was full of good smells, of green and luscious growing things from shore, the tang of salt and iodine and tidal odors from the strand, raw wood from the dockyard, and the scent of pitch and hot pine tar as some ship was repaired to windward. It should have been a delightful day in which to be alive, but it was most definitely not.

That was one of the drawbacks of a man-of-war; the lack of privacy when you had to let go and drop to the deck and weep, not only weep but thrash, curse, scream and pound your fists on something at the unfairness of life until you were spent. But no one was going to walk around you until you were through and then ask if you felt better for doing it.

So Alan stared at the shore and gripped the intricately carved taffrail until his hands were white. There was nothing he could say or do in the face of Treghues' moralizing that would make a difference. He was going to become a leper, Treghues had made it clear that he wanted him gone as soon as the Navy could let him, and would also hound him from the Fleet. A captain set the tone for his ship. How long would it be, Alan wondered, before Treghues' open dislike spread to Mister Monk, Railsford, Peck, Dorne, Cheatham and the rest? Perhaps even David and little Carey would start walking wide to avoid him.

Well, he had not planned to make the Navy a career, anyway. He had hoped to make Lucy Beauman, and her father's money, a career, but even being so close to that was no balm for his shattered spirits. Much as he at times hated the Navy, he did not relish being thrown out of it.

If he were to leave the Navy it would be at his own time, and with his pride and his prize money intact, not as a rejected midshipman but at least as a half-pay lieutenant, which would allow him to hold up his head in public.

And there was his perverse streak to consider—loathe the life of a sailor as much as he wanted to, curse the demands of the Navy and the deprivations one had to suffer, it was the only thing that he was good at. He could roister and romp with the ladies, play buck of the first head in a company of fellow-cocks, dance, drink, wench, run wild in the streets and spend money with the best of them, but that was not a career without a peer's purse. He could navigate as well as any—even with a sextant, one hundred miles out of your reckoning was considered fairly accurate—he could stand a deck watch, could hand, reef and steer, handle a small boat, could handle all the paperwork, much as he despised it, had learned enough to make a good sailor and a fair midshipman, and he was very good with weapons. Where else was he going to be able to do all that? After the Navy, clerking for some firm would be damned dull. No one in his right mind would go for a soldier, and he couldn't afford to buy someone's commission. There was nothing suitable for a gentleman that he could do, or hope to undertake at eighteen-years-old.

He would have to accomplish something, soon, something that he could point to that even Treghues could not demean, that would gain him so much favorable comment that he would be safe in the Navy.

God Almighty, listen to what I'm saying...I'm beginning to sound like I want to stay in and be made post...

Even if that was his goal, and he seriously doubted his own sanity if it was, he still had four-and-a-half years as a young gentleman in training before he could stand for a lieutenantcy. The rules called for six years on ship's books, two of those years as a midshipman or a master's mate, and proof of age no less than twenty. In another ship he might be chosen as a master's mate, which had a salary to it and would lead quicker to a commission, but would not Treghues' opinion of him follow him in his records? He had seen other midshipmen of twenty, thirty, had heard of men in their forties still midshipmen—too good seamen to be cast out but unable to pass the exam, or having passed, had no luck or interest working for them to obtain a berth as an officer.

Damme, but this is a hard life, he thought miserably. *But why should I expect it to be fair? I'm not stupid. Would it be better for me to fight back by being cruel and unfair myself, more than I am now, at any rate? Is that the way to succeed?*

CHAPTER

14

DESPERATE was at sea, reaching north with a soldier's wind on her starboard beam. For once she had company as she followed the thirty-two gun frigate *Amphion*, and was in turn trailed by two sloops of war, Commander Ozzard's *Vixen*, and another sloop of war named *Roebuck*. They had sailed north from English Harbor after making their offing, destined for Anegada, a low sand-and-coral island at the eastern end of the British Virgins. Once there, they had to be careful to avoid the Horseshoe Reefs, where hundreds of ships had come to grief over the years. Commander Treghues had sealed orders, which he had not shared with anyone as of yet, but the presence of four cruising-type warships in company bespoke a major effort of some kind, and rumors were rife in every compartment.

Rumors were also flying about what Treghues had said to Lewrie in his cabins. The captain's clerk and steward were silent about the matter, mercifully, and Treghues was also tight-lipped, but it did not stop the wildest speculations.

People were indeed curious, and expanded on the slightest hints. Treghues behaved as if Lewrie were not there. He paid not the slightest attention to him during the course of his duties, had absolutely no comment about his navigation work when he inspected the midshipmens' slates at noon sights, indeed barely glanced at Lewrie's, and as *Amphion* led them around Horseshoe Reefs into the lee of Anegada at dawn of their third day at sea it was Carey who had charge of the leadsmen in the foremast chains, Forrester who had charge of the cutter that probed ahead of them, and Avery by the wheel, leaving Alan to bide his time restlessly aft by the taffrail with a signalman.

Once safely in deeper waters all four ships hove to, cocked up to windward and gently making leeway on the tide to the west, while all captains were summoned to the temporary flag frigate. The conference lasted two hours, at which time Treghues came back aboard and went below with Mister Monk, leaving Railsford to get the ship underway again. During the course of the day the squadron reached north and south behind Anegada, not straying too far north, nor coming too far south so that they could be seen from Virgin Gorda.

It was dusk before a conference was held aft, a conference in a hot and stuffy cabin with the transom windows covered, in a ship that burned no lights except for the binnacle lanterns. Treghues had included the midshipmen, master's mates, master, Marine officer and Railsford. Lewrie sat far back from the glossy desk, where a chart was spread out. Treghues gave him a single darting glance of malice before opening the meeting.

"Tomorrow, we raid the Danish Virgins," Treghues said.

"But they's neutral, sir," Monk said in the buzz of excitement that followed Treghues' pronouncement.

"Aye, they are, Mister Monk. Neutral, but culpable," Treghues said wryly. "Admiral Rodney was most clever to seize St. Eustatius, and keep the Dutch flag flying. He took over 150 ships intent on running our blockade. But now the word is out and that traffic has shifted to other harbors. At first the Danes winked at privateers using their islands, and the local governors had little military force to control the traffic. We complained diplomatically and they ordered belligerents and smugglers to move their operations to Puerto Rico or Cuba, but they never seem to put any teeth in those orders as long as the privateers are subtle about their doings. Now our job is to stage a lightning raid as though we are part of the ships based on Tortola and put the fear of God and the Royal Navy into these people, scour them until they concentrate somewhere else, and force the Danes to play fair."

"Most clever," Forrester said loud enough for Treghues to hear him, which brought a smile from their captain.

"By first light *Roebuck* and *Amphion,* with local pilots, shall be far enough down the Drake's Passage to look into Coral Bay on St. John, and then run down to the west and snap up everything that moves off the port of Charlotte Amalie," Treghues went on, using a pair of brass dividers to sketch a course, tapping at the great hurricane hole and bay on the southeast coast of St. John, which island had been made desolate by a slave rebellion years before and pretty much left to go to ruin.

"We shall enter the open waters south of the island of St. Thomas and head for the island of St. Croix."

Everyone leaned a little closer to look at the western end of the Drake Passage, which was littered with rocks, possible shoals and the mark of a wreck or two.

"Mister Monk advises the Flanagan Passage for us, south of the island of the same name," Treghues continued. "*Vixen* shall lead our little flotilla and shall be inshore of us off Christiansted, going no closer than two leagues to avoid entering Danish waters. We shall be further offshore snapping up one prize after another. Coming from the east as we shall be, with the sun behind us, with the Trade Winds behind us and with the westerly setting tide flow, we can catch anything at sea. All ships and prizes shall concentrate here, later in the day, off the island of Vieques in the Passage Group to the east of Puerto Rico."

"This'll be a bitch, sir," Monk said, scratching at his scruffy chin. "Drake Passage is as lumpy as a country road.

Now, there's twenty-four- to twenty-five-fathoms, safe as houses, down Drake's Passage. It's here off Norman Island, it gets tricky. The chart don't show it but somewhere off the point here nor'-nor'west o' Pelican there's a shoal with a deep channel between that an' another shoal. There's deep water between Flanagan an' The Indians an' Ringdove Rock, 'bout fourteen-fathom at high tide. An' ya can't go too far inshore o' Peter Island to avoid the shoals. I'd feel my way down with the fores'ls, spanker an' forecourse, an' keep the tops'ls at three reefs until we're in the clear."

"We shall be following Commander Ozzard," Treghues said, disliking the advice. "So, I think we should not have too much difficulty."

"But if he sets on one o' them shoals, sir..."

"We shall depend on your skill to guide us, Mister Monk," Treghues said, moving on to other matters. "Prize crews. First will be Forrester and a bosun's mate... Weems, I think, and ten hands, if she's big. Next, Avery and Mister Feather. We'll be in deep water, so the third crew will be Mister Monk, young Carey, and some men, depending on her size. Lieutenant Peck, if you should be so good as to provide four private Marines to each prize, in full kit to cow any resistance, I would be much obliged."

"Delighted, sir," Peck said. It was rare that his Marines had a chance to wear their scarlet uniforms at sea; usually they were dressed in slop clothing much like the hands, to save wear and tear.

"Should we be so incredibly fortunate as to take a fourth ship as a prize, I shall send the first lieutenant and Mr. Toliver, which will still leave me a master's mate aboard. Bosun, see that each crew has a quartermaster's mate or senior hand able to steer, and let's get all our boats down for towing tonight."

"Aye aye, sir."

There were a few looks in Lewrie's direction, he was rated as able to stand as an acting master's mate, had done so already, in fact, and yet had been pointedly left out of their captain's reckoning.

"If a chase is too small, burn it. We can also ignore the many local fishing boats unless they seem to be heavily loaded, or act suspiciously, or show too many white faces."

"What about putting captives overboard, sir?" Railsford asked.

"Any ship engaged in illicit trade, you may spare the blacks, Danes and neutrals. But any belligerent nationals, and especially any American rebels, or rogue Englishmen, be sure to retain so they may be taken to court for their activities. The French, Spanish and Dutch deserve to be placed in chains, as do any rebels. And any Englishman partaking in this business deserves to hang for treason."

BY first light Lewrie was on the gun deck below the gangways, swaying uncomfortably as the squadron seemed to fly down the Sir Francis Drake Passage. The Trades were steady and blowing quite fresh. With the wind nearly dead aft it never felt like they were making much gain over the ground since they had no noticeable breeze. The only way to judge was to stand on a gun breech or the jeer bitts and watch the many isles and rocks slide past. There was a heavy chop in the passage, six-foot waves seemingly about six feet apart, and the frigate's 450 tons thumped and pounded through them, flinging spray halfway up the jibs.

The crew had gone through the motions of dawn quarters, the daily scrubbing of decks, like automatons, but now there was a tingle of excitement in the air as they stood easy to their guns. They were piped below to their breakfasts but didn't stay below long and came back up still chewing, to stow their hammocks and resume their waiting among the artillery.

"Mister Railsford, I'll have chain slings rigged aloft on the yards," Treghues ordered, finding work for them to do in the meantime. "Bosun, lay out the boarding nettings and prepare for hoisting."

Lewrie had been on the quarterdeck earlier and had gotten a good look at Mister Monk's chart, much marked and doodled on from his years of experience in these waters. He could recognize Norman Island off their larboard bow, could spot the hump that was Pelican Island.

The locations of those two shoals, of which Monk was so leery, were shadowy guesses in dark pencil markings, and Alan tried to triangulate a possible way to avoid them.

About five cables ahead of them, half a mile, *Vixen* tiptoed her way a little closer inshore, and *Desperate* leaned slightly as she wore to follow her around. The leadsmen were alternating tossing the lead from either foremast chain platform, calling out their soundings, which had remained stable at twenty-four- or twenty-five-fathoms. *Desperate* drew nearly four, so she was still safe if the charts were right, though that was a big if. Further ahead and off to starboard a little, *Amphion* and *Roebuck* were threading the gap between Flanagan Island and Privateer Point and would soon be able to look into the deep bay which might shelter enemy merchantmen or a privateer ship or two.

"God Almighty, he's found a shoal!" Monk shouted, and Alan took a peek over the bows. *Vixen* was wearing almost due south, coming about hard and beginning to heel to the stiff breeze.

There was collective relief as *Vixen* continued on her new course and a signal flag went up to her mizzen truck, a numeral 8.

"Safe, by God," Monk said loudly, leaning over his chart and pencilling in another bit of arcana for the Admiralty to peruse some day in future when he handed in all his charts upon paying off.

Vixen hoisted another numeral group; 25. She had found their deep water passage to the south of Flanagan Island, and from what Alan could remember, would encounter nothing shallower than twelve- or thirteen-fathoms from then on. *Desperate* wore early, cutting the corner slightly on *Vixen's* course until they wore due south right in her wake.

"Hands aloft!" The bosun sang out. "Hands aloft an' make sail! Lay up an' let go tops'ls!"

They threaded the Flanagan Passage—the Indian Rocks
to their east, Pelican Island off their larboard quarter, waves
breaking over Ringdove Rock and shoal water shading off
from dark blue to turquoise and aqua and pale green. That
they did it at nearly seven knots and gaining added a certain
piquancy to it all, even though they had found deep water.
By the time the preventer backstays and jiggers had been
freed and triced up, and the tops'ls hauled down and
puffed full of wind, they were on their best point of sail
with the Trades on their larboard quarter making over nine
knots, heading sou-sou'west half-west, the leadsmen steadily
calling out twenty-fathoms or better. It was a bumpy ride, as
Monk had predicted, but most pleasant all the same.

"Sail ho!" The lookout called almost immediately. "Two
points off the larboard bow!"

She was *Vixen's* pigeon, and obviously a belligerent from
the way she hauled her wind and turned to run. But there
was no escaping the fleeter sloop of war, and before half an
hour had passed they could see puffs of smoke as *Vixen*
opened fire.

Treghues had his little band strike up a tune. The young
drummers and fifers countermarched back and forth by the
quarterdeck nettings over the waist, and a couple of lands-
man-fiddlers joined them to entertain the crew.

The seas between St. Thomas and St. Croix were working
alive with shipping that fine, sparkling morning, and the
crew danced their hornpipes exuberantly at the thought of
action to come.

They were bearing down on the nearest chase, a full-
rigged ship painted like an Indiaman and showing two rows
of gun ports. She hoisted Danish colors but continued to
flee, which made her most suspicious for a neutral.

Desperate cut inshore of her as she fled to the west, gybed
to the opposite tack and began to close her rapidly. She was
deeply laden, so the lower row of gunports was most likely
false.

"Still," Railsford bellowed through his speaking trumpet,

stopping the people capering and dancing. "Gun crews, stand to to starboard!"

Once within two cables, Mr. Gwynn was sent forward to the carronade on the forecastle and Lewrie drifted up in that direction to take his stance halfway up the ladder to spot the fall of shot. They had not used the carronades much since "The Smashers" would have made kindling of most of their earlier prizes, but here was a suitable target for the heavy and destructive ball they fired.

In went a powder cartridge, four-and-a-half pounds of powder. Then a thirty-six-pound shot, hollow-cast and filled with powder and a mixture of grape shot and musket shot. Gwynn fiddled with the lay of the gun, and the hands tugged on the swivel platform to adjust it. Gwynn hummed along with the musicians as he slid the quoin out slightly. A carronade had little range due to the light powder charge.

"Ready!" He called, stepping clear and raising his fist.

"Fire as you bear!"

The gun captain touched the vent hole. The quill took light and sparked down into the charge. The gun barked and recoiled on its wooden slide. The ball struck their chase squarely.

The massive ball hit the foe just at the break of the larboard gangway and the quarterdeck, a little ahead of the mizzen chains, and burst with a terrific energy and a satisfying puff of smoke, shrapnel, dust and splintered wood. The chains shivered and the heavy shrouds parted. Her mizzen t'gallant and topmast snapped and heeled over to starboard, yards crashing to the deck and smothering her wheel.

The masquerade of being Danish ended. French colors appeared for a moment, then fluttered down to the deck as people waved tablecloths in surrender. Both ships hauled their wind and rounded up. Forrester clumped his way down into a cutter and was off to take his prize. Even as the rowing boat was cast off, *Desperate* was paying off the wind and gathering way once more to pursue a second ship closer inshore that the *Vixen* could not reach.

This vessel they did not even have to fire into. Her crew abandoned her quickly and began to pull hard for shore, hoping the current did not set them so far west they missed St. Croix altogether. Their chances in the nasty coral reefs on the north shore were iffy enough. Before *Desperate* could think of taking her, a heat wave shimmered over her and smoke began to flag downwind.

"I'd drop this'n, sir," Monk warned. "They want off her awful bad. Might be loaded to the deck-heads with powder..."

"Still, they won't have her, lads," Treghues shouted with false cheer at being cheated of a prize. "Let's go get another."

It was fortunate they did, for once they were about a mile downwind of the abandoned ship, and she had become a raging inferno, she suddenly blew up, tossing timbers hundreds of feet into the air.

The next prize came within an hour, but she was only a lugger, run by a mulatto and crewed by blacks. She was local but carried barrels of salt meat with French markings. Being too small to bother with, she was burned, to the distress of her owner.

An hour later they came within range of a brigantine, and after two broadsides she lowered her Spanish colors and surrendered. This time, Avery and Feather had success and took eight hands and four Marines over to her happily. Like most merchant ships she had a crew barely sufficient to work her, so Avery would have no trouble from them. They left her far behind as they chased after still another prize as four vessels came north from Fredericksted and tried to run.

By lunch they were up to the first, a racy looking brig with raked masts, obviously American-built. She hoisted rebel colors and wore to open her gun battery, about four cables off on their starboard side. The other three vessels continued to flee, and this American acted as if he would trade his ship for their safety, or attempt to delay the British frigate as long as possible.

The brig opened fire first, damned accurate fire. *Desperate* drummed to the shock of iron hitting her hull from the brig's six side guns.

"Mr. Gwynn, fire as you bear," Treghues ordered.

Desperate's nine-pounders began to speak; with a stern wind taking the sound and powder cloud away, it sounded like the slamming of heavy iron doors. One at a time the guns rolled back inboard to snub against the breeching ropes, and the crews sprang to serve them while shot began to moan overhead or strike their ship once more.

The brig was not built to take such heavy punishment. When she was struck by round shot her scantlings were punched clear through and clouds of splinters erupted from her.

"Hands to the braces, Bosun. Close her!" Treghues ordered. The frigate swung until the wind was dead astern, went a point further and swung her yards about to gybe gently. The brig wore at the same time, so that their courses were aimed for a convergence.

At three cables the rebel brig fired again, and this time she fired high. *Desperate's* foret'gallant mast came crashing down, ripping down her outer flying jib, tangling her running and standing rigging in the foremast tops'l and course yards.

Desperate replied with a full broadside fired on the uproll, all nine starboard side guns and the starboard carronade together. The brig staggered as she was struck between wind and water, and the carronade shot blew her forecastle to pieces of lumber. Yet there were still men over there to serve her guns, and she struck back, ripping chunks out of *Desperate's* bulwarks and hammock nettings.

Lewrie was almost downed by a Marine that was flung off the starboard gangway to drop like a beef carcass between the guns. Three gunners screamed and clawed at their flesh as long thick wood splinters were driven into them.

"Loblolly boys!" Lewrie called out. "Here, you, take this man's place as rammer man."

"Oh God, sor, don' lemme be took ta the cockpit, sor," a

gunner said as he was picked up. One splinter stood quivering in his upper right arm, and another in his lower chest, driven sideways under skin.

But Lewrie motioned for him to be hauled away, and kicking and fighting, he was dragged to the midships hatch. The Marine's body was stuffed under the fore jeer bitts.

"Shot your guns!" Lewrie ordered as Mr. Gwynn busied himself at the carronade. "Run out! Number four, overhaul that sidetackle now!"

The carronade slammed aloud once more as Lewrie supervised the battery. Gwynn gave a cheer as his latest shot went home somewhere in the brig.

"Prime your guns," Lewrie commanded. "We shall fire together on the uproll."

Carey was there at his side. "The captain wants you on the quarterdeck, Lewrie."

"Aye. Point your guns."

The range was now about two cables, and even a linstock-fired gun with no sights of any kind could be devastingly accurate that close.

"On the uproll...fire!" Lewrie shouted, feeling the scend of the sea through his feet. The first gun bellowed, now hot and leaping straight back from the sill. He ran aft with the broadside, since some gunners did not get a clean ignition on the first uproll, and had to wait for the second, each gun captain now doing his own aiming.

"You wanted me, sir," Lewrie said after gaining the quarterdeck.

"Mister Lewrie, Mr. Gwynn or the gunner's mate are in charge on the gun deck, and I'll thank you to remember that," Treghues told him.

"Mr. Gwynn is dealing with the carronade, sir, and the gunner's mate is below in the magazine, sir—"

"You shall return forward and remind Mr. Gwynn of his duties as master gunner, and you shall summon the gunner's mate from the magazine for the forecastle gun. I shall not have any of my midshipmen circumventing the proper chain of command."

"Aye aye, sir," and Lewrie doffed his hat. Treghues turned his back on him, and Lewrie was left staring at Railsford and Monk as they shook their heads. He put his hat on, shrugged to them with a smile that seemed to say you-figure-it-out and ran back forward.

Gwynn really would much rather have played with his carronade, but he sighed and went down the ladder to the gun deck. Lewrie took time to see that the brig was taking a real beating, half her larboard side pitted with shot holes and her sail-handling gangway torn away. There were gun ports that no longer held a six-pounder or a gun that was recoiled but slewed about almost fore and aft on the centerline.

Lewrie ran below down the midships hatch and rapped on the hatchway to the hanging magazine on the orlop deck. The gunner's mate stuck his head out through the slitted felt curtain.

"The captain wants you to help Mr. Gwynn supervise the guns."

Robinson spat. He and the Yeoman of The Powder Room were busy enough passing cartridges to the ship's boys to run up to the guns, and no one ever allowed many cartridges to be made up, so he was busy filling silk bags and tying them off to service the hungry artillery. "What's happenin' up top?"

"We're shooting hell out of a rebel brig."

"Then whadduz 'e want me for?" Robinson asked.

"He doesn't want me running the guns, Mister Robinson," Lewrie said with another eloquent shrug as Robinson squeezed through the felt curtain and followed him toward midships.

"No pleasin' officers," Robinson said. "Nor figurin' what they want, neither."

Once on deck there was really nothing for Robinson to do, since they had closed to within half a cable of the brig and the remaining Marines were having a field day shooting in volley from the hammock nettings, ramming and spitting ball down the barrel, cocking and stepping up to the nettings, aiming and firing two rounds a minute at their hottest pace.

The brig was still fighting back gamely. Her colors now flew from her maintop, the gaff of the spanker having been shot away. It looked as though the flag had been nailed to the topmast.

"Damned tough, they is," a quartergunner shouted to Robinson. "Cap'n called on 'em ta strike, an' their master tol' Treghues ta go fuck 'isself."

"They're Englishmen, by God," Robinson said. "May be rebel Englishmen, but they're our sort, game as guinea cocks."

There was another volley from the brig's guns, three distinct barks from all her surviving guns, and three hard knocks that rocked *Desperate* as though she had been kicked by a giant.

"Prime yer guns," Robinson shouted. "Point. On the uproll..."

There was a flurry of gunfire from the rebel ship, swivels and musket fire that struck quills of wood from bulwarks and decks.

"They've men in the foretop," Lewrie yelled to Lt. Peck but could not make himself heard.

"Christ!" Robinson grunted. He had been struck by a ball in the knee.

"Mister Gwynn," Lewrie yelled. "It's Mister Robinson."

"On the uproll...fire!" Gwynn commanded, finishing the sequence that Robinson had started.

"They'll take me fuckin' leg, I knows it," Robinson groaned as he rocked and shivered with agony. "I had ta leave the magazine fer this...?"

There was another volley of musket fire and two Marines went limp, falling back over the starboard gangway. Lewrie remembered what he had tried to tell Peck, and jumped for the gangway, levering himself up in clear shot to speak to the Marine officer.

"Sharpshooters in the foretop, sir."

"Rifles, by God!" Peck called out, spotting where the fire

was coming from. The men aloft on the enemy ship were dressed in some kind of uniform, rifle-green tunics with white facings and buff breeches, and round hats pinned up on one side. This was no expensively outfitted privateer or a merchant vessel feeling overly aggressive—this was a rebel warship of the so-called Continental Navy!

"By volley, at the foretop," Peck ordered, pointing at the target with his small sword.

"Mister Lewrie!" Gwynn roared. "Lay the carronade on them!"

It was an order he was glad to obey...he had not yet been allowed to play with the carronades and it relieved him from standing about like a supernumerary.

"Quoin out, gun captain," Lewrie yelled in the man's ear after failing to get his attention any other way. "Lay on her foretop!"

"Too close, sir, won't bear that high."

"The larboard gun."

"Aye, might reach."

"Even if you hit the mast, that'll bring 'em down," Lewrie said, running to larboard. The carronade mount could be swiveled about in a wide arc, so it was easy to lay it in the general direction. But their activity attracted the sharp-shooters, and a powder boy screamed as his eleven-year-old life was snuffed out with a larger caliber rifle ball through his spine.

Lewrie dove for the powder cartridge and shoved it into the muzzle, standing aside as the rammer man thrust away. They got a ball down the muzzle, but then the rammer man gave a shriek and spun about, a bullet through his brains.

"Jesus Christ, save us," the gun captain said, picking up the rammer and giving the ball a few taps.

"Quoin out, there!" Lewrie told the man behind the gun. He felt a breath of air on his face, heard a hum like a summer bee and saw the larboard rail toss off a burst of tiny wood chips as a rifle ball nearly divided his skull.

"Hot work, sir," the tackle man nearest him said with a gaptoothed smile.

"At least you're getting paid," Lewrie said, lost in a fighting fever.

"Stand clear!" the gun captain said, lowering his linstock.

Up close, the explosion of the powder charge was like having one's head down the muzzle, and Lewrie's ears rang and ached, but he saw the foretop shattered by the explosion of the carronade shot, and the cluster of sharpshooters was torn away in pieces as the topmast came down in chunks as well and her rigging draped her like a netting.

The foremast gave a groan, and then the thick column of the lower mast began to split like a sawn tree that had been felled badly, pivoted forward with the pressure of the wind on a loose forecourse yard and came down with a crash across the enemy's forecastle, crushing the bow chaser gun crews that must have been firing at them at that point-blank range but had gone unnoticed in the general tumult and chaos.

The brig was now almost alongside, her gangways slightly below *Desperate*'s taller railings, and the Marines were having a great time shooting down into the enemy ship's waist.

"Boarders," Railsford yelled, drawing his sword. "Repel boarders..."

"Holy shit on a biscuit," the carronade gun captain shouted. "I don't believe these people."

Lewrie seized a cutlass from a weapons tub and went to the starboard forecastle rail. The brig was bumping into *Desperate*, and such of her crew as had survived were tossing grapnels to hold their ship against the frigate even as the Marines' volleys cut swathes out of their closely-packed ranks.

A gawky thatch-haired young man leaped up in front of Lewrie with a cutlass, and Lewrie engaged with him as more poured over.

The man was strong but clumsy. Lewrie beat his guard aside and cut back across, slashing the man's throat. The man fell back into the sea, blood shooting out like a claret fountain. The next man up took a boarding pike through his stomach and also fell into the sea. The third, Lewrie had time to skewer with the point of his cutlass, and he too raised a splash alongside.

The enemy had gained the midships gangway but were being cut up by boarding pikes and Marine bayonets, and the enemy's stern was pivoting away from *Desperate*.

Lewrie waved his cutlass attracting more angry bees that rushed by him. "Fend 'em off the forecastle..."

With rammers, with handspikes, crows and boarding pikes, about a dozen hands were there with him, some slashing the air with cutlass steel, others fighting like wild Indians with tomahawks. The rebels who had gained the forecastle began to fall back, leaping for their own decks. A Marine corporal came forward with ten privates and began to volley into them.

"Do we board her?" the corporal asked.

"Won't trap me over there," a gunner said.

"I think she's sinking," Lewrie said. "Look how low in the water she is."

The brig was indeed very low in the water now, the sea almost up to her gun ports; her wale and chain plates were already under. Lewrie could see the tangle of bodies on her forecastle and forward gun deck, piled up like slaughtered rabbits after a successful hunt; how two guns were shot free of any restraints and rolled back and forth on the bloody deck.

But they were still firing. Swivels and light four-pounders on her quarterdeck, where the only resistance still stood, an occasional musket or rifled gun, and pistols popped.

"Cut her free," Lewrie ordered the tomahawk men. "We'll not be able to save her, and if we roll over she'll have the sticks out of us."

The three-inch lines grappled to *Desperate* were already iron-hard and taut, groaning and crying with tension, and each time the brig slunk into a wave there was a pull downward on the frigate.

Once cut with an axe, the lines twanged like bowstrings and almost snapped a man's right arm off as they parted. The brig's forecastle was level with the sea, and her beakhead and jib boom was under, sinking quickly now by the bows. She would not last long. Ominous rumbles came from her as the surging waves explored her innards.

"Strike!" Treghues yelled. "In the name of humanity, strike!"

"Hell, no, you British duck-fucker," their young captain yelled back, cupping his hands and standing foursquare on his shattered deck. "You tell the world, we were the brig o' war *Liberty*, Continental By God Navy..."

Then with a foamy surge the ocean broke over her bows and she tilted up by the stern, gear and shattered timbers and loose guns and internal stores screaming in pain and bulkheads battered into ruin. She slipped beneath the sea, leaving a few survivors swimming in the light flotsam. Her mainmast was the last to go under, still bearing the striped rebel colors with the starry blue canton nailed to the mast. She had lost her fight, but it didn't feel so.

They fetched up and went over with a boat to pick up survivors, but there weren't a dozen men left and the young captain was not one of them. Treghues offered them dry clothes and rum and put them below.

Lewrie wished that the day was over but it was not to be. Once they had swayed up a new t'gallant mast, roved a fresh outer jib stay, took down the damaged tops'l yard, fished it with a stuns'l boom, rehoisted it and bent on a new sail, they were off once more in search of prizes that lay tantalizingly to leeward.

After their labor a late meal was brought up from the galley, cold meat and cheese and biscuit. The rum ration was doled out along with as much small beer as they could drink. Their dead were hustled below out of sight by the loblolly boys and the decks washed clean of blood and offal to keep up their fighting spirit.

They came across another brig beating up to windward for Fredericksted from the west, unaware that anything was happening, and did not notice that *Desperate* was British until it was too late. She turned out to be French, come for a load of stores to smuggle, and was crammed to the deckheads with rum, molasses and naval stores. There was no resistance, and Mister Monk went away with Carey in charge of her, leaving Alan as the last midshipman still aboard.

Let it be over, he thought in weariness, and the awful letdown he had come to know as his normal reaction after each hard fight. All he wanted to do was find a patch of shade and go to sleep as some of the hands could, never mind slinging a hammock below. They had finally stood down from quarters ... every sail still in sight was hull down over the horizon running for their lives.

By late afternoon even Treghues had to admit that they had run out of hope of future prizes, that they had seemingly swept the ocean clean. On their way nor'west toward Culebra and Vieques Islands they could see sails jogging along behind them, and in trail of the other warships, perhaps ten captures in all, in which all the frigates and sloops would share. Actually in material terms they had not made a real dent in the volume of imports to the rebellious colonies, but perhaps the audacity of the raid would give the smugglers pause, or make them choose new areas in which to operate.

Lewrie stood by the taffrail, reveling in the quarter breeze now that the strength had gone out of the sun. The wind held his coat open, and he spread his shirt wide below the neckcloth to allow the cooling wind to play on his chest and sweaty ribs.

"Getting indecent with the mermaids, Mister Lewrie?" Lieutenant Railsford asked, coming aft to join him.

"That would be a novel experience, sir," Lewrie said, taking off his hat to cool his scalp.

"That was good work you did up forrard today, Lewrie," Railsford told him, letting his own coat spread open.

"Thank you, Mister Railsford, I am grateful that someone appreciated it."

"I do not mean to pry, Mister Lewrie, but..." Railsford now spoke in a softer tone since Treghues' cabin skylight was slightly forward of them, and was open for a breeze...

"I get the feeling our lord and master no longer approves of you."

"No need to worry, sir, I'll bear up."

"Take a round turn and two half-hitches?" Railsford grinned.

"And as Mister Monk says, sir, the more you cry, the less you'll piss," Lewrie bantered, his eyes overbright and his mood a bit too chipper to pass unnoticed.

"The captain has his...moods," Railsford said, treading on soft ground...there had been officers who had been court-martialed for a habit of criticism. A captain could demand obedience from his officers and also a united front of one mind once he had determined what opinion should be held.

"If it is any comfort, Mister Lewrie, those moods can be swift to change in most instances." That was as far as Railsford would go in criticism of the captain. Any gossip passed on would undermine both Railsford's, and Treghues', authority.

"Aye, sir."

"Remember, every captain has something to teach you, for good or ill. Life in the Fleet can be a series of disasters to be born sometimes."

"I shall bear up, Mister Railsford. Thank you for that..."

Desperate took in her t'gallants and brailed them up, lowered the yards to the caps, took a reef in their tops'ls and got the speed off her for evening sailing at the rendezvous, as well as to allow her prize vessels to catch up with her. Then it was clear-decks-and-up-spirits, supper, evening quarters and hammocks below for the night. At dusk the masthead lookouts came down, and hands took up upper deck viewing posts.

Amphion ordered all prize vessels gathered in an impromptu convoy, with the sloops off to windward to guard the flank. *Amphion* brought up the rear and *Desperate* worked out ahead and to leeward of the convoy as they set off sou'east for the nearest British ports.

Lewrie had had his dinner alone. Both master's mates

and all the other midshipmen were away in prizes. The steward brought him some boiled salt pork, a couple of new potatoes, biscuit and Black Strap cut with water. Aft, the officers were celebrating loudly, those still on board. Their steward came through several times with bottles which had been cooling on the orlop, while Alan ate and drank in isolation, which condition he was sure was to be permanent.

He had the evening watch, and Mr. Gwynn stood in for a deck officer with him. The sky was clear, littered with bright stars, and though there was no moon, the sea shone at each wave top, now and then breaking into a white chop. Lewrie made a tour of the lower deck with the ship's corporal and master-at-arms to inspect the galley and lanterns to make sure all fires were out, then went back to the quarterdeck and loafed by the forward nettings. The Trades sang sweetly through the rigging, and the hull held at a slight angle of heel to starboard, hissing and groaning as she made her way toward home.

Gwynn was near him, looking up at the stars and the sails. There was a gurgling noise as Gwynn pulled on a pocket flask of rum, and the sweet odor wafted by like a woman's perfume.

"Summat ta keep yer eyes open, Mister Lewrie?" Gwynn offered.

"That would have me snoring on the deck, Mister Gwynn, but I thankee," Lewrie replied. "God, I am so tired."

"Allus like that after a hard fight," Gwynn said. "God, they fought grand. Can't remember the Continental Navy showin' that much bottom. Privateers get the best men. Rebels're too independent ta take ta Navy-style discipline."

"If they'd had nine-pounders, or carronades, they'd have done for us, I think, Mister Gwynn," Lewrie said, nodding in agreement.

"Right enough."

Treghues emerged on deck from aft, and the pair of them went down to leeward to give him the entire windward side of the quarterdeck for his pacing. Treghues was in breeches and open shirt, quite informal for a change, a spooky apparition in the faint starlight, pacing back and forth quite regularly; not as though he were in deep thought but as if it was a duty to walk for a while before retiring. To escape, Lewrie went forward to tour the lookouts on the forecastle and gangways and make certain they were more awake than he was. He had to shake a couple of men into full wariness. By the time he had returned to the quarterdeck, Treghues had gone below and only a dim glow could be seen from his skylight. And then as Alan watched, that was snuffed out.

"Ever'body chipper up forrard?" Gwynn asked.

"Aye, Mister Gwynn. Sleepy but trying."

"Here, what's got the cap'n onta ya?"

Not you, too, Alan thought. "I do not know what you mean, sir."

"He come over an' asked me what ya was doin' runnin' the guns as ya were today, like ta give ma a cobbin' about it. I told him ya was as good as any gunner's mate but he didn't wanta hear it."

"The captain has his moods," Alan said uneasily.

"Moods, shit!" Gwynn stuffed a quid of tobacco into his cheek and tore off a large bite. "Fickle as me old lady, 'cept fer Mr. Forrester an' Railsford. Takes a great hankerin' fer somebody an' then turns on 'em an' nobody knows why. Been in *Desperate* near two an' a half years an' it's been like that ever since we commissioned."

"Let's just say he doesn't like my choice of fathers," Lewrie said after Gwynn's indiscretion. "And it seems I'm too big a sinner to wear a Navy uniform."

"Aye, that's one reason we don't have a chaplain aboard." Gwynn laughed softly. "With him aft, we don't need one." Lewrie gave a grunt that might have been a mirthless laugh, or a sign of agreement, and Gwynn walked off to find the spit kid by the binnacle.

Six bells chimed softly from the belfry up forward, and Alan checked his watch against it—11:00 P.M. and only an

hour to go before he could go below and sleep four unin-
terrupted hours until the morning routine of a man of war
claimed him once again.

"Sail ho!" one of the forward lookouts called. Lewrie
shook himself into action, trotting forward to join him.

"Where away?"

"Two points off the larboard bow, Mister Lewrie," the
lookout said quietly, almost afraid to raise his voice. "He's
on the opposite tack an' comin' north. He'll run right into
the convoy!"

Lewrie hefted the heavy night glass, which showed
images upside down and backward. He found their
stranger, what seemed to be a full-rigged ship ghosting
along under reefed tops'ls, inner jibs and spanker.

"Run aft and wake the captain," Lewrie said. "Tell Mr.
Gwynn we've a full-rigged ship coming right for us. Quick,
man."

Lewrie studied the stranger for a while longer, then
shouted for the bosun's mate of the watch, Toliver. "All
hands on deck, Mister Toliver, no pipes or we'll lose the
chase."

"No pipes," the runty little man repeated before running
off to shout down the midships hatchway to the off-duty
watch. It was noisy enough as the hands rolled out of their
hammocks and thudded to the deck to thunder up topside
on bare feet.

Lewrie hurried back to the wheel and stood by Gwynn,
who was using the other night glass to search for the
strange ship.

"Have I your permission to close her, sir?" Lewrie asked
him.

"Yes, let's see what he's doin' runnin' dark out here."

"Duty watch to the braces! Quartermaster, put your helm
down and lay her two points closer to the wind!" Alan
shouted.

"What's this about a strange sail, Mister Gwynn?"
Treghues demanded, emerging on the quarterdeck.

"Here, sir, take a squint. Ship-rigged an' runnin' without a light, sir. Thus, quartermaster! 'Vast heavin'! Belay every inch o' that, Mister Toliver!"

"Harden up on the heads'l sheets," Lewrie called to the foc's'l captain. "Now belay!"

"Mister Gwynn, I have the deck," Treghues said, still dressed in a night shirt. "Lewrie, stop that caterwauling like you know what you're doing. Judkin, fetch me up my breeches and sword."

"Aye, sir."

"Shall we clear for action, sir?" Gwynn asked as Railsford and Peck joined them.

"Aye, load and run out the larboard battery," Treghues told him.

"I'll need Mister Lewrie forrard, sir,..." Gwynn said. "Robinson's lost his leg, ya remember, sir."

"Oh, very well," Treghues said after a long pause.

"Mister Lewrie, do take charge o' the forecastle an' the carronades, if ya please." Gwynn was smiling in the darkness.

"Aye, Mister Gwynn."

"All hands to quarters!" Treghues shouted.

It was hard to see how the men could even see what they were doing as they unlashed the guns and rolled them back to the centerline, overhauled the side tackles and freed the train tackles, brought gun tools up from below and began to light fuses in the slow match tubs.

"Damn fool," Lewrie said, hearing Treghues' musicians get going at "Hearts of Oak".

"Afternoon wadd'n enough fer ya, Mister Lewrie?" the larboard carronade captain joshed with him as they removed the tompion of their gun and freed the lashing on the swivel platform.

"Wanted to see what they looked like going off in the dark," Alan shot back. "Here, can we manhandle the other gun over here?"

"Take some doin', Mister Lewrie, but I kin lash the breech ropes ta the cathead, iffen ya want it."

"Load yer guns," Gwynn called from aft on the main gun deck.

A squad of Marines under their sergeant came trooping forward along the gangway to take station from the forecastle aft.

The strange ship came awake. The wind brought them the faint sound of bosun's pipes playing unfamiliar calls, and the sound of men running to stations. The wind also brought a brassy aroma mixed with the smell of a barnyard.

"Lord, what a stink," Lewrie said. "What's he carrying?"

"Moight be a slaver, sor," the starboard gun captain said.

"He's putting about," Lewrie broke in, almost able to see a faint shadow that was darker than the night. "Going on the wind on the starboard tack."

"Stations for stays!" Railsford ordered. "Stand by to come about."

"Helm alee!"

"Rise tacks an' sheets!" Toliver yelled. "Clew garnets!"

"Mains'l haul!"

Desperate came up to the eye of the wind, her sails shivering and her yards creaking as the hands leaned almost parallel to the deck to fetch her around without missing stays. The focs'l captain shifted his heads'l sheets to larboard, and the backed fore yards provided enough wind resistance to force her bows off the wind as the other yards drove her forward. She tacked smoothly, losing little speed in the dark, and hardened up on the same tack as the other ship, laid within six points of the winds and beginning to beat hard to weather.

"Waisters, harden up the tops'l braces. Now belay!" Railsford called, wanting to put a slight spiral set to the yards, the tops'ls more acutely angled to the wind than the courses for the most efficiency.

The stranger was now off their starboard bows, perhaps a mile off. Lewrie could barely make out ghostly specks of light like tiny candles along her leeward side.

"Slow match," Alan said. "They'll make a fight of it."

"Hope they ain't like that last batch," someone said.

"Gun captain, prepare the starboard carronade. Shift the larboard gun up abaft the roundhouse. Breech rope to the hawse buckler and the cathead," Alan ordered, wanting to put both his "Smashers" to work.

He looked aft now to see an amber light burning on the taffrail, a fusee that smoked and flared like a holiday rocket, the night signal for danger. It would also warn the other prizes in convoy of where they were so as to avoid collision in the dark. Hurriedly, the rest of the ships began to light their taffrail lanterns.

"That's *Roebuck* or *Vixen* out there, sir," a hand shouted, waving a hand at a distant light to windward. "Bet he'll tack agin."

"Belay shifting that carronade."

Within moments the dark shape of their quarry shortened and put her masts in line, tacking across the wind once more, but *Desperate* performed her own tack at the same time. And had the chase missed stays on that maneuver? They suddenly seemed much closer to her.

"Give me a point free," Treghues ordered. "Stand by the larboard battery." Lewrie's men secured the starboard gun and shifted once more, lashing the larboard carronade back into position.

"Can you reach him yet?" Lewrie asked.

"'Bout another cable, sir," the gunner said, squinting at their spectral foe.

"Number one larboard gun...fire!" Gwynn called, and the nine-pounder closest to them below the larboard gangway fired. It was a spectacular sight at night to witness the tongue of flame that stabbed out through a nimbus of gunsmoke, and the sound seemed much louder than during the daytime. Lewrie was almost blinded by the flash. When he looked for their target it had disappeared for him, though the experienced gunners still peered at it intently.

The enemy ship returned fire, a single gun from her stern-chaser, and the ball moaned into the night without hitting anything. By then *Desperate* was rapidly closing the other vessel. The main guns began to bark regularly, though it was hard to tell if they were achieving any better results on their target than the enemy had.

"I kin hit him now, sir, I think," the gun captain said.

"Blaze away!"

"Stand clear."

The carronade lurched inboard on its slide. Seconds later the sure sign of a solid hit on the hull flashed into life, and the night was full of the thin sound of screaming.

"Jaysus," a hand said.

"Mules, sir. Or horses. No wonder he stinks."

"God help the poor beasts," Lewrie said, and the men around him echoed his sentiments. For the enemy, they would have no mercy, yet could weep real tears over their birds and dogs and manger animals.

Desperate was now within a cable, and one could discern the foe clearly in the starlight well enough to aim true. They put another ball from the carronade onto the poop of the enemy, and this time the screams were men, not dumb beasts. There was a hail of musket and swivel fire from the quarterdeck, and the ship's guns, sounding like nine-pounders, began to fire irregularly, but their aim was incredibly poor and did little more than raise great splashes close aboard.

Close enough to see people... Lewrie could make out a mass of men in white uniforms on the quarterdeck, almost a full company of troops that were firing by volley with their muskets. A ball from the carronade took a third of them down like a reaper. *Desperate*'s guns were speaking as regular as a tolling bell from bow to stern, about ten seconds apart, each shot painting the water between the two dueling ships blood red and amber and lighting up their sides. The carronade fired again, providing enough of a light as the ball exploded to see the men with muskets writhing in agony as another third were scythed down and the remainder were faltering in their musket drill, falling back from the rails as *Desperate*'s own Marines began to volley into them.

"Second carronade to larboard!" Lewrie called out. "Lash her down to anything that'll hold."

Once more that day, musket balls began to buzz about Lewrie's ears and strike the deck and rails with solid thuds. There were more men across the way in white uniforms, now on the gangways and forecastle, loading and firing their muskets regular as clockwork. Their own Marines were taking a toll of those people with musket and swivels.

"That bunch, gun captain," Lewrie ordered.

The carronade spoke once more, and the range was so close that the bursting of the shot was almost instantaneous, flicking whining bits of shrapnel around their own ears, but the well-drilled platoon of men on the gangways disappeared in the flash and the bang.

There was a narrowing tide race of channel between the two ships, and *Desperate*'s guns were spitting blazing wads at the enemy ship in addition to the solid shot, firing point-blank across the foamed breadth of water as their bow waves merged.

"Starboard gun's ready, sir."

"Reload larboard gun and stand by. There's some men on her forecastle. Take 'em down," Lewrie said.

"Grapnels! Prepare to board!" Railsford called out from aft.

There was little return fire from the enemy ship now, her gun ports silent and not a muzzle showing, though the resistance from her musketeers was still hot. There was a dense knot of them on the forecastle, first rank kneeling and second and third ranks alternated, lowering their muskets for a volley.

"Fire as you bear!" Lewrie ordered, his testicles shrinking up inside him at the sight of glittering bayonets and musket bores.

The carronade belched fire and smoke, and when the residue blew back over them downwind there was nothing left on the forecastle but a pile of bodies in white uniforms painted red with gore.

"Bow chaser, sir."

There was a light cannon on the forecastle, and the sailors in slop clothing were running to man it while more men in uniform ran forward with them to where the two ships would bump together.

Lewrie tried to attract the Marine sergeant's attention to them, but he was busy directing musket volleys further aft. Alan saw the other crew removing the tompion of the bow chaser.

"Load, Goddamnit! Kill those people!"

A musket barked, and the larboard carronade rammer screamed and fell to the deck, the rest of the crew shrinking away.

"Load, damn you, *load.*" Lewrie plucked a heavy Sea Pattern pistol from a weapons tub, checked to see it was primed and drew back the heavy cocking lever.

There was a volley of musket fire that spanged off the carronades, driving men into hiding behind the bulwarks and taking down two more men. Lewrie turned to face the enemy. He could see a man passing up a powder charge, leveled his pistol and took aim. He fired, and the ball hit the barrel of the bow chaser, spanging off with a flash of sparks and took a side-tackle man in the stomach. The rammer man was now tamping down his charge.

Lewrie took up another pistol and aimed for the man who cradled a bag of musket shot. Not only did he miss him, he punched a scarlet bloom dead in the chest of a man with a handspike on the other side of the gun.

"Shitten goddamn pistols!" He threw the thing across the gap, which by then could not have been fifty feet. If that bow chaser went off, they were all dead.

He was amazed to see the heavy, long-barreled (and wildly inaccurate) Sea Pattern pistol knock the teeth out of the gun captain with the slow match ignition fuse and drop him out of sight.

"Stand clear!" the carronade gun captain finally barked out. The men on the opposing forecastle began to shrink away.

"About bloody time," Lewrie said in profound relief as

his life was spared once more, but his relief was lost in the explosion of the powder charge and the bursting of the shot.

As the two forecastles nudged together, and grapnels flew across to lash the two ships together, it was nearly as silent as the grave.

"Boarders!" Railsford ordered by Lewrie's side, waving his bright sword. "Away, boarders!"

Lewrie scrabbled for a cutlass from the weapons tub and then was borne forward like a pinnace surged onto a beach by a powerful burst of surf as the men who had gathered forward went over to the enemy ship in a howling mob.

He had no choice but to leap across the narrow gap—either that or fall and be ground to sausage meat between the hulls—where he was immediately tripped by a bight of shredded heads'l sheets and fell to the deck, to be almost trampled by his own people as they screamed and whooped and fell on the enemy.

Haven't I done enough, dammit? he thought to himself, feeling the pain in his knees and shins. There was a strong arm lifting him up, a flash of smile in a dark face from one of the West Indian hands, and then he was stuck into it whether he cared to participate or not.

He headed aft for the larboard forecastle ladder and began to descend, but a pike head came jabbing out of nowhere, bringing a scream to his lips. He thrust out in the general direction of the pike's wielder, and his sword met meaty resistance.

The pike was withdrawing for a second thrust, and he grabbed the shaft behind the wickedly gleaming point and was pulled into the enemy, his cutlass sinking deeper into whoever it was. Suddenly there was a shrill yell almost in his ear, a hot and garlicky breath on his face, and he slammed into the man.

There was enough light to see that he had his cutlass sunk hilt-deep into an enemy sailor, and it could not be withdrawn. Lewrie let go the pike shaft and twisted and pulled, bringing another shriek of agony. The sword came free, as did the man's entrails, slithering out like some image from a nightmare.

The entire waist of the enemy ship was a heaving mass of men who were clashing blades like a tribe of Welsh tinkers. Steel flickered and struck, knives flashed, bayonets and pikes dipped and thrust and came away slimed with blood. Underfoot there were already bodies enough, sailors and soldiers ripped to pieces by carronade shot, the decks gleaming wet and sticky. Pistols spat, muskets barked, giving little flashes of light on the scene.

Alan left the waist, going back to the silent forecastle, and made his way aft along the larboard gangway, picking his way across tangled rope piles and torn nettings and bodies. There was hardly any fighting there. He would have liked to have assisted but wasn't sure who was friendly and who was an enemy. He advanced slowly, his cutlass ready.

"*Salaud!*" someone snarled, leaping for him. Alan clashed blades with him, using both hands to go into the murderous cutlass drill, and also trying to remember his poor French ...had the man just called him a 'dirty beast'?...The man stumbled backward from a hard blow, and Alan brought the blade flashing down once more, catching him on the side of the neck, slicing down through the collar bone. This time the cutlass could not be dislodged, so he bent down and took the man's rapier and a pistol from his waistband, pulled the gun back to half-cock and went on aft.

By the main chains he got into another melee. Three men in slop clothing were falling back from about half a dozen men in white infantry uniforms, mostly armed with short hangers.

"At 'em, Desperates," Lewrie yelled, partly to let them know that he was not a foe to be chopped into chutney sauce, and partly to encourage them. He found himself at the head of the pack, slashing away with abandon. One of his men struck forward with a cutlass and ripped the groin out of a foeman, which brought such a shriek that the others turned to run. Alan chopped a second man down across the spine as he faced away but could not escape past his friends.

A musket thrust for him, its bayonet sharp and hungry. He put up the pistol to bind with it, slashing backward with his rapier and opening up the man's chest. As the man stumbled and went down, Alan struck again across the neck, then vaulted the body as it sank to the deck.

Now he was on the quarterdeck as British Marines and sailors swarmed up the ladders from the waist in a rush, and Lewrie's people took the crumbling opposition in the flank, doing great damage before they were spotted.

Lewrie faced off with a boy, perhaps a midshipman like him, and almost without thought beat the young man's guard aside and ran him through with the razor-sharp rapier.

Next there was a real swordsman, an officer by his clothes and breeches and good stockings and shoes, with a rapier and what looked like a poignard.

"To me!" Alan screamed, but he'd been cut off by the swirling fight, almost backed up against the larboard bulwarks and nettings. The man was fast and strong, his wrist like an iron bar as their blades met. Alan retreated slowly, parrying the sword with his rapier and trying to keep the poignard away from his belly with the long barrel of the pistol.

The French officer stamped and lunged, and Alan beat him aside in *quartata*, but the Frenchman was there with the poignard going for his throat, and they binded, thrusting forward at each other. The poignard snapped the gun back to full cock and Alan took aim in the general direction and pulled the trigger. The powder in the pan flashed, but the gun hung fire, the muzzle not three inches from the man's head...

The Frenchman actually smiled as he leaped back, devilishly quick on his feet, before driving forward again. Lewrie held him off with the rapier, going onto the attack to keep the poignard away. He still held the gun pointed at the man, hoping it would make up its mind to fire.

Then they were almost chest to chest again, and Lewrie had to lower the pistol to deflect the poignard. The gun went off. The French officer grunted and fell backward, all his strength gone. The pistol had finally discharged, in the man's groin.

"Quarter," someone yelled in English. "Give 'em quarter, I say..."

It was not that easy to turn aside the mens' blood lust. Three Marines ran past Lewrie, muskets held right forward, stabbing, slaughtering broken men like rabbits.

Alan leaned on the railing and became aware of a pain in his gun hand. The Frenchman's poignard had cut deep into his fingers on the butt as he had tried to fend off sure death from that dagger.

"Goddamn it, give 'em quarter," Railsford was shouting. "*Stop that.*"

Slowly the fight drained out of the men as they realized they had slaughtered and butchered from the forecastle to the after quarterdeck, and that there were very few enemy left standing. The ship was alive with cries of agony and terror, and the screaming of those horses or mules continued from the first moment they had opened fire.

"Mister Lewrie, is that you?" Railsford demanded, coming toward his side of the quarterdeck.

"Aye, Mister Railsford," he shouted back through a cracked and dry throat.

"Take a party below and roust out the survivors."

Lewrie found half a dozen Marines and sailors and went from one compartment to another, down into the orlop and the holds in search of those who had hidden from death. They ran about ten men topsides.

"What's below?" Railsford asked him.

"Gun caissons, limbers, gun carriages, looks like six- or nine-pounder artillery, sir," Lewrie said, his hand throbbing now. "There's draft horses, sir, shot up and screaming."

"Toliver," Railsford called.

"Aye aye, sir?"

"Take a party below and put those horses out of their misery."

"Aye aye, sir."

"Hollo, what's happened to your hand?"

"Cut it, sir. French officer over there with a dagger."

"You go see Dorne, then report right back to me, hear?"

"Aye, sir."

The two ships were now lashed firmly together, heading south on a soldier's wind on the beam, as they tried to sort things out. There was a hatch grating lashed to the bulwarks over which Lewrie scrambled to his own ship, still gripping the strange rapier. He went below to the orlop and found surgeon Dorne busily cutting and sewing, his leather apron awash in blood, with gore up to the elbows. There were few of the *Desperate* present, but plenty of unfamiliar faces were on the deck twisted in pain.

"Bide a moment, Mister Lewrie," Dorne said, his head bare for once in the dancing light of the lanterns over the operating table made of chests. He was removing the arm from a French soldier, which had been shattered by grape shot. "No, can't help this one anymore. Lewrie, come here. Anything wrong?"

The soldier had died and was being lugged out by the loblolly boys to be tipped over the side without ceremony.

"Ah, flex your fingers for me," Dorne said, peering at the cuts. "Everything still works. Drink this."

There was a mug of rum, barely cut by an equal mixture of water, which Alan drank down greedily. Dorne sponged his hand with seawater, got out his sewing kit and began to stitch the worst ragged tears while Alan set his face in a mask. Life was full of pain, anyone could tell you that, and it had to be borne as best as one could, without a show of fear. Men had been operated on for the stone, had their limbs severed, and never uttered a peep...they knew that pain could be stood, and once stood, was over.

"Once you are through with that, sir, I have a pair of

breeches need mending," Alan said tightly, looking off into the middle distance at Frenchmen in much more pain than he.

"Give it a week and you'll be sewing yourself," Dorne said. "There. Soak daily in salt water, which is an excellent prevention of suppuration. The stitches will weep for a while, but no lasting damage has been done. Hogan, wrap this in clean cloth, will you? And you come see me if you have any discoloring or odorous discharge."

"Aye, Mister Dorne," Lewrie said, happy to escape that place as another man was slung onto the table with both legs slashed open. Once Hogan had bound his worst cut finger and wrapped a bandage around his whole hand, Alan went back on deck, reeling from the drink.

He reported to Railsford and was soon in charge of a working party hoisting out the dead horses. The cook was slaughtering them and carving them into chunks of roughly four pounds apiece for fresh meat for each mess. Other teams were identifying *Desperate*'s dead and wounded, carrying them aboard for burial or surgery, tipping dead or badly injured Frenchmen over the side and shoving offal over from shattered bodies.

"Whole company of French infantry," Railsford said as dawn began to tint the eastern horizon. "And a battery of artillery going to the Virginia colony. Not a corporal's guard of them left."

"Virginia, sir?" Alan asked, reeling once more, this time with exhaustion as they labored to set the ship to rights for the prize crew to handle.

"Aye, I thought we had that safe, but things must be happening up north," Railsford told him. "There's a French officer left, but not for long, that man over there in the green coat and red breeches, War Commissary Corps to Rochambeau and Lafayette... He makes it sound like the whole bunch of Southern colonies has been stripped bare for some major fight in the Virginias."

An older French officer had been wounded in the belly and was propped up as comfortable as possible near the double wheel by his orderly, who was sponging his brow.

"He won't last," Lewrie said.

"I know, but he's full of information and cares little for keeping it to himself. You understand French, Lewrie?"

"Just barely, sir. There's a lot would go right past me."

"Well, I'll keep at it, then," Railsford said. "God, I wish we had our people here."

During the night the convoy of prize ships had plodded past the ship and *Desperate,* once *Amphion* had assured herself that they had things in good order. The larger frigate had given up half a dozen hands and a master's mate into *Desperate* to help work her, but this prize would require thinning out the crew further.

"Anything more you want me to do, sir?" Alan asked.

"Check the cargo manifests. Toss any drink over the side that the prize crew might be able to get to. We shall have to get underway."

Lewrie went aft under the poop to the master's cabins. There had been some minor looting done and furniture was overturned, but the glossy desk was still in good order. Lewrie opened drawers until he came across the ship's log, manifests and daily books.

Their prize was a merchantman owned by Mulraix et Fils, Bordeaux, named the *Ephegenie,* chartered by the Royal War Commissary on Martinique and Admiral DeGrasse to carry a full battery of artillery to Rochambeau. Alan scanned the manifest. Twenty-four draft horses, now mostly dead and soon to be dinner, worth their weight in gold in the Colonies; a line company of replacements for the *Règiment Soissonois,* which explained the soldiers in white uniforms with rose facings; a full artillery company of men in dark blue and buff, both sorts also mostly dead. There were stands of muskets for Washington, crates of swords, bales of uniforms, new boots and gaiters, field tents, horseshoe blanks and farrier's equipage for Lauzun's Legion of Dragoons, over 200 kegs of wine, tons of biscuit and salt meat, a field bakery and wagon (disassembled), over two tons of six-pounder artillery cartridges and half a million rounds of musket shot, premade into paper cartouches.

When the wine kegs were broached the hands groaned to see good red wine go cascading over the side. Cheatham took several kegs into *Desperate* for issue at six-to-one dilution, but the rest had to go; no officer could keep order in a prize crew with such a temptation.

The sun was well up before the prize was rerigged well enough to sail for Antigua or another British port. Alan made one last tour of the cabin to see if he had missed anything. He probed into the transom settee lockers, and found personal wine stocks.

There was also a wooden box with holes in the side, holes in the lid which fit down inside the box like a wine press, though Alan didn't think the late French master would squeeze his own grapes. He fetched it out and found canvas-bound packets wrapped up in ribbons like Naval orders, weighted down with grape shot sewn into the canvas binders.

He read the first. DeGrasse to Rochambeau: what sounded like a reply to a request of some kind, full of all the flowery gilt and beshit compliments Frenchmen were capable of. Agreement with plans, fleet being assembled . . . There was a second letter to Washington, also in French, but of much the same tone.

Lewrie hurried on deck to find Railsford and quickly showed them to him. Railsford read closely, his lips moving with the effort of translating a foreign language to himself.

"Have we found something important, sir?" Alan asked, eager to have done something clever.

"Indeed we *have*," Railsford said, almost clicking his heels as he bounced about the deck. "This DeGrasse bugger is going to sail north with a fleet to meet Rochambeau and Washington, somewhere in Virginia or Delaware . . . either Delaware Bay or the Chesapeake . . ."

"And the rebels won't know it," Lewrie said.

"Oh, there's probably half a dozen sets of these that have already gone north, so one of them would make it through the patrols," the lieutenant said. "But we've intercepted one, and if we can get word to Hood he might just be able to square DeGrasse's yards before he gets anywhere with his plans. Get over to *Desperate* and show these to the captain at once."

Lewrie had not seen Treghues for some time, so he assumed that he was aft in his quarters. He raced up to the Marine sentry and was admitted with the usual ceremony of stamping, slamming and shouting.

"Damn you," Dorne hissed at the Marine sentry. "Lewrie, what's the call for all this noise?"

"Papers from the Frenchman that the captain must see, sir."

"Alright, but make it quick."

Dorne pointed to the small cabin to the port side, where Treghues had a hanging bed box, chest and dressing area shared with a nine-pound gun. Lewrie stuck his head in, and there was Treghues, in bed, his chest bare and his head wrapped up in a bulky bandage. His steward Judkin was holding up a mug of watered wine for him to sip, and Lewrie caught the scent of fruit juices mixed into it. Treghues' face was puffy and marred with a massive bruise on one side from scalp to jaw.

"What is it?" Treghues snapped, not exactly cheered to see Lewrie and obviously in some pain from a heavy blow to the head.

Lewrie blurted out his news but Treghues was off in his own little world, from the injury or some medicine that Dorne had given him. He could only rave and quote scripture about fornicators and Absalom's rape of Tamara, and all through it cob Lewrie for a miserable sinner of the worst stripe.

"Just thought you'd like to know, sir," Lewrie said, and left the cabins, knowing he was not going to get any sense through to the captain in his state.

"He acts out of his wits," Lewrie said to Dorne in the passageway to the upper gun deck.

"Some French gunner laid him out with a rammer," Dorne said. "I have given him laudanum to let him sleep.

Best treatment for now. I have good hopes he shall recover his senses in a few days."

"Let us pray he does," Lewrie said with a solemn expression that was expected, but secretly was delighted. Him whom the Lord loves, he chastiseth, he quoted to himself wryly. Pious bastard.

He reported back to Railsford, still holding onto the letters.

"We must get word to Antigua quickly," Railsford said after a long moment. "And if Commander Treghues needs further medical treatment he must have it soon. *Desperate* must go direct to English Harbor. The prize can catch up the convoy for safety, and pass word to *Amphion* regarding our discovery."

"Aye, sir," Lewrie said, handing Railsford the packets.

"I recall you have stood deck watches and run a schooner before, Mister Lewrie."

"Aye, sir." Alan replied, beginning to quiver with joy.

"I shall give you Mister Toliver, an acting quartermaster's mate, and a dozen hands. Transfer the physically able prisoners to *Desperate* where I can guard them the better. The prize is yours."

"Thank you, Mister Railsford!"

"Might take your sea chest," Railsford suggested. "No, don't think I want to get rid of you, but you may be separated from the ship for some time and will need your things. Mind you, I'd be proud to have you aboard after what you've accomplished, but our captain may not see his way to being reconciled to your presence."

"Thank you, Mister Railsford. I appreciate your good opinion of me," Alan told him, and meant it, appreciating such kindness from a man he had not overly cultivated.

"On your way, then."

An hour later *Ephegenie* cast free of *Desperate*, and the frigate began to surge past her, spreading her tops'ls and the hands tailing on the jeers to raise her t'gallants to the accompaniment of a fiddler's hauling chanty.

Alan watched her go, stout oak hull gleaming brown, her

wale a black curve at the waterline, her gunwale streaked bright and jaunty green, her taffrail carvings and gold leaf gleaming in the sun. She was home, for all her frustrations, and she was leaving. He got a lump in his throat at the sight of her.

I never realized that ships could be so beautiful, he thought. Hard work and ruptures, bad food and no sleep, so complex and nothing goes a day without needing fixing, but they can be so Goddamned lovely!

"We'll be back aboard again, don't you fret, sir," Toliver told him, working on a quid of tobacco.

"Get the ship underway, bosun," Lewrie ordered. "Quartermaster, lay her head sou-sou'west, half-south."

"Hands ta the braces," Toliver bellowed. They braced her yards around first, short-handed as they were, then went aloft and shook out reefs in her courses and tops'ls. The convoy was ahead of them but not sailing fast. With all plain sail they could catch them by nightfall.

Lewrie looked at his pocket watch. Eleven-thirty in the morning. Time to think about feeding the men some of that fresh horsemeat before it spoiled. He found a man that claimed he could cook, a former waiter at an inn that had been caught poaching on his squire's lands.

"Boiled horse, an ammunition loaf of that fresh bread per man, an onion, watered wine and an apple to polish it off," Lewrie directed. "Same for me. I'll take my dinner aft."

"Rum issue, sir?" the cook asked.

"Mister Toliver."

"Aye, sir?"

"Supervise the spirits issue, if you please. A pint of wine, if there's no rum."

"No rum, sir," Toliver said, "I checked."

"I'm sure you did." Lewrie smiled slightly. "Carry on. And don't give out more than a pint. And make sure the dinner wine is mixed six-to-one. I don't want to have to flog anyone for drunkenness."

"Aye, sir."

The bosun's call piped and Toliver shouted, "Clear decks an' up spirits!"

"And Toliver?" Lewrie said, standing by the wheel with his hands in the small of his back, watching the luff of the main course.

"Aye, sir?"

"Use the kid. Don't spit tobacco on my decks."

CHAPTER

15

IPHEGENIE jogged along in convoy bound for Antigua, last in column behind the earlier prizes. Lights out had been piped and the off-duty half-dozen had turned in, with room to swing a hammock for once in the echoing lower deck. Toliver had the watch as the stars came out in a sultry tropical night. It was getting on for hurricane season once more, but for now the sea was calm enough and the wind was steady.

Alan lounged in the master's cabin aft under the poop, on the transom settee by the stern windows, hinged open for a cooling breeze, and relishing command.

He had fetched the convoy just at the beginning of the second dogwatch, had gone close aboard *Amphion* and had shouted his news to Captain Merriam, explained that *Desperate* was dashing ahead to carry the news to Hood and that he was to join the convoy.

Alan burped gently, appreciating the supper he had eaten; boiled horse, more fresh bread, a good and filling pease pudding and a raisin duff their temporary cook had created.

He had opened a bottle of the French captain's own wine

and was slowly sipping at the last of it, a most pleasant red from a St. Emilion vintner. They were reefed down for the night, with the main course taken in and the forecourse at two reefs, two reefs in the tops'ls as well and fair weather at least until morning.

Coin-silver lamps swayed over the desk at which he had dined, making the spacious cabin seem like a palace. There was a good carpet on the deck spread over painted canvas, the paneling was glossy white with much gold leaf and the furnishings were exquisitely carved and detailed. After a hammock it was going to be like sleeping in the Palace at Versailles, even if he was going to doss down on the settee, which was as wide and soft as any bed he had ever experienced.

"This is what I should have... to be rich enough to have fine things around me, a whole house in London this nice, a place in the country with a good stable of horses and if I do have to be aboard ship, to have all this room and finery..."

Which, of course, wasn't going to happen, he realized. Treghues would come out of his rantings and remember that he hated Alan worse than cold boiled mutton, and he would be casting about for another ship, this time without Sir Onsley's immediate influence. And there was always the possibility that he would be turned out of the Navy and sent home, or left to make his own way in the Indies. Ways could be found, reasons invented to ruin him, if Treghues really disliked him so much. Perhaps the best thing would be to go into another ship, where he could start fresh with no prejudice against him. Alan sat up and finished his wine, then walked out through the cabins for the quarterdeck, restless and worried.

"Evenin', Mister Lewrie," Toliver said, knuckling his forehead.

"Evening, Mister Toliver. Everyone dossed down?"

"Aye, sir. Watch and watch ta Antigua's gonna be a bitch, sir, but we'll cope right enough."

"Seems calm enough for now. Call me just before midnight for me to relieve you. I'm going to turn in."

"Aye, sir."

Alan went back aft. He blew out every lamp but one, shucked his clothes and found a clean linen sheet for a cover to make his bed. He also discovered the need to visit the quarter gallery.

Privacy for his bowels was another luxury to which he was unaccustomed, having to share the beakhead roundhouse with the other inferior petty officers, or the open rail seats if he was caught short. But here, the French master had a cabinet much like a regular jakes back home in a round quarter gallery right aft under the larboard taffrail lanterns, a spacious closet with a door he could shut, windows above the shoulder to provide a view of the sea, a small chest that held soft scrappaper for cleanliness, a bucket of seawater for a steward to sluice down the seat and pipe which conveyed wastes overboard, even a small lamp if the former captain felt like reading.

Lewrie leaned his head back wearily, watching the starlight play on the sea, felt the ship ride beneath him with a steady, reassuring motion. He bumped his head gently on the deal with the rock of the sea.

It sounded hollow.

He squirmed about and rapped on the walls to either side. Solid. But right behind the necessary, it sounded hollow.

Once finished with his needs he fetched his dirk and began to thump with the pommel at the partition behind the seat. There was more quarter gallery below him for the officer's mess, set more forward than his but in the same turreted tower built into the side of the hull. His disposal chute would pass aft of their seats, partitioned off from view. Which meant that there was a room perhaps the size of the closet behind that hollow partition, above the wardroom necessary.

He switched ends, probing between the deal planks with the point of his dirk, but with no success. He went back to the day cabin and lit another lamp to improve his vision.

To the inboard side of the closet there was a tiny nick in

the deal next to the day cabin bulkhead, a fault in the wood and in the paint. Alan inserted his blade there, pressed down on it. There was a faint click that could have been the lamp swinging. But when he pried with his blade, the deal gave a little. He pried more, and it looked as if it might hinge outboard, but he could not get it to move. Finally he leaned against it, and felt something give, like a latch letting go.

The entire panel behind the jakes swung outboard, a square of perhaps three feet by three feet, its edges masked by the wainscoting. Inside was a stout lining of oak perhaps six-inches thick. And in the space remaining there was an ironbound chest with a lock as large as a turnip hung on a hinged hasp.

Lewrie took hold of the handles and pulled it forward. It was fascinatingly heavy and gave off a faint metallic rustle. Lewrie staggered out of the quarter gallery with the chest until he could drop the burden on the transom settee.

He rifled the desk and tried every key he found before discovering the one that fit the lock. There was a well-oiled clanking of the tumblers as the huge lock sprang open.

It was nearly as delicious an emotion to raise that lid as it was to lift a woman's skirt. Once inside, there was a wooden box on top that contained a fine set of dueling pistols, which he set aside. There were some letters, mostly personal from the late captain's family, some orders from the firm of Mulraix et Fils but nothing of any import that he could discover with his poor command of French. There was, however, a folded bit of canvas ... and then—there was *gold*.

Bags of it, rolls of it, little wooden boxes full of it, with the amount and the denominations and nations of origin inked onto slips of paper tacked down to each parcel with wax or tied as labels to the bags.

There were Spanish *pistoles*, Spanish dollars, French *livres* and *louis d'or*, Dutch *guilders* and Danish *kroner*. And there were sovereigns, golden guineas, two-guineas, five- and ten-guinea pieces, bright shining yellowboys in rolls and boxes and bags.

It was too much to be the late captain's working capital for the voyage. It was enough to purchase a dozen Indiamen!

"Merciful God in Heaven," Lewrie whispered in awe, letting some loose coins trickle through his fingers. He was not sure of the value of the foreign coins in comparison to the guineas, but it seemed like an awful lot...a most temptingly awful lot. But sadly it was a devilishly heavy and unconcealable lot. He left the gold and went forward to the doors to the quarterdeck, listening to see if anyone had discovered him in the midst of his temptation.

The sight of all that gold made him open the master's wine cabinet and pull out a bottle of brandy. He poured himself a large measure with shaky hands and went back to the chest.

There was a paper inventory stuck at the back of the chest. Altogether it seemed as if there might be over £80,000 there if the foreign coin had the same value as the guineas.

He let the heavy coins trickle through his hands again, and thought about it, hard.

It'd have lain there, undiscovered, except for me, he reasoned. Not on the manifest, not listed when we turned the ship over to the Prize Court. Some surveyor or shipyard worker would have found it, if they'd have found it at all. And none of this squadron would ever see a penny of it, and some silver-buttoned whip jack or lard-assed landsman would go home richer than a chicken-nabob...

That settled in his mind, he counted up the number of inferior petty officers in *Desperate*, and in the squadron, that might share in this unbelievable bounty, and came up with roughly eighty men to share £10,000—£125 apiece. Fair wages, he decided, but not the financial security he was looking for.

There was absolutely no way he could get that chest off the prize and ashore. Three men couldn't heft his seachest if he stored it in there. It would be years, perhaps, before he returned to England to pay off, and no way he could keep that much gold safely hidden for that long. No prize agent ashore could be trusted not to peek, and then questions would be raised as to where he had gotten so much foreign coin, not to mention high-denomination guineas.

Once a week for the last year and a half first Captain Bales, then Lt. Kenyon, and now Commander Treghues had read the Articles out at Divisions, and by now Alan could almost quote Article Eight verbatim:

"No Person in or belonging to the Fleet shall take out of any Prize, or Ship seized for Prize, any Money, Plate or Goods, unless it shall be necessary for the better securing thereof, or for the necessary Use and Service of any of his Majesty's Ships or Vessels of War, before the same be adjudged lawful Prize in some Admiralty Court; but the full and entire Account of the Whole, without Embezzlement, shall be brought in, and Judgement passed entirely upon the Whole without Fraud; upon pain that every Person offending herein shall forfeit or lose his Share of the Capture, and suffer such further Punishment as shall be imposed by a Court-Martial, or such Court of Admiralty, according to the Nature and Degree of the Offence."

That was pretty clear. If they catch me I'd be flogged aound the fleet. Rodney would have had me hung up in tar and chains until my bones fell apart. But...

He got to his feet and went to peer up at the poop deck skylight. It was closed. He listened intently for any sound from above, scared someone like Toliver might have been peeking on him. He decided that all anyone could see from the best angle with the skylight shut was the forward edge of the desk, not as far back as the transom settee and that dirty, great chest. He went back aft and sat beside the chest, hefting several of the bags of gold coins. He took up a *rouleau* of coins in his fist and pondered on the possible repercussions.

"Money is the root of all evil," he recited, remembering

his nursery school days, the catechism of good behavior that had been lashed into him at Harrow (and other schools). One-hundred-twenty-five-pounds is nothing to turn your nose up at. But then... neither is this little *rouleau* of two-guinea pieces...

That was £210 he held in his fist, twice his yearly allowance from Pilchard, and who knew how long that bequest would last. And this roll of a hundred five-guinea coins was really £525. And this small box that held two hundred coins was worth £1,050!

He pawed through the contents, setting aside the ten-guinea yellowboys with a deep sense of regret. He sorted out four rolls of coins, and two boxes, all one- and two-guinea coins. That was over £1,000.

Call it a finder's fee, he told himself, claiming a final roll of five-guinea coins. He rose and went to his sea chest, which had been stored along the after bulkhead near the coach. Using his dirty shirt as a screen, he opened the chest, pawed down through his belongings to a secure depth, and stashed his find, emerging with a clean shirt that he made a great production of shaking out and inspecting for serviceability for the morning. He closed his chest and went aft, laying the shirt out on the desk.

"This has to go," he whispered, staring at the inventory list. He shredded it as he stepped out onto the stern gallery into the wind, fed the tiny pieces into the wake, hoping that they were too small to be legible if blown onto the poop deck or officer's gallery below. Once back in the cabin he restowed the contents of the chest, still a mind-numbing mass of yellow metal. He checked carefully that there was no other accounting of the chest's contents. He read all the business and personal letters, found no mention of the gold in any of them.

Only then did he relock the chest and stagger back into the necessary closet with it, sliding it back into its niche and closing the secret panel on it with a wooden click of hidden latches.

He slid the keys back into the desk, then had to search it all for any paper that might explain the presence of the gold.

God, was it mentioned in those papers Railsford has? he suddenly asked himself. "If it was money for Rochambeau or Lafayette, DeGrasse would have mentioned it, might have given an accounting..."

Alan had planned to "accidentally" discover the chest in the morning and take it over to *Amphion*, but now he was not sure. If he pretended to find it, and some of it turned up missing, he would be blamed for any shortage.

In that case I should take more of the guineas, he told himself. What if no one ever finds it? Then nearly £78,000 goes to waste until this ship is scrapped or lost.

No, it was too much of a risk to take more, especially foreign or large-denomination coins he could never explain. And he could not "discover" it.

God, how awful, he thought. What a hellish dilemma I've put myself in. I should put those guineas back and hope for the best part of my legal share. But he didn't, of course.

"STAND by, the anchor party," Lewrie shouted as *Ephegenie* rounded up into the wind. Short-handed as they were, they barely sailed further into English Harbor than under the guns on the point, a single jib standing, and courses already brailed up, and only one tops'l set to draw wind. She was sluggish to turn, barely under steerage way, but they were home free.

"Back your tops'l," Lewrie ordered. "Keep her on the eye of the wind, quartermaster."

"No helm, sor," the man said, idling the spokes of the wheel back and forth.

"Let go." The bower cable roared out the hawse and the anchor splashed into the harbor. "Let go braces and veer out a full cable."

"Done fine, sir," Toliver said quietly in encouragement,

and Alan felt a relief so great that it was almost like a sexual release. For a week he had been nervous as a cat, unable to sleep with the secret knowledge of the gold, unable to relax with the prize so poorly manned, afraid of making a mistake in managing the ship or losing her to a sudden squall. They had run into rising winds for two days, which had kept him wide awake and mostly on deck. They had run through rain and the threat of foul weather, until the skies had cleared and the Trades had settled down to balmy behavior once more.

Now *Ephegenie* lay as still as a stone bridge in the lee of the capes, her anchor firm on the bottom, and a boat-full of dockyard men pulling strongly for them to take charge of her.

"I never knew running a ship would be so hard," Alan confessed to Toliver.

"Short-handed as we were, it was, sir," Toliver said but with an assuring tone. "With a full crew, it's all claret an' prize money."

"We were fortunate," Alan said.

"Average sort o' passage. But I reckon we'd have done just as good in a full gale, sir... Busy damned place, ain't it?"

"What Railsford carried to Hood must have stirred up the Fleet."

The harbor was working alive with rowing boats servicing the needs of the many warships anchored in the outer roads. There were several ships of the line that Alan knew had been based on St. Lucia to the south. There were three 3rd rates in a row warping themselves out of the inner harbor up the row of pilings getting ready for sea, an entire fleet of fourteen sail-of-the-line, preparing for something.

And here was a midshipman with twenty dockyard hands from the Admiralty Court. Were they there to arrest him for theft? The midshipman was elegantly turned out, his breeches and waistcoat and shirt as white as a hammockman could bleach them, his mien serious and superior, and Alan recognized himself from times before with a grin.

"Who is in charge of the prize, may I ask?" the midshipman asked with a lofty accent.

"I am," Alan said firmly, almost swaggering in his stained and faded uniform. "I expect you want the manifests and ship's papers. I have them aft."

"Very well," the other man said. He was a full man, over twenty and possibly passed for lieutenant already, or an aristocratic coxcomb too stupid to pass it. "Much bother?"

"Not after we took her." Lewrie shrugged. "Hard fight."

Alan led him to the master's cabins, made generous with the claret while the other midshipman went through the papers.

"Has the *Desperate* frigate come in?" Alan asked casually. "Is she still here? I should like to rejoin my ship if possible."

"Yes, she's here, further up the roads," the midshipman said as he mumbled his way through the French manifests. "If you would sign this I shall take possession of the prize for the Court of Admiralty and you may leave her. You may use my boat and crew to remove your people."

"Gladly."

"Much of a fight?" the other asked, trying not to sound too curious but itching to know in spite of how much it might hurt.

"A company of line infantry from a French regiment... *Soissonois*. A full battery of artillerymen, plus her crew, of course. Hot work for a while, our captain wounded and already nearly forty hands short from other prizes," Alan said with ease, as though it was an everyday occurrence. "There're big doings up in the Americas. Might be a big land battle soon, and Hood seems to be getting ready to face DeGrasse, too."

The other midshipman by then was looking crushed to be a shore stallion, resentful of being denied the chance to live such a grand life.

"Is that all you need from me?" Alan asked with a wave.

"Yes...quite."

"Then I shall take my leave of you. I'd like a brace of

hands to help with my chest, if you don't mind."

"Certainly!" The other said through pursed lips.

IT was a delight to climb through the entry port and doff his hat to Lt. Railsford, to see all the familiar faces back aboard, to see his chest safely swayed up with a stay tackle and thump to the deck without spilling gold or jingling.

"Welcome back aboard, Mister Lewrie," Railsford said pleasantly. "How was your first real command?"

"Hectic, sir. I don't believe I slept a wink."

"Good training for you. We're going north as eyes for the Fleet. Hood himself received me. Already knew from Admiral Graves that something was up and was getting ready to sail for New York, but our news was welcome, nonetheless."

"Did we get all our people back, sir?" Alan asked as they went aft.

"Yes, fortunately. We shall need them."

"And Commander Treghues?"

"Recovering. Once he was lucid, I explained what good service you had rendered, but..." Railsford shrugged.

"At least he allowed me to rejoin," Alan said quietly.

"After Hood learned it was you discovered those secret papers, he had little choice. I wrote the report before Dorne would allow him to deal with ship's business."

"God bless you, Mister Railsford," Alan said with feeling, and wanting to watch the progress of his valuables below but forced to stay on deck.

"Now, what about the gold?"

"What?" Lewrie almost jumped out of his skin.

"That French War Commissary officer, remember?" Railsford said. "Before he died he revealed that the prize's master had thousands in gold hidden in his cabins somewhere for Rochambeau and Lafayette."

"In the cabins?" Alan was about to faint in terror. "But I slept there. I mean—"

"It was well-hidden. Even the late colonel knew not where," Railsford went on. "Bribe money to certain well-placed rebel political leaders, he said, to give France influence enough to ask for one of the southern coastal colonies should the rebels succeed in their aims."

"My word, what a dirty business," Alan declared, finding his wits at last. "I can see them taking British Florida, but—"

"And you slept soundly and did not suspect a thing! It might have been right underneath your head!"

Or other bodily parts, Alan thought. "How much, did the man say, before he passed over?"

"He did not have an accurate count, but he believed it to be greater than fifty thousand pounds. And I'll lay you any odds you want that the Admiralty Court will have her torn down to a pile of timbers until they find it. Just think what our share will be, even diluted by the other ships in sight when we took the prize!"

"God, that is wonderful news, Mister Railsford!" Alan laughed, in intense relief, wiping his sweaty face. "I cannot tell you how good..."

"Are you well, Mister Lewrie? Touch of Yellow Jack again?"

"Oh, no, sir. Just about done in with exhaustion, though. I tried to do too much, I think."

"Couldn't bear to leave your first quarterdeck, eh?" Railsford smiled kindly. "Should have let Toliver handle her, he's a good mate. Can't do it all yourself, and you have to trust your people or you'll wear and worry yourself sick."

"Aye, sir, I've learned a good lesson from it."

"Best get below and have a bite while you can, then. We're to sail in the forenoon, all the way to New York to join Admiral Grave's fleet, and God knows what after that."

"I shall do that, sir, and I thank you!"

God bless blind shitten luck, Providence, and all the saints, including the Welsh ones, he rejoiced with a glee and sense of relief as intense as any he had ever experienced. I'm safe! Safe and rich! God help me, I'll never do such a thing again, I swear on what little honor I have left.

* * *

"ANCHOR'S hove short, sir. Up an' down."

Alan stood by the larboard gangway ready to swarm aloft with his topmen and make sail. All the Fleet was hove short, waiting for the signal to hoist anchors and be off, all eyes on *Barfleur* for word from the flag.

Treghues, the bosun and Mister Monk were pacing about the ship, making a last-minute inspection to see that all was in order. Treghues glared at him briefly.

"Our bad penny has turned up again, I see," the captain said.

"But a most lucky penny, sir," Monk said with a grin. "All that gold he brought safe to us."

"Umm, perhaps," Treghues softened slightly. After all, his eighth of a reputed £50,000 would restore any family's fortune of itself. He did not fully relent, however; Lewrie was too large a sinner in his cold grey eyes for that, and Alan knew he would still get rid of him at the first opportunity to preserve the purity of his ship's officers, and his Navy.

Monk gave him a friendly tap on the arm as he went past, once the captain could not see, and the taciturn bosun actually smiled at him, and Alan knew that he had friends aboard still.

And, he told himself, they were off on a great adventure. On the gun deck the Marines and strongest men stood ready by the capstan bars. The ship's boys waited with their nippers to pass the lighter messenger from the capstan to the bower cable. Below, hands were ready to handle the cable as it came in, into the cable tier to dry, and stink up the ship. Landsmen and waisters waited in their subdivisions by the jeers to raise the tops'l and t'gallant yards, by the halyards for the heads'ls, by the sheets to draw down the leaches of the sails as they were freed.

There was a single bark in the outer roads from *Barfleur*, the signal gun to get underway, and a signal pendant went up her mast.

"Heave on the capstan," Treghues ordered. "Hands aloft and make sail. Drive 'em, bosun, the flag's watching."

"Hands aloft. Trice up and lay out."

Music came from the boy band and the fiddlers, not just in *Desperate* but from every ship in the Fleet. The men breasted on the capstan bars and the pawls clanked as the bower cable came in.

"Anchor's free!"

The pawls began to rattle like a drumroll, and then men ran the cable up, and the boys were a blur of activity to keep up as the smelly thigh-thick line came in.

"Loose tops'ls! Tops'ls, jibs an' spanker!"

The entire bay thundered with the sound of canvas being whipped by the wind. *Desperate* began to pay off the breeze, the halyards and the jeers sighing through the blocks aloft. While the sails were hauled down, all about her little sloops of war, frigates of the 5th rate, cruisers and line of battle ships began to move and stir, gathering way and avoiding each other with easy skill, all aiming for Cape Shirley and beginning to take up cruising dispositions. Thousands of men, hundreds of guns, all bound in search of desperate battle.

"Hands to the weather braces! Haul away handsomely! Thus!"

Desperate leaned to the wind and began to drive along under full control. Once past the Cape she hoisted t'gallants and the men laid out on the yards to cast off the brails so she could take her position ahead of the fleet as one of the first eyes that would see the enemy. She went hard to weather for her offing, leading other frigates, leading the liners of the 3rd and 2nd rate.

"Lay in from the yards! Another pull on the fore weather braces! Now belay every inch of that!"

Lewrie idled on the main topmast cap as the rest of his hands laid in and began to slide down the stays for the deck. He looked aft to the west as the Fleet rounded the Cape in columns and beat to windward in the frigate's wake.

In a moment he would be expected to descend to face once more Commander Treghues' pious disapproval, Forrester's enmity and the mind-dulling routine of a ship of war. But for this brief pause, he could watch all those proud ships form columns, columns of the mightiest, most intricate and demanding creations that man had ever had the wit to build.

He did not know what this Fleet would face on its way north to the American colonies, but he could not picture anything other than victory. There was a possibility that he would not survive, but he had faced risks enough before to know that life was full of chance.

He felt certain that he would see action, more action than he could ever have imagined when reading about naval battles as a child, and he was more curious than fearful as to what it might be like to see two gigantic flotillas trading broadsides.

He knew that he was on his way to a sight that, if he survived it, he would remember all the days of his life, a chance for fame, honor and glory, amid all the horrors of a sea fight.

Do I really hate this so much anymore? he wondered. Dull as it can be, some people think I'm good at the Navy. If all my other plans go for naught, I could make a career of it, I think. No, anything I've ever really liked or wanted, I've lost. I can't admit to any want of this, or it's gone, too. But I know my place here, and there's some who've told me I do have a place. Maybe just until the war's ended, and then I can concentrate on something more rewarding, something not as depriving. But I'll go with fame and honor, and not when they tell me, damme if I won't—

"Starboard watch below! All hands prepare for Divisions!"

Lewrie swung out and grabbed a stay for his descent.

He reclaimed his discarded hat from the larboard gangway from one of his topmen, and stood by the rail drinking in the view of the island so green, and the many bright azure colors of the ocean.

Is this life really so bad? he wondered, shaking his head at his own rise of sentiment. But would I have seen anything like this in London? Would I ever have learned anything back home half as fascinating as this? Well, I may not be a real tarpaulin man yet, but damme if they ain't made some kind of sailor out of me!

He felt a surge of pride in himself. He felt a tweak of pride in his Service. And he realized that for the moment, he felt content and happy with himself and his station in life.

But then, being Alan Lewrie, he wasn't so sure that Life would let him hold any such sentiment for very long.